M000278633

Ark

Book 1 in the series

Return of the Templars

PJ Humphreys

This book is a work of fiction. Names, characters, places and incidents are either the product of the author's imagination or are used fictitiously. Any resemblance to actual persons, living or dead, or to actual events or locales is entirely coincidental.

ARK: RETURN OF THE TEMPLARS
Book 1 in the Series: Return of the Templars

ISBN: 978-1-527220-38-6

Compiled by: Rod Craig
10.07.2020

Stay in Touch:

Facebook:
www.facebook/returnofthetemplars
Website:
www.returnofthetemplars.com
Instagram:
returnofthetemplars

Be sure to leave a review on Amazon!

This book is dedicated to:

Joanne, my wife, my support system, my literary critic and to Jonathan and Francesca for all of their hard work.

Contents

Chapter 1

The Fallen Knight

Date: December 2007
Place: Washington DC

She had no idea there was a contract on her life. The word on the street was her throat was to be cut and her eyelids removed. Had she known, she would not have gone to the meeting that day, but she did and everything changed – just not in the way everyone expected it to. In the end, what they would need was a miracle.

He had given her the address where the meeting was to be held and had said, be there by noon. Courtney knew there would be plenty of people about: his instructions had been explicit and calculated. She was nervous. She wasn't trained for this; basic training yes, but this was different – she was on her own. She knew the decision to meet the man might well turn out to be the worst decision she had ever made, but if she wanted to get the information she needed, she had no choice.

Courtney sat and waited.

Busy people rushed by her; Washington DC's commuters were out on the streets in full force. It was lunchtime and they had left the labyrinth of office blocks in search of their favourite bars, cafés and restaurants. It was a breezy, frosty, grey December day. Ten days before Christmas, Seventh Street was decorated with Yuletide pomp; it had been for weeks. The sun broke through the grey sky and the slight breeze died, but the chill air still hung around as a reminder of the season. Winter was well and truly ensconced in the capital.

There were sixteen tables outside La Bohème, a small trendy eating-place directly opposite the park in Constitution Gardens. He had said to take a table in the middle. She'd arrived early to make sure of a place, but there was no real need. There were plenty of empty tables; because of the cold, most people ate inside.

Grey office people rushed by her in a sea of expressionless faces. Courtney tried to stay focused and calm, but it was impossible. Every face could be *his*. The longer she waited, the more anxious she became. A cloud was masking the sun again and she pulled the collar of her coat up around her neck, shuddering with the cold. The sickness she felt in her stomach was nerves, she knew that, an edgy apprehension that churned away like a bad foreboding. She felt exposed and alone, but it had been her choice. She just hoped she wouldn't regret it.

He had been watching her for three quarters of an hour from across the street in Constitution Gardens. He had been there a good hour before she had arrived: he wouldn't take any chances. He never did. He'd watched her take her seat. She looked nervous. That was good. If she were hiding anything, he would soon know. Edgy body language never failed to expose a lie, sooner or later. He waited. He needed to be sure it wasn't a trap. Staying alive was his number one priority; getting her to tell him what she knew, his second. He threw more corn to the ever-hungry pigeons that strewed the ground and blended in with the crowds in the park.

He looked like just another plain grey office-dweller, walking in the park on his lunch break, feeding the pigeons. But of course he wasn't and he, and his life, were far from grey and plain. He smiled at the semi-tame pigeons, bobbing their heads backwards and forwards in a comedic motion. Nothing spooks you, he thought. You don't bother to fly away when people pass you by. You don't even look. Nothing fazes you. Throwing the last of the corn on the ground, he discarded the empty brown bag in a trash can.

He buried his hands deep into his overcoat pockets, searching for warmth. Even with his gloves on, his hands felt cold. He moved along, casually and without hurrying.

The waiter, a young, good-looking Croatian with a shock of black shoulder-length hair, brought over her third cappuccino. She tipped him another dollar; he pocketed it with a smile. She worried the man wouldn't show. She'd only spoken to him on the phone once. It had been a short conversation; no pleasantries, just business. He'd timed the call and hung up long before a trace could have been made – but one wasn't. The man was careful and she already liked that about him. She admired professional work in any context, even this. Across the street the park was full of people out walking and jogging. She watched them, trying hard to calm her racing nerves. I must get back into an exercise regime, she thought, making a mental promise to start in the New Year.

The man waited for a lull in the traffic, then walked across the street. He was about a hundred yards away from her now. He stood in front of a shop window and lit a cigarette, his eyes everywhere, ignoring the Christmas bargains on display. He gave it a few minutes, long enough to be sure, but not too long to be conspicuous. Then he made two passes by her position. He walked, not too fast, not too slow, his eyes seeking out anything and everything. His training had taught him to trust his feelings, no matter what was happening around him. He watched the people who were moving and those who were stationary. Old men, young women, lovers in embrace, mothers with children, friends in conversation, shoppers and window-shoppers, office-dwellers with no time: he watched them all. He watched her.

A car horn blew on the corner of Seventeenth and Constitution Avenue. She turned her head, only for a moment or two, but when she turned back, the man was there.

She had practised this speech a hundred times since he had agreed to the meet, but her heart was pounding. She could feel it, hear it, and the well-rehearsed speech deserted her.

"Coffee?" she managed to ask. She could hear unease in her voice. Annoyed that the moment had got to her, she tried to compose herself. The stranger looked calm and relaxed.

"I'll take the same as you," he replied, indicating towards her cappuccino, but his attention was on her.

His eyes never left her. He watched her every move, every facial expression. He listened to every tone change and intonation in her voice, and this made her self-conscious. She caught the young waiter's eye, happy for an excuse to turn away and try to compose herself. She held her cup and pointed to the man next to her; the waiter nodded then went off to get the coffee. What had she got herself into? Doubt sped through her mind.

"May I?" His words were calm and unhurried.

The man next to her reached over and frisked her. It took him five seconds. It was quick and thorough; clearly he'd done it before.

"And the bag," he said, pointing to her black Prada shoulder bag, which was strung over the back of her chair.

She handed him the bag. Inside were a small red purse, a return subway ticket and a set of house keys. He gave her the bag back, then relaxed into his chair. Thank God I'd removed my badge and diary from my purse, she thought. She had kept a diary ever since the age of eleven. It had started as a schoolgirl thing, but now it was a habit she just couldn't break. She rallied her thoughts back onto him; she needed to focus now.

"I'm not carrying," she whispered, slightly learning forward. She could still hear the tension in her voice, almost embarrassment that he could even think she would consider bringing a firearm.

"I wasn't looking for a gun. I was looking to see if you were wired," he said. He didn't bother to whisper, or lean forward. There was no need: no one paid them any attention and there was no one close enough anyway. The diners were all cosy and warm inside La Bohème.

"You said no wires." Again the hint of tension laced her voice.

The man pulled out a packet of Marlboro Lights and a disposable lighter from one of the pockets of his black overcoat, which he had unbuttoned and left open, despite the cold. She noticed that he hadn't removed his gloves. She knew he wouldn't when the coffee came. He wouldn't leave any fingerprints.

"I've said a lot of things to a lot of people over the years and I've learnt that not everyone feels the same need to keep their promises. Thank you for following my instructions, though. I appreciate that."

The young Croatian brought over the coffee. Again she tipped him a dollar. She watched the man sip his coffee. She studied him, but learned nothing.

"I'm surprised you didn't frisk the waiter," she said, her hands wrapped around her coffee cup, enjoying the warmth and comfort it gave.

The man smiled and looked over at the young man, who was now far enough away to be out of earshot. "I already frisked him, about an hour ago. It's okay, though. He's clean."

Of course you frisked him, she thought. God, Courtney, get a grip. Again she rallied her thoughts to focus. "An hour … you've been here a while?"

"Watched you arrive."

"You frisked all the waiters, of course?" He didn't need to answer.

The man raised a smile. She was a spook. He had no doubt about that. From an Agency, probably FBI, not CIA or NSA. Either way, he was sure by her nervousness that she was no field operative. He had known that just by watching her from across the street. She had to be FBI, he thought, given the subject of their mutual interest and because of one of the principals involved. He sensed the meeting had all the hallmarks of a rogue meeting: an Agency operative doing something they shouldn't, and telling no one about it. She intrigued him, though. Why would she put herself in danger? She didn't seem the rash type. The opposite, in fact, and obviously clever and seemingly honest – definitely not -CIA!

He considered her attractive, with a sexy smile that seemed to light up all on its own. Her hair was black, long and curly. It had that wild Mediterranean look about it, and so did she. She had that same look as his wife: his dead wife; his kidnapped, tortured, raped and murdered wife. The wife he had grieved for every day for the last twenty-one years.

He liked the way she was dressed, conservatively, office fashion: black two-piece, but smart, really smart. He could tell she took care about how she looked. Her manner was engaging, warm, like the girl at school everyone wants to take to the prom, but with a personality that had a hint of mischievousness about it. She was easy company and he already knew that, in different circumstances, he would like her, but not today. The last thing he wanted right now was anything or anybody to be connected with him. He eased himself round to watch the traffic lights turn green, making sure every car pulled away at the lights.

She figured he could handle himself should the need arise. He was polite and articulate, graceful in his manners and was obviously well educated. Every now and then an accent was just detectable in his speech, perhaps Irish or Scottish, she thought. He wore trainers and jeans beneath his black overcoat. She noticed the Redskin's sweatshirt. She smiled, trying to ease into a conversation with him. She saw her opening.

"My brother's crazy about the Redskins. He's a priest over in …"

The man was quick to end her sentence. He turned his gaze away from the traffic lights and onto her. He was sharp, taking her by

6

surprise. "We agreed no personal details. I don't want to know anything about you, and you don't want to know anything about me. Trust me, it's safer this way."

Annoyed with herself, she rallied her composure. It was a stupid mistake. She wouldn't do it again.

He still couldn't be sure she was FBI, but it didn't matter anyway. She had something he needed, and he had something she needed: it was a straight trade, no complications. An easy swap of information and then done. He was prepared to gamble that she had no interest in him and that all her interest lay in one person. However, there was no choice. He had reached a dead end and he needed her. He needed her badly.

"I've been posting messages all over the Internet and chat pages for you for weeks," she said.

"I've seen most of them: *S E D bought old papers, wondering why. Original vendor required for chat.* Not very original and pretty thinly veiled. If I saw it, then he saw it. You should be careful." There was a certain vulnerability about her that he found engaging.

"Can I ask you how you know about our mutual friend, S E D?" he asked.

She was ready for the question. Not too much information, she thought, just background. *Take this slow, Courtney.*

"I take an interest in Middle East affairs." She would not elaborate on why; she knew he wouldn't waste her time asking the question. He didn't. "Anything that involves that part of the world is of interest to me. And in this case, it's antiquities. How much do you know about the black market of antiquities?"

"Let's assume nothing," he said.

"Okay. About a month or so ago, I discovered that some extremely rare papers had been sold in Egypt. Their provenance, as is sometimes the case, and often the case in Egypt because of their low legitimacy thresholds, was unknown. Mysterious even. This is not altogether surprising because the world of antiquities is extremely secretive, not to mention murky and at times dangerous. But there was something really odd about this trade that caught my eye. I found out that the papers had been around for sometime. Eventually, I was able to track them from when they were first sold back in 1996, in South America, then to Ireland, then Berlin. There's a missing time frame once they left Berlin, but then they turned up for sale in amongst a bundle of ancient Coptic codices, in Cairo, Egypt.

"The person who was selling them is a well-known illegal Syrian dealer who has shady offices just off Khan el Khalili souk. You can buy anything in the Khan el Khalili souk. After six centuries, it's still the largest market in the world and it still operates much as it did during medieval times.

"One in every eight Egyptians is a Coptic Christian. This means that there would have been a large number of people who would have known the codices, along with the papers, were for sale.

"The antiquities trade is highly specialized and the number of dealers, expert enough to know what to buy, is relatively few, outside the world of universities, museums and academia, that is. I was intrigued at first. I wanted to know who the principals were at the meeting when the sale was done, but no one was talking.

"Antiquities are real big business. It is estimated that the illegal trade of classical Egyptian antiquities amounts to some 250 million dollars annually. Since the law 117/1983 was issued, prohibiting the illegal trade in Egyptian antiquities, the US courts have tended to recognize the legitimacy of Egyptian claims to treasures that were stolen over the decades. So the whole thing is very much underground these days. I wasn't overly surprised that people didn't want to talk, but someone always does, for the right price. Strange thing here was, no one, and I mean no one, talked. All I know is that someone with the initials S E D bought the papers, but not the codices. This is pretty odd in itself. Rumour is someone paid over the odds for what they bought. I also believe that the papers are still in Egypt. Normally they would be long gone by now. So it got my attention.

"Then, not long ago, those initials, S E D, came up again. This time with a tenuous link to a Republican politician who seems to have an unhealthy interest in Colombia. So I started digging, found some stuff out, but not enough, not enough to tell me who the initials belong to and how he's linked to the senator. It's the senator I'm now really interested in. That's why I wanted to meet you. I presume, as you answered, you are the original vendor of the papers. I want you to tell me why this S E D would want those old papers so badly. Why he would pay over the odds for them. What was in the papers, who is S E D, and ultimately what is his connection with the Republican senator and Colombia?"

The man turned on her sharply. "I never said I was the vendor. Presuming things can get you killed, lady."

"Well, I … you answered the internet messages, didn't you? You agreed to meet and you're here. I just …"

"But I never said I sold them." The man opposite her inched forward slightly. "Have you any idea just how dangerous a thing you're getting into here?"

"Let's just say I got an insurance policy," she said.

"Problem with insurance policies, normally you have to die before you can get to use them."

"Look, all the stuff I got is on an audio tape. It's safe. If anything happens to me, it all goes to someone I can trust. That's my leverage. So, shall we get on and do what we both came here to do?"

He thought about it, his eyes and ears still absorbing everything around him, watching for the slightest thing out of place, searching for any sense of trouble. He needed to get the scrolls back. She could help him, but he knew he was going to have to tell her more than he wanted, more than he should. Time was not on his side. If the new owner could eventually decode the scrolls, then people would die and that would be entirely on him. He had to get them back before they were decoded. He would have given anything to walk away from this, but it was his problem to sort out. He had created the mess; he had to clean it up.

"And what do you want?"

"I want to know why our friend is so interested in some old papers. I want to know who he is, what he's like; but more importantly, I want to know, what his connection is with the senator?" she said.

The man shook his head. "They're not old papers, they're important scrolls, perhaps more important than you can imagine, certainly far more important than the codex papers."

"Whatever you want to call them is fine by me. I just want to know why he wanted them."

"You're building a psychological profile on our friend, aren't you? You're building a profile so that you can catch him. Standard FBI procedure."

"You said no detail."

He smiled.

"You're right, that's your business. And if I tell you why he is so interested in the scrolls, you'll tell me where they are in Egypt?"

"Other than a short gap, I can tell you everyone that handled them from the time they got sold to the first broker in South America, and yes, I can help you find them in Egypt."

"And you have no interest in the scrolls?"

"My only interest is in our friend with the initials S E D and the senator. As for the old pa … the scrolls, I have no interest in them at all. When we get them, they're yours to keep. I just want S E D and the senator."

It still didn't add up to him. Why was she so interested in the man who now had the scrolls? Why would she risk going it alone, which he was pretty sure she was now doing? He needed to know more before he was willing to go any further.

"You're going to have to give me a bit more, I'm afraid."

"Let's just say," she started, "if my suspicion is right, then S E D and the senator are responsible for bribing a number of people that are holding down pretty important jobs, people I work for. If I can get to S E D and the senator, then I can get to them."

"You're with an agency then?"

"That's all you're getting. Now it's your turn."

He smiled. "What's your name? Figure I should know that at least."

"Courtney, "she replied. "My name is Courtney Rose."

He sat back. He knew the name straight away. Now it all made sense. Now he knew why she was there. He had picked up the low, rumbling rumours out on the street because of the peculiar way the contract killing was to be done. He had seen that kind of murder before and he knew who had issued the contract on her. If he didn't help her, she would soon be dead. He breathed in deep. He would tell her about the contract that was out on her life and he would help her. But to get what he wanted, he would need to tell her *the* secret. The secret that was so profound, so dangerous, that very few people in the world knew about it. This was not going to be easy.

"I'm going to trust you, Courtney Rose. You've got honest eyes." He smiled. "So here it is. This is why our mutual friend wanted the scrolls so badly. You should prepare yourself, though, because everything I am about to tell you is true. You just remember that when I start speaking and you start doubting."

The man in front of her fascinated her. She was totally hooked; it would have taken an earthquake to move her from her seat, even though she still had no idea what this had to do with the men she was after. Courtney took one of his cigarettes from the packet on the table and lit it; she hadn't smoked for twelve years, but she now felt the need to.

As the grey office-dwellers went about their business he never stopped monitoring what was happening around them.

"Centuries ago," he began, "there was an order of warrior monks called the Knights Templar. Nine Knights started the Order. The King of France sent them to the Holy Land in 1119 to protect pilgrims as they travelled their dangerous paths. Whilst in the Holy Land, they housed themselves at the site of the Temple Mount, the temple of Solomon. There are those who say that they chose that spot so that they could excavate the ruins of the holy temple there, looking for treasure, looking for *the* treasure, and that speculation has raged on for many centuries.

"In 1129 AD, Hugues de Payens, then the Order's Grand Master, was summoned to the Council of Troyes by the Cardinal Legate of France – the council of Troyes was infamous throughout France. It was made up from the country's most senior clergymen and ecclesiastical scholars. There could only be one reason for them to have summoned de Payens: the rumours of untold treasure had reached their ears. Despite intense questioning and threats, de Payens dealt with every question without disrespecting the senior gathering, but, more importantly, without revealing the Templar secret. Luck was with de Payens that day because the Templars' patron was also there, a man called Bernard, Abbot of Clairvaux. Respected and admired, his patronage and presence helped them survive the scrutiny.

"In the ensuing years, the Order of Warrior Monks rose to great prominence in international politics and the affairs of the state. Their standing was so great that in 1139 AD Pope Innocent II granted the Order *Omne Datum Optimum* – International Independence. This meant that the Templars no longer answered, or paid taxes, tithes or dues, to any royal house in any land. Such was their chivalry and honesty, they were granted vast regions of land throughout many countries and their wealth grew. It wasn't long before the Templars became the most influential body the world had ever seen. The Templars put their Order's money to work. They established the first banking system and became bankers to kings and queens all over Europe.

"Then strange things started to happen to the French skyline. Great architecture began to appear. The technical brilliance of the building work was unparalleled throughout the western world. Notre Dame de Paris was started in 1167, in line with hermetic teachings: 'as above, so below'. The cathedral replicated the constellation of Virgo. Chartres cathedral was started in 1194 and Amiens in 1221. These and many more rose from the earth with such exquisite excellence and design: they were years ahead of their time. Incredible heights were achieved and the geometry and mathematics confounded the most gifted builders of the day.

"They say the Templars used Hiramic knowledge, which comes from Hiram Abif – Solomon's master mason and the complex character upon which Freemasonry is based. They say they used secrets in geometry and mathematics. The Templars taught a whole army of craftsmen and created guilds, which were quantified by degrees of knowledge, just the same as Hiram Abif had done centuries before. The techniques they were using astounded everyone. No one thought it possible to build so high, to span so wide. Their labours were to become recognised as the finest monuments adorning the French skyline.

"Many people said that they used this hermetic alchemy to build the cathedrals; others said that their knowledge was deeper and they had used the *Spiritus Mundi*, the breath of the universe. Some quoted Revelation 21:18-21 and likened the splendour – not the material. Others said that they had used a sacred science of numerology, geometry, architecture and mathematics; that they possessed thousands of years of study by the ancients, the lore and law of the universe.

"Years passed. In 1307, France had a very different king. His name was Philippe IV and in that year he finally faced up to the fact that he was, to all intents and purposes, bankrupt. The king owed all of his debts to the Order of Knights Templar. Whilst he and his predecessors had frittered away the country's money, the Templars, over the decades, had used theirs wisely and invested well. The King had not been able to tax the Templars because of the decree of

International Independence by Pope Innocent II in 1139 AD. The King was frustrated that the Templars were so wealthy and that they had never disclosed the source of their esoteric knowledge. Remember this is now 188 years since they first went to the Holy Land. The incumbent pope, reluctant to do the King's bidding, mysteriously met with a nasty end, whereupon the King appointed his friend as pope, Pope Clement V.

"What followed was one of the greatest tragedies in history. The king, along with one of the most powerful churches in the world, headed by his new ally, the pope, drew up horrendous charges against the Templars. The facts were against them. They clearly possessed an insight into geometry and mathematics that was far superior to any orthodox knowledge. The executions began.

"With Jacques de Molay, their Grand Master, and most of the Templars dead, the King sent his army in pursuit of the few Templars that had escaped by ship from the port of La Rochelle. The king tried to persuade his son-in-law, Edward II of England, who was married to Philippe's daughter Isabella, to hunt down the Templars who had escaped across the water to Great Britain. However, the Templars had landed in Scotland, on the Mull of Kintyre and Islay, and were now being protected by Robert the Bruce. The Bruce's people had been conquered by Long Shanks, Edward II's father, although fiercely resisted by the Bruce and Wallis. Robert the Bruce had long held admiration for the Templars, but had nothing but hatred for the English King. In 1314 the Templars repaid the protection of the Bruce by taking arms with his men at the battle of Bannockburn.

"Slowly, as decades went by, the Templars began to disappear from history and, like many other secret societies, their knowledge was thought lost. During the reign of King George III, the Hanoverian Government introduced the Secret Society Act of 1799. The Act banned any teachings and worship higher than the Masonic degrees of York; this meant anything higher than second degree. And so, over time, many of the original ceremonial meanings of Freemasonry were lost; meanings and knowledge that had previously been preserved for centuries, since the time of Solomon. However, the Secret Society Act of 1799 did not afflict all. The Order of Knights Templar, which by then had long since disappeared from public consciousness, had learnt that their survival relied upon their ability **not** to exist.

"Now here comes the bad part. A few years ago two scrolls were taken from the Templar archives, archives that contain thousands of ancient accounts. One of the scrolls was written by the Templars just fifty years ago, which means if it can be decoded, it proves that the Order of Knights Templar still exists today. Their anonymity is no longer secure, and that's not a good thing, as you are about to learn, Courtney.

"The second scroll that was taken is older, centuries older. The person who took it didn't realise at the time the nature of its contents. You see, the second scroll contains details of the biblical artefacts the Templars took with them during the time of the crusades: artefacts from Solomon's Temple. These artefacts are of major importance. Our mutual friend, S E D, has always believed that the Templars still existed. And, he thought he had a pretty good idea what they have in their possession, but he could never prove it. If he could prove it, he would hunt them down. He would use all of the resources at his disposal, and they are considerable. He would kill the Templars to get something that he believes they have. Something that has been the secret Order's most sacred 'Charge' for centuries, something they have protected with Templar lives, many times." He looked her straight in the eye so that there would be no confusion. "If he can decode the scrolls, then he proves his suspicion of who possesses the greatest biblical relic known to mankind. He has killed trying to find it. And, make no mistake about it, he will kill again. Its whereabouts has devoured him, driven him like an all-consuming cancer. He has searched for it for years. S E D, the man you are after, the man who uses a corrupt senator, and many others, for his gains, seeks the greatest icon given to mankind: he seeks the biblical Ark of the Covenant."

She looked at him, then laughed. "Get out of here! You're shitting me!"

"No, no I'm not."

He sipped the last of his coffee. She lit another cigarette, the second in twelve years. Her head was a whirl. "Just who are you, mister?" she asked.

"You don't need to know my name, Courtney."

"Well", she said, "man with no name, just suppose you are telling the truth, and, boy, you need to know this is one big suppose, because I'm not known as the religious one in our family, I still don't get it. I don't get the link with our mutual friend and the senator. Why this senator? And, whilst we are on things that don't figure, if someone really had these scrolls, and they really could prove something like that, why the hell would they sell them in the first place?"

The young waiter was hovering, but the man looked away, watching the flow of traffic at the lights on the corner of Seventeenth and Constitution Avenue. He did this every time they turned green to ensure every car pulled away with the rest of the traffic.

"Why, ah well, now there's a question," he said without turning back. He paused; she was now on the edge of her seat and he lowered his voice again. "It was one of the Templars own, a fallen Knight, who sold the scrolls onto the black market in 1996. He did it for money; it's as banal and as stupid as that. He was so desperate to get out and lead a normal life that he took the two scrolls and sold them. He believed that they would be put into a private collection and would never be made public. That was the deal he made, but the deal was broken and now the scrolls are in the hands of a ruthless and violent criminal, S E D."

He lit another cigarette and then let out the smoke in a great cloud, which hung in the chilly air. Her mind was racing, trying to piece together what he was telling her.

"And you," Courtney asked, "what's your part in all of this?"

"To get the scrolls back. Simple as that."

"That makes you either a broker or, the guy who sold them, this Fallen Knight and a Templar, or at least, ex-Templar."

"It doesn't really matter who I am. What's more important is I get the scrolls back and you get him, if that's what you really want. I can help you. Our route will be through the senator, a man called McGregor. I presume McGregor is the one you want?"

She nodded.

"Then we're in luck. Every year about this time the senator sends out invitations to the great and the good of Washington to attend his charity ball. It will be held at his home on Christmas Eve, so we don't have long to get ready. I strongly believe our friend will be there, low key and anonymous, of course, but he will want to be there. He uses the senator to meet influential people. Then he befriends them, helps them; simple things at first, small things. He does them a favour here, a favour there. Covers up a small indiscretion, helps with a problem they would rather not have. Then, before they know it, they are in his debt, far in his debt. Then he bleeds them.

"I can get you an invite. I can get you in." She looked at him, enquiring. "It doesn't matter how. Just leave that to me," he said. "But you're going to need an escort. It'll look better, more natural. I can't do it, so you're going to need someone who you can take who won't ask you too many questions. The less they know, the better for them. Someone plain and natural, fits in, ordinary like. You got someone like that?"

She nodded. Who was more natural than her brother, the priest?

"We have no idea what this guy S E D looks like, so you will have to watch the senator. Get to him and stay on him. I am guessing that he'll be near to S E D. But no heroics: these people kill. You're going to get one chance at this, so make the night count."

What he didn't tell her was that, if she went, she would be the bait. He was leading her into a trap, but it was the only way he could help her stay alive. That was the paradox of his plan: because of the contract on her life, she had to die. It was the only way he could keep her alive!

She started to give him reassurances about no heroics, but he wasn't listening. Something had distracted him. The pigeons across the street in the park took flight. His eye caught their movement. They had been spooked: those park pigeons never got spooked. His ears picked up the crack – the distinctive sound of a gun being fired. The young waiter had made his way to their table. He had leaned forward and smiled. He opened his mouth; the word cappuccino started to come out – just about the same time the bullet entered his skull. The Croatian fell. The man next to Courtney pushed her hard to the floor. She fell, grazing her knees. He lay on top of her, shielding her. Her face pressed against the hard stone surface of the sidewalk. His gun was now out of its shoulder holster and ready.

"You were followed?" he shouted above the panicked and screaming pedestrians.

She looked at him in disbelief.

"Look, lady, there's a contract out on your life. Word's been all over the street for days. Surely you must have known?"

She shook her head. Her stomach churned and her head spun. He looked around furiously for an escape route for her.

"Listen to me: you've got to get out of here. There, inside." He indicated inside La Bohème. "Find a back door and get out of here."

"But what about you?"

"Get out of here!" he yelled.

There was another crack of fire.

"Go, Courtney, GO!"

She kept low. She didn't look back. Once inside La Bohème, Courtney Rose headed for the back door, stepping over the screaming diners lying prostrate on the floor. She found the door, hit the emergency push-bar and ran, her body shaking. She heard two more shots, then she hit the subway.

Chapter 2

A Disbelieving Priest

Date: Ten days later, Christmas Eve, December 2007
Place: Washington DC

The night that Courtney Rose died it snowed hard and Washington DC was awash with festive activity. The central highway was bumper to bumper with commuters trying to get home for the Christmas holiday. Seventeenth Street and Fourteenth Street had become one big traffic jam. Cars were backed up all along Constitution Avenue, the fumes lingering in the cold, crisp night sky like a toxic cloud. The only thing moving was the icy Potomac River below. Thousands of people gathered in President's Park South (Ellipse) and Lafayette Square, close to the White House. The holiday season had started. Inside the opulent mansion of Senator McGregor, a twelve-piece band had struck up a Glen Miller medley: *Moonlight Serenade, In the Mood* and *Pennsylvania 6-5000*. The wealthy gathering was oblivious to the Christmas chaos outside on the streets, just as they were oblivious to the music inside being played to entertain them. The ambience faltered with every note. No one was listening. They were doing what wealthy socialites do best at parties, practising the art of superficial posturing and being seen. Warm and safe inside, they wallowed in the decadence of the party and in their own self-importance. Outside, the Christmas shoppers continued in last-minute mayhem; drivers revved their engines, hit their horns and moved nowhere.

Father Jonathan Rose complimented his sister, Courtney, as they entered the mansion and joined the party. She was stunning in her evening gown; black always made her look elegant. She smiled and thanked him for the compliment, but she seemed uneasy. He had meant to say something about it on the way there, but he hadn't had the chance. He had already spoken to her twice that day, and on both occasions their telephone conversation had been short. She'd been preoccupied and distant. Since their parents had passed away, five and three years ago, they had become closer. He knew that she had a problem, he just didn't know what it was.

Courtney told her brother she needed to say hello to a couple of people, but she would be back. She hugged him, then seemed to hesitate, apprehensive, before making her way into the crowd. He watched her go, weaving in and out of the wealthy crush and quickly disappearing from his view. She seemed made for this world, he thought, natural and at home in the splendour and refinement. He was not. He hated this kind of event. He felt out of place and clumsy now that he was alone and left to fend for himself amongst the decadent throng. It was going to be a long night.

The Christmas Charity Ball was the first party he had ever attended whose guest list read like a who's who of American politics and A-list socialites. He fidgeted with his white dog collar, which tonight seemed intent on hugging his windpipe.

Father Jonathan Rose was a priest and a schoolteacher. The people around him were neither: they were rich and famous 'somebodies'. He stood awkwardly, spoke only when someone addressed him and tried not to make eye contact. He had no intention of making small talk to these shallow people.

He watched the guests hugging and kissing each other, spilling out compliments and false platitudes. Many must have waited all year to make their grand entrance. He shook his head as he watched the gold and diamonds worn gracefully around the room on their rich owners. Designer clothes, top fashion accessories: the scene was complete. The only photographer invited to attend the party, Thomas Kilroy-Downing, a top fashion photographer from *Life in Washington* magazine, snapped away in a haze of flash and glitter to eager faces. His photographs would be vetted later by security; he would be allowed to use only the ones the senator approved.

Father Jonathan stood close to a six foot high cardboard cut-out of a thermometer, with dollars instead of Fahrenheit markers. It was placed at the foot of the marble stairway, in the main reception area of the McGregor mansion. It showed that the charity ball had raised the sum of one million dollars and all of it, the legend at the bottom of the barometer read, 'raised by the good citizens of Washington DC, for the city's homeless children'. This was the only reason he had agreed to go. He had seen too many kids drop out of school and end up on the streets of the capital. However, when his sister had first suggested they attend, he had done everything he could to get out of it, but Courtney had been insistent. In fact, she had been a little too insistent and he couldn't help thinking that her motives were more than just a bout of festive guilt: her being in the FBI had done that to him. After days of his holding out, she had finally worn him down and he had agreed to go. He could suffer one night with the shallow elite he disliked so much.

His sister, four years older than him, had never married, despite his constant hints. She often relied on Jonathan to act as her escort whenever she had a function to attend. She was proud of her brother, the priest, who taught world history and religious studies at a local high school. She took every opportunity to show him off, something he hated, but never said.

Senator Thomas McGregor's mansion stood in the tree-lined Vale, a salubrious suburb reserved by the developers for the wealthy and the very wealthy. The senator was in the very wealthy category and so were most of his guests. The son of a rich landowner out of Salt Lake City, his family had all the right connections; they moved in 'those' kind of circles. The senator knew the value of good PR. The charity ball, which he held every year, was just another predetermined strategy to help him on his way to the White House. '*By Invitation Only*' would ensure that only the rich citizens of Washington would get in. The homeless were not invited to share his Christmas fare in person. Instead, the six foot high cardboard barometer represented them. Father Jonathan didn't know how his sister had managed to get invited to Washington's party of the year, but she had.

Courtney Rose had been a Harvard graduate with a double honours degree in criminology, as well as a doctorate in computer sciences, working as a desk-based FBI agent on one of the most powerful computers in the world. She liked science, math and puzzles and Jonathan had always admired her because she was logical, clinical and rational. Though she never said so, he gathered that she was now a rising star in the FBI. She worked hard at her job as a Middle East Theatre Strategist, a job that required a very powerful computer linked to the FBI's cloaked mainframe, Colossus 1, and an intellect only found in the top three percentile of the world's population. Jonathan felt she worked too hard and he would often tell her that he had never known a man or woman say on their deathbed, 'I wish I had spent more time at work', but she never listened.

He himself didn't have the skills that Courtney possessed; neither did he have her drive or ambition. He was content with his faith and his teaching job, in which he found all the fulfilment he needed.

Of medium build, he stood five feet ten, with light brown, well-kept hair, green eyes and boyish looks. His ideal week consisted of a few beers midweek after school with friends from the old neighbourhood and watching a football game, the Washington Redskins, on Saturdays. On Sundays he assisted the regular parish priest for both morning and evening mass at the local church.

Father Jonathan was a good and popular teacher who taught his students based on two basic beliefs: 'never look at children for what they are, look at them for what they can become' and 'teach them how to think, not what to think'. His sister loved these qualities in him; she said he always looked at people through a generous lens. He acquiesced, was considerate and would compromise rather than seek confrontation. He liked his uncomplicated life: a life he would not have swapped, given the choice.

The police found Courtney Rose's body at 3 a.m. the following morning, fifty miles away from the McGregor mansion, nearly two hours after her brother had reported her missing. Despite the fact the body had received ninety-five degree burns, the coroner recorded the corpse as that of Courtney Rose. His report indicated that her throat had been cut – the incision measured ten inches long – and both eyelids had been removed. After burning at intense temperature, the body having been thoroughly soaked in a highly inflammable industrial solvent-based liquid, identified as Zaliform Om2, the charred corpse had then frozen in the unusually heavy snowfall that fell on that Christmas Eve. The time of death was recorded as midnight.

At first the police suspected her brother, despite the obvious fact that he was a priest. The two homicide detectives struggled with the case: no motive, no witnesses and no reason for her to have left the party without her brother.

At midnight, about the time of Courtney's death, Senator McGregor had stood on the wide marble stairway in the main reception area of his mansion and proudly announced to his 470 guests that they had raised in excess of one million dollars for homeless children. Father Jonathan, standing right next to the cardboard barometer, was remembered by some of the guests. His awkwardness stuck in their minds. They could tell that the priest was not one of them, not one of their kind, and so the police's suspicions of him were short-lived.

Father Jonathan had last seen his sister at around 11 p.m., talking to two men, near to the main entrance. One of the men was Senator McGregor and the other a Middle Eastern-looking man in his mid-fifties. He was tall with silver hair, sharp features and piercing black eyes. Father Jonathan remembered seeing her with the two men because, against his better judgement, he had been trying to hold a meaningful conversation with a group of wealthy stockbrokers. He had no interest in moneymaking talk and they had no interest in his views on the under-funding of the education system. He had tried to attract his sister's attention. He needed rescuing, but she was too engrossed in her own conversation and didn't see him. He would later regret not trying harder.

Just after midnight and the speech by the senator, balloons fell from the ceiling onto the throng and the band struck up *For he's a jolly good fellow.* Father Jonathan had searched the crowded room for his sister, but she was nowhere to be found. Outside, her car had gone and none of the parking valets could remember her or her car. At this stage he hadn't felt any panic. A valet called him a cab and he went straight to her house, arriving there at about 1 a.m. The house had been broken into and ransacked: his sister was nowhere to be found. Now the panic set in. Fearing the worst, Jonathan called the police. The name Courtney Rose was entered onto the missing person's list. Two hours later, her frozen, charred corpse was discovered. Her file was then transferred to two detectives working in homicide: it had become a murder case.

Date: Christmas day, December 2007
Place: Washington DC

Meeks had been with the Federal Bureau of Investigation for twenty-two years. As an African-American, he'd had to work hard to move up the FBI's ladder of promotion. He had been one of the first agents to be informed about Courtney's death. The duty officer at the Bureau knew that Meeks had been a friend of Courtney's, so he figured he would want to know. Meeks had been at home asleep when the call came through.

In the early days Meeks had taken Courtney under his wing, before she got promoted and specialised. He had seen it all in his twenty-two years with the FBI. He'd lost colleagues before, but Courtney's death hit him hard. Despite this, he made the late night trip back into the Bureau offices to search Courtney's desk. He only had a matter of an hour, maybe two at the most, before the internal investigation division would get there to clear her desk and start reassigning her cases. It didn't take him long to find what he was looking for. Although she'd never admitted it, Meeks knew Courtney kept a meticulous diary. He also knew her well enough to know where she kept it. He had warned her many times about keeping a diary; now he was thankful she had.

Ever since he found out about it, he had been suspicious about Courtney's motives for going to the McGregor party. There were rumours in the Bureau about a senator, and Meeks knew she had pulled files on a number of senators, including McGregor's. In fact, she had pulled McGregor's file several times in the last six weeks. But Courtney had been one of those people who could never leave anything alone once she started something – she always had to scratch that itch. Meeks had tried to talk her out of going to the party but, as always, she had given him one of those cute smiles of hers and told him that it was just a party.

Meeks knew the senator kept unhealthy company. More than that, he knew who bankrolled the senator's political campaign. He worried that sooner or later, if she dug deep enough, Courtney could stumble across the man behind the senator: and he figured that must be exactly what she had done. Meeks was angry with himself. He should have known better. He should have done something, tried harder to dissuade her. Perhaps he should have told her everything, but now it was too late and it troubled him deeply. He, her friend, had failed to protect her from her killer: the killer whose name Meeks knew only too well, the name that belonged to the initials S E D.

On the drive home from the Bureau's office buildings, Bill

Meeks grew increasingly frustrated. He just couldn't piece it together; none of it made any sense. He guessed that Courtney had found out about the senator and his friend's activities. He didn't know how much she knew, but it had been enough for her to start digging. Courtney, a natural and talented operative, had one of the best investigative minds he knew. Once she had one or two pieces in place, it wouldn't have taken her long to begin to figure things out. Then, slowly she would start to see lies, deceit and bribes, now rife throughout the Bureau. She would have made the link between the senator, his friend and those in the Bureau that had gone bad. But why had she been killed? That didn't make any sense to him at all; something must have spooked the senator or his friend. Something didn't fit though; whatever it was, he was missing it and it gnawed away at him.

Later that night, at home, Meeks started to read her diary. Half an hour later he had his answer. The entry read:

... my mystery man finally contacted me, after all these weeks

... my mystery man has agreed to meet. He sounds
PROFESSIONAL. Take care ...

... must know who S E D is. Why did he want the old papers
His link to the senator?

... then it's time to clean house!!!!

Meeks's stomach sank. He knew the initials S E D and immediately he knew what the words 'old papers' meant. On top of Courtney's death, this was the worst news he could have received.

Meeks had to get word to his friends in Scotland – friends the FBI knew nothing about. Thanks to Courtney, he now knew that the scrolls were out in the open and in S E D's hands. This changed everything. He made the call from the secure line installed in his home and within two hours his friend in Scotland had made the eight calls to destinations all over the world: *they* were now gathering.

Meeks resolved not to make the same mistake again. Secretly he kept watch on Jonathan. In his grief Jonathan was cold and impervious to the world, but Meeks knew his retribution was waiting to surface. He could read the signs: the grief was like an express train coming. Jonathan needed answers and there was no one to give him any in Washington. He would have to go to Scotland for that. An amateur in a deadly game, he would be driven by his grief and he would end up getting killed.

Date: December 2007 (Three days after the murder).
Place: A remote castle in Scotland

It was bitterly cold, a frosty white blanket stretching out as far as the eye could see. The castle, restored in 1972, bulged high above the white panorama. The structure, with two-metre-thick walls, was solid and inspiring, a haven and sanctuary for its owners over the years. Semi-isolated from civilization, the castle stood in hundreds of miles of bleak Scottish wilderness, accompanied on three sides by bracken-covered hills and by a dense meandering spruce forest on the other. A magical place in summer, but a desolate and barren place in the winter, it was seldom visited in any season.

Payne St Clair made his way up the dimly lit, spiral stone stairs. The draught from an open embrasure made his breath visible as he exhaled. The steps were worn from age and a lifetime of use. At the top he stopped and turned a large iron key. The solid oak door moved when he pushed against it, the three large ornate hinges creaking. He moved out onto the battlements and leaned on the waist-high parapet wall. The wind howled and drove its chill into his eyes, making them water. Some way off, he heard the noise of rattling braziers, pots and pans, the clatter filtering intermittently through the harsh roar of the wind. A convoy of rural gypsies made their way around the narrow winding lane, just east of his position. Past the spruce forest the land was dispersed, dotted every now and again with little-used tracks. Grassy plateaus, now snow-covered, and ranks of dry stonewalls, rambling glens and floundering bracken stretched out before him. This was the Scotland he loved, a scenic infinity that was wild and unspoiled.

Seven were inside. They had come because he had called them. They had travelled thousands of miles to be there. He had made contact with them just three days ago, after Meeks had telephoned with the grave news and now they were there, waiting for the last of them to arrive.

The car had been visible for over two miles. St Clair had watched its progress along the lane that led to the castle. He knew who the driver was and it pleased him.

The driver parked by the side of the other vehicles. Slowly, he eased his frame from the car, groaning with the stiffness in his legs after a long drive. He raised his hand to the silver-headed man standing on the battlements in gesture to his old friend. He was the last of them to arrive: now they were nine.

André Sabath, a small, rotund figure with short-cropped hair, stood on the frosted cobbled courtyard below and smiled up to his friend. The gaze between them was held for only a few seconds, their understanding tacit. They had been friends for over thirty years and had faced many dangers together. Now more Knights of their Order would have to put their lives at risk. It was the reason he had come; it was the reason they had all come. He shook the chill from his body and went inside.

St Clair looked up again and squinted. He could no longer see the gypsies. The January wind now veiled the sounds of their cooking implements, as they banged and crashed in harmony on the undulating lanes. The eight were inside waiting for him. He was the ninth of The Nine Worthies. The Higher Council of the Order of Knights Templar had gathered and he, their Order's Grand Master, would join them. He left the battlements, locking the solid oak door behind him. Shutting out the wind, he made his way down the stone spiral stairs to the great hall. The fire, already raging in the hearth, gave out a welcome warmth which extended beyond the hall.

St Clair paused outside the door to the great hall and checked his dress in the tall seventeenth-century French mirror hanging on the stone wall. He adjusted his white surcoat, centralizing the distinctive red cross of the Templars. Just as there is distinction in Benedictine and Cistercian Orders, the Knights Templar wore white to signify purity, symbolizing their abandonment of darkness for light, evil for good. He looked into his own eyes, breathed deeply and then exhaled ruefully. He could hear the voices of the eight inside, old friends who seldom met. Once, maybe twice a year was all they would risk; they had too many secrets to protect. He turned the black iron ring handle and entered the great hall.

Payne St Clair, the Order's Grand Master, took his seat at the head of the table. Four Worthies were seated to his left and four Worthies to his right. After the ceremony of welcome was complete, they each took the Eucharist, the embodiment of Christ. Now they sat silent in contemplation and expectation. St Clair eased himself out of the high-backed Jacobean chair to address them. He stood tall and proud, a man who personified reverence and dignity.

"Brothers, by God's grace we are called again. May our Lord watch over this Council and give us the wisdom we will need."

He lowered his head in respect and then began, his tone deep and meaningful. As they listened the incredulity on their faces grew. Meeks had telephoned with news that the stolen scrolls were now in the hands of S E D, Salah El-Din. The erosion of their Order's anonymity was just a matter of time now, and their Charge, which they had protected for centuries, was now in extreme danger.

Their ultra-secret network, scattered all over the world, was put on code red vigilance. They had been monitoring Salah El-Din's criminal activities for some time, but The Nine Worthies had decided not to take the ultimate action against him. They were still not sure that the criminal had the resources to discover their Order and its

Charge. Some feared, however, that it was just a matter of time, but the next step, a death sanction, meant taking lives. They would need to be sure.

Date: March 2008 (Three months later)
Place: Washington DC

Father Jonathan Rose's life had fallen apart. Despite their enquiries, the police were no further forward with what had happened the night of the murder. He had no idea why his sister had left the party without telling him. Why was there no sign of a struggle at the scene of the murder? Who had killed her and who had wrecked her house? All the police knew was that her body had been found by the side of a railway track, by a night watchman, fifty miles from the Vale. The night watchman had seen nothing other than her burnt body, lying next to her car. Her blood was found on the crime scene, but there were no fingerprints, and no clues. The keys were still in the ignition of her car; her purse, on the driver seat, had not been touched. Without eyelids to protect them, her eyes had frozen into a fixed stare.

At first, and on most days, Jonathan telephoned the two detectives from homicide, Detective Sergeant Billy Thomas and Detective Brent Walker, and every day he received the same reply: 'no progress'. It angered him that he always rang them; they never rang him.

Three weeks after Courtney's funeral, Father Jonathan had returned to work, but his life was in shreds. He felt he was slowly going insane as the constant unyielding grief ripped at his insides. He blamed himself. He blamed everybody, but most of all he blamed God. Unanswered questions tormented him. Why had she left the party without telling him? Why had God allowed her to die, and in that way? She had her whole life in front of her; why would God want to take her? It ate away at him like a cancer. His colleagues at school did all they could to help, but his malaise and depression only grew stronger. As the weeks went by, he became progressively worse.

His archbishop wrote a number of caring letters, but he left them unopened. The church, used to dealing with grieving parishioners, found it difficult to justify Courtney's death to one of their own. Jonathan had heard all the words before, even said them himself: those words now held no comfort for him. He became more and more distant from his priesthood. His faith had been tested in the most horrific way, and he had found it, and his God, wanting.

Days passed slowly and his interest in himself and life ebbed. He acted out living, but it was false: he was a thirsty man without a drink; a walker without a road; a priest without faith – alone. He had not worn his priest's collar since the night of the McGregor party and as each day passed it became easier not to put it on, not to think of himself as a priest. His faith, like his priest's collar, no longer seemed part of his life, no longer important. God had not answered his questions, so he stopped speaking to God, his faith lost to him.

His resignation from the priesthood surprised no one. He had taken his sister's death harder than anyone could have imagined. His holy vows seemed like empty words to him now. He had once resolved that, whilst he was worth his room on earth, it would be given over to God. Now he had no such resolve. He felt no worth; he could no longer reconcile his faith and considered himself exempt from even trying any more. He had attended many funerals in the past and had felt what he took to be true empathy, but now he knew that it had been just well-meaning sympathy. There had been no real understanding of what the mourners were going through; now, of course, he understood. He had once told his students that to know what water was like, first you had to get wet. Now he knew what grief was like: every day he was drowning in it.

Then, two weeks before the festival of Easter, the church decided to make a final attempt to bring Jonathan back into their fold. Father Mark James knew him well. They had spent a lot of time together at seminary and had both been ordained at the same time.

Like Jonathan, Father Mark was a teacher as well as a priest. The letter from the diocese had arrived a week or so ago, but, like the rest of his mail, it had remained unopened.

Surprised by his visitor, Jonathan reluctantly let his friend into his house. It was a bright day, fresh and alive with colour, but Jonathan took little notice of its beauty. Father Mark, dressed casually and not in a cassock, still had that same lolloping walk that used to amuse Jonathan. His feet, pointing out as he walked, hovered above the ground before being placed gently down, but there was no amusement today. Father Mark was on a mission from the bishop.

The conversation was cordial to start with, but inevitably it turned to religion. Father Mark did his best, but he was quite unprepared for Jonathan's anger towards God.

"God cannot be held responsible for every death, Jonathan. You know that as well as I do."

Jonathan had been plagued by uncertainty well before the loss of his sister. Her death had merely polarised it and now it was about to spill out.

"Can you honestly tell me that you have never questioned our Bible, Mark? You know as well as I do that many of the scriptures no longer match with scientific and historical facts. But then again," Jonathan said almost as an afterthought, "how could they? The Testaments are just stories written over vast periods of time, in conflict with each other; disparate ideology, culturally diluted fables."

"But …" Mark interjected, "stories of no less value and importance because of their age."

"Age has nothing to do it with it, Mark, and you know that." Jonathan rounded on him sharply. "They have been changed from their original texts because of poor translation. And in a lot of cases they were deliberately changed by interfering clerics, infected by politics and manipulating monarchs. As priests, our whole reason for being is based on a book that has been tampered with by generations of self-effacing, power-hungry bigots."

Jonathan raised his hands in his perceived futility of it all. "For pity's sake, Mark, we don't even know the real name of Jesus Christ. That name is Greek, Iesus Chrestus, added to the scriptures much later as an attempt to translate the Jewish title, Messiah, the bringer of salvation. And even that wasn't true. It wasn't the bringer of salvation; it meant a person who will be the rightful king. But despite all this, our church's ecumenical nonsense persists even over a name."

"You know that the same events of the birth and death of Jesus can also be found in other cultures? The religion of Mithraism comes from the Roman Empire. It is widely believed that Mithras was born in a stable, of a virgin, on December twenty-fifth and his resurrection was celebrated by the Romans at Easter time. Mithras's story predates Christianity by 600 years. And what did our Lord Bishop tell me when I asked him about it? He said that it is known that the story was devised by the devil, to deliberately fool the people of the time."

"Adam and Eve: go look at the creation story of Sumer, in modern day Iraq. It was written centuries before Genesis, yet it is almost identical."

Father Mark shifted uneasily in his chair. He was a priest, not a theologian. He'd had no reason to seek out such data.

"Does it matter, Jonathan?" Father Mark began, in an attempt to quell Jonathan's frustration. "I mean, does it really matter? Just because you don't know a person's name, does it make them any less a person? Just because there are similar stories in history, does it make the Bible any less true?"

Jonathan laughed. "It's not the name, Mark. It's not even the story of Mithras or creation. It is the point of it. Don't you see, if the name is wrong, if there are other identical stories in different cultures, how much more is wrong?

"The Old Testament was written in Aramaic and Hebrew between 1200 and 165 years BC. It was then translated into Greek. The Greek language had several different dialects, so translation was difficult. Do you not think there were additions and changes, or maybe interpretations made throughout those centuries because of errors, church politics, even incompetence? We know whole new passages were put in and left out: Tobit, Wisdom, Ecclesiasticus, the history of Susannah, the prayer of Manasseh."

Father Mark shrugged his shoulders. There was little else he could do. His belief was under attack and he was struggling to hold his side of the argument. This was the first time he had argued with another priest about his faith in this way and it wasn't pleasant. Jonathan still wasn't finished, though. There was more frustration waiting to surface.

"Please read Rabbi Manny Jacob's new book. It starts with a simple question: what was the name of the man who was released at Jesus's trial? The man accused of being a Jewish rebel, the man who was chosen by the crowd to be freed, instead of Jesus?"

"Barabbas."

"But what would you say, Mark, if Rabbi Manny, using new techniques in translation developed at the University of Haifa, had discovered that Barabbas was not the name of a man at all, and that he and his highly respected team of archaeologists have defined the name Barabbas as meaning the Son of God?" Jonathan didn't even wait for a −reply. "It would mean that if the Son of God was released, he did not die on the cross. Which fits with one of the world's oldest religions that preaches that Jesus did not die, but another took his place. The Koran, Sura 4:157: '... *We killed the Christ Jesus, the son of Mary, the apostle of Allah − but they killed him not, nor crucified him, but so it was made to appear to them.'*"

"Surely in the Old Testament you can still find meaning, still find faith?"

"Our Ten Commandments, perhaps?" asked Jonathan, rhetorically.

"There were supposed to have been two tablets of stone, but Exodus does not give their shape or size. However, in the Jewish Kabbalah, it says that the tablet of Testimony was a divine sapphire called Schethiya, which Moses held in the palm of his hand. The

Kabbalah also says that Abraham is said to have received the Testament of a Lost Civilization which was said to have contained 'all that man had ever known'. Kabbalistic writing also refers to the 'Table of Destiny', inherited by Moses and subsequently passed onto King Solomon.

"Melchizedek was the priest who presented bread and wine to Abraham, but when the Dead Sea scrolls were found at Qumran, Khirbite Mird and Murabba, in Judea, they contained fragments of a scroll called the Prince Melchizedek document and it indicates that the Archangel and Melchizedek were one of the same. Have you never wondered how that can be?

"And what should we priests make of one of the most blatant acts of wilful religious vandalism, ever?' Jonathan continued without skipping a beat. "Turkey, May twentieth, 325 AD, the Council of Nicaea. King Constantine, who, despite worshipping Sol Invictus, the Sun God, convened the first International Council of Christians to establish a single view concerning Christianity. Up until then, our religion was plagued by multiple fractious beliefs. Constantine brought together leaders from all over the ancient world to debate doctrinal differences. The time for nuance was over and what came out of the meeting forms the order of things today.

"Constantine's meddling, fabrications and fanciful meanderings did not restrict themselves to him alone. Even his mother got in on the act. The Empress Helena decided she would take it upon herself to locate all religious sites in Jerusalem, and thus sent an army of servants to find them. Of course, eager to please, these early day detectives made some miraculous discoveries. Or so we are told. Christ's tomb was found beneath Jupiter's temple, the site of the crucifixion a short distance away. Helena herself discovered the True Cross and even the spot where Jesus ascended to heaven. What is most miraculous is that they did all of this 300 years after the events took place! And 250 years after the Romans had destroyed the city!"

"That's not new and you know it, Jonathan. Even the pope is …"

"Ah, finally we get around to the pope! A position founded on the fact that Jesus said to Peter, 'You are Peter, a rock, and I will build my church upon you. I will give you the keys of the Kingdom of Heaven.' After his resurrection, Jesus said to him, 'Feed my lambs. Feed my sheep.' So what did they translate this as? That Jesus made it clear to Peter that by these words he was to be the first pope. The man the Romans crucified upside down. And in turn, Peter passed on the mantle to the Bishop of Rome, and so it prevails today with every successive pope. But don't you think it perhaps a little odd that, according to the Acts of the Apostles and Letters from Paul to James, the younger brother of Jesus took the leadership role? And, in fact, the first ten bishops of the Jerusalem Church were all circumcised Jews, who used Jewish liturgy for their daily prayers? Not a Latin speaker amongst them!"

"I have never heard you speak of these things before, Jonathan. I always thought your faith in the Lord Almighty was as strong as anyone's, but now, now I know I was wrong."

Jonathan lifted his head, weary. "Mark, can you not see the litany of changes for the sake of perpetuating a belief system that gives its masters, the church, our church, great power and wealth, as long as the population believe? I have never before questioned the existence of God. That's why I became a priest. Yes, I always had issues with the Bible because I always knew that men with ulterior motives had complied and decided its order. Yes, I believed in God, then God abandoned me, He abandoned my sister, and now I have abandoned Him. Quid pro quo, my friend, quid pro quo."

It was late when Father Mark left Jonathan's house. It was dark outside and he shuddered with the chill. Wearily, he started the engine of his old Ford Dodge. The engine growled and spluttered before easing into a steady rhythm. He wound down his window and held out his hand; Jonathan grasped it and shook it.

"So what now, my friend? What are you going to do?" Father Mark asked.

"What do you mean?"

"Jonathan, it's clear you no longer want to be part of the church and you're not teaching anymore. It seems to me that you have two choices. You can try to reconcile your pain and your faith, or you could try to find out what really happened to Courtney and why, and perhaps that path will lead you to peace."

"I wouldn't know where to start. Where do you start? Look at me, I'm …"

"I don't mean you, Jonathan. You're one of the most easy-going people I know, the quiet, unassuming type, not the gung-ho sort. Find someone to help you, a professional, a private investigator, or something like that. I'm just saying, I don't think you will find any answers sitting locked inside your house all day."

"You mean revenge?" Jonathan frowned.

"No, Jonathan, I don't mean revenge. That's not what I'm saying. I mean answers. This thing, this sorrow you have, it's eating away at you. Why don't you look for the truth? That's all I'm saying."

Clouds blanketed the darkening sky as Jonathan watched his friend drive away towards the city. Going back inside, he closed his door and slumped into the armchair. He closed his eyes and fell into a deep but -troubled sleep. His dreams were full of images of death and of pain. But a voice in his head gave hope. It was a deep low melodic voice, repeating over and over again, (Revelations 22: 23) *He seized the dragon, the ancient Serpent, who is the Devil, or Satan and bound him for a thousand years. He threw him into the Abyss, and locked and sealed it over him, to keep him from deceiving nations anymore…*

Chapter 3

Walker

Date: Summer 2008
Place: Washington DC

Months after the murder the police had moved on. Their caseloads grew and the Rose file moved further and further down the pile. For everyone else, it seemed that this was just another unexplained death, but for Jonathan, the express train that Meeks had seen coming was gathering speed.

Jonathan was angry with Meeks and he was angry with the FBI. It seemed that, like the police, they were treating his sister's death as yesterday's news. Despite the tension between them, Meeks went by the house every week, but their meetings were always strained.

The police had told Jonathan that they had interviewed everyone who had attended the party that night, but had no leads. The DC elite had given their statements, shaken their heads with disbelief at the gruesome details, and then got on with their lives. Courtney Rose and the plight of homeless children were other people's business now. Senator McGregor had sent a condolence card, which was read out at Courtney's funeral. It said that he would do all he could to help. Jonathan never heard from him again.

By midsummer Jonathan had given up everything that was his life before the murder. He no longer went to ball games and he no longer drank with his old friends from the neighbourhood. He missed his sister: he missed her terribly. His house was left untidy and the once-tended lawns grew without opposition. He found it hard to sleep, his dreams ravaged by her death, and he struggled to make sense of it all.

The insurance company, Nesbit and Morgan, acting on behalf of the government, had paid promptly on Courtney's FBI life insurance policy: no fuss and no visit. As the next of kin, Jonathan received all of the money. It lay untouched in his bank account. Then, a few weeks later, another insurance company contacted him. This time they wanted to send someone to fill out some forms and check some details. He didn't know that his sister had private insurance. A petite woman, dressed mainly in black and in her early thirties, called at the house after the appointment had been made. The woman, who was tanned and attractive, introduced herself as Roan Jones, Regional Claims Officer for Diggby Price and Goldstein. She was somewhat curt and pushy, Jonathan thought. She asked lots of questions about Courtney. He never did receive a cheque from Diggby Price and Goldstein, but, preoccupied, he never gave it another thought.

In June, Jonathan read in the national newspaper that Senator McGregor had been shot in Salt Lake City. It said that it had been a professional killing. The suggestion was Mafia, but nothing could be proven. The only clue the police had was the bullet that had lodged in the senator's heart. It was a .40 calibre round. The bullet came from the same Glock 27 handgun associated with several other killings, both sides of the Atlantic. It was known to be favoured by at least five known international assassins. The assassin took only one shot; he or she couldn't have been more than ten feet away from the senator. A police spokesman said that that kind of close quarter hit was rare; most assassins prefer the long shot, with a rifle and high calibre round. Few had the steel for such close-quarter work. As a result of the assassination, security around every major dignitary was doubled. Some stayed away from their offices for a few weeks, others left for early vacations, and the FBI and the CIA were extra busy.

Reading the article, at first Jonathan's concern was for someone who had once sent a condolence card to a funeral, his sister's funeral, but something about the picture in the newspaper bothered him some. He looked at it hard: then it struck him. The picture the paper carried of the senator was six months old. It was a picture of the senator and his family, taken in Salt Lake City airport on Christmas Day, the last time the senator was there. The airport clock in the picture was clearly visible. It showed the time at 11 a.m. and the date of the 25th December 2007. He knew from his conversations with Sgt Thomas, one of the homicide detectives assigned to the case, that they had interviewed McGregor for two hours on Christmas Day – the day after the party and the death of his sister. They had done this in his home in the Vale. Jonathan couldn't understand how the senator could have been in Salt Lake City, when he was being interviewed by the police in Washington DC.

Jonathan walked to the refrigerator and ripped the top off a can of Red Stripe. He studied the picture again: there was no mistake. His breathing accelerated.

He made the call to the precinct. A female voice told him that Detective Sergeant Billy Thomas had retired from the force two months earlier; he would have to go all the way to Arizona if he wanted to talk to him. Jonathan asked for his partner who had worked on the case with Thomas. He was put through. He told Walker what he had just found.

"You know, Father, now you come to mention it," Walker started unconvincingly and with obvious unease, "I seem to remember something about the senator being out of town and Billy had to interview him over the phone."

Jonathan didn't know what he was expecting to hear, but it wasn't this. Thomas had clearly told him that he had interviewed McGregor, face to face, at his home on Christmas morning. Jonathan was not going to be fobbed off. "I am not a priest anymore, detective, so please don't call me Father," he said, conscious that he sounded curt.

Walker apologized, but Jonathan hadn't finished.

"So, what you're telling me is you interviewed someone who was a key witness to this case by phone? You know that McGregor and the Middle Eastern-looking man were the last people I saw talking to my sister."

Walker, curt in return, reminded him that McGregor had never been a suspect in the case anyway. He had a cast-iron alibi because, at the time of the murder, he was standing in front of over four hundred guests, but Jonathan knew that already. He had only been a few feet away from the senator himself. However, the lie was clearly there. For the first time he had something to hold onto, and he wasn't about to let go.

"So why did Detective Sergeant Thomas tell me he had interviewed him face-to-face in his home, on Christmas Day? Why didn't he just tell me the truth, instead of some bullshit?"

Walker's guard went up. The 'bullshit' seemed more damning coming from a man he knew as a priest.

"It's not bullshit. It's called a screwed-up and under-funded system, is all. Too many bad guys and not enough cops. This may come as a surprise to you, but the general public really don't give a damn, as long as they don't have to pay more taxes for more cops and the crime doesn't involve them, so we do the best we can."

But Jonathan was not about to give up on the only thread he had.

"But I distinctly remember Thomas telling me that he had interviewed McGregor, at his house on Christmas Day, and now you're telling me he was lying?"

Walker snapped back. "He was wrong Fath ... Mr Rose, is all. He did it over the phone. It happens sometimes."

"And when McGregor got back from vacation, was he interviewed then, by any chance?"

"You will have to speak to Billy Thomas about that. It was his baby. I had other witnesses to interview."

"You could check your case files."

"Look, Mr Rose, your sister is dead. Let her rest in peace. Leave the police work to the police. If we find anything we will let you know."

The express train picked up pace some more.

"What, I should just sit here knowing that a murderer is walking around free? You think it's easy visiting my sister's grave, knowing her murderer is still enjoying life? I should tell her what, detective? Don't worry, the police are on the case, still!"

"I can't help you, Mr Rose," Walker said. "As far as the city is concerned, this case remains unsolved."

"You mean closed."

The phone went dead. Jonathan stood holding the receiver, his heart pounding. For the first time since the death of his sister he felt a purpose. He wanted to cling on to it. He rang the precinct back, but the female voice said that Walker was out. He couldn't have left the building that quickly. She had been well trained. He would ring again first thing in the morning. He would not let this go.

It was 10 p.m. when the front doorbell rang, waking Jonathan as he dozed in a chair. His head lurched forward and he opened his eyes. It was a still summer's evening; the smell of freshly mown grass permeated through his house, but it wasn't his grass, which remained uncut. A well-built man with collar-length blond hair, parted in the centre, stood on the porch. He wore no jacket and his brown trousers and white short-sleeve shirt were viciously creased from another long, hot, sticky day in the capital. His craggy looks hinted at a stressful job. He loosened his collar and drew on the cigarette he was smoking.

"Mr Rose, I know it's late … do you mind if I come in?" He was uncomfortable standing outside where he was visible. He showed Jonathan his badge, but Jonathan had already recognised Walker.

Walker had been inside the houses of hundreds of victims' families. They all had that same sense of emptiness and pity. He could smell it in Jonathan's house; he would never get used to it.

Brent Walker had thought about the Rose case a lot since his partner had retired. He had never been happy with the way it had been dealt with back at the precinct. He was a good detective and the Rose case had always bothered him: something about it had a bad taste. Billy Thomas, older in years and longer in service, had told him to forget it, do what they had been told to do and leave it alone. Walker had had every intention of leaving it alone, until Jonathan's phone call. Now he couldn't do that.

"You want a Red Stripe, coffee or something?"

Walker lowered his big frame into a chair and groaned with the pain in his back.

"Sure, Red Stripe would be good."

Jonathan brought a six-pack from the kitchen. Walker pulled the ring off one of the cans and drank in large gulps. He had a thirst that needed quenching. He looked around the living room.

"You got the place looking like shit, if you don't mind me saying so, but I know how it is. My wife ran out on me two years ago. Don't think I've washed the dishes since. Place is the pits, but it's home."

Jonathan raised half a smile and the slight tension that had been there was eased a little. Walker swallowed hard again. The beer was cool and it felt good. He finished it and took another.

"So you quit on the cloth, eh? Seems real weird not calling you Father."

"No, actually God quit on me, or my sister would still be alive."

Walker got the message. Small talk had no place in Jonathan's life, just answers.

"I guess you're wondering what I'm doing here?"

Jonathan nodded, encouraging Walker to do the talking.

"It's not easy," Walker began. "I mean, with all the shit we have to deal with. It's like a cattle market down there some days. Caseloads mount up and more come in every day. If it ain't drugs, it's rape, extortion, murder; you name it, the city's got it. Kids no older than ten

43

wielding machetes or pulling shotguns defending their turf, run down, sewer-ridden, filthy buildings no one else would give a shit about, but they are willing to kill each other for it and we are supposed to stop it."

He paused. It was true but he knew it sounded lame. Jonathan was looking at him.

"But you don't want to hear that do you?"

Jonathan shrugged.

Walker finished his second Red Stripe and put the empty can into the over-spilling waste-paper basket by the side of his chair. He took another can and drank some more.

"The night your sister died, Billy and me got the party guest list from the staff at Senator McGregor's mansion. Then we interviewed them, all those rich bastards. It took us nearly three weeks because they had to find time in their fucking social diaries for them to see us."

"Three weeks?"

Walker's guard went up.

"Hey, these ain't ordinary Joes here., Some of these people are pretty powerful. You can't just walk across their lawn and demand to interview them. That shit only happens on television. The point I'm getting to is, we never got to McGregor because we got told to leave him alone."

"What do you mean, 'leave him alone'?"

Walker moved back into his chair.

"You know ..." he said, knowing that Jonathan wouldn't. No one outside of the Force could know how things worked sometimes. "Out of bounds, don't touch him, leave the senator alone. It came from the top. The brass upstairs said they would deal with it. So we just figured that, because it was a senator, they didn't want Billy and me raining all over his parade. They said this guy was heading for the big time in politics. So, Billy and me thought that the mayor was looking out for one of his friends and because he was not a suspect, we thought hey, why not? Problem is, it never did get dealt with, and he was never interviewed, to my knowledge. I checked with a friend of mine at the FBI. Normally, when one of their own goes down, they're all over it like a rash, but he said that their case file was also being dealt with higher up and, to his knowledge, it was still pending, somewhere."

Rage boiled up inside Jonathan. "Well, that's just great." He was already preparing his speech to Meeks.

"No, Mr Rose, it ain't great, because this shit gets worse. When I said we interviewed all the guests, we did, except one."

Jonathan reached for the newspaper containing the photograph of McGregor in Salt Lake.

"I'm confused. We still talking McGregor, right?"

"Wrong. There was one other person we never got to interview."

"Why not?" It was a simple enough question. Walker gulped at his beer.

"Because, officially, we have no idea who he is. No ID, jack shit. All we know is that there were four hundred and seventy guests that night. We interviewed four hundred and sixty-six. Now add you, your sister and the senator, and that leaves us with one missing, our mystery person."

Jonathan was not a slow thinker, but he was trying really hard to make sense of what Brent Walker had just told him. This was the first time he'd had any facts about his sister's murder in six months, but these facts were making no sense. He told Walker that he and his sister had to show their invitations to get into the mansion. The security checked off everyone's name against the names on their list. Security had been tight. If Walker could get the list then they would know who the person was. But Walker hadn't finished.

"Like I said earlier, we had the list, got it on Christmas Day. Trouble is, someone had tampered with it. A name had been erased."

45

"Erased! So what does that give us?" Jonathan asked.

"That gives *us* jack shit, because there ain't no *us*. Officially, I'm off the case. In fact, I ain't even been here tonight. However, Mr Rose, it might give *you* something, if you want it."

Suddenly Jonathan grew anxious. "What do you mean, 'if I want it'?"

"Because only you can do this. If you don't, seems to me that no one else is going to. Just do some digging, nothing heavy. I got a couple people that will help you. Couple of ex-cops I know who have their PI licenses. Look, all you got to do is find some hard evidence. They'll help you do that."

All of a sudden Jonathan felt trapped. He had no idea what to do, how to do it, and if he had the courage and the resolve to do it and it scared him. He had no knowledge of how this stuff worked; he had never been involved in any conflict in his life. His stomach churned and he tasted bile.

"I've spent my life in classrooms with books and students. I've dedicated my life to the church. The last fight I had was when I was seven and it was over a tortoise! I drive a beat-up old Beatle car. I eat takeaways and watch football. I listen to The Who and The Stones. I'm an ordinary man ..." His words began to taper off. "I ... I don't even watch horror movies on my own ..." But he knew he had no real choice. "Look, Walker, if I do this, what ..."

"Mr Rose, it's OK. I'm gonna help you, but first let's agree that we never met tonight. If anyone got to hear that we have had this talk, then I would be in real trouble, along with my kids and that bloodsucker wife and her alimony. I figure that this is that serious. Something is off here and it's going to get a lot worse. For the sake of my kids, I cannot afford to get involved."

"But why, Walker, why isn't anybody doing anything?" Jonathan just couldn't understand it. This was modern-day America, not the 1930s.

"I don't know why," Walker said. "All I know is, you have a

simple decision to make because it ain't gonna be no summer camp, but without you this case dies, sadly, just like your sister. I'm afraid if you want answers, then it's down to you to go get them."

Jonathan sat motionless, feeling anger in a way he had never felt it before. He was angry about Courtney's death, angry at the incompetent system and angry that someone, somewhere, had stopped the investigation into his sister's murder. It was crazy. The police were supposed to be the good guys and all that the police and the FBI were doing was paying lip service to the investigation. His resolve grew, steadily and slowly.

"OK, detective, tell me what you know."

Walker pulled out his notebook and leaned forward on the chair, his manner serious as he peered down at his notes.

"OK, you said in your statement that you saw your sister talking to the senator and a Middle Eastern-looking guest, around about 11 p.m. and that was the last time that you saw her?"

Jonathan nodded.

"So, that would mean that we should have some kind of Arab name on the guest list, right?"

Jonathan nodded again. The conclusion was an obvious one and he didn't see the relevance.

"OK, here's the thing: there was no Arab or even foreign name on the guest list. This means that his name must be the name someone tampered with, the one they tried to erase."

Jonathan thought he saw the fault in Walker's thinking straightaway. "But the guy may well have had a western name. This doesn't mean anything, does it?"

"Sure, he could have had a western name, but you see we didn't interview any Arab or foreign-looking guy!"

Walker let this sink in for a few seconds, and then he continued with his revelation.

"So we know that the missing guest is the Arab you saw with McGregor, talking to your sister. Now we need to figure out why he would want his name erased from the guest list. We answer that and we know where to start looking."

Jonathan had stopped listening. He sat with his head bent down and his eyes shut. He had suddenly realised that in all likelihood he had seen his sister's killer: the realisation stunned him. The self-accusations, the blame and chastisement screeched through his body like a car wreck. He had been so close. Why hadn't he called to her, got her away or recognised something in the man's face? He should have known. He was her brother: he should have done something. Guilt engulfed him and tears welled up in his eyes. He shook himself hard as anger began to rage in his body again. He had to get a grip. He clenched his fists and beat the arm of the chair. There was no time for remorse now, no time for self-anger. He tried to concentrate on Walker's words, to bury his guilt; he would shelve that mental anguish for later. He sat, bedraggled in his jeans and T-shirt, crying with the pain at the loss of his sister.

Walker's tone became softer. "You need to stay with me, Mr Rose. You need to listen. This gets complicated and you need to know this stuff. You gotta get past where you're at if we want to make progress."

Jonathan raised his head, wiping the tears from his eyes. He took two or three deep breaths. A renewed steely resolve suffused him. He was ready to hear what Walker had to say.

"About two years ago," Walker began, "I was working undercover on the West Side, on a job with the narcotics squad. Me and this guy from the Unit had got ourselves in real nice like. It had taken nearly eight months, but we got close to the centre, to a capo called Donald Cert, or 'Donny The Mouth', as some people called him, on account he bragged a lot."

Jonathan looked at him blankly.

"Capo, capo regime, Mafia … you've seen the *Godfather* films, ain't you? Jees, man, where've you been? A capo is a lieutenant in the Mafia. It was the Mafia we were infiltrating. They control everything on the West Side. Well, as I said, Cert liked to boast a lot, had that big mouth, fortunately for us. So he tells me one day, when I was driving him to a drop of a senator who lived in the Vale, said the senator was on their books, which meant that he took bribes. I checked it out and McGregor was one of two senators living in the Vale at that time. The other was a real bible-puncher called Pugh, ex-judge, so work it out for yourself."

Jonathan didn't need to.

"We left McGregor alone because we were after Cert's boss, Mr Big. We had nothing on him; he had no record and he had never been photographed, so we needed Cert to lead us to him. Now we know that our missing guest is Arab-looking or is an Arab. We know he knew Senator McGregor. We know that McGregor was on the take from the Mafia. Cert confirmed this. We know that our Arab friend wanted his name off the guest list. I think it's safe to assume that our missing friend is Mafia or has pretty close links with the brotherhood. Now, what we do have are two letters from his name, 'El', followed by a dash; that's all the lab boys could get from the tampered list. They were lucky to get that.

"And, here's the real interesting thing. The day I was driving Cert to the drop, he told me that the main man was going to a party at the senator's house, in the Vale and that he, Cert, had been invited by his boss to accompany him. It was a big honour for him to be asked to go. So he starts shouting his mouth off about it and, he let it slip, the only time he ever let the man's name slip, Salah El-Din, his boss."

Jonathan saw it. He didn't need Walker to say any more, but Walker did.

"I figure that the guy you are looking for is a big time crime boss, maybe Mafia, maybe not, but if he's not, then he is definitely working with them because Cert was Mafia; and he is real high up and carries major, major cred all on his own and his name is Salah El-Din."

"Shit."

49

It's fortunate he's left the cloth, thought Walker. The guy's developed a helluva foul mouth for a priest.

"Fucking damn right, shit" said Walker, "because I ain't ever heard of an Arab being let in close to the family like that, not at that level. You don't earn that kind of respect in the family for helping old ladies across the street. The only way to 'get made' is become part of the family and then no one can touch you. No one can order a hit on you, unless they get full permission, is if you are Italian or Sicilian. Even then they have to check your blood line right back to the old country, just to make sure there are no blood feuds with anyone else in the family.

"So two years ago, this same senator threw a party for some charity or other. A reporter by the name of John Dukes was there, with his wife, as guests. She was twenty years younger than him; she was some minor celebrity on the catwalk or something. So she gets an invite out of the blue one day and no one suspects. Her husband, Dukes, had been real vocal in his newspaper column at that time about organised crime. Trouble was, he was writing about Cert's turf, the West Side. Dukes made a lot of enemies; I mean a lot of bad enemies. Cert told me that the main man, our friend Salah El-Din, was real pissed about it. It was all over the neighbourhood that Dukes showed no respect, so someone was going to take care of it. According to police records, Dukes' wife disappeared from the party and was found dead the next day, throat cut and eyelids removed. Sound familiar?"

"You're saying he's done this before?" Jonathan gasped. "Walker, why didn't the police pick him up? Why didn't you arrest him the first time?"

Jonathan held his head in his hands, distraught. If only someone had arrested the man the first time his sister's murder could have been avoided. His nightmare, the hell he was living, had just got worse. How could a known murderer walk around free? He felt betrayed by the system, and by the government his sister had worked for.

Walker had known the question would come, but he had no answers. He tried to explain that most of what he had was hearsay. They were just words from Cert. He'd had no proof to arrest anyone. He waited for Jonathan to compose himself, then pulled a piece of paper from his pocket. Written on it was John Dukes's last known address. He gave it to Jonathan. Walker knew the risk he was taking, but he felt good about what he was doing and sometimes, he mused, it came down to that, how you felt about a thing and not what you were told to do about it.

He had stayed long enough, but before he left he made Jonathan promise *not* to keep in touch.

Jonathan no longer blamed Walker or his partner; all the blame was concentrated on himself, and God. He had seen his sister's murderer and had done nothing: and neither had God.

Walker's car slipped away into the hot, sticky night. He only switched on his headlights once he was half a block away from Jonathan Rose's house. He didn't look back.

Meeks kept in the shadows. He recognized Walker as he left. He had no idea what he had been doing there, but it wasn't hard to piece together. He knew Walker was on the Rose case. He knew Walker and his partner, like their counterparts in the FBI, had been told that the case would be dealt with higher up the chain. He'd heard that Walker was a decent cop, not on the take: clean. Whatever Walker knew, Meeks figured Jonathan now also knew. He would need to watch Jonathan more carefully.

Later that night, Jonathan had trouble sleeping. Too many thoughts whirled around in his head, clamouring for attention. He tried to remember the man's face, the man he'd seen talking to Courtney, but that night had become a congealed blur of wealthy faces, anger and regret. He had spent so long trying to forget it, now he found it hard to remember anything about it.

There was no air in the room. His bed, now a mess of crumbled sheets, was an irritation. He flicked the switch on the small blue bedside lamp and opened the bedside cabinet drawer. Ignoring the bible, he fumbled for his sleeping tablets, now a habit since the death of his sister and, before long, he slept.

The front doorbell ringing shrilled into his consciousness. At first the sound was in his dream and he wrestled with it. It didn't fit with the multitude of frenetic images swirling inside the dream. The ringing came again, this time louder. He opened his eyes and the sun hurt them with its brightness. Easing slowly out of his bed, he made his way through the hall to the front door. The USPS man smiled and pushed an official-looking form in front of him to sign.

The brown envelope, marked 'recorded delivery', had been secured with tape and it took him a few seconds to open it. Inside were two audiocassettes. He took the one with his name on, in his sister's handwriting, and put it into the stereo, nervous at the prospect of the emotions hearing Courtney's voice might stir in him.

Her words floated out of the two speakers, filling the room with her presence and for a fleeting moment, it was as if she were there with him and all was well.

"My dearest Jonathan ..." her voice half whispered, *"if you are listening to this tape recording then I am in need of your help and the help of Bill Meeks. I am so sorry. Please forgive me."*

There was a pause and he could sense her breathing; there was no sound, but he could tell she was still there. He closed his eyes and her image entered his head. Desperate to cling on to her, he held the image in his mind; ironically it was her voice that pulled him back again to the bleak reality of what had happened.

"Jonathan, I want you to do something for me now. You have to listen carefully to what I am going to say and follow my instructions. Please, I wouldn't ask if there was any other way."

She then said the date; there was a slight pause again. He saw an image of her looking down at her watch; the watch he had brought for her for her birthday. She would never look at it again. She gave the time and her voice came back into the room.

"Once I have finished the recording, I am sealing the cassettes into an envelope addressed to you. I am going to place the envelope with a small firm of lawyers down town. They will have one instruction, Jonathan, to post the envelope to the address on the front if I have not retrieved it from them within six months, which should be long enough.

"Jonathan, you have to give the second tape to Bill Meeks. You can't send it to him through the mail or discuss it over the telephone. You must arrange to meet him away from the office and the house, somewhere public. This is very important: you must give it to him in person. Don't worry, Jonathan. Bill will know what to do. I'm sure everything will be alright. Trust in Bill, Jonathan. He will be able to sort all this out. Take care, little brother, and I promise I will see you real soon."

The silence didn't register; her words lingered even though there was no sound coming out of the speakers. Around and around they spiralled. It had been so long since he had heard her voice. He fumbled with the second cassette and abruptly the silence was broken again: this time the tone of her voice was more troubled. This time she did not hide her fear.

"Bill, I don't know where to start. I don't know who to talk to. You are the only one I can trust. If you have this tape, then I guess I am in real trouble." There was a short pause.

"I'm going to start from the beginning. A few months ago I was working on my computer in the office, trying to find a report that someone had not saved correctly in the hard drive. I ran a random search and accidentally stumbled on a report filed by some of our field agents out in Algiers. The report contained transcripts of a wiretap, dates, a name and some initials. It was restricted, but there must have been a security breach because it let me in. Curious, I ran

the names for a matching sequence and bingo, one of the initials matched with a covert operation Interpol and British MI6 were carrying out in the Swiss Alps. Then the screen went dead and all the data disappeared. As far as I can tell, I think I must have accessed the data at the very moment someone was wiping it clean. It could only be someone from the inside the Bureau; that's why the security cloak was down. I checked for both files again the next day, but there was no record of them. According to the mainframe auto data log, the data never existed.

"Bill, you know we never lose data. Even when we wipe the files the data is always iced into a holding vault in Colossus 1. Someone had deliberately wiped data, one of our own, and they have to be high up in the Bureau. Fortunately, I wrote down the information before it got wiped. Bill, the initials appeared in both reports. I've it seen them before, S E D. Whoever S E D is, a while back he went to great lengths to buy some old religious papers that came onto the black market out in Egypt. The only other bidder for the old papers, a nasty piece of work called Fayad Ali Sulima, mysteriously disappeared and has never been found.

"We don't have anything on this S E D, that's why I never followed it up. Now I think I know why: someone inside the Bureau is protecting him. I don't know who S E D is and, with no record, it's going to be difficult to find him. I have placed ads on Internet sites and the dark net, and am using all of my contacts to try to get in touch with the person who originally sold the old papers that he bought. I figure if I can find him, he may lead me to S E D and, once I have him, I can get to the people inside the Bureau who wiped the files. We need to catch them, Bill. We need to get them and put them in prison. Who knows how wide this is spread and how high it goes up.

"For days I have been running multiple random scans on associated words. I have scanned everything I could in the mainframe, but found nothing. At home I have been scanning thousands of web domains and e-mail systems. Then, two days ago I got lucky. Someone else from the outside was doing the same thing. They were scanning

international police agency records for the same information and initials I was looking for. I'm almost certain that it's another agency because of the method they were using, but I don't know who. They're smart, Bill, very smart. Whoever they are, they know what they are doing.

"It's none of our lot and I don't think it's the British; doesn't have their trademark on it. The only thing I got on them was two Internet comms. I was able to hack into them because they were scanning multiple webs at the time and it made them vulnerable. I managed to slip past their first firewall, but they had a secondary cloaking device, one I had never seen before, so I couldn't track the comms back to origin. I was only onto them for about ten seconds, then they burned me and I lost them. The comms were coded, but I got the same initials again, S E D and the name Senator McGregor. I also managed to decipher the word 'Unity'. Bill, the names Unity and McGregor were also in one of the files that got wiped from our own system. I have spent hours trying to decipher the rest of the two comms and all I have is one more name, or maybe the name of a place, St Clair. That's it. I don't know if I can decipher the rest. It's the best I've ever seen and I am really struggling with it.

"Bill, you need to be careful and watch your back. If I'm right, this thing is pretty high up in strategic ops. Who else could wipe files and get away with it? It could even go right the way up to the Justice Department. Whoever is behind it all must be a major player from the outside. None of these guys would ever have the nerve to organise this on their own. My guess is, senior Agency guys are being paid big money to lose certain information as it comes into the Bureau. Somehow, this all fits with the comms I hacked into and the files, but I don't know how, not yet anyway. Oh, and there are a couple of supervisors from black ops who have been over friendly since I pulled the McGregor file a few weeks ago. You'll have to be careful.

"Bill, I have hidden all the information I have inside the Colossus 1 mainframe, at the Bureau. I figured it was the safest place

to hide it, in plain sight, right under their noses. You will need to get access to it through the main intra net system on G plus G. Once you're inside, find a program called 'metal-desk-twenty-one'. That will get you into my department's intranet drive, in strategic ops. Then, look for a file called 'Winter Snowman'. Once you have it, enter the password 'Simple Simon'. The program will start to shut down. Do nothing until the computer asks you for the shut-down password, type in 'Jonathan'. The computer will reboot and take you directly into the file you want. Press enter and you're in.

"I wish I could give you more than I have, but every way I turn there are ten more false trails, I don't know how deep this thing goes.

"That's it, Bill, that's all I have. Be careful, my friend, and take care of Jonathan for me until this thing is sorted out. I don't want him being involved."

Jonathan played the tape time and time again. He couldn't believe that the FBI had senior people who would do this. It was like some horror story; no one would believe it. His sister had a desk-based job. She wasn't a field agent, or a spy. She had no training for this, no experience or knowledge. He just couldn't understand why she would get involved. He knew she loved her job, believed in what the FBI did, what it stood for. She was a patriot, an American who was proud of what she did. But why hadn't she got help? Surely someone, somewhere, could have helped? Meeks? There were too many unanswered questions and, like his sister, he had no experiences that would help him find out the truth.

Jonathan decided not to give the tape to Meeks; he no longer liked or trusted him. For all he knew, Meeks might be part of *it*, whatever *it* was. He would try to do this on his own. The odds were stacked against him. He didn't know what Courtney had been afraid of, and he couldn't get access to the FBI mainframe computer, Colossus 1. Her detailed instructions to Bill Meeks meant nothing to him. He loathed technology; he wouldn't know which button to press to turn the computer on. In fact, he had never owned a cell phone.

Without his God, Jonathan knew that he had become cold and impervious to the emotions that had once driven him to teach the gospels and the word of the Almighty. Now he had only one thing on his mind: to find his sister's killer. Nothing else seemed to matter anymore.

Chapter 4

Dukes

Date: June 2008
Place: Washington DC

John Dukes had once been one of the best freelance reporters in America. When he wrote, people read. He wrote the stories that people wanted to read. He said the things people wanted to say. He exposed organised crime throughout mid America and told the nation all the sordid details.

Dukes could command huge fees for his features and had all the accruements of success: money, fast cars and a wife some twenty years younger than him. Via Reuters, his work was syndicated throughout the world. It was read in millions of households and in hundreds of countries. He seldom drank, kept long, unsociable hours and revelled in his success. Dukes had been a skilled wordsmith. He had built a following of loyal readers who adored his plain-speaking investigative journalism. His stories sold newspapers and he was at the top of his game: but that was before the demons came. Now he found it hard to get any work at all and even the more downmarket newspapers refused him the courtesy of returning his calls.

Dukes drank heavily to keep the demons at bay. He was unreliable and the occasional freelance story that was accepted barely kept him in bourbon and food. It had been eight months since he had last worked. Friends and colleagues had long since stopped giving him handouts. The State had no time for him. He owed

$65,000 in taxes, which he had no way of paying. He was a manic-depressive with an erratic behaviour disorder, which had gone from mild to acute in less than two years. His unpredictable, animated outbursts scared people. His involuntary jerking, twitching and sudden fits made him a social outcast. His life was miserable and he lived it amongst the rest of the lowlifes in a no-hope part of town.

The address Brent Walker had given him turned out to be right. Jonathan recognised his loneliness and bitterness as soon as Dukes opened the door. The man before him hadn't shaved for days and, by the smell of him, the shower was not a place he had seen too much of. His breath smelt strongly of drink. His sunken eye sockets played host to jaundiced eyes, and his severely dilated pupils viewed Jonathan with disdain and distrust. Underweight for his height, over six feet, his ashen face was gaunt and wrinkled. His white, unwashed hair hung where it wanted to hang, unchecked. He shuffled in worn, dirty trainers that had no laces. His torso, bent forward, suggested an arthritic hip. His trousers were peppered with cigarette burns and the remnants of past meals and spilt drinks.

All this Jonathan took in within moments. He really didn't want to be there, but he knew he must do this. The street outside was dangerous; he could feel it, as if a thousand eyes were piercing his back.

"Mr Dukes?"

The jaundiced eyes remained fixed. Dukes didn't bother to answer, to confirm or deny.

"Mr Dukes, I'm sorry to bother you, but a friend of mine said you might be able to help me get my story published in one of the papers and maybe even help me write it. Of course, I am willing to pay you."

Dukes's yellow eyes flickered. Pay was good. He was on his last bottle, with no credit at the 7-Eleven on the corner, It had been on his mind all day, plaguing away at him. He needed the drink. He would need it when the night came: he always did.

"And who the fuck are you?" Dukes rasped. He had no time for social pleasantries. He didn't like people and they didn't like him. Jonathan put out his hand, but Dukes ignored it.

"Jonathan Rose. Brent Walker gave me your address."

It was the only association between them. Jonathan had no choice but to try it, and amazingly it worked without need of clarification.

Dukes eyed him, the hostility marginally lessened.

"Well, you can come in, but you ain't stopping. You hear me? You ain't fucking stopping." Dukes hesitated at the door, then rubbed at his scalp with both hands in a violent manner, then stopped as abruptly as he had started, turning to yell obscenities at the local miscreants who had been watching them from across the street. "And fuck your mothers, you lowlife shits!"

Jonathan was glad when the door closed. For the time being at least, the piercing eyes were removed from his back and the dangerous street was left to its own devices.

They moved down the gloomy hallway of the tenement building. Dukes stopped to look down at the occupied mousetrap; the occupant was still fresh on the spike, its hind legs twitching. "Fucking cats. Two of them can't catch a fucking mouse between them."

Dukes lived in a ground floor apartment, a one-room hovel with two cats and two months worth of dirty laundry. There was little furniture in the room: an unmade bed, a table with two unmatching chairs and an all but empty wardrobe, doors slightly ajar; and that was it, the sum total of one man's life. There was nothing to cook on and no refrigeration. Jonathan winced at the grim living conditions.

They sat at the ring-stained table. The ambience of the room was beyond depressing, but Dukes appeared not to notice it. He hadn't, Jonathan guessed, noticed much for a long time.

Jonathan hadn't made a plan. He would stick to the story about Walker and hope for the best; that was all he could do. Dukes was his only lead; without him he had nothing to go on. He was nervous, but he hid it as best he could. Dukes filled a stained glass with cheap bourbon from the half-empty bottle on the table and drank without constraint. Jonathan needed a drink almost as much as Dukes, but he would let Dukes do all the drinking. He needed sobriety more than bourbon right now. The stale air smelt of cat urine, –cigarettes and human depredation. Newspapers lay strewn all around the room, hundreds of them scattered over the floor. There were piles more stacked high in corners. Empty boxes lay on top of each other, while plastic refuse bags full of old clothes remained where they had been left. Next to the unmade bed, a shopping trolley held more newspapers, yellow with age. Empty bourbon bottles lay discarded. Jonathan counted at least twenty-three. He shifted his attention, keen to do this as quickly as possible. He didn't want to spend any more time in the room than he had to.

Dukes lit a cigarette.

"I appreciate your time, Mr Dukes, and it's good of you to see me. Do you mind if I ask you a couple of questions?"

Dukes shook his head and gave out a deliberate tut. It was not a good start. "How old are you, son? Eighteen, nineteen?" Jonathan wondered whether or not to say that he was thirty, but he was not given the chance to make the correction. "Let me put you straight before we go any further. I ask the questions, you give me the answers. I write the story; we all make a buck. Simple really. I give you the co-operation you give me, or, you can fuck off." Dukes emptied the glass and poured another. "Now, tell me what you got."

Outside on the street, a car backfired. Dukes jumped, his cigarette falling from his hand. He was frightened, Jonathan realised. More drink was poured down his throat to dull the pain.

"Well?"

Jonathan hoped that whatever was about to come out of his own mouth would be plausible enough to get Dukes to talk. Dukes lifted the cigarette from the floor and inhaled more blue-grey smoke into his lungs.

"I normally teach … I'm a school teacher, but at the moment I'm on a sabbatical because I want to write." He eased himself into the lie. "My interest lies in organised crime, mainly Mafia and especially what happens here in DC." He eased a bit more. "During my research, I have uncovered information that I believe should be made public, but I just don't know how to go about getting it into the newspapers, well, not in the correct way." *Now drop the name into the conversation again*, he thought. *It got me through the front door.* "Brent Walker thought you might be able to help me."

He was quite pleased with himself. For a man who hadn't known what a capo was until Walker had told him the night before, he thought he'd done well. He knew that if Dukes asked too many questions, his story wouldn't hold up. However, at the moment Dukes was impassive. Jonathan began the embellishment of the lie.

"Of course, the information might be nothing, but I don't think so because it proves a link between two murders and a member of a crime organisation here in Washington. I think I can prove who committed the murders."

Dukes's stare remained fixed. There was an old notepad in front of him and a blunt pencil by its side, but Dukes didn't touch it. He didn't write anything down. The pencil and the notepad remained firmly on the table.

"The man has a very distinctive name, foreign. I think Middle Eastern. He's called … Salah El-Din."

The glass slipped from Dukes's hand and smashed onto the bare floor. The noise shattered the silence of the room.

"Mr Dukes, are you all right?"

John Dukes' face had contorted, his cheekbones tensed. He tapped his left foot on the floor with great pace. His agitation manifested itself in several parts of his body all at once. His face twitched quite violently. His head snapped back three or four times; his breathing became more pronounced. Jonathan worried that Dukes was having a fit, but he rallied and he turned on Jonathan.

"You ain't on no goddamn sabbatical," Dukes spat, in between the jerking movements. "You're the priest, the priest whose sister got killed at the McGregor party last Christmas."

Jonathan hadn't considered that Dukes might know who he was and he cursed himself for missing this important point. Walker had told him that John Dukes had once been one of the best investigative reporters going. The newspapers taking space in Dukes's room should have been warning enough, but Jonathan hadn't taken in the possibility that Dukes read everything. Courtney would have noticed it straightaway; she would have done her homework.

Dukes shuffled to the sink, kicking glass slivers out of the way. He found another glass in amongst the dirty dishes; flies hovered over the sink. Not bothering to rinse the glass, he poured more bourbon and drank it in one mouthful, and then he lit another cigarette. One of the two cats appeared from behind the wardrobe to see what all the noise was. It came out head first, then gingerly it took two or three steps. Dukes roared at it. "Fuck off, cat!" The cat shot back, closely pursued by the scruffy notepad and blunt pencil.-Dukes returned his attentions to Jonathan.

"And you want me to help you find this person because you believe I know something you don't?"

Jonathan nodded. That was about it. He should have come right out with it at the start and saved himself the ordeal, he thought. With no more reason to lie, he told the truth. "Mr Dukes, my sister died in exactly the same circumstances as your wife. The same man was at both parties. It was the same senator. Same kind of party, same kind of murder, everything was the same. If you …"

"Always bothered me, you know," Dukes interrupted and continued without pausing for breath, "the way we use the word 'kind' like that. 'Kind of murder'. Strange, isn't it? We use the word 'kind' in the same sentence as murder. Doesn't seem right somehow."

Dukes's bad mood wasn't getting any better. He rubbed his scalp erratically with both hands. It was unnerving because he kept on talking, seemingly oblivious to his involuntary movements.

"You really thought you could come in here with this bullshit story and I would believe you? Do I look like a fucking idiot? His rubbing continued with frenetic viciousness and at the same time his leg was going up and down like a banjo player's wrist. Jonathan didn't need to answer the question, Dukes was doing that all on his own.

Then Dukes stopped, as abruptly as he had started. He laughed, but it was full of cynicism. His laugh brought on a bout of coughing, and then his scalp received some more attention. He was clearly a very sick man and Jonathan didn't know how much more he wanted to take of this.

"How do you think I got like this?" Jonathan said nothing. It was another rhetorical question. Dukes coughed again and spat blood and yellow mucus into a rag he pulled from his trouser pocket.

"Look at me, for Christ sake. I'm all fucked up, a drunk who can't even look after two cats. You want to end up the same way? I know who killed my wife and, yes, I know what he did to her and there ain't a fucking thing I can do about it, and you, Mr Fucking Bible Basher …" The leg started again and, as if on cue, his cheekbones flexed repetitively and in harmony with the free-spirited leg. "You have the same problem. You already know who killed your sister and all the fucking gory details and there ain't nothing you can do because if the police were interested, then you wouldn't be sat here wasting your time with me. You don't need my help, son, you need a miracle and, as you can see, I'm fresh out of them. Go find the murdering son of a bitch on your own and leave me the fuck alone."

He shook violently in a crescendo of involuntary movements, then drank some more – it seemed to help. He was a man whose life had lost all purpose, a feeling Jonathan knew only too well. Walker had given him a glimmer of hope and Dukes had just almost snatched it away, but he wasn't about to give up now. He wasn't done yet. Dukes had nothing to hang onto; for him there was nothing left but suffering. His hands went for the scalp again, but turned course halfway and grabbed the bottle. He poured more bourbon and drank.

"Shit, Rose, he's gonna eat you up and spit you out without going near you. He'll fuck with you. Play his shit games with your life and, if you're lucky, he'll just kill you. Either way, if you go looking for him, you'll be in a world of pain."

There were no windows open and it was another hot day. The smell of cat urine had grown stronger and the cigarette smoke was stifling. Jonathan needed some air. He desperately needed to get away from Dukes and his erratic scalp-rubbing, but he didn't move. He equally desperately needed to know how to find the man who had killed Courtney. He had no experience that would tell him what to do next; she might have known, but he didn't. Dukes was all he had to go on.

"You believe in the devil, son?" Another rhetorical question. "Me, I believe in the devil because I've seen him. He killed my wife, seems your sister, too, but no one gives a shit about the devil anymore. No one gives a shit about you or me. We're just case files at the bottom of someone's workload. You know what fear is?"

The rhetorical questions flowed. At least he was talking, Jonathan thought, he had no idea what about, but he listened.

"You know those times, when there is no one around, just you and the dark. There's nowhere for you to go, sitting alone, night after night in a place full of dark shadows and screaming lunatics. You look for the cries, your eye catches the mirror and you see that the screams are yours. You're the lunatic. You try to hide, but it's no use trying to hide from yourself because yourself always finds you. Pretty fucking scary, eh? Keep digging, Father, and you will find out all about fear."

The silence came abruptly as Dukes stopped. Even his scalp was rested from its torment. Jonathan understood Dukes. He could have taken his own life and ended his suffering, but he knew that Dukes wouldn't. He had to live this way because it was his way of paying penance for his wife's death. Dukes's life was riddled with shame and guilt. His wife had been murdered because of what he had been writing and the self-blame racked his soul. Tormented, he suffered every minute of every day, but death was not an option for him: he needed to live out the pain. It was his sentence to serve.

Jonathan felt sorry for the man, but he needed to know more. He needed Dukes to tell him everything; he couldn't leave until he had it. "Mr Dukes, I need your help and I have money. I need to find where Salah El-Din is. I just need to know what you know, then I'll leave, I promise, and I will never bother you again."

Dukes sighed. "You haven't been listening to me. I'm scared, Father." Dukes's face was full of anguish, his voice a whisper, almost pleading. "I get these nightmares. They never leave me, even when I'm awake. I scream out on the streets; it doesn't matter where I am, I have no control over them. People move away from me like I'm a disease. I'm in purgatory here, Father, and he's done it to me, the man you are after. He's evil. Not like all the other fucked-up scum around here. I mean real evil. You can't fight him with the law because he has the law, probably has half the government, that's why no one will help you.

"Fuck, I get this mail, Rose, it comes every week, same day. A sealed envelope that has nothing inside it and the name on the front isn't mine, but the address is. Who the fuck is Nathaniel? That's the name on the envelope, Nathaniel. I ain't ever heard of a Nathaniel. I've sent them back. I've written the mail people. I've gone down and screamed and shouted at them, but they say it's not them. What kind of person does a thing like that, every week, constantly without fail, why?"

Dukes paused and wiped water from his eyes, then poured more drink. Jonathan knew of one Nathaniel, but he shuddered at the thought of what it meant. "I hope you like bourbon, Father, because it's the only friend you're gonna have, if he lets you live."

Jonathan was beginning to wonder if there was room behind the wardrobe with the cats. He had been there for nearly two hours and he still had nothing from Dukes. He would have to push him. He didn't know how long Dukes would be able to keep a hold on reality. Looking at him, he didn't know how long the poor man would even stay alive. Surely he must have cirrhosis of the liver.

"Just tell me where to find him, that's all I want."

"And then what?

Jonathan hoped this was another rhetorical question, but it wasn't. There was an uneasy pause.

"Then I don't know. I guess … I guess I'll find a private detective to track him down, get some information." It was feeble and Jonathan knew it.

"Fucking great plan. Where were you two years ago when I needed you? Private eyes: they'll rob you blind or they'll end up dead. What you need, son, is a small fucking army, knights in fucking shining fucking armour!"

Dukes smiled slightly and for the first time his bad mood subsided. He emptied the last remaining bourbon into his glass and drank it. Then he placed the glass down in a purposeful manner. "Shit, empty," he said. "Get your money out, Father. Only reason I let your sorry arse in here. There's a 7-Eleven on the corner. Bastards won't give me any more credit. Fucking foreigners, should fuck off home, fucking Koreans."

"I'd buy you a distillery if it would get you to help me."

Dukes shook his head. He looked tired and beaten. "I don't know where he is, Rose, and no one will talk., You know, their fucking precious *omertà*. Even his capos are scared of Il Capo Di Tutti Capi, the boss. After my wife's death, I spent months trying to find a way into his organisation, but I didn't even get close. I got jack shit. I ain't even sure he's Mafia now; in fact, I pretty much doubt he is. This guy's got a style all of his own, not like the family. Besides, can't see him answering to anyone, let alone the Italians. Wouldn't surprise me if he wasn't an independent operator and if he is, it means he's pretty fucking powerful. The shit I did get was worth nothing and besides, no one wanted to listen anyway. All those doors I used to open were slammed in my face.

"The only time I ever saw him was one time too many. It was at a distance and I couldn't really make his face out because he wore his coat collar high up and a hat low down, but his eyes … I remember his eyes, black as night. I mean, those things felt like they were looking straight into me. I'd staked out this nightclub that I hoped he would visit. It was a big club. I guessed he had an interest in it because it was on his patch and I figured if he did, he would have to go there eventually. All the big crime bosses need to be seen. Guess it gives them security, to show their face, I mean, let all the smaller guys know they're still there, just in case they get to thinking. I got lucky because after two days he turned up with two bodyguards, two African types, built like fucking mountains, looked identical, twins. They stopped the car right outside the club. Then he got out. He was tall, thin-looking with silver hair, short-cropped. I had no photographs of him. No one knew what he looked like and if they did, they weren't saying. People said he did all of his communications through the bodyguards; he seldom met anyone. But I knew this was him. I sensed it. And he knew I was there, he fucking knew."

Dukes paused for breath, as if that night had crept back into his life. Jonathan closed his eyes and desperately tried to recall the image of his sister talking to the senator and Salah El-Din. He needed to see her killer. Now that he had some kind of description he needed to see his face, the face of the man who had so brutally murdered her. But however hard he tried, Jonathan couldn't visualise him. Dukes yanked him out of his thoughts.

"He didn't go into the club straightaway. He stopped on the sidewalk and turned, then he looked right at me. I was hiding in the back of a van, with blacked-out windows, about a hundred metres away. I felt those black eyes looking straight into me. And the bastard just smiled. He just smiled. Then he went inside the club and I left.

"Next day, my assignments got cancelled on some bullshit

grounds and no one would hire me. All of a sudden I was the unwanted red-headed stepchild of the newspaper world. All my credit got stopped and I lost everything. My so-called benighted friends stopped calling and eventually the police stopped taking my calls. Six months later my nightmares began. Sometimes I wake up in the middle of the night and the bed is soaked in blood. I have no cuts, nada. Jack shit. Nothing. Just blood and I've got no fucking idea where it comes from. I don't know if it's me or that bastard or some voodoo shit or something, or ... Can you imagine how fucking frightening that is?"

Jonathan didn't want to try. He felt the need for bourbon, but Dukes's liver was marinating in the last glass of it.

Nothing was said for an age. Dukes looked at the stained table, his thoughts his own, but Jonathan knew what he was thinking: he was thinking the same. Jonathan held the image of his sister in his mind for as long as he could. Every day that went by seemed to fade the picture. Like himself, Dukes was scared that one day he wouldn't be able to see the image anymore.

Dukes had told Jonathan just about everything he knew, which, as far as Jonathan was concerned, was just about nothing. Then Dukes spoke.

"I met a man, Father. Think he was FBI. He called me and wanted to meet; he said a public place. We met on a Sunday, in a park; it was full of people. The guy stayed for less than five minutes. He told me I would find answers if I left the States. He gave me a one-way airline ticket, the name, St Clair and an address. The address was in Scotland. I don't have the address anymore."

Jonathan saw the connection straightaway: the name St Clair had been on the tape that Courtney had made. He was about to tell Dukes about the tape recording, but then stopped. He figured Dukes was not the best person to tell anything to. He was in a different place to Jonathan, a dark place that had no way out. And if there was any hope for Dukes in the future, he would surely burn that bridge himself when he got to it.

"And that's it, that's all I got, Father."

Jonathan thought about it for a second or two. "Scotland?"

"That's what the man said."

"Scotland, United Kingdom?"

"Well it's the only fucking Scotland I know. Thought you were a schoolteacher?"

Dukes's mood was returning to its normal black state.

"Scotland, and that's it. You haven't got the address, a first name, anything?"

"I told you, Rose, that's all I got, right!"

Now would be a good time to leave, Jonathan decided. He'd had enough. He was tired and he needed time to think. Jonathan got up from the table and offered his hand. This time Dukes shook it before following him to the front door, shuffling his tired body. Outside it was beginning to get dark and the street was alive with drug traffickers and prostitutes. This was not a neighbourhood to linger in. He was thankful his car was still there and in one piece. A gang of teenagers, wearing their colours, had gathered twenty yards away. Really time to go. He shook Dukes's hand again; it was sweaty and weak.

As he left, he asked Dukes one more question. "Do you know the name of the man who you met in the park?"

Dukes thought about it. "Think the fellow said his name was Deeks or Meeks, something like that." Dukes eyed the gang of teenagers. "Fuck off! Fuck off and fuck your mothers." He hurled drunken abuse at them, his body contorting with every fresh salvo. The bourbon was beginning to work its numbing qualities and his brain was slowly being purged of any words that made sense. Jonathan left him to his black nightmares.

Jonathan's head was spinning as he pulled away. The mention of Meeks's name had completely thrown him. The permutations went around and around in his head, but there was no rational sense to it. Nothing about Courtney's death had any sense to it. Why hadn't

70

Meeks told him about Dukes? If Walker saw the connection between Courtney's death and the death of Dukes's wife, clearly a trained FBI agent of twenty years would.

He checked his rear-view mirror and thought he saw Meeks on the sidewalk. A few minutes later he thought he saw Meeks following in a black sedan: paranoia was setting in. Meeks was everywhere, in his head, in the car behind him. He was beginning to feel like Dukes. He breathed slow and deep, trying to get control. He focused on the man in Scotland, already planning his trip. He pulled left out of Jiniwin and West Street and onto the freeway. He wound down the window and breathed in the air, which made him feel better.

Meeks wanted to hang around, just in case Dukes got into trouble with the local hoods, who he was still viciously lambasting, but he had bigger problems on his mind. He didn't need to tail Jonathan; he knew where Jonathan was heading.

He sat alone in his car, playing the cassette for the second time. He had found it in Jonathan's house earlier that day, whilst Jonathan had been at the grocery store. He had searched the house before and had found nothing; he had searched Courtney's house, with the same result. However, he had become increasingly suspicious of late because Jonathan seemed to know more than a well-meaning amateur should. The cassette proved that his suspicions were correct. Courtney's voice filled his space with her sweet tone. He missed her. He now understood why she had wanted to go to the McGregor party. He understood why she hadn't told anyone: because she no longer trusted anyone.

Dukes finally slammed his front door on the hoods and went inside. Meeks started the engine of his car, the cassette still playing Courtney's voice. He punched the dashboard hard with his fist. What a waste, he thought. What an absolute waste of a life. He sped away and headed home.

Meeks lived alone in an apartment building near the river. The layout, like his mind, was orderly and logical. After punching in the alarm code, he hit the lights, then went straight to his den. He removed his grey suit jacket and slung it over the back of a chair. Then he poured himself a drink and prepared the audio system.

He made the secure call. He punched the seven-digit number into the phone. It rang three times, then the call automatically routed to an address in Islington, United Kingdom. The computer in electronically protected shell (ESP) in Islington checked the call's authenticity. Then it checked the caller's location against its worldwide GPS system. It matched the location where the caller was meant to be on that day's location list.

The fifty-old woman watched the computer with careful scrutiny. As 'controller', her job was to ensure that no one from the outside was hacking into the system. She checked the meter on the cloaking software. It was normal. She had been the one who had detected Courtney's interception of their comms and had been forced to take immediate action to block her out of the system. Somehow, Courtney had made it past the powerful 'cloak' and because of that all controllers were now extra vigilant.

The computer directed Meeks's call to a private number in Scotland. The conversation would take place between the two men via the computer. The computer would cloak and scramble the conversation. If the EPS room's security was breached, the scrambler would protect the caller's identity and the contents of the conversation.

Meeks told his friend in Scotland that Jonathan had been to see Dukes. He told him that he thought it might have been Walker that had given him Dukes's details. Then Meeks played the audiotape he had found in Jonathan's house earlier that day. His friend listened with unease. When the tape had finished playing, he asked Meeks if he had anything on the report filed by the field agents out in Algiers. "Nothing," Meeks said.

"And the covert operation Interpol and MI6 carried out in Switzerland?"

"Same: the reports no longer exist. Courtney was right, they got wiped. This thing goes deeper than we imagined. What about the scrolls? Do you think ...?"

"I don't know, Bill. If she did meet him, then, I guess ... I just don't know, Bill."

There was a silence. Then the voice on the other end of the phone asked Meeks to replay the middle section of the audiotape again. Meeks pressed fast forward, then hit the play button.

"... *the people inside the Bureau who wiped the files. We need to catch them Bill*... Meeks let it play to the end.

Again the pause came. The darkness outside seeped into Meeks's room. He switched on another small desk lamp and waited for the voice in Scotland to speak

"There's no doubt S E D had the files removed from the FBI computer. I guess we have to assume that whatever Courtney knew, he now knows. That's why he had her killed."

"I'm afraid we may also have another problem." Meeks's voice lowered. "Her brother's house has been searched – a professional job. I think they may have found this tape. If they did, they made a copy and put the original back. That means they have everything in the tape as well and ... they have the name on the tape, your name. What do we do about it?"

"There's nothing that we can do about it, Bill. If he knows the name, he knows it."

Bill Meeks then asked the question, the question that had been hanging in the air for the entire telephone conversation.

"So it's time?"

"Yes, it's time, Bill," said Payne St Clair. "I will call them all tonight."

"And Jonathan," Meeks asked. "What do you want me to do about Jonathan?"

"Do nothing, Bill. From what you've told me, we already know where Jonathan is headed. Can you get the file Courtney left for you on the FBI's computer?"

"Tomorrow is Saturday. I'll go in then, when it's quiet."

"You take care, old friend."

The phone went dead and Meeks sat alone in the dark. He poured himself a large whiskey, and then eased back into his chair. The permutations of what had happened raced across his mind. All he knew for certain was that the Nine would now gather and something would happen. I It was no longer a matter of if, it was just a matter of when.

Date: Saturday (The following morning)
Place: Jonathan Rose's house

Jonathan telephoned the precinct and left a message for Walker: *Seen Dukes. Going out of town. Have a lead. Dukes told me what I needed to know.* He didn't leave his name.

Place: FBI Buildings, Washington DC

It was Saturday, and because of that there were few people around. It wasn't unusual for Bill Meeks to work on a Saturday; he had no family. He was known as a 'lifer' – married to the Bureau. Courtney could only guess that a major criminal had been behind the security breaches within FBI, but her guess had been right. She was right, too, about the fact that people in the Justice Department were also taking bribes to supply information and to make sure certain information was removed from the records. She could not have known the sums of money involved in the deceit, but she had known it would be large; none of these people would ever risk their jobs or their freedom unless the amounts were substantial. However, she could not have known that it was their sordid secrets that had led to the extortion and blackmail, drawing them ever deeper into the criminal underworld. They now lived their lives by deceit and lies, an ever-decreasing spiral that would end in one conclusion and one conclusion only. But they, like all those sucked into criminal activity, believed that they could get away with it. They thought they could control it, but it was just a matter of time.

Meeks was already onto the two people Courtney had warned him about on the tape: the two supervisors from black ops who had been over-friendly towards her since she pulled the McGregor file. He had used Templars to carry out sustained surveillance on them and it had paid off. He already had enough on them to indict them, but for the time being he would allow the supervisors to believe they were still safe. Sooner or later, they would lead him to the bigger fish.

Meeks booted up his desk computer. Within seconds his seventeen-digit password was accepted and he was into the FBI's Colossus 1 mainframe computer. He punched in another series of digits and he was into the main intranet system, on G plus G. There, as Courtney had instructed on her audiotape, he found the program called 'metal-desk-twenty-one'. He opened it and he was into the intranet drive in strategic ops. After a couple of minutes searching, he found the file he was looking for, 'Winter Snowman'. He entered the password Courtney had given, 'Simple Simon'. The program started to shut down, and although she had said this would happen, his heart skipped a few beats; he was not skilled enough in computers to know what to do if the program did shut down completely. The screen flashed and asked him for the shut-down password. Meeks typed in 'Jonathan' as she had instructed. The computer rebooted and the cursor flashed, Meeks hit the enter key and the file opened up. Less than ten minutes later Meeks had copied the file onto a memory stick. He then went into the main operating system and deleted his actions.

The traffic was now getting heavy. He turned into Ninth Street and past Ford's theatre where Abraham Lincoln was shot, then past the Martin Luther King memorial library. It was only when he was past the DC Convention Centre that he started to relax. He was home by 9 a.m. He sat at his computer in the den and read the file for the third time. Courtney was right: it was a labyrinth of lies and deceit. There were a hundred false trails. These guys had covered their tracks, but Courtney had done her job well. She had enough for Meeks to go on. The new intel supported his own information. Templar surveillance and patience had yielded a lot of evidence. Courtney's file filled in most of the missing links and gaps. However, the decision on what to do with the information was down to the Council of their Order. They still didn't know what Salah El-Din's end game was; how he intended to get at their Charge. It was presumed he had formed Unity so that he would have the manpower, reach and resources to seek out their Charge's location, but nothing could be taken for granted, not now.

Date: One week later
Place: Washington DC

Dukes had spent the money Jonathan had left on the table for him on five bottles of bourbon. Three weeks later he was found dead by his landlady. The decomposing body had been stripped of most of its flesh. The two starving cats had survived on the meat from Dukes's face, eyes and his tongue. The Coroner's report said that it had taken about three hours for someone to skin the body. It said that Dukes had been tied and gagged, but had been kept alive and conscious throughout by the introduction into his body of a sedative narcotic which kept his vital organs going. Whilst there was loss of blood, it was minimal, considering the butchery. An expert had removed the skin, slowly and with skill. It would have taken Dukes nearly twelve hours to die. The cause of death was recorded as petrified hysteria, which finally brought on a massive seizure. His landlady reported that she thought she had heard him screaming, but had ignored it because she often heard him screaming.

The police told reporters that whoever had killed Dukes had daubed the wall with a message, written in Dukes's own blood. The message read *Nathaniel, so it is again*. The police had no idea what the words meant. However, the Templars, who heard about Dukes's death the following day, did.

Nathaniel, also known as Saint Bartholomew, was a disciple of John the Baptist. He was on the lakeshore when Jesus showed himself after the resurrection. He preached the Gospel in Arabia and India and he suffered martyrdom in Armenia. He died when his skin was cut from his living body.

No motive was recorded for Dukes's death. No one attended the funeral, except Brent Walker, a cop from homicide and an FBI agent called Bill Meeks, who remained at the back of the funeral parlour. He left before the end. Jonathan didn't get to hear about the death of John Dukes. By the time it hit the papers, he had already left America.

Chapter 5

The Sanction

Date: June
Place: Glennfinch. The remote castle in Scotland

Even though the castle had electricity and had done so for many years, the great hall smelt of burning wax. The Higher Council held their meetings by candlelight – a tradition important in Templar life. The atmosphere conjured by their light and shadows was intoxicating. The castle was empty but for The Nine Worthies, the Higher Council of the Knights Templar.

The only staff that were employed on the estate were a local family. Their ancestors had served the Templars when they first acquired the castle centuries before and the family had looked after the Order ever since. They cleaned and cooked for the Templars; acted as a public face. Dealt with anyone appearing unannounced at the castle; dealt with the payment of bills and repairs. They kept the Templar's secret. They kept the castle's secret. There were places inside the castle that were consecrated ground, embodiments of spiritual grace. It was a sanctuary that was as sacred as the innermost subterranean passageways and catacombs of the Temple Mount, the Holy of Holies. Tapestries depicting medieval adventure and stoic heroism decorated the tall stonewalls in the great hall. History radiated from every direction.

Carved into the stone hearth were the words, *'Nil nisi clavis deest, Templum Hierosolyma, clavis ad thesaurum, theca ubi res pretiosa deponitur'. (Nothing is wanted but the key, the Temple of Jerusalem, the key to the treasure, a place where a precious thing is concealed.)* It is the same Latin inscription that once adorned a precious jewel held by the Royal Arch of Freemasonry many centuries ago.

The Nine Worthies represented the Higher Council of the Order of the Knights Templar, the most secret Order of ancient and modern time. People knew of the Thule society, the Rosicrucian Fellowship, the Golden Dawn and the Freemasons because they had all experienced public exposure in the twentieth century. The Templars had remained hidden, obscure in their isolation from the eyes of the world.

The Worthies were pious people, dedicated to the holy vows of righteousness; warrior monks, who worked in the shadows, dedicated to the sacred science of the Qumran – the original Nazarene church.

Calling them all together had been a difficult decision for St Clair. They had last met in December, less than six months ago, when St Clair had told them that the scrolls were now in the hands of Salah El-Din. Now he had called them together again, but this time it was to sanction someone's death. It was a grave matter, and he knew approval would not be a forgone conclusion. Over the years there had been many sanction approvals, but there had also been many rejections. They, the other eight members of the Higher Council, would need to consider it at length, even though the sanction was for the man who now had their scrolls, Salah El-Din. If approved, the sanction would be the first of 2008. St Clair hoped and prayed that it would be the last: experience, though, had taught him that it wouldn't.

The vows he had taken many years ago were explicit and absolute. They left no room for compromise, no second thought. Once pledged, they were forever followed. His commitment to his vows emanated from everything he did. His life was dedicated to the sacred science and the protection of the Order's Charge. He had made many sacrifices over the years, but his life was not his; he had already given it to the Holy Order of Knights Templar.

The Nine sat silent. At their head hung the *baussant*, the black and white chequered war banner of the Knights Templar. They had already donned their white surcoats with the distinctive red cross during their initial welcoming ceremony of intoning chants and secret gestures. Now they sat around the long mahogany table which dominated the great hall of Glennfinch Castle.

Some of the Worthies had arrived by ferry, others by plane into international and provincial airports, but all had arrived as they would depart, separately, a habit formed over many years.

As always, Payne St Clair sat at the head of the table. Four Worthies were seated to his left and four to his right. After the ceremony of welcome was complete, they each took the Eucharist, the embodiment of Christ. Now they sat silent in contemplation and expectation.

After a respectable silence, St Clair finally eased his frame out of the high-backed Jacobean chair to address them. "Brothers, by God's grace we are called here again. May our Lord watch over this Council and give us the wisdom we will need."

He lowered his head in respect for a few seconds and then he began. St Clair told them that he was seeking a sanction to take the life of one who would seek their Charge for evil purposes. One who had killed and caused great suffering to others. Low voices wove together as they spoke to each other. The staccato flames of the candles danced on relentlessly. The room was heady with purposeful whispers, words of concern and importance.

After a while, St Clair raised his hand and silence fell. He told them that the sanction he now sought was for the termination of a violent and ruthless criminal, a man known to have killed more than forty people by his own hand and countless others by his direct orders. But, St Clair warned, this would not be an easy sanction; for this job he would need to use only their best Knights. He told them that their very own existence was now at stake. In addition, he continued without pause, he would need to recruit two new people.

One would be a highly trained specialist with combat experience and one other. He breezed over the second of the two, giving no name, no detail. He saw the surprise on their faces, but he did not elaborate, nor would they question him when the time came to vote. They knew their Order's Grand Master would have good reason not to give any additional information at this stage. The two new people, he said, would join the four Knights he was about to propose for the sanction team.

The Worthies listened as St Clair told them about the telephone call he had received from one of their Order in Washington, Bill Meeks. Meeks had given details of the most recent activities in Washington of Salah El-Din, a man their Order knew well. For a long time, Salah El-Din had been working to unite major crime organizations from all over the world. His quest was to bring them together into one all-powerful organisation that would control crime in principal cities and major capitals.

From his humble beginnings as a small-time criminal, Salah El-Din had grown into one of the most influential underworld criminals in London, Washington and Cairo, where he mostly operated. In those cities he had systematically set about removing his rivals in order to take over their operations. He made no secret of his intentions: for him there was no code of honour, no brotherhood. Wives and children, even aging relatives, all were fair game to get to the people he wanted and he killed without thought or remorse. His murdering was brutal and the death toll rose. The criminal gang leaders found an adversary who was truly evil, one who enjoyed the torture and death, and they began to run scared. It wasn't long before those who were left joined him, deciding it was better to be part of his organization, with a smaller share, than looking over their shoulders for the rest of their lives. With his wealth increasing, he paid off judges, politicians and senior-ranking law enforcement officers, including the FBI and the Attorney General's office. By 2001, with the help of people like Senator McGregor, he had become one of the most powerful figures in organized crime.

The news they received in January from their Knight in Washington, Meeks, regarding the lost scrolls, had been grave, but now the audio tape Meeks had played to St Clair meant things were much worse than they had thought. The tape had shocked St Clair. Now his companions were feeling the same horror. Salah El-Din had formed Unity. Now in London, Washington and Cairo, the Mafia, Teamsters, Yardies and a mix of other criminal factions had all come together under the overall chairmanship of this one man, Salah El-Din.

St Clair told them about the death of John Dukes. As an organisation they had tried to help him two years earlier, but Dukes had already begun the slow journey into madness by the time Meeks met him and he had ignored their warnings and offer of help. Now he was dead.

The Nine Worthies knew that if Salah El-Din was able to break their coded scrolls, he would have the manpower to seek out their secret Order and, take their Charge, that which the Order had protected with their lives for centuries. The Worthies were all familiar with his name. Over the years they had watched him grow from a small-time gunrunner into a ruthless and violent criminal. Now he had succeeded in the unthinkable, the forming of Unity. A combined underworld of pariah and vermin, it could only have one outcome: the bleeding of cities and the suffering of many, in order to find their Charge.

Salah El-Din had been powerful before, but with Unity he could now extend his search for that which had eluded him for so long, the Ark of the Covenant. With an organization of tens of thousands, he would stop at nothing to get it. They knew that he'd been searching for it for a long time, searching for them, but he had failed at every juncture. Their veil of secrecy was impenetrable, but now all that could change.

St Clair told them that they must assume that Salah El-Din had a copy of the tape, the tape Courtney had made and, if so, he had St

Clair's name. Even if he didn't have the tape, he told them, Dukes had been tortured and he would have given his torturers St Clair's name and the location: Scotland. St Clair acknowledged he had made a crucial mistake in trying to help Dukes when Dukes was of unsound mind. It now put their Order, and their Charge, in great danger.

As was their Order's way, St Clair bowed his head when he had finished his report from Meeks. He couldn't see their eyes, but he could feel their intensity.

Down the years Knights had given their lives courageously to defend the innocent and in the unwavering protection of their Charge. Giving one's own life reflected the final act of faith. To outsiders, this devotion would seem to border on insanity, but to the Nine, this was something they had committed to in their vows of absolute fidelity to their faith.

Now more Knights would be asked to risk their lives in the sanction team and St Clair wanted to be one of them. He knew it was against their Order's unwritten rule. 'Active' Knights, those who undertook sanctions, were all below the age of fifty. The Nine Worthies, most of whom had been Active Knights in their day, were now considered too old to undertake a sanction. However, St Clair would press hard on his inclusion.

St Clair produced the list of Knights he wanted for the sanction team, laying it before him on the mahogany table. He ran through the names on the list. The first person he proposed was the American Indian, John Wolf. He had served the Order on many sanctions. If he were approved, word would be sent to him in the usual way: a short telegram with their Order's sign at the bottom left-hand corner. St Clair's voice still hushed, he then proposed to recruit a new Knight to the Order. He was a man who had served as a captain in the Russian Special Forces for nearly eight years, in Afghanistan. He owed the Order a debt of honour, inherited from his father. St Clair told them they would need his special combat skills. But first, he would need to get him out of a Russian prison camp, deep in the wastelands of

Siberia, where he was incarcerated. He explained that one of the Council, André Sabath, had finally tracked down the man's whereabouts just under a year ago. Since then, Sabath had only been able to communicate with him intermittently because of the prison authorities' security measures. However, Sabath and a small group of Templars had been planning to help the Russian escape during the short summer of that year, when the temperature rises slightly, just enough for him to have any chance of surviving the frozen wasteland.

However, with their Charge at risk, St Clair wanted to act now. The Russian and the Indian would have to take out Salah El-Din's infamous and highly dangerous bodyguards. Both Knights were trained for this type of work. St Clair fell silent and waited for the two men to be approved. After some debate, approval finally came in the usual manner. Each of the eight Worthies made the sign of the cross across their white surcoats and when everyone had done this, in unison they whispered, "By God's grace and by his word, that which was cast in stone, we humbly seek your forgiveness. Amen."

The girl, Dominique, had not been on a sanction since the South African sanction in 1996, when she was shot, badly wounded and very nearly died. It took a long time for her wounds to heal and, because of what happened to her as a child, it took longer for her mind to recover. However, he told them she wanted to become active again and he believed that she was ready. He proposed that she would oversee communications and transportation. Again, after some debate, this was also approved.

Their ghost man had been an active Knight for many years. He had trained in counter intelligence and espionage, courtesy of British intelligence in a past life. He was already planted inside Salah El-Din's organization, in London. This precautionary move had been approved almost a year ago, as part of their surveillance on Salah El-Din's illegal activities in the United Kingdom.

Now St Clair, with his head still bowed, broached the subject of his own inclusion on the sanction. Whilst no one argued that he had been one of their most effective active Knights in his day, his age now troubled them. It could put the sanction and him at risk. As was customary, St Clair, as the Knight proposing the sanction, did not take part in the discussion; it was left to the other eight Worthies to decide. His head remaining low, he strained to detect the mood of the debate. The table was long and their voices carried, but they were almost inaudible. For what seemed like an age the debate went on, but he remained silent and still.

Finally, his wait was over: because of the severity of the situation, their approval was reluctantly given.

Now there was only one more person for the sanction team. St Clair told them that he would need to recruit one more new Knight to their Order. He wanted their approval to choose the final person later. Again he did not elaborate. St Clair's judgment was beyond reproach. He had recruited many new Knights over the years, as they had all done, and his request was not unusual. What was unusual, however, was the fact that he wanted the new knight to be mission-active straight away. The other eight Worthies knew their Grand Master well and they knew that he must have his reasons for such a request. He had led them in a manner befitting their religious Order. It was this leadership that formed the foundation of their approval for the request. They gave their approval.

It was now time for them to vote on the sanction itself. Despite agreeing the sanction team, the sanction itself was always left until last. This was their way: the most important issues were always left until last. It was a most grave thing to sanction the termination of another's life. The Order, steeped in tradition and ceremony, now followed with ancient custom. St Clair made his case one more time, then each of the eight Worthies would remain seated at the long table to signify their approval, or they would leave the table, signifying their disapproval. Every sanction had to be unanimous. St Clair stood motionless. He didn't know if they would approve the sanction, despite the overwhelming evidence. Again, as the Knight proposing the sanction, he did not move now or speak; he left them to their intense debate. Most of the eight had been active in their time. They knew the risk St Clair and the other Knights would be taking. Salah El-Din, violent and ruthless, was well armed and well guarded.

They had intelligence that Salah El-Din had evaded two assassination attempts on his life already. Two Israeli undercover agents from Mossad had attempted to kill him. However, the assassination did not go to plan. One agent's body was eventually found by Bedouin nomads. The dead man had been bound hand and foot, tortured, and then beheaded. A Puma helicopter, from the Sultan's Royal flight in Oman, found the body of the second agent. He had died in the searing heat of the desert. There was no explanation of how he had got there or why. Both bodies were returned to Israel and buried in private, but with full honours.

Then, in 1990, Salah El-Din made a series of drug deals with a Spanish crime syndicate based in Madrid. It was worth fifty million US dollars. Salah El-Din had flown to Madrid to supervise the deal personally. The cocaine had been tested by the Spanish criminals and had tested pure. However, when they tested the last three batches, back in their laboratories, they found that it had been cut so fine it had halved its street value. Three men were sent by the Spanish gang to the hotel where Salah El-Din was staying. The Inspector of Police, talking about the horror that followed, reported that the fire that had swept through the Madrid hotel that day and had killed thirty-three people, including the three henchmen, had been started by accident. Salah El-din's bodyguards knew differently and the Inspector of Police was paid the equivalent of two years' salary.

No chair was moved. Approval had finally been given and the sanction was on. The three Templars, Dominique, the Indian and their ghost man, would be contacted at once and, as always, given the choice to take on the sanction or not. The Russian would be difficult because he had been incarcerated for such a long time. St Clair would help, but the Russian would have to do much on his own. Now that the mission was sanctioned, St Clair could not risk sending Knights to help him. The Russian faced an almost impossible task of escaping from the snow-bound fortress that held him. Whilst St Clair had never met him, he felt that the Russian had the grit, fortitude and resolve he would need to stand half a chance of executing a successful escape.

If St Clair's hunch was right, he figured that the sixth member of the sanction team, the new Knight without a name, would arrive in Scotland by late June, about the same time as the others. But first he needed to turn his efforts to the Russian.

Chapter 6

The Russian – Part 1

Date: June 2008
Place: Ural Mountains

The morning roll call brought with it its usual tensions: there were new prisoners in the camp. The authorities would have already tortured most of the newcomers and many would now be informers. It was the only way the prisoners could ever hope to have their sentences reduced from the living hell that was now their internment. It was not surprising that when a new intake of Zeks arrived at the camp, everyone was treated as an informer. It was usually more than a year before any of them could be considered safe to talk to, and by that point, the other Zeks would have found them out. Most people's spirit broke within a few days; few lasted more than six months.

The Gulag was called Perm 35. It lay deep in the Ural Mountains, 800 miles east of Moscow, one of the diminishing numbers of Soviet labour camps for political prisoners. Once Gulags had lain scattered all over the USSR, forming part of the infamous Gulag system.

Nickolin Klymachak, a Leningrad Christian like his father before him, was one of the 600 Zeks at Perm 35. Nickolin, an ex-solider, had been court-martialled and then imprisoned for refusing to carry out a direct order from his commanding officer: to destroy a small rural village during the Russian occupation of Afghanistan. The village was known to contain women and children only. Their men, part of the militia, were fighting in the Hindu Kush mountain range in the north.

Afghanistan had once been Nickolin's righteous war. He had been part of the forward task force back in 1979, when Russia had first entered the country and installed the PDPA leader, Babrah Karmal, after executing the existing incumbent, Hafizullah Amin. Nickolin believed in the glory and humanity of their war. In a country where the life expectancy in men was forty-three years and the average literacy rate 29 per cent, he believed that, for a country that survived on exporting dried fruit, nuts, and opium, Mother Russia was their saviour. He was eighteen years old then and the ravages and futility of that war had yet to show its repugnant face to him.

In 1986, whilst still fighting the war in Afghanistan, his young wife – who he'd left back in Russia – was finally persuaded to take their two children from Russia to her parents' home until he returned. As so many times before, she had not wanted to leave their home, but in early 1986, she agreed to go: her parents' hometown, in northern Ukraine, was called Chernobyl.

In 1986 two huge central reactors exploded in Chernobyl, breaching the 1000-tonne roof. Thirty-three people died that day, mainly plant workers and fire fighters, but many more would die from the aftermath. Nickolin's wife and two children perished within a few months; it was a slow and painful death for all three.

In the early part of January 1987, the news of Chernobyl and the death of his wife and children had finally reached Nickolin, on the outskirts of a small village. The news had been intentionally delayed in Moscow for months. Nickolin was twenty-six years old and had been fighting the war for nearly eight years.

The order to destroy the village, by detonating high explosives in its centre, was given by his commanding officer on the day Nickolin received the news about his family. The order had been given twice, and twice Nickolin refused to carry out the order. With desertion in the field an ever-increasing problem for the Russian commanders,

Nickolin was made an example of. Stripped of his command and rank, he was shipped back to Russia, where he spent the next four years held in a military prison whilst awaiting trial. Then in 1991, at the age of thirty, and two years after the Russians withdrew from Afghanistan, the authorities finally brought his case to closed court. Nickolin was court-martialled, found guilty, and imprisoned in a labour camp for fifteen years.

Once, Nickolin had been the toast of Moscow, decorated and accorded recognition as a national hero. Now he had been left to rot in jail, forgotten by the comrades and the country he was once so proud to serve. His father never saw his son's incarceration. He had died the year before Nickolin went to war, but Nickolin's ultimate destiny had already begun many years before and his father was to play a pivotal role.

Date: 1963
Place: Paris, France

In 1963, when Nickolin was only one year old, his father, a loyal member of the Communist party, was working in the Russian Embassy in Paris as the Chief Clerk. A diligent, fastidious man, he worked with great skill through the myriad of daily tasks required to keep the affairs of the embassy operational. An efficient and effective administrator, he didn't make, or tolerate mistakes,

Work was rarely out of his mind. Long days and late nights, streams of coded communications to and from Moscow and a never-ending sea of papers for the ambassador to sign made his life frenetic. Trustworthy and loyal, he was a factotum at the hub of everything. Back home, he had left behind a wife and four children: Nickolin and three older siblings. The subject of his family accompanying him on this, his third overseas posting, never came up for discussion. Without distraction, tirelessly he kept the paper-mountain moving from the in tray to the out tray, ensuring that everything that needed to be done was done. Life at the embassy was one of strict routine and discipline. Secrecy was a byword for everyone who worked in the embassy: it was etched into their work ethic. He, and the other seventeen-strong staff that worked for him, represented Russia and no one took their work lightly. The Iron Curtain remained veiled and the consequences of any failure would be punitive.

Nickolin's father strongly disliked his ambassador, a flamboyant bureaucrat who minded his own future. He was a career diplomat who revelled in the finer things in life, all of which he could find in Paris, and none of which existed at home in Russia. Integrity and diligence were words Nickolin's father would seldom use when thinking about his ambassador. It seemed to him that the country would be better off without such transparent men, men without principle, but he never said. No one would dare speak their minds. The ambassador knew too many party officials and high-ranking military officers back in Moscow. His post was secure, theirs were not and Russia was not a country known for its free speech policies.

Paris was a strange place for Nickolin's father. His other postings had been to communist countries where he had met and worked with comrades of a different nationality, but they were comrades all the same. In France, there were fewer comrades and, although he tried hard to find the imperialism in France he had been warned about, he found none. The West, he had always believed, suffered from social diseases, greed and degenerative capitalism, but all he found were ordinary people. Parisians living freely, abiding citizens going about their everyday business, people just like him. Old doctrines die hard when they have been ingrained from childhood. He tried to block out the reality of what he saw, but the thought kept coming back. Maybe Communism was not alone as a plausible way of life; maybe there were other workable social and economic systems and Marx's '*Jeder nach seinen Fähigkeiten, jedem nach seinen Bedürfnissen*' ('From each according to his ability, to each according to his needs') was just as achievable in a non-Communist society. But he kept his thoughts strictly to himself. He buried himself in paperwork and stifled his wandering mind by yet more work. He would not disgrace his family, and he would not disgrace Mother Russia. However, eight months into his posting his life took a dramatic turn and the events that followed would eventually help an American priest called Jonathan Rose, over thirty-six years later.

The ambassador finally made the mistake some knew he was destined to make. Working later than normal one night, Nickolin's father found a document on the ambassador's desk. The ambassador had forgotten to take it with him in his attaché case when he left for the night. The document, just a single piece of paper in a manila file, written in the ambassador's handwriting, detailed transactions between the ambassador and four people. Nickolin's father recognised their code names immediately. All four were known spies of foreign governments, operating out of France. As he read, his life began to fall apart. He checked the office diary, sweat now soaking through his shirt. He checked it again and again, but there was no mistake . The horror of what had happened hit him full on. Unwittingly, many of the clerks who worked for Nickolin's father had been used as couriers by the ambassador. It was the clerks who had unknowingly made document drops to the foreign agents. The same clerk was not used consecutively and so suspicion was never raised. The crushing feeling swirled around in the pit of Nickolin's father's stomach and then erupted when he came to the sixth and ninth entries: his own name was scribbled beside the dates.

He'd had no way of knowing what was in the packages he had been asked to deliver; he would never have asked. In the malevolence of the cold war, Russian embassies were always in covert mode, so it was not unusual for packages and documents to be channelled through a series of couriers back to Russia. Only these documents were not bound for Russia; they were Russian secrets bound for foreign governments. The ambassador's plan was simple and not, as it turned out, particularly well thought out: sell secrets to foreign spies and use the clerks at the embassy to do it. Given the black market rates for a state's secrets, and the kind of information the ambassador was privy to, he would, the ambassador had calculated, amass enough money in less than a year and a half to defect and live out a pleasant life in the West, where he could find all the finer things he craved. The foreign governments would not give him away because the publicity of the defection was valuable currency for whichever government got him. The realisation that he, as Chief Clerk of the embassy, had passed Russian state secrets to German and French agents, made him despair with the finality of it all. If he told the authorities in Russia, what he had discovered, he would surely be as guilty as if he had been a willing accomplice: the Iron Curtain prevailed with unforgiving menace and who would believe him against an ambassador?

Alone that night in his tiny apartment, he tried to find a way out of the disaster that had just taken over his life. The ambassador would deny all knowledge and that would leave him and the others to face the retribution of the infamous KGB. He needed help, but there was no one to help, no one he could talk too. Thoughts of his impending death troubled his sleepless night.

The following evening, when everyone had left for the night, he opened the ambassador's secret wall safe. He wasn't supposed to know the combination, but he did – he was good at his job. With the night-guards firmly ensconced in a mild debate about the best whores they had slept with in Paris, he went through the ambassador's private papers. He knew that he was committing a crime, but now he had nothing to lose. The document he had found on the previous evening was tucked away at the back of the safe. He made a copy, then replaced it. He continued to search amongst the other papers and files. His eye caught an envelope he had not seen before. Inside the envelope was a letter, clearly marked 'Komitet gosudarstvennoy bezopasnosti' (KGB). He opened all correspondence from Moscow, which arrived at the embassy in the diplomatic bag. This had obviously arrived by another covert channel. The letter consisted of a small paragraph, neatly typed:

Comrade Ambassador

Utmost attention must be given to our current problem in Paris.

You must confirm the whereabouts of the KGB defector, Anatoly Petrov.

Imperative we have confirmation and details by month end.

Two comrades will arrive by the 30th to terminate the problem. Afford them full co-operation.

Last known address of target ...

Nickolin's father had just found his way out. He made a note of the address and put the envelope back. He locked the safe and switched off the lights. Passing the guards, he bid them goodnight, his voice calm. But beneath his overcoat, his body shook.

He walked far enough away from the embassy building until he felt safe, then he found a public telephone box, from where he called the telephone exchange. The telephone operator checked the address he had written down. It was listed. She gave him the phone number for the address. He dialled the number straightaway. A French woman answered. She denied that Anatoly Petrov lived in the house. It took him nearly ten minutes to convince her that he was not the KGB.

Just after 11 p.m. Anatoly Petrov arrived at the street café, as arranged through the French woman. The street was still busy. Nickolin's father and the KGB defector talked for just over two hours. Nickolin's father told him about the communication from Moscow and that two KGB operatives were due in Paris on the 30th and Petrov was their target. Anatoly Petrov didn't seem surprised. He told Nickolin's father he had met the French woman a year ago and they had fallen in love. Now he wanted to leave his old life behind to be with the love of his life. He wanted a family. He wanted to be free.

Nickolin's father offered to help Petrov in return for his help. He would help him by acquiring false papers and passports and would ensure his safe passage out of France. Then he would give him a bank account number. The account would contain 10,000 US dollars. Acquiring false documents and depositing black money was all part of the job for a Chief Clerk. He often moved money around into different bank accounts. Transactions were seldom checked by the ambassador, whose job it was to check all transactions. Mother Russian ensured all of their embassies had large sums of money for their clandestine political activities. In return, the man would help expose the ambassador to the KGB. Nickolin's father gambled that, because the man had worked for the KGB for over twelve years, he would know how to expose the ambassador without implicating him or the rest of his staff. His not being branded a traitor by the KGB and about to be shot was now in the hands of a man who was in hiding. It had all the hallmarks of a plan destined to go wrong, but Nickolin's father had no other choice. He didn't have the man's specialist knowledge or the contacts for this kind of thing. He gave the man the copy he had made of the ambassador's handwritten note, which contained the evidence, and then he left.

The man left Paris two days later on the false passport and papers Nickolin's father had sent to the French woman. Less than two weeks later, the French woman left Paris to join her Russian boyfriend, who had just recently acquired a new bank account, with the sum of 10,000 US dollars deposited in it by an unknown source. Four hours after the man was safely out of the country, Nickolin's father was contacted at his apartment. The caller, a small rotund man of Egyptian and French origin, introduced himself as Sabath, André Sabath. He gave Nickolin's father assurances that he was not connected to any government. He said that the organisation he represented had no interest in the affairs of foreign governments, but, should his organisation decide to help in this matter, a debt would be owed. Nickolin's father agreed, then he told Sabath everything. It took the Templar just three weeks to wire and tape meetings and to tail and photograph the ambassador's nocturnal activities – amassing enough evidence to seal his fate.

The Communist party back in Russia, upon receiving detailed documents, tapes and photographs from an unknown source, called Nickolin's father back to Moscow. There he lived out his life. The ambassador, also called back to Moscow two weeks after Nickolin's father, disappeared from public life, reportedly retiring to the country, but he was never seen or heard of again. Years later, the KGB confirmed his execution.

Nickolin's father owed the Knights Templar a great debt, but he was never able to repay them. Despite staying in contact with André Sabath, he was never called upon to discharge his debt. Upon his death, the old man told his son the story of what had happened to him in Paris and the little he knew about the Knights Templar from his communications with André Sabath over the years. The debt, considered a matter of honour by his father, was then passed onto Nickolin. André Sabath attended the old man's funeral, at which the seventeen-year-old Nickolin made him the solemn oath that, if he were called upon, he would, without hesitation or recourse, discharge his father's debt. It was the year before Nickolin went to Afghanistan. It would be many years later before Nickolin would be asked to discharge that debt, but that time had now come for the Leningrad Christian.

Chapter 7

The Indian

Date: September 1981
Place: Kentucky

His father squeezed his hand tightly, and then he let it go. He smiled and told him not to worry. Not to wander off onto the prairie, but to wait for him there; he wouldn't be long. He told him a man had come to help them with the people who were trying to steal their ancestors' souls, a man from Great Britain. He told him he would meet the man and all would be well with their people again and their ancestors would rest in peace. He smiled at him and promised he would be back soon.

The boy watched as his father drove off into the distance, the Ford pickup truck engulfed in clouds of dust as it left the reservation. He still felt his father's hand in his. He felt safe. He waited. The boy couldn't say how long he waited. People came, but he stayed. He told them he was waiting for his father. It got dark and he strained his eyes for the first glimpse of the headlights of his father's pickup. It got chilly, but he waited. His father was a man of his word. His father didn't lie; he was his friend.

The night noises came. Distant voices of wild coyotes called to each other in the blackness. At this age the night scared him, but he wouldn't show it; he was his father's son.

Three police officers gathered around him. He didn't recognise them, but they seemed to know him. They spoke his name and looked sad. His mother moved through them and embraced him She was crying. His mother seldom cried. She took his hand as his father had done, then led him away. He didn't want to go; he wanted to wait for his father, his friend.

His mother cried at her husband's funeral. They told him that his father wasn't coming back. They said that his father had gone into the spirit world, to hunt with their ancestors for buffalo and white elk. The boy didn't understand: his father had promised to come back. He had told him to wait and he had waited. He didn't cry at the funeral because his father had told him that only a fool bathes in his own tears. He was his father's son: he would never cry again.

Date: Late June 2008
Place: Kentucky.

John Wolf, a thirty-seven-year-old Shawnee Indian and a mission-active Knight Templar, intoned a prayer in his native Onondagon language because the spirits of his ancestors had been disturbed again. The land around him lay marked with hundreds of probe holes and mounds of fresh brown earth: the Indian relic hunters had been out again that night. His father, Grey Cloud, would be saddened: the father that hunted in the spirit world with his ancestors, for buffalo and white elk: the father who never came back.

John Wolf closed his eyes and saw himself as that ten-year-old boy watching his father drive away for the last time. He looked up at an eagle descending in spirals. He wiped the sweat from his forehead and the image of the boy was gone, but it would return. It always did. Twenty-seven years had passed, but the pain of losing his father was as strong as it ever was.

John Wolf held the official position of 'Protector of the Western Kentucky Indian Burial Sites'. He had been appointed by the Sheriff's Department back in 1993, when Wolf was just twenty-two years old. It was a post funded partly by the State and partly by the American

Indian Movement. His job was to protect the ancient Indian burial sites that lie hidden by the brown earth on the prairie and farming land. Protect them from weekend surface hunters, para-archaeologists, grave robbers and an increasing number of commercial operators.

John Wolf, like his father before him, stood a proud man, tall and lean with solid broad shoulders, shoulder-length jet-black hair, parted in the centre, chiselled and weathered features with deep-tanned skin. His brown eyes were the eyes of a hunter, the eyes of a man who could survive on the ranges. He looked and was the embodiment of the wild and rugged land on which he lived.

John Wolf was also a prominent guest speaker at the local university, where he lectured on Indian culture and Native American heritage. Whilst Wolf was a popular speaker, he remained aloof from the mainly white bookish educationalists that worked there. He disliked their bigotry, their indifference to the way in which the Indians had been, and still were being treated. Their own forefathers, they would tell him, were not wholly to blame for what happened to the Native Americans. They raptured away in their textbook worlds, arguing that even history wasn't immune to exaggeration. Wolf was confounded by their ignorance: such learned men, advocates of knowledge, such stupid men. 'We gave them the telegram and a railroad,' he was once told. 'Perhaps they didn't want the telegram and a railroad!' he had replied.

At his lectures, students hung onto his every word. He kindled passion in them and the rights of the Native American Indians seeped through his lectures and resonated in the hearts of many. He stirred his young audiences and converted hundreds of supporters to the American Indian Movement, supporters of all creeds.

John Wolf had a presence about him seldom awarded to a man. Wild stories about the Indian loner sprang from the fertile imaginations of the young students, who, flocking to see the tall, dark figure hold centre stage and to hear his rich, gravel voice talk with a passion no other lecturer had. Many of the students saw John Wolf as a latter-day hero, straight out of the old west.

Wolf enjoyed lecturing at the university. It meant he was able to educate a whole new generation of Americans. But his heart lay on the vast reservation where he was born. However, with the post greatly under-funded by State parsimony, he struggled to maintain vigilance over the many thousands of acres of land that lay within his jurisdiction. Visits from the curious surface hunters, who came down from their homes in cities at weekends, were easier to deal with than most. Stern words from the imposing figure of Wolf, with his long-range rifle strung across his shoulder and a fourteen-inch bone-handled knife holstered in its sheath by his side, soon convinced them to leave. However, the commercial operators, made up of greedy businessmen and an increasing number of organised crime syndicates, were much harder to deal with. These people were the real jackals. They played hardball and like his father before him, Wolf rubbed them up the wrong way – and the abrasion festered. The travesty was there for all to see. Numerous reports in the press stated that since the early sixties a profitable business had grown up in the trade of Indian artefacts. Most of these were being sold on the open market – merchandise for the tourists and city dwellers. But the rarer finds were reserved for private collectors who paid thousands of dollars. Commercial operators would bid for the 'lease digging' rights from the farmers. They knew that was where the good sites were, around the Ohio River, where Wolf lived.

How Thomas Grey Cloud, John Wolf's father, had first met Payne St Clair, the man from Scotland, was never discussed. However, in 1981 they arranged their second meeting. This was, as it turned out, to be their last. Back then, commercial digging operations had just begun and a criminal syndicate from Chicago was quick to see the opportunity. It wasn't long before Grey Cloud had become a thorn in their side. He thwarted them wherever he could. Raising public awareness and speaking out in as many newspapers as would print his words, he brought their seedy operation into the spotlight.

In the Fall of 1981, St Clair and Grey Cloud agreed to meet in the Western Hotel in Frankfort city. St Clair arrived at the hotel, direct from the airport by cab, at around sunset. He made his way to his room, where they had arranged to meet. The door to the room, which had been reserved by telex a week earlier, was already open. Inside the curtains were drawn and the lights were off. Something was clearly wrong. St Clair discovered Grey Cloud lying face down on the floor just outside the bathroom. He had been beaten, and then shot twice through the mouth with a .38. The gun had been fired through two pillows to muffle the shots. The police report said that it had been the work of a professional hit man. The body, hideously beaten, or 'symbolically embellished', as the police report read, was someone's way of saying that Grey Cloud had been killed because he had spoken out.

Four weeks after the funeral of Grey Cloud, three members of the Chicago crime syndicate, who had been supervising the commercial digging operations in the area, were systematically assassinated. Each body was found with a small red cross painted onto each victim's forehead, the victim's own blood having been used to make the mark. The police had no clue who had carried out the killings.

After the death of Grey Cloud, St Clair and the Knights of his Order watched over the dead Indian's family. They paid for his son, the ten-year-old Indian boy known as John Wolf, to be educated upstate, away from any possible reprisals after the murders. The boy attended college until the age of eighteen. St Clair made many trips to the US over the ensuing years, spending many summers with the boy and becoming like a second father to him. St Clair tempered the anger Wolf felt over the death of his father, and helped shape and hone the young boy's spirit.

With the passing of each year, John Wolf grew in size and in maturity. He had natural ability for the skills he would later need in life: a life he would choose to lead, a life that would often take him away from his tribe and a life he kept secret. As the boy grew, St Clair made arrangements for specially selected teachers to tutor him. The tutors who were sent to America were masters of their craft. The first to arrive was Luther Coates, a survival specialist who had been with the British SAS. He taught Wolf to shoot with the accuracy of a highly trained sniper. Under Luther's supervision, Wolf learned how to handle a range of firearms. When he left, he gave Wolf a specially modified .357 Magnum handgun. This would become Wolf's favourite firearm.

Next to arrive was Master Hang Ma Chow, from Hong Kong. He was sent to Kentucky to teach the boy the art of self-defence, including Chinese kick-boxing, Kendo and Aikido: the boy excelled and Master Chow left early. Dr Steve Barns had a double honours degree in psychology and held a doctorate in sociology from Manchester University. However, his real specialism was close combat strategies in hostile theatres and 'Hearts and Minds' campaigns in multiple warfare scenarios. Of all the many tutors who were sent to America to teach Wolf, it was St Clair who taught him his most important lessons. These were the lessons normally reserved for a father to teach his son: empathy, humility, integrity and honour.

John Wolf achieved excellent grades at college, majoring in American history and conservation. He was never ridiculed because of the colour of his skin and he was never bullied. He had been set upon only once, by a group of four seniors, when Wolf was still a freshman. The sight of the four bloodied seniors and one unmarked freshman was warning enough. He was never bothered again.

Just after his nineteenth birthday, St Clair invited John Wolf to the castle in Scotland. There he was introduced to the Order of Knights Templar and told about their association with his father back in 1981, when the Order was helping to find and destroy the criminal syndicate operating on tribal burial grounds. He learned about the origins of the Templars and about their secret work all over the world. At his own request, Wolf was initiated into the Order and by the following year, he was mission-active: a Knight who can be called upon for a covert operation at any time and in any part of the world. John Wolf soon became one of their most effective Knights.

Wolf was used to receiving the telegrams from St Clair. He would normally get three or four each year and each started with the same line: 'May God guide you by His grace'. He had already been on three missions, the last in April, and was eager for his next job. A small red cross always appeared at the bottom of the telegram, the sign of their Order. It was the same red cross St Clair had marked on the foreheads of the three dead men in Chicago, after he had received the sanction and shot them dead.

Wolf was returning home from three days in the field when he called into town for some supplies. The postmaster gave him the telegram. Wolf retuned home, packed a bag and caught an international flight out of Louisville International airport early the following morning. He had been called to arms.

Chapter 8

The Russian – Part 2

Date: June 2008
Place: Ural Mountains

Nickolin Klymachak had lost track of the number of years he had spent in Perm 35, but he knew it was longer than the fifteen-year sentence he had been given. Nickolin was forty-six years old, a big man, broad and powerfully built; at six foot five he towered over the other Zeks. He had short-cropped black hair with hints of grey and brown eyes. He had a square chin and a deep scar over his left eye, remnants of a knife fight with three Zeks in his first year at Perm 35.

Most Zeks kept out of Nickolin's way, but a small quiet man in his late fifties, who slept in the bottom bunk below Nickolin, was always at his side. It was rumoured that the small quiet man had been very wealthy on the outside. His crime, as he told it to Nickolin, was to have made 'some' money; he never defined 'some'. Unfortunately, he had forgotten to share it with his partners, two corrupt senior party officials and a certain commander in the KGB.

The small quiet man bribed the prison guards to smuggle in his money every month, for which favour they kept two thirds. With the remaining third, the man bribed other guards and brought rations of meat and vegetables, which he shared with Nickolin. Nickolin, for his part, made sure that the man was never bothered by other Zeks in Perm 35. It was a good arrangement and one that kept Nickolin alive through the relentlessly harsh winters. His body had become like iron and his hands like leather. He was fit and he was mean.

Nickolin spoke five languages fluently, including English, Arabic and Hebrew. Of above average intelligence, he had graduated from Moscow University top of his class. However, he turned his back on the life of an aspiring lawyer in search of adventure in Russia's most elite commando force at the age of eighteen, rising to the rank of captain by the time he was twenty-three years old.

Perm 35 was a different world. Here he was the enemy of the state, not its darling. He worked eight hours a day, six days a week, in the prison workshop, for which he and the other Zeks were paid 200 roubles a month each, none of which he saw. The camp's Commandant, Lt. Col. Vladimir Mikhailov, kept the money the party provided for working Zeks, considering it his. Mikhailov didn't like Nickolin. Mikhailov didn't like any of the prisoners. They were scabrous eyesores on the face of Mother Russia, but he hated the ex-commando more than the others. Nickolin's resolve was legendary at Perm 35 and Mikhailov took it as a personal and professional challenge to break it, which included ignoring Nickolin's release date.

During his first three years in Perm 35, Nickolin had spent much of his time in the *shizo*, an isolation cell with no windows, no heating and no blankets. He never complained. His silence was his weapon against them. Depression and despair, he had once told the small quiet man, robs people of the power to plan and, whilst many of the Zeks were slowly parting company with reality, he remained true to hope. When Zeks cursed at their potato puree and borscht meal, which, they complained, was unfit to feed to animals, Nickolin sat and ate in silence, smiling.

The KGB interrogators left him alone. They were only interested in political Zeks, dissidents and radical reformists. These they sought out, torturing them by starving and freezing them to death.

Large metal gates and rolls upon rolls of razor wire on top of the ten-foot high walls that surrounded the camp kept the Zeks incarcerated. If they wanted to die, as some did, it was easy for them: they just had to step over a small barbed wire fence, which stood about five feet from the wall. A bullet from the turret tower would find its mark and the camp's half-starved guard dogs would finish off any life left in the wretched body.

In the old days Zeks dug ditches, built roads and railways, many dying from malnutrition, tuberculosis or the cold. Fifty years on, nothing had changed. People were still dying. Every day Nickolin watched as more bodies would be carted off to makeshift graves outside the camp, but there were always more new intakes to take their place.

Life dragged in Perm 35. It was a living hell that tormented the Zeks from sunup to sundown. At night they would lie freezing in their beds, with just a thin, dirty blanket as protection from the sub-zero temperatures: grown men shivering uncontrollably and sobbing. Few Zeks ever left Perm 35 and of those that did, many died within their first year of freedom. Some died from diseases they had contracted whilst in prison, but mostly because of the hopelessness of their lives. Despair and depression marked them like a scar and suicide accounted for the deaths of over 95% of all released prisoners.

The morning that Nickolin was listed as absent from the roll call, there were no new Zeks, no one to watch for the next year. It was also the morning that Lt. Col. Vladimir Mikhailov's body was discovered: his neck had been snapped whilst he slept. At the time and because of the incompetence of the prison staff, the two incidents were not thought to be linked. Mikhailov's clothes were not discovered missing until a week later, when investigators finally arrived from Moscow and searched his room, which had remained locked as a crime scene, but by then it was too late.

They knew that with over 200 miles of snowbound wasteland between Perm 35 and the nearest civilisation, Nickolin would either freeze to death in the sub-zero temperatures, or he would be killed by wild bears, or the packs of rabid wolves that terrorised the area. Only ten people had ever managed to escape from the camp in its fifty-year history and of those, no one had ever managed to get more than five miles. Wolves had eaten six, two had been mauled to death by bears and two had been found frozen solid, not more than three miles from the camp.

Nickolin, surviving in the layers of civilian clothes he had stolen from Mikhailov's room the night he had broken his neck, and with the food he had stored away over weeks, brought for him by the small quiet man, made it to the railway station. The locker contained new papers and a passport, a visa for the UK, an airline ticket and money, just like the Templar Sabath had instructed in his letter.

Nickolin had received Sabath's letter only one week ago, but it had already lain on Mikhailov's desk for nearly two. It was written in Hebrew and Mikhailov hadn't bothered to get it translated. His prisoner had received at least two letters every month in the last year. All the other letters had been translated and contained nothing, just some trifling news items from some Jewish aunt. His clerk, finding the letter on the floor one day, presumed that Mikhailov had already done with it and so passed it on to the prisoner.

Nickolin had had no hesitation when Sabath had written asking if he was now ready to fulfil his father's debt, but the trip over the frozen wasteland had nearly killed him.

It had taken him just over six days, walking at an average of thirty miles per day in sub-zero temperatures, laden with a heavy pack containing extra spare clothes and food. He had kept to the treeline most of the way and had only left its safe haven when there had been no alternative. Being caught out in open space would have given him nowhere to run.

The woodland was dense and dangerous. Bears and wolves roamed the timber wilderness unchecked. Starvation drove them and the Russian would have made a welcome meal where food was in such short supply. However, Nickolin was clever. Digging up pungent roots, he ground them down into a paste, then spread the paste onto branches he towed behind him on vine ropes, some three metres back. Whilst wolves tracked him and he could hear their nearby howls at night, the ground roots confused their finely tuned sense of smell. The branches dragged along in the snow also helped cover his tracks in case of human followers.

The cold hit him the hardest. The wind chill drove its icy spikes into his body and by the end of the first day his body temperature was in shock. Walking thirty miles a day meant his body would heat and sweat, but the icy wind blasted through his clothes and he would shiver endlessly. At night the temperature dropped even lower. He never rested at night, catching only two hours sleep a day, and always at noon, when the temperature rose slightly. He had made the mistake on the first night of resting after dark. A lone wolf, an old alpha male who had been evicted from the pack, had stayed steadfast on his trail. Wet, cold and shivering, Nickolin had lain dozing inside the hollow of a rotted tree trunk. The old dog's snarling had woken Nickolin seconds before the animal lunged at him. With no weapons, his instinct was to raise his left arm to protect his face and throat. Then he threw his mighty fist down onto the wolf's jaw in one simultaneous movement. A sharp crack echoed through the wood, the sound of breaking bone. It was followed by a high-pitched yelp. The wolf ran off into the blackness, its lower jaw hanging loosely. Nickolin packed quickly and moved on. Fifteen minutes later he heard the screams of the old dog. No longer able to defend itself, it was torn to pieces. A pack of wolves ate well that night. From then on he no longer rested after dark; he no longer walked without dragging branches smeared in pungent ground roots.

By the fourth day Nickolin was beginning to dehydrate and suffer from the first signs of hypothermia. It was only his resolve, his sheer willpower that got him over the icy wasteland. It would take his body a long time to recover from the gruelling hardship he had just endured, but he would have walked it again, ten times over, or died trying, to honour his father's debt.

$$* \quad * \quad *$$

Nickolin took the money and the papers that had been left for him, then walked into the crowded train station. There he bought a ticket. His train would leave within two hours, but it would travel in the opposite direction to the nearest airport. The plane ticket was an open ticket. He would book his flight soon, but first there was something he needed to do.

The train followed the Dnipro River through Smolensk, Mahilyow and Chernihiv. There were many stops. Faceless stations came and went, the hypnotic sound of the wheels on the iron track his only company. He spoke to no one and no one spoke to him. He was just another bedraggled-looking peasant bound for somewhere and no one cared. It was early morning when his train finally pulled into the 800-year-old city of Chernobyl, sixty-five miles northwest of Kiev, the Ukrainian capital.

Nickolin viewed, at a distance, the forty-mile-wide area circled off by a fence: this was ground zero. Once it had been home to 160,000 inhabitants; now it contained a monument to hell, the steel and concrete sarcophagus of Reactor No 4, 180 tons of uranium fuel and ten tons of radioactive dust trapped within. Nickolin had no way of knowing where his wife and children were buried. No one had ever told him. Perhaps in the city, nine miles away, but it didn't matter; their spirits were there. He no longer sought retribution for their deaths; besides, the operators and supervisors who were blamed had gone to jail. Five in all. The others were amongst the poor souls who died on that day, and of the rest, their painful suffering would be their penance.

His wife and his two children had lived with her parents in Opachychi, fifteen miles from ground zero. Their proximity to the disaster would have been enough to kill them anyway, but his wife had taken the children, along with her mother, father and two other sisters, to join the thousands of people recruited to clean up the area in the early days of the aftermath. No one knew any better and it was paid work. Some received radiation doses of more than 200 rem, enough to cause acute radiation sickness and a breakdown of the body's systems. Officials ordered the people monitoring the site not to report anything over 25 rem and so daily the check sheets were returned at recordings of 24.5 rem, the considered safe dosage. The clearance workers didn't stand a chance: their ignorance and a corrupt authority had signed their death warrants. Nickolin's family's death warrants.

At Eastertide, tradition says that Ukrainians should visit their deceased. Nickolin had missed many Eastertides. Now he had come to pay his respects, but he would not linger. He would carry the spirits of his family with him, wherever he went. They belonged to him, not to Chernobyl; he would keep them in his heart, safe.

The day after arriving in Chernobyl, he booked his flights from Kiev to Vienna, then from Vienna to London, with a connection to Edinburgh on a Euro hopper. He arrived at the castle just two days before the Indian, John Wolf. There he was briefed, his wounds were looked after and he was initiated into the secret world of the Knights Templar. Nickolin Klymachak had accepted the death sanction on Salah El-Din and, like the other Knights who had gathered, he trained and waited for the sixth member to arrive.

Chapter 9

Act of Remembrance

Date: 29th June 2008
Place: Scotland

Strange noises hurled themselves out of the public address system of the Arrivals lounge of Glasgow airport. Guttural words struggled with each other in the same sentences. Someone was making an announcement: Flight BA 762 from Luton had just landed. Jonathan Rose strained to listen. Occasionally he caught a word or two that he recognised as English, but as for the rest, to him they were just throat sounds in turmoil. He noticed it was catching. Other people around him were talking in the same strange language. It was, Jonathan mused, like jazz: a group of musicians on stage, seemingly each playing a different piece of music. The Scottish accent would take some getting used to, especially the ochs, ayes and noos. He left the Arrivals lounge sounds to their verbal combat and went to look for his rental car.

The small two-seater car presented him with his first challenge since arriving in Great Britain earlier that morning – driving on the wrong side of the road. He kept repeating to himself, 'passenger nearest the sidewalk', 'passenger nearest the sidewalk'. It was strange changing gear with the wrong hand. It was strange being in Scotland with its strange language.

Jonathan hadn't slept during the long haul flight from Washington to Heathrow and the four-hour wait for the connection to

Glasgow had merely added to his fatigue. His body clock was in disarray. His senses wanted to shut down and rest, but adrenaline and copious amounts of coffee were keeping him going.

It was a wet morning and a grim introduction to the land of the Celts and he hoped it would get better. The grey sky hung gloomily as he found his rental car and pulled out of Zone D of the airport car park and headed for the Civic building in the city: Births and Deaths Department.

Jonathan followed the map he had studied so meticulously during the never-ending flight to Great Britain. Precariously, he made his way onto the main road. It was still early and he was thankful the traffic was light. The engine of the small car groaned in protest, until his left foot found the clutch. He changed up into fourth. Tall stone office buildings sidled up to ominous-looking tenement blocks along his route and he was reminded, oddly, of the place where John Dukes lived. He wondered if this city had dangerous streets. Building shapes barely broke up the bland grey masonry and in the distance the city's profile blended into the grey sky.

Jonathan drove along the M8 motorway towards the city centre. He found navigating the roads surprisingly easy. He followed each direction he had written down on the map and, much to his astonishment, found that it took him to where he wanted to go. He had never been a great map-reader.

The traffic progressed in and out of the city with more élan than Washington traffic, although he knew both cities shared similar populations, around half a million. He discovered that Glasgow was laid out in a grid system, in much the same way as most major cities in America. By counting the squares, instead of blocks, he drove into and around the city with relative ease. Four blocks down, then left on Renfrew Street, two blocks and right into Killermont. It worked perfectly and he kept to his route without getting lost. At George Square, a central point of the city, he found parking and from there he had a short walk to the Civic building.

The strange throaty noises he had heard uttered at the airport had followed him into the city. The streets were now busy with people who all seemed to speak and understand the harsh brogue he struggled to comprehend.

However, Jonathan liked the sense of solitude he found in this sea of strangers: he knew no one and no one knew him. Here there were no reminders for him to stumble over, no places, songs or smells. Here he could think of his sister when he wanted and not when a fleeting association with a sound or a smell, place or song, triggered a memory in his subconscious. Here he could push the sadness away and focus on the reason he had come.

Once inside the Civic building he made his way to the second floor where Births and Deaths was situated. The woman behind the counter smiled politely at Jonathan and checked her computer screen. He had one lead and one lead only: it was a name Dukes had given him, the name on the tape, St Clair. Now all his hopes lay with the city's records.

Now he was beginning to get used to the accent that had perplexed him when he had first arrived. They spoke it in the Civic Building, but this woman, presumably accustomed to dealing with ancestor-seeking Americans he thought, was different: she spoke slowly and distinctly for him. He was in luck. There were five St Clairs listed in the births records and none of the people had been registered as deceased, yet. His luck held. She told him that all the people had been born and baptised in the same place, Grogan, a small village just south of Edinburgh. He knew that some families lived in the same village for generations; it was the same in some parts of Ireland and Wales and even in some parts of the Southern States in the USA. He hoped that the St Clair he wanted still lived there. The woman gave him a list of their full names: two men and three women. He looked down the list, hoping something would identify the person he was looking for, but of course it didn't. She told him that he should ring directory enquires because the operator would be able to tell him how many St Clairs were listed with current telephone numbers and even current addresses. Without her help, he would have been back on a plane to America, with no more leads, no avenues and no hope.

The drive to the Sternforth Hotel took just over twenty minutes. The hotel was more like a motel than a hotel, with all of the rooms detached from the main building and arranged like chalets.

Even though it was still early evening, he knew he would have no trouble sleeping. He calculated that he was at least two days late in going to bed, give or take a time zone or two. However, sleep was not the first thing on his mind. He made a tentative telephone call to directory enquiries. He explained that he was an American visiting Scotland to search for relatives who had emigrated many years ago. He gave the operator the five names in full. The girl at the other end of the phone was patient and helpful. This was not an unusual request, he was sure. She would have received calls from many Americans in search of lost relatives. He could live with his white lie.

The operator found three St Clairs listed out of the five and all with Grogan addresses. His luck, in part at least, was still holding. Jonathan pressed her for the other two names, but she could only find three. She told him that she had tried the Highlands, Lowlands, Borders and Islands. Jonathan thanked her and then hung up. He took the key and opened the minibar. There was an array of alcoholic miniatures on offer, but he thought of Dukes and took the Highland spring water. Jonathan thought about ringing the numbers the operator had given him, but he decided not to. He figured Courtney wouldn't have left anything to chance. His sister would have wanted to see their faces. He decided he would drive to Grogan the next day.

Settling down into his single bed, he surveyed the bland room with its typical hotel- style furniture and its unimaginative décor. It could have been anywhere. Only the tartan curtains and the array of tourist information pamphlets on his bedside table gave due notice that Scotland awaited him. On the other bedside table lay the ubiquitous Gideon's Bible; he left it undisturbed. God was not a friend of his. God had let his sister die.

The next morning he was up early. He showered and dressed in his normal attire: jeans and T-shirt. The breakfast room was full of tourists, mostly, it seemed, Americans. He sat at a table for one and ordered black coffee and a little toast. He recognised the tones of a group of loud ladies from Chicago. He didn't look; he didn't need to. He just knew how they would be dressed. A woman in her early thirties, pretty and petite, dressed in black, had been watching him over her newspaper. He caught her looking and she quickly looked away, sipped at her coffee and went back to her newspaper. There was something familiar about her. He tried to look without being too obvious. He thought he'd met her before, but he wasn't sure. Every now and again she rubbed her left shoulder; it was obviously bothering her. At that moment a young waiter dropped a heavily laden breakfast tray over an alarmed diner. When Jonathan looked back to where the woman had been sitting, she was gone. He ate his breakfast in silence and considered how this day would turn out for him.

Just after ten, Jonathan paid his bill, checked out and went to his car, remembering to open the right-side driver's door. Scotland covers an area of approximately 78,470 sq km and Jonathan still didn't know how much of it he would have to traverse. If the person he was searching for turned out not to be one of the three on the list, then he could be looking for weeks. He didn't relish the prospect.

Bracken, fern and heather lay either side of the road he was driving down, stretching out of sight like a rustic carpet. This was indeed a most beautiful country, he thought; the silence and solitude of the Highlands were the epitome of calm.

In the distance he could see the craggy ranges of the Moorfoot Hills and the Pentland Hills, which stood like bulbous mounds on the horizon. He turned off the main A701 and passed through Mount Lothian. There was nothing out there past his windscreen and yet there was everything. The land captured him and he revelled in its being. And then, in what seemed like no time at all, he was there.

He found Grogan village to be quaint. Small, it was mainly made up of stone-built houses. He estimated that it had fewer than forty dwellings in all and one antiquated post office, which nestled snugly in amongst a legion of rhododendron shrubs. All around herbs of basil, chive and mint grew in abundance. Their fragrance filled his lungs as he parked in the small car park at the side of the post office. The rich smells made him heady and he stood a while just breathing in their scent.

He liked the village, but by 2 p.m. all that had changed and he reached his lowest point since arriving in Scotland. He had found and spoken to the three St Clairs on his list. He had made the decision not to telephone them the previous evening, but now he wished he had and saved himself the trouble of the long journey. One of the people was accommodating, but clearly, at ninety-two, too old to be the person to have saved John Dukes. The second, he had concluded within the first two seconds of meeting him, was a halfwit who had left his senses in the bed he had slept in. The man, dressed in dirty underwear and a panama hat, was happy to talk. It was just unfortunate that his words, riding high on the worst case of halitosis Jonathan had ever experienced, revolved around the fact that the aliens were coming and encouraged Jonathan to wrap himself in silver foil and hide. The third person was downright rude. Annoyed at the intrusion, she had summoned her rather large dog and Jonathan left. He had come to the end of the road and had used up all of his enthusiasm; disappointment had sapped it away.

The polished brass bell above the post office door announced his entrance. A small wiry woman, probably in her early eighties, peered from behind an old-fashioned oak counter and smiled. He was thankful for a friendly face, after the last house he had visited.

"Och, now, you'll be an American gentleman."

Jonathan smiled. The old lady had probably served behind the counter nearly all of her life and with that came the uncanny ability to know a lot about a person, just at a glance.

"Good afternoon, ma'am. Grogan is a lovely village," he announced. He looked out of the window at the peaceful hamlet.

"Aye, so it is. Been in the village all me life. See noo reason tee move; wouldn't feel right in the city with all those cars and those gadgets. Noo, take noo mind of my manners. Yee didn'a come in here tee chat. What will I get yee?"

The last few letters of every word she spoke peeled off in an ascending tone, punctuated with ayes, ochs and noos. But her brogue was soft, like the Scottish mist, woven like the tweed she wore. It was more pleasing to the ear than the harsher Glaswegian accent, the strange Arrivals lounge language his ears had been subjected to when he had first arrived in Scotland. He felt obliged to buy something: he had a feeling that he wouldn't be allowed to leave until he had handed over some of his money. The old lady had that cunning look about her that all good traders have when they see a potential customer. He bought a newspaper, the *Scottish Dispatch*, and a packet of mints, which he placed on the oak counter.

"Och, yee'll be on holiday then, noo?"

"No, ma'am, I'm in Scotland looking for a relative," he replied. "Unfortunately, the three addresses that I had turned out to be the wrong people. So I guess my relative is one of the two St Clairs I have no address for."

He then told her the whole story of the five St Clairs, from the Births and Deaths Department at the Civic building. And the three addresses the operator at directory enquires had given him. He went through the three St Clairs he had seen that day. She smiled at the one who was helpful, but too old, shook her head with embarrassment at the fool in his underwear and panama hat and gave a tut at the one with the dog, who had been rude and curt.

"Och, you bear no mind of that last one. Miserable, that's what she is. Been like it since childhood. Morag St Clair has noo spoken tee me since, och let me see now, must be nearly twenty years. Came in here one day and all that I said was that I liked her shoes, practical-looking, not pretty mind, but the red dress she had on, I told her I would have walked right by that in the shop and paid it no mind. She didn'a seem tee like my comments and she has noo spoken tee me since. Och, noo then, what am I thinking? You need tee talk tee the gillie up at the croft. He'd have a view on the other two people on yee list. Knows everyone around these parts, does the gillie."

"Gillie?"

"Och aye, 'tis what we folk call him. 'Tis what he is. Looks after the deer out on the glens and the fine trout in the river. Gillie, that's his job. We're a National Park, yee noo." She said it with some pride.

"Gillie will know what is tee be done for yee. Noo, yee tell your story tee Gillie, he'll know. There's many an isolated farm round these parts. Your kin could be anywhere."

Jonathan couldn't hide his joy. Perhaps he was not at a dead end after all. A broad grin replaced his frown. She moved from behind the counter to show him the way. Her step was sprightly for her age, her face wrinkled and kind, and her silver hair was brought up in a tight bun on the back of her head.

"Noo, if yee go up that thistle-lined road a ways, yee'll come tee a stile. Take its path and yee will come tee the croft. Oh, and yee may want tee keep an eye open for Albert!"

Jonathan had gone from despair to upbeat in a matter of minutes. Now he was eager to move on and find the man at the croft.

"Ma'am, I can't thank you enough." Jonathan moved towards the door.

"Yee could start by paying for yee goods, young man!"

The path that led from the stile was a dirt track that twisted and turned. It rose slowly and led over brown-covered mounds. Here the bracken and fern stood more than four feet high, but the path was well worn. The frequently trod cow tracks made the ground underfoot undulating and Jonathan occasionally fought to keep his balance. He was not from the countryside and without sidewalks he struggled. He had a rough idea of what a croft was, a small Scottish dwelling, but had never seen one. However, he knew from the isolation that he would not find anything else along this path.

No sooner had he thought this than he had to adjust his ideas. The beast stood about the same height as Jonathan. Its long brown, shaggy hair, matted with weathering, gave it its bulk and its long horns gave it its menace. Jonathan stood motionless. He had not seen it until he had all but bumped into it; it was a stand-off and the Highland bull was not going to move. *Albert*, he thought. He hoped it knew the difference between a Sassenach and an American. But he couldn't be sure. Jonathan's spirits started to flounder and he was beginning to wish he'd stayed at the hotel an extra day or two, at least until Albert had roamed off somewhere else.

Jonathan tried to ease around Albert, but the bull turned in the same direction. Not good, he thought. This is not very good at all. Come on, Rose, you can do this. It's just a cow, after all. You've eaten enough of them. He looked around for an escape route. It was the dense fern and bracken or the path, and the bull stood on the path. Slowly, Jonathan made his way through the dense fern and bracken. The bull watched him until he was out of sight, and then went about its business of doing nothing, its matted, shaggy hide swaying as it plodded along in perfect ignorance of the world.

Jonathan's hands had become badly scratched and bloody. He had no idea that the vegetation could cut so much. He tried to keep his hands above the fern and bracken, but stumbled and they fell back to his side to steady himself. It was slow going and his legs ached. It had been a long time since he had physically exerted himself as much.

The croft was what he imagined, a bland stone building with a thatched roof, quaint enough, but not very inviting compared to a hotel room with a hot bath. He rapped on the wooden ledge and brace door and waited. Nothing. No answer and no sign of any presence; he tried again with the same empty result. Around him an army of bees plagued him. He swatted but missed and they buzzed on.

The sun was starting to sink below the horizon. Jonathan had no intention of walking back in the dark, not with Albert skulking about. He found paper in his pocket and wrote a brief note for the gillie, advising him that he was looking for a person called St Clair and that he would be back the next day and would welcome the chance to talk to him. He stuck the note under the horseshoe that was nailed to the ledge and brace door for good luck.

The village shop was still open. Through the window Jonathan saw the little old lady busying herself behind the counter. Once he had cleaned up his bloodied hands he would ask her for directions to the nearest hotel. With luck he would not have to travel too far. The car had a first aid kit in the trunk, but he didn't get to it. A note on the windscreen made him halt. He looked around and saw no one. The village was empty of people. The note, neatly written, had been folded and placed under his windscreen wiper.

'To find the man you're looking for, follow the map.'

Below the words, the anonymous author had drawn a small map.

The unease around him began to suffocate him. He remembered the words John Dukes had used to describe Salah El-Din. Jonathan shivered. He needed to get out of there. He fumbled getting the keys into the ignition, but finally he pulled out of the car park and, following the map's directions, headed north.

Dominique picked up the Russian as he emerged from behind the post office, still pulling pieces of dead bracken out of his clothes. They followed Jonathan at a distance.

The journey took Jonathan just under two hours; he had stopped only once, for petrol. For the last twenty minutes of his journey the roads had been deserted. The castle's shape loomed in the dusk. With each new twist and turn in the road, its imposing bulk filled more of the skyline. Even in the fading light, the structure, with its two-metre thick walls and large keystones, looked solid and safe.

And then, finally, he was there.

Stationary, the engine of his car turned over at an idle rate. He peered through the windscreen and into the castle's courtyard. It was empty. A mixture of curiosity and anticipation moved his foot onto the accelerator and the car crawled forward. In the courtyard he turned the car around one hundred and eighty degrees, facing the way out: the thought of having to make a quick exit crossed his mind. He switched off the engine and the silence unsettled him. There was no one around. Dim lights seeped out of the castle's lattice windows, but there was no sign of life within.

He stood in front of the large arched, double oak door. studying the bell. He hesitated, running through his options: he could find an open window, if there was one, and sneak inside, but he wasn't good at sneaking. He could call 911, but figured Washington's finest would take a while to get there. If he knew the number he could also call the local fire brigade and tell them that there was a fire at the castle, so that when they evacuated the castle he would be waiting to see who came outside. He liked this scenario, until he remembered he would need a telephone to execute his plan. Each new scenario he came up with was more convoluted than the last. Almost involuntarily, his hand moved towards the bell. Then, all of a sudden, a hand grabbed his shoulder. His whole body dismantled and reassembled itself in the space of a millisecond. His heart nearly burst out of his ribcage and the shock sent him six centimetres off the ground.

"Holy shit!"

The man behind him was tall, about six feet or more. He wore an Australian herder's trench coat which smelt of wax. His arms folded in front of him, his top half bent slightly forward towards Jonathan.

"No, not holy shit. St Clair, Payne St Clair and you are on my doorstep, friend."

Jonathan had to look twice at the man in front of him. "You ... you just look like ..." He was stopped in mid-sentence.

"I swear," St Clair started with clenched teeth, "I will do harm to the next person who tells me I look like him."

"But you do," protested Jonathan. The resemblance was uncanny. St Clair was the double of the actor Sean Connery, sporting a well-trimmed white beard and moustache.

"Enough of this rubbish. I've no time to bandy words with you. Tell me your business and get to the point. I know how you Americans like the sound of your own voices and have a habit of parading your accomplishments with embellished results. I met an American from Texas on a flight once who spent the entire flight from the UK to the States telling me about how Donald Duck paraded around wearing a towel at bath time to hide his duck bits, only to dry off, don his clothes, a hat and a waistcoat – no trousers!"

St Clair opened the right side of the large oak double-door, which had been unlocked all the time. The sun had now completely disappeared.

"Well?" exclaimed St Claire, pausing inside the doorway. "Do you want to come in or are you going to stand out there all night with your mouth open?"

Inside, the castle was spacious but sparsely furnished. Jonathan followed St Clair into a reception room that had a welcoming log fire burning in a stone hearth. Two armchairs were placed in front of the fire. They looked inviting and Jonathan rubbed his aching legs. The walk to the gillie's croft and the last two-hour drive were beginning to take their toll on his unfit body. Off to one side of the room, on a large wooden table, stood an assortment of honey pots brimming with golden honey. The walls of the room were almost bare, but for a few old pictures, which were too small to make out. The wattle and daub ceiling, perhaps a later addition to the room in an attempt to retain the heat, was yellow in patches from the smoke of countless log fires. The floor was made of light-coloured flagstones, about four inches thick and partly covered by a large blue ornate rug that took away the coldness of the stones. Three doors leading off to other parts of the castle remained shut. The whole place was neat, perhaps too neat and orderly, Jonathan thought.

The fire hissed as the flames licked the fresh wood, evidence that it had been lit recently. Clearly St Clair had been expecting a visitor.

After removing his wax-smelling coat, St Clair sat in one of the chairs in front of the fire, "Sit down, man. I won't bite. Sit down and we'll have leisure to talk."

Jonathan eased himself into the soft furnished green chair. It felt good. St Clair's Scottish accent had a rich vein of mellowness to it that made it soft and palatable, unlike the receptionist at his hotel. She had made no effort to make herself understood: she practically chewed her words on their way out of her mouth. No sooner had St Clair sat down, he was up again. From the table with the honey pots, he produced a small brown jar of ointment. There was no label on it and no lid.

"Here, rub this into your hands. It will heal them. Looks like you've been walking through the rough bracken, friend."

He gave the jar to Jonathan. Instantly, smearing the salve into his hands, the sharp stinging went away.

"This is good cream. What is it?" he asked.

"Well," St Clair began, like a chef reciting a cordon bleu recipe from memory and with pride. "Let me see: of course, there's zinc, ground peat moss, fresh honey, a blend of *ocimum basilicum* – basil, *aconitum napellus* – monk's hood and wolfsbane, *glechoma hederacea* – ivy, *hypericum perforatum* – St John's wort, three rooks' eyes, ground of course, and a helping of bull sperm." And then, almost as an afterthought, he added, "There's a donor south of here, great beast of a bull locals call Albert. Mind you, I don't do the collecting myself." St Claire laughed.

Jonathan looked at his hands and couldn't decide if he was happier when they were untreated and stinging, or now that they pained him no more. He made a mental note to scrub his hands the moment he got the chance, and then every day for a month after that, maybe even every day for two months after that.

"So," St Claire enquired, "tell me why you are here? No one comes this way unless they're lost or … no, you couldn't be, could you? Tell me you're not one of those artists looking for inspiration. Last fellow spent three days camped in one of the lower fields. His paintings were useless. Can't stand artists and writers, self-indulgent fools."

Jonathan smiled. "No, Mr St Clair. If you had ever seen any of my attempts at essay writing and art, you would know that I'm not one of those. I'm a schoolteacher from Washington DC, my name is Jonathan Rose and I am very pleased to meet you. I have come a long way to be here."

"A schoolteacher," St Clair said. "Well, that's a new one for these parts. What's an American schoolteacher doing way up here in the Highlands?" His question was direct and therefore warranted a direct answer.

"Looking for you, I think," Jonathan said.

St Claire's expression didn't change; he showed no sign of surprise, nothing. Jonathan was disappointed; he'd been expecting to see something that would confirm that he had the right man.

"And what business would you have with me, friend?"

The fire spat and the flames danced their merry dance around the logs. Jonathan moved forward on his seat. Physically, he already felt much better. The ache in his legs had gone and his hands troubled him no more. Mentally, he felt safe, strangely comfortable in the calm presence of the Bond lookalike and his new surroundings. For his part, St Clair sat motionless, giving nothing away.

It took Jonathan almost an hour to tell his story to St Clair, although he had no sense of time. It just all came tumbling out. He started with the Christmas Eve party at Senator McGregor's mansion in the Vale. He recounted Courtney's murder with great difficulty, but he got through it without embarrassing himself. He told St Clair about Meeks, then about the contents of the tape recording, the erased files and the corresponding names. He told him about the fact that he hadn't given the tape to Meeks, as Courtney had wanted, and he felt bad about that. He went through his conversation with Detective Walker and how it was Walker who had helped him by giving him Dukes's address. He related his meeting with Dukes and the obvious similarities with the death of his sister and Dukes's wife. He told St Clair everything that Dukes had told him about the man Salah El-Din. He left no detail out; he told it all exactly as it had happened. When he had finished, he sighed, relieved. It was the first time he had talked about these events with anyone. His thoughts and his emotions had been locked away inside his head since that Christmas Eve, and now they were shared.

St Clair eased himself out of his chair. Jonathan couldn't detect his mood; he had said nothing and done nothing throughout. But Jonathan now knew that he was talking to the right St Clair. There was no doubt in his mind that this was the man who could help him. This must be the man who had arranged for the map to be placed under his windscreen wiper so that he could find him. Jonathan felt great relief, but even more than that, he no longer felt utterly alone.

Now he had finished speaking, the stillness and isolation of the night penetrated the castle. Silence was sometimes the loudest noise and for Jonathan it could be deafening. He had travelled a long way; he had followed one lead, the only one he'd had. That one lead had kept him going; made him travel halfway around the world. Without St Clair he would have nothing. Without him being the right St Clair, he would be back searching for the last name on the list, and he didn't relish the thought of starting all over again, but he would have done so if he had to.

St Clair made his way to a small maple drinks cabinet that stood against the wall. "Presuming I have something to give and, am willing to give it, tell me why you're on this journey, this quest of yours?

Why you are doing this? You don't strike me as a rash man, big heart maybe, but to get involved, put yourself in harm's way, that's another matter. There are massive risks and you will not be able to detach yourself from the responsibilities you will have to others. Your life might well have been torn asunder by tragedy, but grief and anger will not support the resolve and courage you will need when things get bad: and things will get bad! Any help I might be willing to give is conditional and that condition is, I need to know why you are doing this."

Jonathan hadn't thought why; there hadn't been time. Options ran through his mind. He had been totally caught up in finding St Clair, the man whose name his sister had spoken on the tape recording, the man Dukes had been told about by Meeks. Why was he doing it? Was it hate, revenge, justice … what? He remembered telling Walker he wanted justice. Maybe it was as simple and selfish as peace of mind, but right there, right then, in the presence of St Clair, those reasons seemed meaningless, trite and shallow. He struggled to tell St Clair why he was doing it. He struggled to know why himself.

"Seems to me you have got yourself into something that most people would want to stay away from," St Clair said after a while. "So you need to ask yourself, are you really sure this is what you want? You can walk away and in time, although it may not seem like it now, you can get your life back again. It will not be as it was, but you're not the only person to have lost someone close. Many others have and they have gone on to rebuild their lives. For me to even consider helping you, you need to know why you are doing this, because it needs to be worth it to you. It needs to be worth the price you and others may have to pay."

It was as if St Clair's words dug deep into Jonathan's emotions, the same emotions he had locked away for so long. The emotions he had not even dared to dwell on surrounding his sister. All of a sudden it became clear and he finally understood why he was doing it. In that split second it all made sense.

He turned to St Clair. "You ask me why I am doing this." He paused; the sense of it put everything into perspective. "I'm doing it because this is my act of remembrance."

St Clair smiled. "You're an honest man, Jonathan Rose. An act of remembrance: well, that's a good and righteous answer. So, I will tell you. I am the St Clair that you have been seeking and, yes, I will help you find your sister's killer and together we will end his tyranny and the terror and death that he fuels."

The frustration and exasperation left Jonathan's body with such an overwhelming sense of relief it almost exploded from him.

"However," St Clair cautioned, "from this point on, there will be no going back. And from this point on you must not contact anyone in this regard, tell or speak about it. Can I assume that no one knows you're here, in Scotland?"

Jonathan nodded in confirmation.

"And no one is expecting you?"

Again Jonathan nodded, but then he remembered the note he had left pinned to the gillie's croft door. He didn't know if it was important and was just about to say something when St Clair started to speak again and the matter of the note went straight out of his head.

"You must realise," St Clair began, "if you tell anyone about what I am going to tell you, then they become your liability; a liability you will have to carry for the rest of your life. Don't expose them. They will be used to get to you. They will get hurt. Don't let that happen; don't involve them."

The night closed in.

Chapter 10

Revelation

'I saw heaven open and there was a white horse. Its rider is called faithful and true; it is with justice that he judges and fights his battles.'

(Revelations 19:11)

Date: 29th June 2008
Place: Glennfinch Castle

They had been talking for a long while. The evening had worn on and, despite the lateness of it, Jonathan felt rested. His hands no longer hurt and the dull ache in his legs from walking to the gillie's had subsided. Even though St Clair was a stranger to him, he felt strangely relaxed in his company. He had no idea why; he just felt safe.

Jonathan's five foot ten frame snuggled neatly into the high back chair. All thought of his teaching life and the priesthood had, for the moment at least, left him and the intoxicating company of St Clair wrapped his emotions up in a safe blanket.

The small maple drinks cabinet held over thirty assorted whisky bottles, each one a different blend. St Clair hovered over them in thought, and then he took one of the bottles and poured two drinks into cut-glass tumblers, before adding a little water from a pitcher. Jonathan sipped at the drink he had been given. The light brown blended liquid felt warm as it entered his body.

St Clair made himself comfortable again in front of the fire, his gaze focusing thoughtfully on the flames. He needed to tell the former priest everything: but *everything* was an awful lot to tell. There was much at stake: their Charge, the lives of Knights and, he feared, the lives of others. Jonathan was the key to his plan, though. He always had been, ever since January. It was a risk, a big risk because it would mean they would have to come face-to-face with the criminal they would now hunt down. To be precise, Jonathan would have to come face-to-face with him. St Clair thought through a myriad of permutations: the multiple preparations, roles, timelines, planning, equipment, data and intelligence they would need for them to have any chance of success. His strategies would mean the difference between success and failure. He cleared the thoughts from his mind and focused back on the teacher-priest. The American looked content. St Clair liked him – he had suspected he would.

"You were a religious man, Jonathan, a pious man and of the cloth, I'm told."

This was the first time St Clair revealed that he knew who Jonathan was. It didn't surprise Jonathan at all; he had a feeling that the past events were intrinsically woven around St Clair.

"I was." He accentuated the past tense with purpose, more as reconfirmation to himself than St Claire. "I took my holy orders so that I could serve God. I did His bidding, preached the gospels and the love of Christ. I gave thanks to the Holy Trinity, gave the sacrament in His name. He was my God and His work was my life. Serving God was the only thing I had ever wanted to do. From as early as I can remember I had wanted to be a priest. But *my* God stood by whilst my sister's throat was cut and her body burnt. He wasn't there when my sister needed Him most and for that I cannot forgive Him. I left the priesthood because of that and because He has failed to answer the only question I need an answer to, why her?"

"And do you miss your God, Jonathan?"

"No." Jonathan fidgeted uncomfortably on his seat. He missed his faith; it had been his calling, his vocation. His life. Having to talk about it now was uncomfortable for him because his anger needed a culprit and, because of his unanswered questions about inaccuracies in the bible, God fitted the vacancy.

St Clair could see that he had much work to do to help Jonathan find his faith again. Inwardly he smiled. He knew that if Jonathan knew what he would soon learn, then there would be no doubt in the priest's mind. One day soon the priest would have that unequivocal proof he needed, but not yet, thought St Clair, not just yet. When he's ready.

"Dukes is dead." St Clair announced.

"Dead?" Johnathan broke in. "How … why? I'm sorry … I didn't know." It was another death. Another reminder of the dangerous game he had allowed himself to join. Poor man, he thought, that poor man. Jonathan knew that for Dukes, like Hamlet, there was to be no volte-face. He was tormented and his 'antic disposition' drew too much attention to him. He knew, deep down, that Dukes's life was always going to end tragically, and now it had.

"If you're going to interrupt me every time I start a sentence, then we will never get done. I thought priests were good listeners. Now, sip your whisky and listen." St Clair filled in the rest of the details. "Dukes was murdered just after you left Washington, God rest his soul." St Clair cupped his hands and moved his gaze skywards in gesture. Jonathan, without thinking, made the sign of the cross over his chest.

"We had warned him about the danger he was in, so he had been given my name and told to come here, to Scotland, where we could protect him. However, he ignored our warning and in the end there was nothing we could do to help him. His death was, I'm afraid to say, just a matter of time. We all knew it, and I think even he knew it." St Clair sipped his drink again and Jonathan seized the chance to find out something that had been troubling him ever since his meeting with Dukes.

"Dukes was given your name by Bill Meeks, yes or no?"

"Yes, of course. How else would Dukes have got my name? Bill Meeks is one of us."

Jonathan had only just made the connection between Meeks and St Clair. He was pleased he didn't have to dislike Meeks any more. He was pleased he could like the man his sister liked so much. But he needed to understand the *us* a bit more.

"One of *us*?" he asked. The question was plain enough, but St Clair ignored it.

"Meeks had been keeping watch on Dukes as we were all concerned for his life. It was Meeks who met with Dukes and gave him my contact details. It was Meeks who informed us in the first week in January about your sister's death. It was Meeks who found your sister's diary and then informed us that our scrolls, which have been missing for twelve years, were now in Saladin's hands."

Jonathan noticed that St Clair had changed the Arab's name from Salah El-Din to Saladin; he stored the question for when St Clair had finished about Dukes and Meeks.

"It was Meeks who told us a few weeks ago that the rumours about Unity were true. Your sister read about it back in December, when she stumbled on the filed reports from agents in Algiers and the Swiss Alps, just before they disappeared from the FBI's mainframe computer. And I'm afraid it was Meeks who broke into your house and found Courtney's tape and made a copy of it for us."

Jonathan was amazed. So all of this had been going on right under his nose. He'd had no idea, no clue. He felt no anger about Meeks breaking into his house. After all, the tape was meant for Meeks and now he knew it was in good hands.

"We know that, for years, McGregor had been approaching people in positions of power. It was a simple plan: the senator would identify venal candidates, those who it was rumoured had a weakness for money, drugs, women, men, children, gambling; those that had heavy debts or out-of-town mistresses. Saladin would apply Unity's considerable manpower and dig out their dirt. The senator would then make the introductions to his paymaster. Over time, when Saladin had their trust, he would help them with their desires, wants, troubles, problems and needs, no matter what it was. Then he would have them. There was no shortage of candidates. It seems that a lot of people in power have a dirty little secret or two they want to hide, or in Saladin's case, dirty big secrets. All the senator and Saladin had to do was find what that secret was, then exploit it with blackmail and extortion.

"At first these people would be asked for small favours, in return for feeding their desires or helping their 'little problems' to go away. However, it wouldn't be too long before those favours grew, then, before they knew it, they would be so far in they couldn't get out. Without McGregor, Saladin would never have been able to get in so deep and so quickly into those players. It was a masterstroke on his part to use McGregor. In fact, our friend, the senator, played another major role for Saladin.

"McGregor was due to fly out to Colombia at the beginning of June. As far as we know, it would have been his fourth trip in the last twelve months. He was heading up an American funding initiative called 'America Aid Against Drugs' – AAAD. Under the official guise of the State Department, he could effectively go anywhere in the country without raising too much suspicion. We now know that over the years he had held covert meetings with several of the most powerful drug lords and had negotiated deals for Saladin, his boss. McGregor was used because Saladin would not risk going back to Columbia. His drug-growing operation was closed down some years ago by the Drug Enforcement Administration, who were acting as advisers to the Colombian Government. Their lucky break came from eight members of the International Congress of Churches, who were in Columbia setting up projects to help local people break free of the drug industry. The group from the ICC were passed information about a coca plantation, which was using kidnapped children off the streets to grow and produce the cocaine. As it turned out, this plantation was Saladin's and supplied his illicit drug cartel in the west.

"The money behind Saladin's ever-growing criminal empire,

Unity, is made through suffering on many levels, but addiction seems the most lucrative for him. It has taken him years to build up his distribution networks that deliver his drugs. It seems that he has concentrated his drugs a lot in the UK and on run-down, deprived council estates there.

"From listening to your sister's tape, we can presume that she must have eventually worked most of this out. If she hadn't seen those files go missing, then maybe she would never have become suspicious and she may still be alive today. We don't know why she risked her own life; she wasn't a field operative. Meeks found your sister's diary and she talked about the lies, deceit and bribes being rife in the FBI and she talked about wanting to clean house. Maybe that was it? I guess we'll never know.

"Then the two of you went to the senator's party. We can only assume that she must have got too close to them that night. Probably asked too many awkward questions because when a victim has their eyelids cut off, it means they have been looking where they shouldn't be looking. Bill Meeks couldn't be sure that your sister actually knew anything before the party. We were in a dilemma and only had guesswork to go on. We didn't know if we should let Meeks tell her what was going on as we were afraid of dragging her in. He advised her not to go, once he had become suspicious about her motives, but she didn't listen. She was a brave lady, but she would have been no match for Saladin. He would have seen right through her that night. He would have known she had been trying to track the people involved in the scrolls. He would have known she pulled the file on McGregor. As far as we can make out, McGregor didn't want her murdered and an argument broke out between him and Saladin. We were finally able to track down a witness who remembers the men arguing. He hadn't given this information to the police at the time because he didn't want to get involved.

"So it seems that the senator had made only one mistake since becoming involved with Saladin, but that was to cost him his life. He questioned Saladin's decision to murder a young female FBI agent called Courtney Rose, on Christmas Eve.

"The shot to the senator's head, in Salt Lake City last Christmas Day, would not have given him time to know what was happening. An assassin, originally from the East End of London called Harvey Walters, known as Grimbone Walters, carried out the hit on McGregor. Walters's trademark is close-quarter hits, in public places. The kind of killing only a handful of hit men undertake. The shot, from a difficult angle, found its mark. One minute the senator was exercising his politician's public grin to a group of young Republicans, the next minute he wasn't."

It was all beginning to fit into place now. The party, the tape and Meeks: it was like a jigsaw slotting together and constructing before Jonathan's eyes.

"The man who killed your sister was Salah El-Din, or, to give him his full name, Al-Malik al-Nasir al-Sultan Salah El-Din. However, he likes the shorter version, Saladin."

Jonathan thought it was now time to ask.

"You mean like the Saladin of the Crusades?"

St Clair sipped at his whisky again before answering. "Precisely. The great Muslim warrior who ruled in the northern Middle East region at around 1191 AD, during the third crusade, the crusade of Richard Coeur de Lion, Richard the Lion Heart."

Jonathan knew a little of the history of the crusades from his training at seminary for the priesthood, but what he really wanted was present day facts. St Clair didn't disappoint him.

"The man who killed your sister was born in Har Megiddo, Israel."

Instantly Jonathan knew the name. To a layperson it might be meaningless, as most would only recognise it by its other name, Armageddon. Apt, Jonathan thought.

"About the time we think he was born, around 1948, like thousands of others in the region at that time, he would probably have been evicted during the resettlement of the Jews and the establishment of their state. The rare snippets of information we have gleaned tell of a tough upbringing. They were a poor family and it seems he was always in trouble with the elders and the authorities. The family moved from area to area as his father tried to find work as a herder. His mother died when he was young, and his father, a religious zealot, was apparently known to beat his six offspring extremely harshly and regularly.

"It seems that Saladin was a violent and troubled child. There is some evidence to suggest that he was involved in the death of a young Christian Arab. Beaten and stabbed repeatedly, the boy's body was found at the bottom of a well in the local village. Because of this and his worsening behaviour, he was made to pray alone every day and was not allowed out of the house. He was whipped every day and given only rice and water as penance for the shame he had brought on the family name. But villagers recall that the boy grew worse. Many, in recalling him, said, 'He was possessed with a wicked Jinn', a demon, and a number said they had been scared of him.

"His family finally ended up in Salalah, in the Sultanate of Oman. There he quickly made his way into mainstream crime. Petty theft at first, then more serious crimes escalating to murder, the skin trade, trafficking arms just across the border into the Yemen and importing cheap slave labour from the nearby continent of India. With a number of less than scrupulous sheikhs on his side, his empire soon grew into the neighbouring and richer states of the United Arab Emirates and into the Near East. He made a reputation for himself because he liked inflicting pain, especially on those who attempted to double-cross him, stand in his way or try to muscle into his territory. Eventually his operations penetrated the affluent and rich pickings of the West. By then he had become sadistic, brutal and ruthless. But, don't be mistaken, our friend is no ordinary criminal. You see, he believes he really is related to Saladin or even is him reincarnate. This makes him a very dangerous adversary, but it could also work to our advantage."

Jonathan was about to say something about the 'our',' we' and 'us', St Clair kept referring to, but St Clair put his finger to his lips.

"Shhh, don't interrupt. All in good time." Suitably chastised, Jonathan shushed and St Clair continued.

"As well as many money-making criminal activities, Saladin has also spent a lot of time and effort stealing certain things, not for money, but for his own collection. His particular penchant is for religious relics and artefacts, mainly Christian, Muslim and Jewish. He has the money; he has the contacts and he is a criminal without conscience, willing to do anything to get what he wants. However, for a number of years now we have become aware that he has become obsessed with trying to get a very specific religious relic. It is the very thing he can never have. Must never have. His relentless, savage pursuit of it gives us a compendious route map to his behaviour; a psychological canvas against which his life is fashioned, and in this there just might be a way for us to get to him."

St Clair sipped at his whisky again. The pause was deliberate. He wanted Jonathan's full attention, but he needn't have worried; Jonathan was fully attentive.

"You see, our friend covets that most holy relic, the Ark of the Covenant. And he believes we have it."

St Clair went silent. Jonathan looked at him expectantly. St Clair had spoken the words 'Ark of the Covenant' in an almost perfunctory manner. They had rolled off his tongue like the word hamburger or shoelace, or any other everyday word. In fact, they had rolled off his tongue a little too easily. Jonathan decided he had now shushed long enough

"Ark? As in the bible's Ark? Spewing fire and light, causing cancerous tumours, severe burns, levelling mountains and halting rivers Ark, that Ark?"

The bible had almost two hundred references to the Ark. Jonathan thought he knew most of them, but he didn't know the story as well as he thought, not the full story.

"Indeed," St Clair replied. "The Ark that rested in the Holy of Holies, Jonathan, or as known in Masonic terms, Sanctum Sanctorum. Hovering above the floor in suspended animation and in total darkness, except for one day of the year, the Day of Atonement. A box made of shittim wood, four feet long, by two feet wide, by two feet high, covered in a thick gold sheet with two cherubs, each with stretched-out wings guarding its contents."

St Clair had a grin of self-congratulation on his face. He considered he had eased Jonathan into the subject of the Ark and Saladin without too much alarm!

There was no doubt in Jonathan's mind that the Sean Connery lookalike was deadly serious, but he couldn't figure out if he was completely mad!

"OK, let me get this right." Jonathan started. "I know this. I know that mention of the Ark had disappeared almost entirely after the death of Solomon and all the evidence I have seen has always suggested that the Ark had gone by the time King Nebuchadnezzar burned Jerusalem and ransacked the Temple of Solomon in 587 BC. I have always thought that it was reasonable to assume that the priests of the day would have hidden the Ark. Indeed, under the 'Assumption of Moses' this is precisely what all priests were instructed to do, to hide their most sacred secrets and their Community Rule documents. The priests of the day would certainly have seen the approaching invaders and acted.

"I know that there are some historians who believe that the Ark was taken out of the Promised Land and into Ethiopia. They say that the Queen of Sheba, whom the Ethiopians say was their monarch, had visited King Solomon in his stronghold of Jerusalem. When she returned to her own land she found out that she was bearing his child. The child was named Menelik, Ebna la-Hakim in Arabic, and when the child reached the age of twenty, he, too, journeyed to the land of King Solomon to meet his father. Sometime later, he and his priests stole the Ark from Solomon and carried it out of the Promised Land into Ethiopia. The Ethiopians say that the Ark remains hidden to this day in a city called Axum. Many people have journeyed to Axum to see the Ark. However, a chosen priest guards it and no other is allowed to see it. He is the only one who is permitted to enter the resting place of the Ark. Annually, the Ark is brought out of its resting place during the ceremony of Timkat, Holy Epiphany, but it is always covered for fear of the untold damage it might cause."

The Ark was just one of the things that Jonathan had been in serious doubt about before meeting St Clair, because of the fragmented facts, hearsay and worldwide speculation. St Clair's revelations merely added to his problem.

"So that's what I know. Not much, but, like most things in my past calling, nothing is concrete but contradiction."

"Tell me, Jonathan, do you doubt the Ark and your religion?"

Jonathan could have spent days explaining to St Clair. He had issues inside his head that plagued him. However, he always seemed to arrive back from where he started. If knowing something means you had to have knowledge and proof of it, then Christianity, which is based on faith, means you know nothing. He decided to try to explain his feelings to St Clair.

"Forget all the big stuff in Christianity like God, the virgin birth, the resurrection, the miracles. There are enough issues in there alone, but even the smaller stuff is so full of contradiction. The Torah, for example, the book of Jewish law, forbids the kindling of fires on the Sabbath, but Jews, even the most pious, ignite their electrical fires on the Sabbath and, the Sabbath was on a Saturday, not Sunday! And, as for the Ark and the merciful God, God promised His chosen people the land of milk and honey. But what of the people who were already living in the land of milk and honey? We now know that they were not a barbaric people. They had roads and social systems, and they traded and grew crops. And, what did God do? He sanctioned their destruction, every man, woman and child. Today such genocide would receive repulsion from the world. The book of Deuteronomy,

Douai version, *And Sehon came out to meet us with all his people to fight at Jasa. And the Lord our God delivered him to us: and we slew him with his sons and all his people. And we took all his cities at that time, killing the inhabitants of them, men and women and children. We left nothing of them:* God was even known to have taken a dislike to some of those who followed him. Exodus 4:24-5: even Moses was on His hit list and if it hadn't been for a flint knife and the intervention of his bride, who begged for his life, he would have been killed. Meddling clerics in later rewritten works changed the story to read that indeed it was not God at all, it was a spirit called Mastema that wanted Moses killed, but what they forgot was that the word 'Mastema', in a number of translations, purely means the hostile side of Yahweh, and Yahweh is God: perhaps a rushed job!

"Apparently, the evil Egyptians used Hebrew slaves to build their early pyramids; someone forgot that there were no Hebrews at that time. Much later, the scattered Semitic nomads were called Habriu – Hebrew. Jesus's first miracle was to turn water into wine at the wedding of Cana, but historians now know that 'turn water into wine' was, at the time, a well-known phrase used to describe something completely different.

"The Roman Catholic Douai bible says that Moses means 'saved of water'. It doesn't. It means born of, like John Moses Smith, John born of Smith. In other parts of the Middle East they use bin, ben ibn, or abu.

"You ask me if I doubt the Ark and my religion. These days I have little faith in anything, and have doubt in much and, for me, the contradictions prevail."

"Then we will have to see what can be done about your faith, Jona ...," St Clair started.

"See," Jonathan interrupted, "now there's that *we* again. Don't you think its time to tell me who the *we* and the *us* are that you keep referring to? I know you can't live in this rambling old castle all on your own and I know the *we* and *us* can't be just you and Meeks. Just who are you, Mr St Clair?"

And so we have arrived, St Clair thought. He smiled.

Payne St Clair knew the question would be asked. For weeks he had thought about how he would answer it. At the meeting with The Nine Worthies he had been given approval to recruit the sixth member of the sanction team. Now that sixth member sat in front of him – although Jonathan didn't know it yet. St Clair looked closely at the teacher-priest, trying to see something that would convince him that he was about to do the right thing. It wasn't every day that a new Templar was recruited, especially one who would be asked to join a sanction team. The American was young and inexperienced. He had no concept of what he would be letting himself in for, but St Clair saw what Meeks saw, integrity and honesty, two of the Templar doctrines – the two St Clair admired the most. He finished his whisky, wiped his white beard and then, began.

"Jonathan," he said, "I, too, am a man of God. This place," he looked around the room, "this castle, I and the people connected with it, are all monks. We belong to an ancient brotherhood, a brotherhood that has survived the eyes of the world for centuries. Our purpose is simple: to protect that which is in our charge. I am the Grand Master of our Order and, along with eight other righteous men, we are the Higher Council of the Order. We are The Nine Worthies."

Here we go again, thought Jonathan. This is like some horrific nightmare. No straight answers. Nothing is simple with this man.

"Our Order began in 1118 AD, when a group of nine knights were given holy vows in the presence of Warmund of Picquigny. These original nine Templars, later called The Nine Worthies, swore a secret oath to find and then to protect the Ark of the Covenant. It was rumoured to lie buried in secret chambers, deep within the Temple Mount, in Jerusalem. Because of where The Nine made their base, on the ruined Temple Mount, they became known as the Pauperes Commilitones Christi Templique Salomonici or, as it was later shortened, the Knights Templar.

"After many years of searching, The Nine finally found the Ark.

For years they kept their secret safe in the Holy Land. But then on the 4th July 1187 AD, 400 Knights Templar lay trapped and surrounded, our Charge hidden within their ranks. At a place called the Horns of Hattin, the Templars stood without food and water and exposed to the oppressive desert sun. Gerard de Ridefort, the Grand Master at the time, ordered a charge at the circling army of over four thousand Muslims. The Knights were outnumbered by ten to one. By midday, hundreds of Templars lay dead and dying upon the arid scorched earth. Most of the Knights who survived were beheaded, but a few escaped with our Charge."

St Clair's pride resonated in his words. Jonathan was just about to ask a question but held his tongue.

"Templars live by a strict code. They are not allowed to seek mercy, unless they are outnumbered by more than three to one. Templars fought many battles in the Holy Land, warrior monks with our *beausant* at their head. The *beausant*, the Templar battle flag, has two vertical blocks, one black and one white, depicting the transformation from darkness to light.

"Because of the Horns of Hattin, the Order of the Knights Templar went back to France and took our Charge into safe hiding. But in 1307 AD, the monarchy, along with the Church, fearful of the standing and power of the Order, arranged to have them tried and convicted. After the death of thousands of Templars and our Grand Master, Jacques de Moly, some of the few remaining Templars fled to Scotland. There they stayed and one of the Grand Masters, Hugh de Payens, married Kathrin St Claire, the daughter of a wealthy landowner. Their names were given to me as my birth names. They are my ancestors.

"And so *we* have remained hidden ever since, silent, secret and vigilant, but unfortunately all that is about to end. Two really important documents were stolen from us by a Knight who has fallen from our Order. We had presumed the scrolls lost, along with the Knight. Now, of course, we know differently. Now we know that

Saladin has acquired the scrolls and we have to presume he will eventually break their code. Once he does, he will know what he has long suspected, that it was the Knights Templar who took the Ark of the Covenant out of the Promised Land and our Order still guards its Charge to this day. He is coming for it, Jonathan, and we, I and my brothers and sisters, brave Knights one and all, must stop him."

Jonathan moved uneasily in his seat. St Clair was now actually saying that he, or *they*, had the biblical Ark of the Covenant. He longed to wake with a start and see the sun come up over the capital, Washington DC. That way he would know that all this had been a bad dream. St Clair did not falter in his explanation; his fluidity unnerved Jonathan because it gave his words credence. His view of what was his sense of the norm faded into the distance, St Clair's words filling the void. Now Jonathan found himself beginning to hope that there was some semblance of truth in what St Clair was saying. Some grain of veracity, authenticity, just something he could hold onto. He so hoped he could even begin to dare to think he might ever believe in something again.

"Saladin has been relentless in his search for the Ark, but so far we have managed to elude him. He has already killed for it and will do so again. He will not stop until he has it, or we have him."

Jonathan nodded. Courtney was not the start of this, but she was his start. He knew that now. The killings would go on. He slowly began to feel part of *it*, he had no idea why, but he did. He considered that he had earned his place, but with a very high price. In that split second Jonathan had just become the sixth member of the sanction team.

"He believes that once he has the Ark," St Clair continued, "he will be master of the 'sacred science'. At first he penetrated the Masonic lodges, who have their founding routes from the building of the Temple Mount, by Solomon and its master mason, Hiram Abiff. Saladin gained access to antiquities and parchments that his Arabic scholars painstakingly translated and, bit by bit, he has been unravelling the jigsaw and getting closer, which means getting closer to us."

St Clair stopped and lifted his glass. "To those who win the victory, I will give the right to eat the fruit of the tree of life that grows in the garden of God; Revelation, message to Ephesus."

Jonathan raised his own glass. "The devil will put you to the test by having some of you thrown into prison; Revelation, message to Smyrna."

St Clair smiled. "I knew I would like you, priest."

It was getting late and St Clair insisted that Jonathan stay. Jonathan was thankful for the offer. It had been a long drive and he didn't relish driving back so late. St Clair took him back into the main reception hall and then up two flights of stairs; he followed without saying anything. He had been given a lot of information and slowly things were starting to make some kind of sense. His sister wasn't a field agent and would never have risked her own life. However, she had gone to the McGregor party. She would only have done that if there were an important reason and now he understood it. She did it because she had realised that once the files had been deleted, there were people in the FBI who were corrupt. His sister had loved her job at the Bureau. She was passionate about the work she did, and she was patriotic and saw her work as vital to national security. When she saw the organisation she had worked so hard for beginning to decay she had wanted to stop that; that had been her motivation. She'd done it out of loyalty, out of patriotism and for her sense of right and wrong. Even Walker thought people in the FBI and the police were on the take. Now Jonathan knew Walker was right.

Jonathan had lived an ecclesiastical life. Now he found himself in the middle of violence, murder and theological history. The future was unclear, but an excitement filled his heart that he had never felt before. Morning could not come soon enough.

Jonathan's room was sparse, but comfortable. He drew back the bed cover and revealed crisp white sheets. They had a pleasant smell of lavender about them. He punched the goose down pillows and sat on the end of the bed.

His surroundings had nothing to do with his once normal and carefree life back in Washington. You can add life to your days, Courtney had once told him, but you cannot add days to your life. She would often chide him because he was content with school and his football games. His ambitions never saw the light of day because he had none. What would Courtney have made of his life now, he wondered.

He had asked St Clair if there was hope. St Clair had paused at the bedroom door on his way out and told him that there was always hope, but sometimes you just had to make hope get up off its backside. He told Jonathan that he was now part of them and part of the race against evil, part of justice and faith. Part of a team of dedicated men and women who would lay down their lives for the protection of the word of God, for His gift to mankind, Moses's legacy and that he, Jonathan Rose, an ex-teacher-priest from Washington DC, was now one of them, a Knight Templar.

It was, he recognised, an overwhelming responsibility for a man who had suffered great grief at the loss of his sister and the loss of his faith, the two mainstays and core of his life. He doubted he was ready; he doubted he was ready for much.

"I just don't want to let you down, St Clair."

St Clair shook his head. "Don't worry, Jonathan. I have every faith that, when the time comes, you won't let me down. You won't let me down at all."

"I hope not," said Jonathan. "You know, I find it incredible that my sister's death is linked to a murdering lunatic running around loose in Washington DC, who thinks he's Saladin from the eleven hundreds and the crusades, and believes the Ark of the Covenant still exists."

St Clair smiled. "Oh, he's not in Washington, Jonathan," he said as he closed the door. "He's right here, in Great Britain. Now sleep well tonight, for tomorrow all the sanction team Knights will have gathered here and we begin our mission to take out Saladin. And you, my friend, you begin your act of remembrance in earnest."

Chapter 11

The Icon

Date: 30th June 2008
Place: Athens

Sweating, Yannis left the small taverna on the outskirts of the city. It had gone midnight but the streets of Athens were alive with a kaleidoscope of flashing lights and a myriad of musical beats. Late-night bars were still heaving with drunken clientele.

Yannis pulled off the main road and wound his beaten-up old Fiat around the narrow back streets of the capital, doubling back on himself twice. By now he should have been feeling better, but he wasn't. The meeting had gone badly and he was scared. He checked his rear-view mirror for the umpteenth time since leaving the run-down taverna, a haven for people who liked privacy and spoke in low voices.

Yannis Kiriakos was a small wiry man, with a sharp face and a pronounced nose. He had jet-black hair and an untended moustache. A small-time thief, his nocturnal activities usually involved breaking into any one of the cheap nondescript hotels in the city. These hotels, with little or no security, were easy pickings for Yannis and his kind. Yannis had started stealing young; at the age of thirteen he had been left to support himself and his mother. His father, a jobbing labourer, had died after falling from the scaffolding of one of the new hotels that were springing up all over the city. He fell sixteen floors.

Yannis was one of the lucky ones: the police had never

caught him. At the age of thirty-three, he had spent twenty years as a professional thief and had no charge sheet.

He parked the Fiat in the usual place, at the foot of the cast-iron fire escape that serviced his building, just in case he needed to leave in a hurry. He went straight to his drab one-bedroom apartment on the third floor. He had meant it to be temporary, but after seven years he was still living there. Extra careful, he locked the door and closed the curtains before switching on the light and phoning Jones.

Harry Jones, British naval attaché in Greece, was fast asleep. His wife, Mary, snored loudly next to him, untroubled by the ringing of the phone. Reluctantly, he reached for the receiver.

"Mr Jones, I'm Yannis here."

Jones pressed the light button on the bedside clock.

"Christ, Yannis, it's gone midnight!" he barked. "How did you get my bloody number?"

"Please, sorry, Mr Jones. I need you help."

Yannis never needed Jones's help; Jones always needed Yannis's help. As a professional thief, Yannis would steal just about anything, for anyone, for the right money. Even though Jones's job didn't involve espionage, he had used Yannis on a number of occasions to 'acquire' certain items for the British government. Normally, this was mundane stuff like documents from international trading corporations in the capital. Sometimes, the task would be to search the hotel room of a visiting diplomat from a foreign country and copy certain files.

Jones sat up. He was now fully awake; his wife slept soundly, albeit noisily, on. Yannis spoke in a hushed whisper, his English broken. He told Jones that he had received a telephone call from a man called Albert Toombago, a Nigerian who had lived and worked in Athens for fifteen years. Toombago fenced stolen goods on the black market, knew everybody worth knowing and, more importantly, was reliable. The Nigerian had told him that two British men, who had arrived in Athens three days earlier on false passports, were looking for a local to help them with a job. The only proviso was that the person had to be familiar with the island of Zakynthos in the Ionian archipelago. The two British men were offering five thousand US dollars. The Nigerian knew that Yannis had been born on the island, so he had contacted him. Yannis agreed to meet the two British men in a small taverna on the outskirts of the city. The Nigerian was paid €500 cash for the contact.

Yannis, who had spent three months in Dartford, England some years before working in a relative's restaurant, and so perfected his broken and staccato English, met the two men in the taverna, as arranged. He recognised their accents as South London. It seemed simple to Yannis and he couldn't believe his luck; this would be an easy job. They were to take the ferry to Zakynthos, drive to the small village of Macharado, just above the island's fertile growing plains of grapevines and olive trees and steal the revered Icon of Mavar. Yannis knew that the icon lay on public view, inset into the old wall of the church.

He was eager to help: the money was good and the work would be quick. Eagerness, as it turned out, was not a wise emotion, because the men went on to tell him that the icon was only part of the job. Their primary objective was to kill the region's bishop. The bishop was due to preach to the congregation there in a few days' time. When he asked why they wanted to murder the bishop, he received no answer. His eagerness faltered and his survival instincts told him to get out, but it was already too late. He knew their plan and, more to the point, he knew their faces – and they knew his. Whilst he had never killed anyone, he was not overly perturbed by the act, but killing a bishop was another matter. Though not a moral man – in his line of work it didn't pay – paradoxically, like most Greeks, he had respect and reverence for men and women of the church.

Jones listened. This was not his area of expertise, but the fact that two British assassins were in Greece made it his business, and the embassy's. He told Yannis to do nothing, just sit tight and wait for his call. Yannis had every intention of doing nothing, except to keep out of sight and pray for his salvation, which, he fretted, was now in the hands of God and Jones.

Jones made a call to the British Ambassador's residence. The ambassador listened without interrupting; when Jones had finished, four more calls were made.

The ambassador made the first call to the home of one of his superiors, a senior diplomat who worked in Whitehall. She then made a call to the Secret Intelligence Service, MI6. The people at the emergency meeting, which was convened less than two hours later, decided that the problem, the two British assassins, would require immediate termination. However, because of the current strained relationship between the British and the Greek governments over the island of Cyprus, it was decided that an outside organisation would have to be used. The British would distance themselves.

The suggestion of using the CIA, who had assisted in the region in the past, was rejected because of the religious element. It was agreed that a specialist outside, private organisation would be needed. Only one organisation fitted the profile that had Omega 1 and Omega 1S clearance. The Chief Director of Operations signed the order to contact Pi, the two-letter code name for the outside organisation MI6 had used a number of times over the years. The head of internal security counter-signed it. The call was made from Vauxhall Cross, London, the headquarters of MI6, to an unlisted telephone number in Islington, thirty minutes after the Whitehall diplomat had first made her call. A woman in her late fifties lifted the receiver and said nothing throughout the call. Putting down the receiver when the caller had finished, she played back the recording she had made using digital magtape telecoms technology. Two minutes later, she punched in the numbers on the desk-phone; the phone rang out in an isolated castle in Scotland. After six rings, the call was automatically re-routed by a computer to a cell phone number, also in the castle. Dominique's cell phone vibrated in her pocket

* * *

Date: 30th June 2008
Place: Glennfinch Castle.

Around one hour before the call came in to Dominique's phone from Islington.

Jonathan had slept soundly. It was only the second time he had slept through the night since his sister's death. Scottish air, fresh lavender sheets and the prospect of what would happen next had cleared and refreshed his mind. His will and resolve were back and the pit of despair he had lived in had been filled with hope. He had risen for breakfast expecting to find St Clair alone, as the previous evening, but there were three other people in the room with St Clair. The Knights had gathered.

The young woman paced the floor. She was stunningly beautiful, petite, with short mousy-brown hair and a tanned skin. She ignored Jonathan as he entered the kitchen. This time, though, he recognised her straightaway.

St Clair greeted him with a warm smile, just like they were old friends from way back, before introducing him to John Wolf. The Indian smiled, a broad grin that lit up his face. His eyes had a twinkle in them that, despite his size and stature, gave away the joker in him. He greeted Jonathan in a rich, gravel voice.

The Russian, Nickolin Klymachak, was a mountain of a man. Even though he was seated, Jonathan could see he had a large and solid bulk. A deep scar over his left eye gave him a mean look. He ate his cereals from a large bowl, shook Jonathan's hand and, in perfect English, bade him good morning. However, he remained aloof from the others as he sipped his coffee looking at the view outside the window.

St Clair, turning to the pacing girl, introduced her as Dominique. She half snorted her indifference at him and ignored them both. St

150

Clair laughed loudly. When Jonathan had last seen her, in the breakfast room at the Stranforth hotel, peering at him over her newspaper and rubbing her left shoulder, he hadn't recognised her. He hadn't made the connection with the bogus insurance firm back in the States; now he did. Her hair was different. Perhaps that was what had thrown him, but now there was no mistake. She had called at his house introducing herself as the claims officer for Diggby, Price and Goldstein Insurers. Jonathan had had no idea that Courtney had held two life insurance policies, one a government one and the other private. Now he knew she hadn't. When Dominique had arrived at his house she had been too nosy and had asked too many questions about Courtney. Jonathan had taken a dislike to her. The only thing he could remember about her was that she was attractive, but cold, and that her left shoulder bothered her a lot. He smiled to himself, realising that St Clair had known about him months ago and that their meeting had been planned. He thought that it had been his gumshoe detective work that had led him to St Clair, but he now realised that he had been led like a parent leads a child across a busy and dangerous street.

So now we are gathered then, thought Jonathan. Four Knights Templar and me, smelling of fresh lavender. This is going to be interesting.

The Indian drank his coffee, smiling. The Russian, who had only just finished his Templar initiation a few days ago, in Southern Ireland, stared out of the window, the Scottish glens evidently captivating him. He ate like a horse and Jonathan lost count of the number of bowls of cereal he had eaten. Dominique said nothing; she paced the floor, sombre and silent; her manner brusque. Jonathan ate breakfast; he sat at the table with the Russian and kept his gaze down. No one seemed overly eager to talk. The previous night the castle had been full of words, full of answers and more questions. The intensity of this lingered with him, but the morning had brought with it a frustrating hiatus, an aridness of words and information. He was desperate to ask more questions, but this was not the time. Everyone had gathered for a reason, the air was thick with it, but Jonathan still didn't know why.

Dominique jumped; her cell phone vibrated in her pocket and startled her. She reached for the small phone and answered it. Everyone watched her, their intensity visible as they strained unsuccessfully to hear the conversation. The caller, from an unlisted number in Islington, was not on the line long. She spoke for about a minute, then played the digital recording she had made a short while earlier. They then spoke for about thirty seconds. After that, the call was ended. Everyone waited. She placed the cell phone back into her pocket and smiled.

"It's confirmed and it looks like Greece as suspected," she announced. "Operation Roulette Wheel is on. This is the break we have been waiting for."

Jonathan felt the tension leave the room. They all knew something he didn't, but he was about to find out.

The Templars already knew, from their source within Salah El-Din's organisation, that Salah El-Din had hired the two hit men from South London just a few days ago. They had kept track of the two men until they disappeared into the hustle and bustle of Athens. One of the men, an assassin called Grimbone Walters and known to be a hit man favoured by Salah El-Din, had been suspected of the murder of Senator McGregor. They did not know the other man.

Based on Yannis's information and Jones's call, MI6 had already established the name of the bishop; he was the only bishop who would be visiting the island over the next six weeks. They had the name and they also knew the church where the hit would take place, but, they didn't have the time or day of the hit, information which was desperately needed. However, getting it rested on a small-time crook in Athens.

St Clair washed his cup, then placed his hands purposefully on the table. "I think its time to go to work, my friends." He turned to

Dominique, who had now finished pacing the floor, her wait over. "Give our guest a cell phone, with the numbers he will need. Then, show him around downstairs."

"Here." She thrust a cell phone into Jonathan's hand, along with a small piece of paper containing nine telephone numbers. One had a Washington DC area code, Meeks, he suspected. He didn't recognise the others.

"Memorise the numbers, then give me the paper back." Her abruptness bordered on rudeness. "I don't want you leaving it in your pocket or losing it for someone to find." She threw a piece of paper onto the table; it was the note he had left on the gillie's croft door, the note with St Clair's name on it.

He took the cell phone.

Courtney always had the latest phone on the market and never went anywhere without it, but he had never owned one, having never seen the need. In fact, he disliked the intrusion into his life. Wherever he went on the subway, he was in a constant state of frustration. It seemed that no commuter could take a train journey without calling up everyone they knew and, in a loud voice, talking about absolutely nothing.

Dominique interrupted his thoughts. "The phone has an integrated memory chip. It works off our own virtual network and uses short and rapid touch pad sequencing to announce instant voice messaging. It's person-to-person and person-to-team, with exchange of free form text messages. Lucid formatting, a full data download facility, fully secure anywhere in the world. All you have to do is make sure you keep the battery charged."

Jonathan looked at St Clair for help, but Payne St Clair laughed and then shrugged his shoulders.

"Don't ask me," he said. "To me it's just a cell phone. As long as you can press a couple of buttons I think it will work just fine."

John Wolf laughed, but he wasn't about to say anything. He had felt the sharpness of her tongue before; he would let the new boy take the brunt of her attention. She shook her head in disgust and ignored St Clair's lack of interest. Jonathan noticed there was something between them; he couldn't put his finger on it, but it was there. The way they looked and acted with each other. The familiarity was tacit.

With St Clair leading the way, the Templars moved from the kitchen into the reception room and through one of the doors that had been closed off the previous night. Behind the ordinary-looking door lay a four-inch steel door that required a retina scan to open it. Jonathan followed. Tungsten bulb lighting revealed an iron spiral staircase. He followed the Indian, who seemed to know every footing. A low hum permeated from the room below.

At the bottom, Dominique moved next to him. "It's our Control Room."

She ushered him around the room like a professional guide. All around them were computers and other technological wonders. Jonathan, a confirmed Luddite, knew nothing of what he saw. 256-way symmetric multiprocessing mainframe running Unix, Linux operating systems, Quad TFT Plasma display terminals. Hard drives with petabytes of storage, satellite uplinks, combined CPU speeds cloaking into terahertz stealth technology: it was all a mess of wires and bits to Jonathan. She might as well have blindfolded him and led him around and she knew it, but reluctantly she gave him a full tour as instructed.

The Indian settled himself at a computer terminal. He obviously had work to do, but Jonathan still didn't know what he was meant to do. He sat at an available computer terminal next to the Indian. The screen was full of numbers in a grid system. His hand toyed with the idle mouse on its pad. He looked at the Indian. The Indian shook his head and frowned.

"I wouldn't!" John Wolf whispered.

"Why not?" Jonathan whispered back, not knowing why he was whispering.

"Just in case you're good at it – better than she is, I mean."

Jonathan looked at him, bemused.

"Apollo," the Indian said, as if Jonathan knew who Apollo was.

"Apollo?"

"Yes, Apollo. He used to like amusing himself by playing the lyre on Mount Tmolos. He thought he was pretty good at it; in fact, he thought he was the best. However, down in the valley there was this shepherd called Pan, who played the flute to his flock. He was said to be a most exquisite player. One day, Apollo got to hear about the shepherd and decided there could only be one great player. So Apollo challenged the flute player to a duel of music. He rounded up some high-ranking judges and the duel commenced. All the judges voted for Apollo, smart move on their part, that is, except for one, King Midas. Foolishly, he decided his ears were more partial to the flute player. So, Apollo turned the King's ears to those of a donkey."

"Donkey?" Jonathan didn't see the connection.

"She doesn't like to think anyone is better than she is on these things, sees it as a bit of a challenge. If I were you, I would wait until I was given permission to touch it. Then I would ask a lot of questions so she feels in control. You don't want to get on the wrong side of Dominique. Don't be a Pan."

The Russian was struggling to muffle his laughter.

St Clair made a call to Morgan Clay. Clay was the Templar ghost man inside Salah El-Din's organisation. St Clair told him that Operation Roulette Wheel was spinning. Then he called the unlisted number in Islington and was fully briefed on the problem in Greece. He listened to the recording, and then he hung up. The next call he made was to Phillip Thornton, director of operations at MI6. Thornton, expecting the call, gave St Clair the telephone number and name of the ambassador in Greece.

The ambassador was in a meeting when the call came through, but he quickly cleared the room. His assistant knew that there was a problem, but not the details. The ambassador did not interrupt or ask any questions; he just listened. St Clair told him that his people would be there the next day and would deal with the problem by termination. There would be three casualties, two British, the other a Nigerian. Someone from MI6 would telex him with a draft press release early next morning; he was to use it once the deaths had been reported. The press release would say that two British holidaymakers had inadvertently been caught in what the British authorities believed was a dispute between rival drug gangs. Vague enough. St Clair gave the ambassador Dominique's cell phone number. He told him to find out the day and time of the hit and when he had it, call that number. After the terminations, he was to forget everything and destroy the number.

St Clair then gave each of the Templars a list of jobs to do. "We need two of everything for the main termination team and one of everything for the car bomb hit in the capital."

Car bomb hit! Jonathan wondered which of the Templars would be going to Greece. He looked at them hard, but they gave nothing away. He guessed the names had already been decided; he was only glad it was not him.

St Clair fired his orders in rapid succession. "Wolf, passports, papers, driving licenses, money. They can get holiday clothes at the airport, but I want two large suitcases, something that looks like they're on holiday for a few weeks. Nickolin, holiday companies. We need two places for tomorrow. Do whatever it takes. Dominique, we will need a gun to be delivered to the main termination team once they get there. It's better if it is local so it fits in with the cover story. Go for a ten-round magazine with a 5.7 calibre or above, double action trigger, perhaps a Five-seven. I want it cleaned and left at the hit. That way when the police retrieve it the story of a local gang shooting will hold some water. I want the explosives for the capital hit to be carried from here. I don't want anything going wrong with bad Semtex. Call Islington and ask them to take care of customs for us. I don't want any hitches at the airport."

Dominique nodded. She booted up her computer and, like

Nickolin and John Wolf, set about her tasks with professional skill. Jonathan watched them all doing something. He sat alone at the computer terminal, not daring to touch it, feeling utterly useless and with his finger hovering over the static mouse.

A large six foot plasma screen on the far wall flickered. Quickly, Dominique keyed the name of the visiting bishop and the details of the island's icon came up on the screen. St Clair asked for everyone's attention. He told them that they had to make the connection with the icon, but more importantly, the bishop and Salah El-Din. Grimbone Walters was not connection enough. They needed to know why the bishop was the mark.

For more than an hour they brainstormed. Every possible angle was processed through the computer and onto the plasma screen, but nothing fitted. It seemed that there was no connection between the bishop and Salah El-Din. The RAM was working overtime and frustration was beginning to settle on the Templars. Jonathan had sat and listened throughout. Most of what he saw on the screen was technological wizardry which he did not understand. The rest was hundreds of facts he had no knowledge of, but he did have an idea.

"Er ... perhaps, I mean ... can the computer juxtapose and then reverse on a grid system?"

The Russian looked blank.

"Two or more contrasting things placed together, so that their differences are highlighted and then, if it can, reverse the juxtaposition so that their similarities or connections are highlighted."

Jonathan thought he saw Dominique smile, but then again, he wasn't so sure she knew how to smile. She tried it. The bishop's name, Alexis Pagiaslis, showed on one side of the screen and thousands of unassociated items, objects and facts flashed and flickered on the other side. Within less than a minute the activity on the screen stopped and the word 'cocaine' flashed ominously. The name Father Eddy O'Brian joined it. Jonathan asked Dominique to check the diocese of the priest. What the computer came back with wasn't diocese, but 'deceased,' flashing in red. They all turned to Jonathan, waiting.

He told them that he knew of Father Eddy O'Brien. He had died from a tragic accident last year. He had fallen under a train, in a subway, in New York. Father Eddy O'Brien had worked with drug addicts and in the murky world of muling – people employed by drug smugglers to ship drugs into countries. There were rumours at the time that his death had not been an accident. A lot of people would have been happy to see the meddlesome priest dead. Jonathan asked Dominique to random-search country names and fifteen seconds later they had the beginning of their answer. Colombia flashed, quickly followed by the initials ICC. St Clair raced over to a computer terminal and typed away furiously, while the others waited.

"Dominique, type in these names, please." He called them out.

Dominique entered the six new names next to the bishop's name and Father O'Brien's. There, on the screen, was their answer: the names of the eight-man ICC team that had gone to Colombia to help the local people rid the area of drugs. Against their names, the word 'deceased' flashed in red. Only the bishop was still alive. Jonathan looked at St Clair for an answer.

"The International UNFDAC, the United Nations Fund for Drug Abuse and Control, along with the International Congress of Churches, co-funded the cost of sending eight senior clergymen, each representing five of the world's main religious groups, to Columbia. The eight ICC members were given information about a coca plantation; as it turned out, this plantation was Saladin's. They passed the information onto the DEA, who were there helping the Colombian authorities. The raid destroyed everything. It was a major blow for Saladin. In order to gain leverage with other criminal and terrorist factions, he needed credibility. The drugs gave him the money and the money gave him the credibility. He had worked for a long time to create Unity, but with his money dried up, the pending fragile union of criminal factions was in jeopardy. Unfortunately, McGregor gave him a way back in."

"So he murdered each of them?" Jonathan asked, but he didn't get an answer. It was now obvious why Grimbone Walters and the other unknown man were in Greece. Salah El-Din had sought his revenge on the eight men who had cost him so much.

Date: 30th June 2008
Place: Athens

The message reached Jones by mid-morning. He was sitting at his desk in the office. His secretary buzzed through.

"It's the ambassador for you, Mr Jones, on your secure line."

Jones flicked the switch and the ambassador bade him good morning, then gave him the instructions.

"Tell your man Yannis to go along with the assassins' plan and say nothing. Report back if anything changes, but we must have the day and time when it's going to happen. It's going to be dealt with by an outside organisation." There was a pause. "Harry," the ambassador's voice lowered, "you need to distance yourself from this one. No meetings with your man, no hint to him of what's happening. They will not be leaving any loose ends, if you know what I mean. Messy business all round, I'd say. Don't want you dragged in, old boy."

Jones knew exactly what he meant, but he was curious. "Do you think they've asked the Americans to deal with it?"

"Don't think so, Harry. I spoke to Carl this morning, before he left for the embassy. Didn't say much to him, just asked him if his boys were doing anything for us over the next few days. He assures me they're not. That doesn't mean to say that they are not involved. Remember what happened in Crete. However, I don't think they are involved. Whoever it is, London is keeping tight-lipped about it and I am happy to keep it that way. Nasty business, nasty business."

Harry Jones had been around long enough to know when not to get involved and he intended to distance himself, once he had called Yannis.

Jones made the call. Yannis trusted Jones, even with his life. Yannis put the phone down and kissed the cross he wore around his neck. He thanked God for giving him Harry Jones. Yannis made the telephone call to the two Brits at their hotel and confirmed the sailing times of the ferry for the next five days. They then gave him the details of the hit, the time and the day. He poured himself a large glass of ouzo. He would call Jones with the information later – right now he needed liquor inside him.

Date: 5th July 2008
Place: Zakynthos

Dominique and Jonathan arrived on the small island of Zakynthos. Jonathan still didn't understand why he was there. St Clair's reason had seemed simple back in Scotland: because he had no experience, he would make the perfect cover for Dominique. He just had to act like a tourist and Dominique would do all the work. Now, however, he wasn't so sure and his stomach was working overtime. The last time he'd acted as a cover for someone, at a Christmas Eve party, that someone got killed. He felt the sweat trickle down his arms.

MI6 had called the local police in the UK and had asked for their help. An hour later a young, newly married couple, Mr and Mrs Terry, packed ready and excited about flying off to Zakynthos for their honeymoon, were being questioned by police for something they didn't do and for something that hadn't happened. With the couple safely tucked away, two new passports were rushed through the passport office in Liverpool and were being couriered down to Birmingham airport, from where the honeymooning couple were due to fly.

The low-cost package holiday in Tsilivi, on the east side of Zakynthos, gave Dominique and Jonathan the flight they needed; it also gave them their cover: honeymooners. They mingled with the crowd of tourists who had just landed, all crammed together in the tiny airport. A building only just upgraded from a 'barn', Jonathan mused, looking at the single conveyer belt for luggage-reclaim. Planes just happened to land there! Dominique carried her own bag. She probably spat, drank beer and ate children as well, Jonathan thought.

Outside, their budget hire car was waiting for them. Jonathan drove. At least he knew how to do that, but he was surprised she had agreed to let him. He wasn't familiar with the make of car and it seemed to him the car wasn't familiar with being driven. It had a mind of its own. She sighed, but said nothing as they spluttered out of the airport car park. All the other passengers who had arrived on the same flight were met by holiday reps and taken to their waiting coaches.

Arriving at the Apollo Holiday complex at approximately 5 p.m., Jonathan found a parking place under a large olive tree that would offer shade when the hot sun rose the next morning. They made their way to the tiny reception, Dominique still carrying her own bag. They checked in and Mr and Mrs Terry were entered into the hotel register. For the first time it dawned on Jonathan how they would spend the next few days. When St Clair had told him that their cover was as newly-weds, on their honeymoon, it hadn't occurred to him that they would be sleeping in the same room. He suspected he'd caught a glimpse of relief on the Indian's face when John Wolf realised that he would not be her 'husband in the sun' for a few days. Jonathan couldn't wait for it to be all over. Despite giving up the cloth, and mainly because of it, his prowess with the opposite sex was minus zero, on any scale. She had clearly sensed his embarrassment and was revelling in it.

The Apollo holiday complex at Tsilivi was a perfect cover. It was purpose-built for families and they were everywhere. Sun-loungers and parents littered the poolside. The ping-pong table and swings heaved with children. Snorkels and facemasks lay where they had been dropped. A constant din hung over the complex. Shouts and screams, talking and laughing, splashing and thrashing blended together to give that most distinct of all sounds: children enjoying themselves.

Jonathan and Dominique had unpacked. Each had a large suitcase big enough to hold clothing for at least two weeks, but inside there was just one change of clothes. St Clair had insisted they take the large suitcases, so that they looked like all the other holidaymakers, and they did. Trying to take his mind off the fact he was sharing a room with a perfect stranger, Jonathan picked up a leaflet left by the reps to help people to get acquainted with the island.

"Did you know," he began, trying to break the unnerving silence, "that Zakynthos is one of the most beautiful islands in the Ionian archipelago? It has a population of just less than forty thousand, but this number swells to four times that amount during the main tourist season, May to October. The island's lush green vegetation and natural beauty makes it an ideal destination for tourists who want the sun."

Dominique yawned, but Jonathan persevered – anything to break the silence.

"Its narrow streets and countless ascending layers of small ornate balconies, potted with semi-tropical plants, compress the ever-decreasing space. Letters on street signs have backward G's and Y's. There is an excessive use of the letter X, As without legs, hyphenated vowels and nouns, unpronounceable place names. Local services are on GMT. Someone has written below, GMT stands for *Greek Maybe Time!*" He laughed.

Dominique, by this time, was totally uninterested in the information the leaflet had to offer and so Jonathan eventually gave up and read to himself.

Their ground floor studio had a small kitchenette, one wardrobe and two single beds in the room. A small door led to the bathroom that only had room for one person at a time. They had each changed into t-shirts, shorts and trainers, purchased at the airport from one of the duty-free shops. Now they sat silent again. She seemed in no mood for idle conversation. Her mirrored sunglasses unsettled Jonathan. She rubbed coconut oil into her skin; her complexion was already deep brown. She looked as though she had been born of Mediterranean parents, or at least half Mediterranean. Her looks were radiant and stunning. She rubbed at her shoulder; whatever was paining her had been there a while. A small round scar was the only visible sign of her discomfort. Jonathan remembered she had rubbed her shoulder a lot when she called on him masquerading as a claims officer from the bogus insurance firm and again at breakfast at the Sternforth hotel. He was going to mention the fact that St Clair had some great cream that had soothed his hands, but just the thought of its contents made his stomach turn.

Jonathan had spread thick, white Factor SPF 100 cream onto his exposed skin, conscious that he felt and indeed looked anaemic.

After a while, the silence was too much for him. Aware of his own breathing, he couldn't stand it any longer. "If we are supposed to be on holiday, don't you think we should be mingling with the others?"

She looked at him as he stood up expectantly. He was dressed in long baggy yellow shorts and a Hawaiian shirt, which, she reflected, must have been designed by a person with a sense of humour, or a deranged mind. He looked like a ghost in his white sun cream – a ghost with a very bad dress sense. Desperately, she tried to hide her amusement. She looked away.

"Fine, OK then," she managed to say in a muffled voice. "Let's go, Casper."

Outside they were husband and wife on honeymoon, Mr and Mrs Terry. They acted like everyone else. They did not draw attention to themselves and did not strike up conversations with people. They were friendly, but not too friendly. Their aim was simple: not to be remembered by anyone. Jonathan had been given these instructions by St Clair and he intended to follow them as best he could.

"They say that rhythm and harmony were invented in Greece by Hermes, Athena, Dionysus and Apollo," he said, as they walked along the poolside. "In the old days their music was played on the bouzouki, it's like a stringed lyre, and the toubeleki, a drum."

She didn't answer.

The music of Wham and the Gypsy Kings was now entertaining the guests, the constant beat coming from the poolside bar. He decided they should head in that direction.

The pool looked and smelt fantastic, blue and deep. A British father floated aimlessly on his back, trying to ignore his three young daughters whose childish voices pierced the poolside din and overshadowed Wham's *Club Tropicana*.

"Daddy, Daddy!" one of them shrieked. "Daddy, Catherine's been nasty. She has spoilt our game, and she won't be a shark."

"Daddy, I will so." Catherine cried in a similar piercing shriek to her sister, but only after swallowing half the pool in her attempt to get her side of the story out before her defence was lost. "But I said I wanted to be a dolphin first, but Mary says that she's the dolphin and so I have to be a horrid shark. I'm a better dolphin than Mary because she has to wear arm bands and I don't."

Dominique watched in amusement, transfixed by the family squabble. Their father just kept on floating aimlessly, his head half submerged so that his ears were partially protected from the bickering of his children. Dominique stood there with a big smile on her face. Perhaps there was a heart inside of her after all, Jonathan thought.

The Russian contingent of holidaymakers was made up of just one person, a woman in her early fifties. She had 'toy boy wanted' written all over her face. She evidently thought she was stunningly beautiful. Her face was haggard with time and even the thick foundation cream couldn't hide her years. Bright red lipstick accentuated her botoxed lips. As she eyed the poolside pickings, her eyes fell on Jonathan. She smiled and Jonathan smiled back. Dominique saw it.

"Are you okay, darling?"

Dominique's words broke his gaze; it also threw him a little. This would take some getting used to, he thought. All of a sudden I'm her darling! However, the affection was short-lived. She learned forward and scolded him in a hushed whisper.

"We don't want to make any friends on this trip. How hard can it be to do nothing? And, whilst I'm on, can you please stop rattling that change in your pocket? It's driving me nuts."

A Greek man, dubious-looking and smelling of sweat, wandered onto the complex. He was selling what were obviously pirated CDs from a worn-out rucksack. He ambled over to their table in a casual kind of way. He had already been to several other tables; no one was buying. Jonathan felt disappointed in himself because he couldn't wait for the Greek to ask Attila the Hun sitting next to him if she wanted to buy some of his dodgy CDs. He watched in splendid anticipation as the Greek approached Dominique.

"CDs, madam. I've a some great CDs, very cheap to lovely lady."

Here it comes, thought Jonathan. Wait until he sees that snakelike tongue come out of her mouth and wrap itself around whatever dignity he has left.

"I'll have five, please."

Jonathan couldn't believe it. He had expected to see the vendor's head rolling towards the pool by now.

The smiling vendor rummaged in his rucksack, then handed her a bag. She took it, put it under her towel and paid the man. Jonathan had made the mistake of thinking he was on holiday and everything he saw was real.

The Greek tucked the money in his pocket and then whispered, "Give my regards to St Clair."

He then walked away. Now St Clair's words echoed in Jonathan's head: 'Get the gun when you are there'. Jonathan now realized what had just happened: she had the gun that was probably going to kill someone.

"Is that what I think it is?"

'Yes' would have been enough for his palpating heart.

"Lightweight, ten rounds, deadly at close range and, local," she said.

It had just become real. He reached for his beer and swallowed hard. Then he headed for the pool bar where he intended to drink more beers than he should. It was the only way he was going to deal with the reality of what had just happened.

At 7 p.m., maintaining their cover, slightly inebriated and somewhat merrier, Jonathan sat by the side of his new bride with about twenty other new arrivals in the reception area of the complex. Patiently, they listened as the excitable Kathy, their appointed holiday rep, went through her script, word-perfect. It was obvious that she had made the same speech a hundred times that season and, despite her best efforts, it showed.

"According to Homer," Kathy began, and then broke off for the obligatory audience participation, "now, who knows who Homer was?"

No one said anything. Poor Kathy stood with a broad grin on her face waiting for someone to answer. Once one person had spoken, the others would follow, but it always took one to start it off. Jonathan, sensing this, moved to raise his hand, but Dominique stopped him with a look which didn't require any words.

But Kathy was a pro. "Yes, he was," she said, pointing loosely to somewhere at the back where no one had said anything. Then she was into the next line of her speech. "Homer was a very famous Greek and, according to him, Zakynthos gets its name from its very first inhabitant. Now, here's a harder one! Can anyone guess who that might have been, who was that first inhabitant?"

Jonathan looked at Dominique and mouthed, "I know this one."

"It's a question for the children, stupid," she whispered.

Jonathan smiled inwardly. He knew who the question was aimed at. He was merry, not drunk, but he had discovered the pleasure of teasing old iron pants sitting next to him.

"Zakynthos," a parent called, in a self-congratulatory tone.

Jonathan looked at Dominique and raised his eyebrows. "Told you I could have answered that, darling." She didn't respond.

Kathy, thankful for any response from the audience, was on her way again. "Yes, that's right. Now he was the son of Dardanois, who was, as some of you may know, the King of Troy." Contagiously enthusiastic and vivacious, she was in full flow and even the antics of twelve boisterous children dancing around the tables and causing a youthful ruckus didn't put her off her stride. She continued, seemingly without drawing breath, taking them through Greek art, gold museums, ceramics… the cultural deluge went on and on.

"Now, I know you will not want to miss our Loggerhead turtles on the smaller islands of Morathonisi and Pelousi. You know it's the temperature of the nest that determines the sex."

Dominique leaned over to Jonathan and whispered, "Bet you didn't know that one, did you, darling?"

He winked at her, amused.

"And our turtles…" Kathy continued. "And our island…."

Jonathan and Dominique nodded and smiled all the way through as Kathy rhapsodized melodically about the wonders of the island's life.

"Do you think we will have time to see the turtles, dear?"

The alcohol was manifesting itself in a mischievous manner again, much to Dominique's annoyance. For the first time in a long time, Jonathan was having some fun. Kathy was quick to seize on the two potential customers for the boat trip. Jonathan surmised that this was because she would get commission on their booking. He had already gathered from overheard conversations around the pool that all the reps were on the same deal and worked hard to sell places so that they could supplement their low summer wages.

"Oh, you must make time to see our turtles. We also have a very reasonably priced island tour, Olympia excursion, Kefalonia, Greek night, Keri Caves and shipwreck."

Attention was now on them, the last thing Dominique wanted. She needed to get them out of there. She threw her arms around Jonathan and kissed him delicately on the lips.

"Thank you, but we won't have the time. We're on our honeymoon."

This time she kissed him hard on the lips. Kathy cheered, the parents cheered, then Jonathan cheered.

Date: 5th July 2008
Place: Athens

Yannis rang Jones and gave him the details: tomorrow at noon at the old church. Nothing more was said, although Yannis wanted to keep Jones on the telephone, wanting reassurance, but that was not the way things worked. Jones hung up. Next, Jones passed the information on to the ambassador, who, after putting down the telephone to Jones, rang the cell phone number he had been given. Dominique answered. The ambassador gave her the new information about the hit before putting the number out of his head.

Date: 5th July 2008
Place: Zakynthos

Dominique took Jonathan's hand and led him away from the reception area and the presentation. They had barely left the room when her cell phone rang in her pocket. Reality was back and, for Jonathan, it was an unwanted intruder. She wouldn't tell Jonathan the details the ambassador had just given her. She would spare him a sleepless night. When she asked him if he was OK, he said didn't know; he didn't know how he felt.

"Don't worry, priest," she said. "I've been an active Knight before. Just stay close to me and you'll be fine."

"And Roulette Wheel?" he asked. "I guess this is it. It's starting?"

"It is."

"And the name: what is the significance of the name?"

"Roulette Wheel? Well," she began, "if you add up all the numbers on a roulette wheel, they add up to six hundred and sixty-six."

"6,6,6!"

From his reaction, she thought, he was now in for a sleepless night anyway

Date: Sunday 6th July 2008
Place: A small church on the island of Zakynthos

Dominique knew where he would be. Every Greek Orthodox Church contains a chair which is specifically reserved for the visiting bishop; it is never used except when the bishop visits.

The bishop sat piously on his chair. He was mildly aware of the church door opening. He saw the two European men approach, a third, a Greek, waited at the back of the church near to the door, which he closed. The Greek had the icon in his hand and looked nervous.

The gun came from nowhere; it was the same GLOCK 27 that had killed McGregor in Salt Lake City only a few months before. The bishop watched, unable to react. The congregation saw the men, then the gun and they screamed, but the bishop remained motionless in his chair. The gun was raised, pointing at the bishop. He closed his eyes and waited for the sound of the gun going off.

A petite lady, her head covered with a black scarf, who had been sitting in the middle of the congregation with a male companion, stood up, both hands wrapped tightly around her Five-seven pistol. She fired two shots. One of the European men fell to the ground, his gun falling from his hand and hitting the ground before his body; he died instantly. Grimbone Walters was dead. The other man had turned and was running towards the exit of the church, screaming at the

Greek to open the church door. At that precise moment Yannis found redemption and salvation. He slammed the door shut and stood in front of it. There was no way out for the European.

The bullet entered his heart and Yannis Kiriakos died instantly, the icon still in his hands. The European turned, his next bullet already in the chamber. The petite lady moved out into the aisle, her eyes never leaving the man. At the last minute she stumbled; the kneeling bench caught her foot and she lay prone on the church floor. Her gun had slipped from her hand as she fell and it now lay a metre away. She shouted for her companion to get the gun. Seeing his chance, the assassin moved closer. Her companion didn't move. frozen to the spot. The assassin crouched. At the last minute the petite lady rolled from her position, scooping up her gun as she did so. The assassin's bullet went wide of its mark. With her in a kneeling position, her bullet was more accurate; the two assassins were now dead.

Horror gripped the congregation. They watched in silence as Dominique bent down over the two dead killers and painted a small cross on their foreheads with their own blood. Then she took the hand of her companion, who was still in shock, and led him away. At the church door she stopped and looked at the Greek on the floor. Her companion knelt down and whispered something in Latin, then made the sign of the cross over the body. Dominique wiped the gun she had been holding before dropping it onto the floor, as instructed by St Clair.

Place: Athens

At about the same time in the city of Athens, a Nigerian criminal known to the police as a fence of stolen goods and the operator of a paedophile website opened his car door. The blast, from a RDX, PETN-based compound, Semtex, blew his head from his body; no one else was injured. A man of Northern European origin, mean-looking, six foot five with short-cropped black hair with hints of grey, a square chiselled chin and a deep scar over his left eye, was seen walking away from the scene by two delivery men. After a telephone call from the British Embassy to the Athens police authority, they later retracted their statements, having each received €5,000 from an unknown source.

The bomber, Nickolin, was back in Scotland within five hours, Dominique and Jonathan arriving just two hours later. The sanction had been a success.

Place: Glennfinch Castle

Later that same night, Jonathan told St Clair that he had been scared on Zakynthos, so scared he had been unable to move when Dominique needed his help, and she had nearly died because of him. They sat alone in the same room as the one they had sat in that first night. St Clair went to the small maple drinks cabinet. He took one of the bottles and poured two drinks into cut-glass tumblers. Then he added a little water from a pitcher, as he had done on that first night.

"It was like something out of a horror movie. It was awful seeing someone killed. I don't think I am going to be any good to you. I am so afraid I will put someone's life at risk, like I did with Dominique. I don't think I will ever come to terms with taking a life." Jonathan sipped at his drink for comfort and steadiness.

"Jonathan," St Clair began, "if it weren't for you and Dominique, a bishop would now be dead. Instead, two assassins are dead. I understand you are struggling with the justification. We all do every time there is a sanction. Our Order only carries out sanctions when there is no other choice, but we are warrior monks. We are at arms, Jonathan. It is what we do and who we are. Those two assassins would have killed time and time again if you and Dominique had not gone to Greece. More innocent people would have died. We do not want the deaths of innocent people on our hands. Our Order doesn't just kill for killing's sake. We take away what is evil. We take away the really, really bad people: and only the really, really bad people. Maybe in time you will see the justice in this, in what happened and, in what will happen. However, you must follow your heart. You must do what you think is right and we will all understand and respect you for that, whatever you decide. As for letting us down, don't worry, Jonathan. I have a feeling that your time will come, and when it does, I have faith that you will know what to do. You just lacked experience in Greece, and experience is something you gain by not having it when you need it. You now have it."

Jonathan went to his room and stayed there for the rest of the evening. As a priest, he could never have reconciled what had happened on the island, but he was changing, slowly. As the long night wore on, he began to find some emergence of justification for their actions. In times of such soul-searching he had always talked with God; now he couldn't. It was strange for him not having his God. That omnipresent dynamic was missing from his reasoning. Now there was just the man, a man who struggled well into the night about his involvement in the deaths of three people.

Chapter 12

Morgan Clay

Date: July 2008
Place: The merchant ship *Efach II*

There is an old seafaring expression, 'If things look bad on the horizon, then they generally are. And they will probably get much worse by the time you get there.' However, there are times when seemingly unrelated events can come together to turn that bad situation into a good one, and in the most unexpected way.

Alan Murry had been a merchant sailor for over twenty years and for the last seven of those years, he had captained a number of ships. Most carried what can only be described as dubious cargoes. Murry, unlike his younger brother in Manchester, had no police record, but he was wanted for questioning by the authorities in France and Holland. The charges ranged from theft, rape, and assault with a deadly weapon. A man of few scruples, he was known by the intelligence agencies as a 'sea mule' – an apt name considering he would carry anything, anywhere, for the right price. He was credited with the shipment of millions of dollars' worth of drugs into the West and, of late, human trafficking. But nothing was ever proven.

Murry had attracted the attention of Interpol. They had mounting evidence that he was trafficking people out of the Congo and into Western Europe. Interpol believed that his human cargo, which included children as young as ten and eleven, were destined for the sex industry and Involuntary Organ Removal. However,

Murry had never actually been caught carrying anything illegal; he was one of those lucky people who had an uncanny knack of getting away with it.

Date: July 2008
Place: Glennfinch Castle

The Templar computers monitored communications between different intelligence agencies around the world. It was a daily routine for the powerful computer system. That morning Dominique had checked the monitors and saw that Murry's photograph, along with those of seven of his crew, had been posted on Interpol's secure site. She scanned the data report. Interpol had replaced the ship's anode, a small electronic device that gives off a low electronic frequency to deter unwanted crustaceans from attaching themselves to the propellers and fouling the blades, with a tracking device. Too small to be noticed and with a frequency so close to the original, it would not raise suspicion on the ship's sonar.

Date: July 2008
Place: Manchester

The housing estate was no different to a hundred other housing estates throughout the United Kingdom: concrete blocks with boarded-up windows and heavily bolted doors, looking out onto an environment bleeding to death. Salah El-Din revelled in such social deprivation; it was a breeding ground for his activities.

Drugs, rape, arson and gang wars, all had become the norm and no one had a mind to involve themselves in the mammoth task of reversing the depravity of such estates. Some had seen the opportunity. Salah El-Din was one of them. He had seen and seized it with both hands. He had laid the groundwork in the mid-eighties, his gangs working the streets with drugs, prostitution and extortion. It built slowly, but it built. His business thrived and ordinary people suffered.

The police remained on the periphery. Odd skirmishes, with high media attention, resulted in nothing but more violence and cries of police brutality. The police were seen as the criminals and the criminals treated as the victims. In the end, the real victims remained unseen, hidden behind bolted doors. Hope had disappeared into the shadows, along with those who had once stood up and spoken out.

Dagmar Grey was only seventeen years old, but already she had been raped, robbed and beaten, and all in her own home. A tall, pretty girl, she had jet-black, short-cropped hair, greeny-brown eyes and a soft oval face. She had learned about estate life early. She lived with her alcoholic mother in a two-bedroom flat on a large brutalist housing estate, along with her seven siblings. Dagmar shared the same father as Tony, her eldest brother. The other children all had different fathers who had come and left over the years.

Her mother's present consort was a man called Bill. No one knew his last name, but everyone on the estate knew his street name, Pit Bull, a name he was proud of. It was tattooed on the side of his neck. He was a career criminal who had worked the large housing estate for Salah El-Din for over five years. A brute of a man, a bully and a drug dealer, he had served nine years in jail for armed robbery before he met Salah El-Din and was currently out on bail on two drug-related charges. A crooked lawyer, Timothy Crowthorp, who worked for Salah El-Din, was paid well to keep the estate bosses out of prison.

Bill was over six feet tall and weighed eighteen stone; he had a shaven head and wore a montage of tattoos from his legs up to his neck. A streetwise hard case, he prowled the streets with his lieutenants and an assortment of firearms, although Bill was infamous for favouring the cut-throat razor. He was feared on the housing estate and surrounding areas for a temper that could ignite without cause or warning.

The night he raped seventeen-year-old Dagmar had been a good night for the Pit Bull. He had taken over twenty-five thousand pounds in drug money and another twelve thousand in protection dues. Since the landlord's wife at the Queen's Head public house had been attacked with battery acid, everyone was paying up.

Both Pit Bull and Dagmar's mother had been drinking excessively since 3 p.m. They had made it upstairs before her mother passed out on the floor of her bedroom. Bill had left her there, lying in her own vomit. Dagmar was in the bathroom when he walked in. There was no lock on the door. There was no point because it had been kicked open that many times there was no frame left for the lock to fit into. Bill's eyes stared. Her muscles seized and involuntarily she stopped urinating. As always, he smelt of drink, sweat and smoke. His eyes remained fixed. His voice was gruff and threatening. He had never sexually bothered Dagmar before, but now he unzipped his black jeans. Dagmar knew not to irritate him for he had beaten her up on many occasions.

His words were curt and of the street. He grabbed at her, her pants still around her ankles. She was helpless against his powerful arms. He sat on the side of the stained cast-iron bath and pulled her onto him.

"Don't scream or I will fucking kill you." He lifted her up effortlessly and onto him. Her face was inches from his, his breathing heavy and potent.

Bill heaved the young girl up and down. His mouth closed over hers and his tongue searched her mouth. He closed his eyes.

Out of nowhere, a baseball bat smashed down on him. His head split open and blood poured down his face. Disoriented, he rocked precariously on the side of the bath. Dagmar freed herself, shaking uncontrollably and bleeding from her vagina. Tony, Dagmar's brother, rounded on Bill again with a second blow that was more forceful than the first and Pit Bull's skull splintered. He toppled back into the bath. Blood oozed from his head, mouth and nose. His eyes glazed over and then Pit Bull was dead.

The police and forensic officers arrived fifteen minutes after Tony had called them. The drug squad and special branch were there twenty minutes later and were being briefed by the crime scene officer. In total, they seized over four hundred thousand pounds in used banknotes, two Beretta sawn-off shotguns, a Cougar handgun and enough cocaine and crack cocaine to make it the biggest drug bust ever recorded in England.

Date: July 2008
Place: 890-923 Knightsbridge Court Crescent, London.

From the outside, the London headquarters of Salah El-Din's criminal empire was just another plush apartment block in Knightsbridge.

The commissioner, smartly dressed in a peaked cap and a deep red uniform, paced around the lobby like a strutting cockerel. The residents were proud of their commissioner; his dogmatic fortitude gave them status. Only invited guests were ever seen in the building; the riff-raff stayed outside, where, of course, they belonged. Good security was a benefit of living in a building owned by a wealthy Arab.

Salah El-Din's operation took the entire top floor of the building. The other residents, who had no idea what went on above them, occupied the other two floors. It was the perfect front for his criminal activities: their respectability was his façade.

The top floor of the building consisted of a series of offices, twenty-three in all. Most of them were involved in running his legitimate businesses. However, some were used to launder his drugs money. Cash from his illegal enterprises would be moved between countries by couriers. The couriers would deposit the cash in a number of banks. Several transactions later, bonds, shares, property, all would be owned by one of his legitimate companies.

Nine offices at the far end of one of the corridors and out of the way of the majority of employees, were strictly for those closest to

Salah El-Din. Here his illegal empire was run. Three suites for guests, furnished to five-star standard, lay ready twenty-four hours a day. At the furthest point of the building was Salah El-Din's palatial suite, complete with side rooms for his bodyguards, who stayed with him around the clock.

His bodyguards were a menacing sight, both over six feet, in excess of nineteen stone, and very powerfully built. They were solid muscle. They were also cold-blooded killers. The bodyguards had been with him for over six years. They were loyal and they were absolute in their duties. Black African twins, they had been mercenaries in a series of civil wars on the troubled continent before Salah El-Din found them. They had no conscience, no morals and no social values. They were merciless, uncompromising, unyielding and bloody.

Morgan Clay had spent over a year infiltrating the corrupt empire of Salah El-Din and, with the help of the Templars and their network of contacts, he had achieved much in that time. Whilst suspicion prevailed on all newcomers, he had succeeded in infiltrating the corrupt world of 890-923 Knightsbridge Court Crescent. He had become trusted. However, despite all this, Clay had never seen his employer. Only three people in the building had: his two bodyguards and Bob Stranks, a distasteful man who worked for the wealthy Arab.

The call about the murder of the estate boss known as Pit Bull came into the headquarters in Knightsbridge at four in the morning. Morgan Clay was on duty. It was the second call that evening. The first was from a man in Athens, saying that the police report he had just acquired stated that both assassins, Grimbone Walters and his accomplice, were confirmed dead. The report detailed the painting of a small red cross on the foreheads of each of the dead men – painted in their own blood. It had said that the killings had been related to drugs and involved rival gangs.

For the second time that night, Clay rang through to Salah El-Din's private suite to give him more bad news, this time about his estate boss. Salah El-Din answered the telephone himself, his bodyguards being in the small kitchen that serviced the suite. Clay reported that the man called Pit Bull was dead and the police had seized the merchandise. Salah El-Din revealed no emotion. He thanked Clay for letting him know. He wished him good night, and then he put the phone down.

Salah El-Din was paranoid about security. However, it didn't take him long to work out that the estate boss's murder was no breach in security. If anything, it was domestic. The failed assassination on the bishop in Greece, however, was another matter. Salah El-Din was no fool. He knew that the deaths of the hit men had been the work of the Templars; he was sure that it was their mark. Despite having no real proof that the Templars actually existed, he had always believed that they did. He had made it his business to read as many reports on assassinations and killings over the years as he could. He had begun to see a recurring pattern. They were always low-key, always a clean crime scene, always the red cross and always the connection with religion.

He knew the Templars were out there. He felt it. He believed they were there with every bone in his body.

Far away, his scholars were working on the scrolls he had purchased and soon they would have them decoded. Then he would find *them* and rain terror on the religious monks. He would destroy them, every one of them. Until the scrolls were decoded, though, he needed the Templars' attention, along with that of the law enforcement agencies, on Unity and not on him. His end game depended on their attentions being elsewhere.

Clay knew the call was a devastating blow. The dead man was one of the top earners for Salah El-Din's illegal drug business in the UK. A small red light flashed and Clay switched his gaze to a monitor. Someone was moving around in the room where the secure mainframe was kept. Bob Stranks was working late again.

The US National Security Agency, the top-secret intelligence gathering centre in Fort Meade, Maryland, had employed Bob Stranks back in the mid-eighties. Stranks was one of the elite mainframe trouble-shooters, until Salah El-Din made him an offer he couldn't refuse. For nearly a decade Stranks, through the programmes he wrote, kept the illegal empire of Salah El-Din going. Twenty-four hours a day data was gathered, assessed and stored. Stranks, greying early at forty-one, was a small wiry man. He had suffered from rodent facial ulcers since the age of twenty-seven. Each time the surgeons had been able to remove the cancerous lumps from his face, but not without having to take deep extractions from areas of his face, which looked beaten. Painfully shy in new company, his lack of social skills had plagued him all of his life. He had been a target for bullies at school. His early life was a miserable existence of loneliness. Then he discovered computers and the Internet, and a whole new world of communication opened up to him. A self-taught programmer and self-confessed hacker, he'd been taken in by the NSA when they failed to stop his repeated hacking.

Stranks had thrived for a time in the NSA; the atmosphere of secrecy and isolation suited his nature perfectly. He acquired the kind of reverence accorded to those young pioneers of Silicon Valley, like Steve Jobs, in the early days of Apple. However, Stranks had one weakness, a weakness that had evolved from the thousands of hours he had spent alone in front of the computer screen. The Internet gave him access to sex, albeit virtual sex. It was something he could never experience in real life because he was unable to interact with people. Night after night, he would download pornographic material from the Internet. It wasn't long before his taste changed and he discovered the slender, sleek bodies of young men. Stranks's weakness did not go unnoticed by Salah El-Din. Stranks was happy with the arrangement: one hundred thousand pounds a year, paid into an offshore account set up for him by his new employer, and all the young slender male flesh he could bed.

Security was intense on the top floor of the building. All

employees and invited visitors underwent in-depth scrutiny. All were issued with plastic tabbing cards – active badges, which omitted a frequency signal picked up at the security nerve centre in the basement of the building. No matter where anyone was on the top floor, the computer would pick up the signal and locate the person's precise position at any time. Even furniture, and every other object that could be moved or tampered with, had a tabbing card attached. If it moved and it wasn't supposed to, then the computer would issue its warning and within seconds, day or night, security would be there.

Surveillance cameras scanned all areas of the top floor. Thermal imaging cameras scanned Salah El-Din's suite; no visual monitoring was allowed inside his own quarters. All surveillance was recorded, then viewed and stored. If anyone was wanted on the phone, the computer would locate the person via their tabbing card and automatically re-route the call to the nearest telephone. The tabbing cards detected heartbeats; if anyone took them off, the computer would know instantly. A dedicated computer screen, constantly showing the blueprint of the top floor, was dotted with small white spots. These were people moving around, people at their desks, people meeting in groups and whom they were meeting with. All meetings had to be approved beforehand. No cell phones or any other kind of electronic equipment were allowed in the building.

Even the drinks dispenser was programmed into the mainframe security system. Once an employee had used it, the computer's mainframe, via the sensory programme, would recall the person's preferred drink, including their exact measurements of milk and sugar. The Xerox machines used new e-paper technology. The paper was wiped and used again and again. There was minimum waste. E-commerce was at its cutting edge inside the building, but outside, it was just another apartment block.

At night, hidden lasers beamed a complex patchwork of micro-thin infrared beams, criss-crossing corridors and offices like an aerial street map of New York City. Alarms were connected to every opening device: windows, doors, drawers; all were linked to the mainframe computer and all were monitored day and night. The computer monitored the amount of paper the office had at any one time, adding the weight of new stock delivered to old stock; the total weight of all stock was known at all times. At the end of every day, every document printed that day would have to be put into a special chamber overnight, so that the computer could weigh them. The difference between the stock weight and the printed weight would have to match the previous evening's balance. Any shortfall would have to equal the waste paper balance, placed in another chamber for weighing, before being incinerated. Every night the calculation had to match. No one was allowed to take documents out of the building. If one piece of paper left the building, security would know.

The phone and computer system had a complicated cloaking device that protected the system from hackers; it controlled phone calls, e-mails and faxes and had a dual back-up system in case of power cuts. All the windows were covered with a silver film to stop electronic intrusion and spying through the glass. To get to the top floor a swipe card was needed. The buttons in the lift only went as far as the residents went, the first two floors. To some it was a technological revolution, to others it was the Orwellian nightmare come true; to Salah El-Din it was the difference between life and death and Bob Stranks was the master of the technology.

Morgan Clay sat quietly monitoring the screens in front of him. Clay was a Templar 'ghost man'. It was a term used in the world of espionage to describe a person who infiltrates an organisation and is able to stay there gathering information without being discovered or killed. The title fitted Clay perfectly. Employees in the nine offices thought that he had actually been there longer than he had. This pleased Clay. It meant he was doing his job, to blend in, not to draw attention to himself and to become part of the furniture. A ghost man can never afford to do things well in an organisation because that would draw praise and therefore attention to them. Also, they cannot afford to do things badly because again this would draw attention to them. They just do, impassively, no matter what, mediocrity their greatest weapon.

Morgan Clay was average looking, average height, with average features and average ways. Nothing ever changed about Morgan Clay – leastways, not outwardly. The kind of man you could see every day for a year and not be able to describe him when asked. He was ideal for the job and the best ghost man the Order of the Knights Templar had ever had.

Clay had learned his craft from his previous employers, the British Secret Service. He had spent thirty years defending the crown, but at the age of fifty, all that changed. During the Spring of 1993, whilst infiltrating a known IRA cell active in London at the time, his superiors badly misjudged a situation that severely compromised him and almost cost him his life. It would be one bureaucratic blunder too many for Clay. Despite his misgivings, which he had relayed to his superiors, they had ordered a raid on the terrorists' safe house, in Putney. Instantly suspicion fell on Clay, as he had feared. Clay had been undercover as an IRA sympathiser for more than fifteen months and had managed to penetrate deep into their UK organisation. He had been getting close to their source of funds in the United Kingdom. But the raid on their safe house closed off all his contacts within the organisation and the terrorists went to ground. Then, about six weeks later, two of the terrorists contacted him. His instincts told him that something was wrong, but he had no choice. He hadn't reported that new contact had been made, fearful of the faceless idiots who sat behind their desks back in Whitehall. Clay was out in the cold.

The two men picked up Clay from the prearranged site and drove to a secluded area near to the Dartford tunnel, on the Kent side of the river. Clay had been in the business long enough to know that this was no meeting, that this was a murder squad, but he couldn't be sure. All he could do was to go along with it – and hope.

He didn't see where the two shots came from. He just knew that the two terrorists, who had been standing behind him about to put a bullet through his head, dropped like stones to the ground. Both men were dead in less than two seconds. This was his first introduction into the Order of Knights Templar, who, fortunately for Clay, had also been interested in the IRA cell, but for different reasons. The lone sniper was an active Knight called Luther Coates. Luther had been charged with following the terrorists. Luther knew Clay was British Secret Service and had, by his actions, blown months of painstaking surveillance to save Clay. Weeks later, Clay met two of the Order's most senior Knights and he liked what the Order stood for. Besides, by then he had begun to despise the fresh-faced controllers that now ran Whitehall. He didn't hesitate to join the Order. Now he was the fifth member of the sanction team.

Clay had presented himself to Salah El-Din's organisation just over a year ago, after being introduced by one of London's most notorious porn kings, Izekl Freeman. Scotland Yard had caught Freeman in a classic sting operation, with enough evidence to send him away for a very long time. Jail not being to his liking, he had cut a deal. All Freeman had to do was introduce someone – Clay – to a particular firm, Salah El-Din's.

Freeman had been paying protection money to Salah El-Din's organisation for a long time. Clay entered the organisation with a glowing criminal record and references from a notorious porn criminal.

Morgan Clay finished his shift. The handover took over an hour, as it did every night. Meticulous checks and double checks were ticked off against criteria laid down in a standard operating manual, written by Salah El-Din himself. Ted Skinner, a Texan by birth, satisfied that all the checks had been completed, hit the buzzer and Clay left the basement by the side entrance, as usual.

An hour later Clay rang St Clair on his secure cell phone, routed via the controller in Islington. Clay told him that the details of the

Athens job had come through. He then told St Clair about the killing of one of Salah El-Din's notorious estate bosses. Whilst St Clair had already heard about the murder, it was all over the law enforcement agencies' networks; he hadn't realised that the man had been working for Salah El-Din. The opportunity that now presented itself could be the lucky break they had been waiting for.

Clay had not been able to get any intelligence on any of the on-the-ground operations, for now he was stuck on internal security. St Claire knew that if they could track down the dead man's associates, then they could start to inflict damage on Salah El-Din's operations in the UK. They had already announced their presence on the Greek island; it was time to send him another message. They needed to draw him out. The hunted were about to become the hunters. St Clair ended the call with Clay and then made a secure conference call to the other eight Worthies.

Chapter 13

Dagmar Grey

Date: First week of August 2008
Place: Liberia. The merchant ship *Efach II*

The cargo vessel *Efach II*, a five thousand tonne merchant ship, left the safe harbour of Port Buchanan, one of the two principal ports of Liberia, under a flag of convenience, Panama.

The Captain, Allan Murry, made the tide. The harbour pilot navigated their way out to open water and all pilot advice/captain's orders were recorded into the ship's log. Slowly they passed the breakwater that protects the chaotic container terminal. Over a five-day period, Murry's ship had been loaded with crates of assorted machinery and farming chemicals, bound for India. The illegal cargo, hidden deep in the ship's hold, Number 4, did not show on the inventory. It had been loaded aboard under the cover of darkness, on the last evening in port.

Law enforcement agencies in both the United Kingdom and the United States of America, were keeping watch on the comings and goings of Unity members. The joint operation, code-named Apple Pie, stretched their already over-stretched resources. In all, there was a total of three hundred and eighty-seven men and women, plus administration support units, involved in Operation Apple Pie.

Unity had attracted the attention Salah El-Din had hoped it would. For years he had worked to make it a possibility. He had fought and killed to ensure that the criminal cartel succeeded Everything he had done had brought him to this point. However, what the authorities didn't know was that Salah El-Din had created Unity as a huge smoke screen. A red herring big enough to ensure that the major law enforcement agencies would be kept occupied, whilst his real plan, his end game, was put into place. Captain Allan Murry was pivotal to its success. Everything was at stake for Salah El-Din. The year's frustration would soon be over. Then he would have the greatest prize of all, the Ark of the Covenant, which he emphatically believed the Templars had. The prize that would make him the most powerful man on the planet and the most powerful man since King David and King David's son, Solomon.

Two junior detectives were assigned to track the whereabouts of the merchant seaman called Alan Murry. Whilst Murry's ship, *Efach II*, had been docked in Port Buchanan, awaiting loading over a period of five days, French navy divers had attached a small tracking device to the propeller of the ship. The two junior detectives' plan was both creative and simple. Murry's ship, like most, was fitted with a small anode which sent out a low frequency emissions to deter barnacles and other crustaceans from attaching themselves to the underside of the hull. The tracking device had a similar low frequency emission to the ship's anode and was therefore virtually undetectable.

The two junior detectives would rely on the French navy, on exercise between the coastal waters of North Africa and the Azores, to track the low frequency tracker and relay back the ship's position. At a set time each day, a window of twelve minutes was made available on a United Nations satellite orbiting over West Africa. The French navy would relay the ship's position, tracked by their powerful sonar, to the UN satellite, which would then relay the information back to Interpol's communication headquarters.

However, cloud cover and bad weather conditions would mean that information was intermittent. By the third day at sea, the ship, heading on a new course, disappeared from the navy's sonar. Random sweep scanning was carried out, but the ship was lost in the relative density of the Atlantic shipping lanes. The search stretched as far south as the Gulf of Guinea, off the west of the Congo. No one guessed that the ship was sailing in the opposite direction of their search, heading at full speed for the Straits of Gibraltar, and into the waters of the Mediterranean on a direct course for Israel.

Date: First week of August 2008
Place: Manchester.

Dagmar Grey eyed the man and women in front of her with some disdain. She had already been interviewed by the police several times and was tired of the questions. She was guarded. It didn't pay to speak at length to the police because the eyes of the estate were everywhere. She knew that the Pit Bull had successors just waiting in line. For the time being Bill's cronies kept away, whilst the police where there. They suspected it was Tony that had killed their boss, Bill, but they couldn't be sure. They would wait. In their warped world they considered that what had happened to Bill was a domestic issue. If it had been business, then Tony would already be dead. Besides, as a user, he was still one of their best customers.

Dagmar had disliked the woman from the start. She was pushy, abrupt and too self-assured to be liked. The man she found cute; and she adored his American accent. It had been three weeks since her rape by Bill. She had tried hard to forget that night, but she couldn't. The constant questions by those she had no regard for, the 'authorities', only polarised her problems.

A young female police psychologist, Dr Glenn Fox, who had been assigned to Dagmar's case, had spent a considerable amount of time with the girl, but progress had been slow. It wasn't just the violent rape she had suffered. It was also her witnessing of the murder, the years of poverty, mental abuse and social deprivation that made Dr Fox's task almost impossible. The girl's future, Fox had concluded in her report, was irreversibly affected by the company her mother had kept over the years.

The two people sitting in front of her had nothing new to ask. Their questions were tedious. She had been asked them a hundred times in the last three weeks. Dagmar was tired of the woman's attempts to get her to say something she had no intention of saying.

Dominique's irritation was beginning to show. Jonathan's job, St Clair had told him, was to help fill in any pauses with bits of small talk and to watch and learn. Dominique had left no pauses. Her questioning was intense and she was getting nowhere. He was finding the experience frustrating.

He thought the plan of masquerading as Special Branch detectives from London was an ill-fated ruse, considering Dominique's impeccable upper-crust British tones and his obvious American accent. It was also plain to see that Dominique was not at ease with the surroundings. The conditions that Dagmar lived in would have unnerved most outsiders.

Dominique's Italian mother and British father had raised her in Italy up until the age of ten, when her mother died suddenly. Then she moved with her father to Great Britain. She had then gone to a private boarding school for girls, Mary Thomas's, in the heart of the Derbyshire countryside. After that she went off to finishing school in Switzerland. She had never wanted for anything. She was independent and strong willed. That this was the first time she had been onto an estate and into a council house was obvious to Dagmar.

A constant thudding three-chord beat came from one of the upstairs bedrooms. Dagmar said that it was her brother playing his favourite CD. Dominique remarked that in her opinion, it wasn't the music he liked, it was the noise it was making. And, either he was profoundly deaf, or soon would be.

The conversation and the questions had become repetitive and it was obvious that Dagmar had become bored. Jonathan empathised with her. As a schoolteacher, he knew how her age group thought and it wasn't the way Dominique was approaching it. He decided he had sat silent long enough. Dominique sat back and watched. Jonathan's words were kind and soft. He had a way about him that put the young girl at ease. Slowly, she began to open up.

The front room was dank and dirty. The red flock wallpaper, an attempt by her mother at some form of respectability, had been torn and ripped. No doubt boredom had struck one of her many offspring. The furniture in the room was old and worn from years of ill treatment. The carpet on the floor looked as if it had been a cheap remnant. It butted up to just one of the four walls. And the only piece of respectable furniture was the widescreen television. Everything they possessed had been battered, kicked and misused: just like Dagmar.

The girl eased out of her ridiculously high blue platform shoes and drew her legs underneath her on the chair, her growing ease becoming more apparent as Jonathan engrossed her in conversation. They talked for over an hour about fashion, school and even music. He found her to be highly intelligent, but she hid it well: it didn't pay to be academically gifted on her estate. Finally, he steered the conversation to the events of that night. There was really only one question he had to ask her. He crossed his fingers.

"But all of this," he started with conviction and easing himself forward slightly, "all of this you've suffered, Dagmar, will be meaningless if there are men like Bill, still raping young girls and supplying drugs on the streets. Who's next, a fifteen-year-old girl, a ten-year-old; your sisters? You have to help us stop this horror. Tell me who Bill worked for and I promise we will put a stop it."

What he didn't reveal was that thanks to their ghost man, Morgan Clay, they already knew who the dead man worked for. What they didn't know was the chain of command. If they could disrupt the chain, they might stand a chance of getting the elusive Arab out into the open. It was the only play they had available to them.

Jonathan smiled, his eyes remaining fixed on hers.

Retribution, she considered, would be justice for what he had done to her. Deep down, she wanted to show those bastards. The bastards like her mother's lover, Bill. Show them that she wasn't a piece of rubbish that they could treat as they pleased. She was a person, a real person: but she had spent long enough on the troubled estate to know what would happen to her if anyone ever found out that she had informed.

"I don't want to get into trouble. If people round here know I've talked, then I'm dead meat. You don't know what it's like. I'll get fucking killed."

Jonathan thought about it for a moment, then, much to Dominique's horror, who up until that point had marvelled at his communication skills, blew their cover.

"We're not Special Branch, Dagmar. We're not even police. I know it and you know it."

"I knew the posh bitch was dodgy," Dagmar blurted.

Jonathan loved the description. He turned to Dominique, whose face was stony. "You have to admit she has a point." The tension had eased in the room in one sentence and only Dominique failed to share in the humour of it.

"So, if you and Miss Selfridge here ain't pigs, what are you?"

Jonathan thought about it for a second or two. Of course, there could only be one answer, the truth. "We are knights, Dagmar, knights in shining armour. I promise the police will never get to hear about our conversation and neither will anyone else. You have my word." He gave another reassuring smile. It worked.

"OK, but you ain't got it from me, right?"

Jonathan nodded.

She lit a rolled-up cigarette and a huge cloud of smoke made its way to the yellow-stained ceiling. She then proceeded to tell Jonathan that when Bill was drunk he used to boast a lot, about his money and his business dealings. She said he was a big man with a big mouth.

She told him that for the past few months Bill had been travelling to New Street railway station, in Birmingham. Before that, it had been Paddington, and before Paddington, it was another main-line station; they changed every couple of months. She said that Bill used to leave the house about 10 a.m., every second Friday and return late. Bill used the stations to make their drops – their drug money – and to take new deliveries of drugs. The Pit Bull had the largest estate to work and often had two to three hundred thousand pounds to drop. He also ran other smaller estates through a network of thugs he called his lieutenants. Coupled with extortion rackets, prostitution and a few clubs, his takings were always high.

Dagmar looked over to the window. Her brother, who had saved her from the infamous Pit Bull, had entered the room whilst she had been talking. The thudding beat was now silent. She nodded to him and he smiled back. Tony hadn't been charged because no one was talking. The murder weapon couldn't be found and the police investigations were hampered at every turn. Tony didn't join in the conversation, but he lingered, making his belligerent presence felt.

Dagmar gave Jonathan the business card of Bill's barrister, a man called Timothy Crowthorp, QC. The barrister's home address and phone number were on the back. She told him that all the estate bosses had one, in case the filth lifted them.

Dagmar's mother had taken to her bed earlier that day, apparently grieving again for the loss of her man, but the house had the smell of whisky about it, fresh whisky. It wouldn't be long before she would have another man in her life; it never was. She was one of those people who attracted trouble and always in the form of men. Dagmar put out the cigarette in the overflowing ashtray and asked Jonathan if he had a woman. Jonathan smiled.

"I have only ever had one serious relationship, but not of the kind you're talking about. My relationship was one of devotion. It was love for someone I could not see, but then they let me down when I needed them, when my sister needed them."

Dagmar didn't understand, but Dominique did. She could see the pain on the ex-priest's face. Then Jonathan, with a mischievous grin, lifted the mood again.

"Oh, and I guess you could say I was kind of married recently, not so long ago, in fact. It was on a small Greek Island called Zakynthos, but that didn't last. The lady had a bad temper and a nasty habit of scaring me to death every time we went into a small church with a bishop!"

Dominique burst out laughing. She did have a sense of humour, then. He liked her laugh. She was radiant when she laughed, but Dagmar completely missed the joke.

Despite liking the American, Dagmar was eager for them to leave. She had told them all she knew. Now she wanted them out of her mother's house. Tony's eyes flicked back and forth between Dagmar and the street outside, nervously watching for anyone taking an interest in their house. It wouldn't be long before one of Bill's cronies would be around to see what the visitors had wanted, and more importantly, what they had been told.

Dominique stood up first. The barrister, Crowthorp, was definitely on their list to visit and with the information they now had, it wouldn't be too difficult to stake out one of the drops. The drops would be where the moneymen would be and the moneymen were always close to the man at the top. Dominique had turned to walk out, having put on her mirrored Ray-Bans – she was rarely without them – but she stopped suddenly. A photograph, in a cheap frame and standing on the TV unit, had caught her attention. She recognised the man's face immediately, even though she had only seen it for a few seconds, on a computer screen, in Scotland.

"Is this Bill, the man they call the Pit Bull?" she asked, but she already knew it wasn't. The man she was pointing to was Allan Murry, a sea captain whose details had been on an Interpol report over three weeks ago. She needed to know the connection between Murry and the girl's family. The answer was more than Dominique had bargained for.

"No," Tony answered curtly, as if the picture was a reminder of all the bad things that had happened. "It's the bastard's brother, Allan. The other fucker is the Pit Bull, Bill Murry. His brother came down last Christmas and we all had to have that fucking photograph taken on some chicken shit camera he had nicked. His brother stayed here for a few days and then they both went off to meet some guy in London. Bill bragged that they would be rich if the meeting went well. He said he was hooking his brother up with a big noise who needed a boat. Now the bastard's dead and I hope his brother gets it as well."

As soon as they pulled onto the M6, Dominique made the call to St Clair. She told him everything that Dagmar and Tony had said and, astonishingly for Jonathan, she even praised him.

"The priest did well, actually, far better than I had expected. In fact, I was sort of impressed, but I don't want him getting a big head or anything." Then her voice lowered. "St Clair, I need you to go into the data records on my computer. Please look at the Interpol file from three weeks ago, or maybe two back. There's a report about an anode tagging ops Interpol carried out on a ship that was docked in Liberia. The ship's captain is a man called Allan Murry; Murry is the brother of the recently deceased Pit Bull né Bill Murry. If what we have just been told is right, then I am sure that Bill Murry introduced his brother to our friend Salah El-Din sometime last Christmas. However, what I can't figure is what our Arab friend would want with a sea captain who has the same criminal tendencies as his late brother. I have a bad feeling about this, St Clair."

St Clair's immediate thought was drugs, but it bothered him. There were a lot of things beginning to bother him about Operation Roulette Wheel and this merely added to his unease. He had learned over the years to trust his instincts, no matter what he saw in front of his face. He put the phone down and started to write on a note pad. *UNITY, Ark, ship, drugs, bishop, McGregor, Courtney, Dukes,*

194

Captain, Murry. He filled the page with more words. He struck off all the words that were related, which left two: *ship* and *Captain.* Why would Salah El-Din need a ship and an unscrupulous captain? It didn't add up.

The journey back to Scotland was long, but the going was easy. Jonathan felt good about what they had just done; what he had contributed to the meeting with Dagmar. However, what pleased him most of all was the fact that Dominique was, for the first time, speaking to him like a human being. The verbal chastisements he had received from her in the first few weeks had now gone. He wondered if he'd earned his spurs.

Jonathan liked Dominique; in fact, he liked her a lot, despite her caustic manner at times. She was pretty, intelligent and had a presence he really liked. He had a sense that there was a softer side to her nature that she rarely showed. Perhaps it was the business she was in that made her the way she was. In some ways she reminded him of Courtney. She seemed to have the same drive, same focus and ambition. Her skin was tanned, like Courtney's, although slightly darker. She always smelt nice, something he had noticed that first day. In all the time they had spent together, though, she had never once asked him about his sister's death, or why he had left the priesthood. However, he guessed that she would have already read his file. He had learnt that they seemed to have a computer file on just about everyone else, so why not him?

The journey rolled on, the miles blending into miles as they made their way across the border and into Scotland. About an hour had passed and neither had said anything. Then she broke the silence.

"A penny for them?"

"Excuse me." Jonathan had been deep in thought.

"A penny for them. You have that expression in the States, right, a penny for your thoughts?"

"We do indeed have that saying. But I have far too many. Too many questions … no, I don't mean that. I mean too many unanswered questions. I'm afraid you would need a small fortune in pennies."

Jonathan still had no idea how many Knights the Order had, where they were, how many sanctions they carried out. How they funded their missions and, the biggest enigma of them all, why would St Clair say he had the Ark of the Covenant? On the night of their first meeting, St Clair had said that it was the Knights Templar who took the Ark of the Covenant out of the Promised Land and "the Order still guards its Charge today". It was the Ark more than anything else that played on his mind.

"Here," she picked a penny out of the loose change in the console, "what's the biggest one, priest? Your biggest question?"

"The Ark, of course. That's the one. To believe that you, the Templars, have the Ark, would be to believe that the Ark is worth keeping."

"You don't dispute it existed then?"

"No, I don't, because there are an overwhelming number of eyewitnesses' accounts from that time, but do I believe it did what it was supposed to have done? That's back to faith. Not my strong point of late."

"Do you doubt that the Ark has actually done what it is supposed to have done, what great tomes have told us it did: a vehicle, transporter, a powerful force unsurpassed on earth, a door to the Creator of man and His secrets?"

"I think I do doubt, yes. There is so much mounting evidence, from archaeologists and historical investigators, that throws new light on those ancient times. Some challenge the Ark."

"Such as what?"

"The Israelites were led through the desert by Moses for forty years to escape the Egyptians. Egyptian history would have some record of the event; it doesn't. There was no trace of the mass exodus and considering that the number of people was almost one quarter of the entire population of Egypt, someone would have noticed! Which means without Moses and the Exodus, then there would be no Ten Commandments, and of course, no reason to make a box to contain them, the Ark of the Covenant.

"My whole Christian belief, like millions of other Christians, has rested on the central core of the New Testament, the resurrection of Jesus Christ. An event we all know is disputed and one that caused great consternation and controversy in the early Christian church. Millions of people believe the resurrection story not to be true, but a distorted literal translation of the truth by the Catholic Church, again! In antiquity, there was a secret Christian doctrine that said the resurrection meant that Jesus Christ was 'reborn' spiritually, whilst still in his human form. To believe it any other way was said to be *'the faith of fools'*. The church, of course, denounced this. But if it were true, then it would eradicate the need for the Catholic Church. The *Treatise on Resurrection*, an ancient Gnostic work, explains that resurrection means the *'spirit dies when we are born but can be found, in life, if the chosen path is righteous'*. In life, not in death!"

Dominique drove on without replying, knowing he needed to get his frustrations out.

"I guess it really all comes down to a central issue, the crucifixion and the resurrection. If the resurrection story is not as the Church would have it, then their claim of apostolic succession, papal succession, is wrong. In *Apocalypse of Peter*, which I have read over and over again, it is written, *'Those who consider themselves bishops or priests and act as if they have received such authority from God are waterless canals as they believe the truth belongs to them alone.'*

"We know that crucifixion is a brutal death. It is a slow death, for the legs of a -victim are able to hold the weight of the body for a long time, for many days. If the legs are broken the victim suffocates as their ribcage is forced up. It quickens the death. So, sometimes, to speed death, the victim's legs were broken. However, the length of time Jesus spent on the cross was short, too short compared to the

197

many other accounts history supplies on crucifixions. If Jesus's legs had been broken, it would account for the brevity of the grotesque ordeal. However, the New Testament states that *'Jesus's legs remained intact.'* The Gospel of John, 19:32 *'The soldiers came and broke the legs of the first man who had been crucified with Jesus, and those of others. 19:33 'But when they came to Jesus and saw he was already dead'.* Really?"

He looked over to Dominique, but again she didn't answer.

Jonathan had sunk back into his thoughts. Dominique knew she couldn't help him with his questions; nor to find his faith again. That was St Clair's department. All she could do was listen and keep him safe. The time would come when Jonathan would know what he needed to know.

He opened the window slightly to let in some fresh air. "Do you think she will be all right, Dagmar, I mean?"

"Not unless someone intervenes. You saw how she lives. If it weren't Bill Murry, it would have been the next thug who moved in with her mother. People have to take care of their futures, because that's where they are going to spend the rest of their lives. The girl needs a guardian to protect her from the likes of Murry. Men like that are wolves in wolves clothing. She needs someone to take care of her future."

"You really think there is hope for her then?" Jonathan asked.

Dominique thought about the question for a few seconds. "Look at Joanne of Arc: she had already been dead eleven years by the time she would have been my age. We can achieve much in a short space of time if we have hope, and a little bit of help."

Jonathan smiled. He liked her analogy.

"You see, I believe there's something for us all to do in this world, priest. She just needs help along the way to find that something, just like you and I."

Jonathan decided that the 'priest' thing needed dealing with, before it got stuck there.

"Why do you all keep calling me 'priest'? I'm not a priest any more."

"I guess," she started, "it's a Templar thing . . . well, actually, it's a St Clair thing. He does it all the time. John Wolf is the Indian and Nickolin is the Russian."

"But," Jonathan replied in mild protest, "Wolf is an Indian and Nickolin is clearly Russian. I'm not a priest."

"Yes, and I'm not a girl any more, but that's my name, 'the girl'. Don't get too hung up on it. St Clair likes you. If he didn't, he wouldn't have bothered to give you a nickname. Take it as a compliment."

Now that they were in general conversation, something that had not happened without a growl or two from her, Jonathan decided to use the opportunity to find out more about her.

"How long have you been a Templar?"

"Over fifteen years now."

"Are you ever afraid?"

"Of course. I was shot in the shoulder and very nearly died on my first sanction, back in 1996 in South Africa. I was twenty." She saw him doing the maths. "Thirty-two, I'm thirty-two!"

He smiled.

"Look, this is the way I see it. We are all born to die; none of us gets out of this alive. It's the only guarantee any of us ever have about our lives. Doing what I do, well, it kind of makes me feel better about it."

"What made you become a Templar? Was it St Clair, like in Wolf's case?"

"In part I guess it was."

"He seems to have that effect on people, in a good way, though. I can tell that you like him."

"I love him," she said.

Jonathan hadn't been expecting that answer and for some reason it shocked him. "You love him?" The words left his mouth at speed, half question and half statement.

"Of course." She looked at him inquisitively, as if taken aback by his surprise. Then her eyes returned to the road.

A bolt of strange emotions hit Jonathan like a sledgehammer. He had not realised just how much he had liked her, but the jealousy was there. He felt it straightaway. He tried to suppress it, but it was too strong. He felt embarrassed, ashamed that he was being unfaithful to St Clair in some way. His feelings confused him.

"That's nice." It was all he could muster, given the circumstances. It was feeble and had about as much conviction as a politician at a campaign rally. His next set of words struggled out of his mouth in the same way. "I don't blame you, of course. He's very charismatic, I also love ... not in that way, of course. I mean ..."

The hole he was in was just getting deeper by the minute and he was the only one with a shovel. Then she did it again, another sledgehammer to his emotions.

"I should think so. My uncle is a good person."

"Uncle!" He looked at her in total astonishment.

"Why have you got that ridiculous look on your face?"

"But I ..." He didn't finish; his brief flash of jealousy beat a hasty retreat, giving way to a new set of emotions.

This was new ground for Jonathan and he was green around the edges, from head to foot, in all ways really. He was falling for her and he so wanted to tell her. He remembered the two assassins in the small church. Whatever had happened to his quiet, peaceful life in Washington DC, he thought.

They made the castle by nightfall

Chapter 14

The Drop Zone

Date: August 2008
Place: Birmingham

The manager of Birmingham's New Street railway station checked the pink official-looking form on the clipboard, then checked the man's security pass and papers. They were all in order and he signed in the appropriate place.

"Someone should take those bloody things down," the manager complained. "We are forever having them fixed."

The man, dressed in the usual white coveralls and who looked like the actor Sean Connery, smiled. He tore one of the triplicate forms from under the pink form and gave it to the station manager.

"Well, if there were no surveillance cameras in train stations to maintain, then I would have nothing to do and that would mean that I would be out of a job."

He laughed and the station manger laughed with him, then left the maintenance man to his work and went to check on a lost briefcase. With the station manager gone, the man in the white coverall checked the array of monitors and switches, then checked his watch. Two more minutes and the Knights would be inside the station. He studied the crowd of commuters rushing past on the screens: nothing out of place. But why should there be? No one knew he was there, but good habits die hard when your life depends on it. He looked again, then took out a small set of stainless steel tools from his hip pocket and removed the control panel cover. He placed two microchip circuit breakers into the relay system; the breakers were fitted with timers and would switch the security cameras back on in seven minutes. He checked the monitors again. They were all blank. The station cameras were down. Whatever was about to happen in the station would not be captured on tape. He replaced the cover. It took him less than a minute to render all the cameras in the station inactive. He left the station unnoticed. Every two hundred yards he stopped and checked his 360 degrees line of sight. He doubled back on himself once. Five minutes later he opened the door to the parked Jaguar, reset his watch and waited.

The Indian, John Wolf, and the Russian, Nickolin, stood inside the station entrance; they had arrived exactly one minute after the cameras had been rendered inactive. The Templars would spot their targets easily. They watched everyone's movements and body language intently. Criminals are edgy people in public places, especially when a drop is about to go down. Yet there is always an air of cockiness about them, as if they are untouchable. They watched for these signs.

With the information Dagmar Grey had given Jonathan and Dominique, the two Knights knew it would happen soon. It was the second Friday of the month. By checking the train times from the nearest station to Dagmar's house they knew they wouldn't have to wait long. They would then have seven minutes in which to complete the operation.

The first of them arrived. It was a little after 2 p.m. and the bustle of New Street Station had lulled. It would start again around 4 p.m. when the homebound commuters would descend on the station once again. They knew straightaway that he was one of their targets. Nickolin spotted him first, but didn't have to signal; Wolf saw him seconds later. A tall black man walked over and stood by a public telephone box. The telephone box was just under one of the security cameras and had a natural blind spot. He was edgy as he looked at his watch. His three minders, male Caucasians, tattooed, with focussed expressions, entered the station just ten or so paces behind him, loitering in close proximity. They might just as well have held up a sign saying 'Beware'. They were menacing just by their presence; it made the other commuters uncomfortable and they were given a wide berth. The fourth minder, was watching their exit route outside. The first of the estate bosses arrived two minutes later. His Manchester to Birmingham train was on time. The Templars had decided to close in once the first estate boss had arrived. That was all they needed. As they had expected, he stuck out from the 'normal' people. The Knights began their move. The Indian made his way past a group of Japanese tourists studying a large electronic timetable on the wall, confused by the array of numbers, destinations and arrival times. They were about the only people not to sense something was happening. Nickolin eased around the corner and stood next to the vending machines. They were both less than fifteen yards away from the black man. He had placed himself in the blind spot to make the drop; he hadn't noticed that the red lights were all off on the cameras. The estate boss moved through the commuters with a purpose. He was a small fat man, heavily tattooed, with a nose piercing that looked sore. He was carrying a little over seventy thousand pounds in collected drug money from the estate he worked for Salah El-Din.

The Templars had decided to terminate only one of the main estate suppliers; this would cause enough disruption to the Manchester drugs chain to have the effect they wanted. The sanction that St Clair had been given by the other eight Worthies had included any and all necessary terminations that might be associated with it. On this occasion, however, the estate boss was to live; he would carry a message to Salah El-Din.

Most of the estate bosses worked for Salah El-Din, especially those on the more notorious estates. They sold his drugs on their patches, collected the money and took their ten per cent cut. Every second Friday in the month, they would make their drop in the prearranged spot and collect a new consignment of drugs, ready for the Friday night's wage packets. The Templars were lucky: one more week and the drop zone would have been changed again. A drop only took place in the same city ten to twelve times before it changed, sometimes less.

Everything now moved quickly. Two railway police, who were busy evicting a noisy out-of-tune busker, didn't see what was going down, but they wouldn't be needed. It would all be over before they had time to react. Wolf moved in from the left. Nickolin closed in from the right. By the time the minders spotted the two large men approaching, it was already too late.

Nickolin's knee caught the first minder between the legs. Wind emptied from his lungs like a plummeting air balloon. Strong arms gripped his head and, with an effortless twist, his neck snapped. The second minder spun on Nickolin, his fist hurtling towards his head, but Nickolin, a trained combat soldier with years of bloody war in Afghanistan, and bloody years in a prison camp behind him, was ready. A straight-fingered jab to the minder's epiglottis made it impossible for him to draw breath. He spluttered, trying to inhale. The palm of Nickolin's left hand was pressed upwards against the man's nose as he reeled. The open palm of Nickolin's other hand hit the back of his left hand with a mighty blow, forcing the man's nose bones up into his skull. Death was instantaneous. As the third turned for the exit, Wolf broke past the Japanese tourists. He caught hold of the minder's sleeve. The man kicked and struck Wolf's thigh. Wolf brought his foot down hard on the man's leg. His shin cracked and he screamed with pain, shinbone protruding from his torn trousers. The man lay face down on the floor in agony. Wolf's fist hit him in the middle of his back, causing instant paralysis.

The tall black man had grabbed a stunned female commuter and had pulled a gun, which he now held at her head. His eyes glazed: he meant business. Wolf's eyes sank into his, his stare fixed and unwavering. Wolf pulled a flat-bladed throwing knife from the back of his belt and in one flowing movement threw it. It hit its mark, embedding itself into the drug dealer's forehead. The gun fell from his hand. By the time it hit the ground he was dead. The hostage ran, her mouth open in a silent scream.

The estate boss fell to his knees; he started crying, pleading for his life. Nickolin and Wolf searched the corpses. They relieved the bodies of all their money, and the drugs. Had they lived, they would have made twelve more drops that day in locations around Wolverhampton, Walsall, Tipton and Dudley. The Templars made their Order's mark, a small red cross on the foreheads of the dead bodies, and then took the estate boss's drug money. He continued to sob uncontrollably, but he would live to tell his story.

By the time the Templars were moving towards the station exit, the whole operation had not taken more than ninety seconds. The station police, like most of the commuters, were stunned into immobility. Wolf and Nickolin threw them the drugs and the money. Then, they were gone into the crowded Birmingham streets; minutes later the station's security cameras came back on.

The car, parked only five minutes' away, carried its passengers safely onto the Aston Expressway, before joining the M6. St Clair, changed out of his white coveralls, kept to the speed limit as he headed north. They drove back to Scotland making only two stops for fuel.

Back in the castle, everyone, including Jonathan, was fully debriefed. St Clair was pleased because this was the first time John Wolf and Nickolin Klymachak had worked together. It had gone well and to plan.

Lying in bed that night, Jonathan was thankful that he had not had to go on that mission. He didn't know if he could watch another death, despite the fact that the victims were all criminals and undoubtedly the world was better off without them. The act of killing had always appalled him and, now that he was personally involved, his conscience was not at ease.

St Clair paced the floor of the great hall where The Nine Worthies had sat at the long mahogany table and had sanctioned the death of Salah El-Din. He cleared his thoughts. Had they done enough to force Salah El-Din out into the open?

He knew that their target was too careful and too clever for them to attempt a long-range kill; he had shown his stealth on too many occasions in the past. And if they tried and failed, he would surely go to ground, and then it could take years before they got another chance and all their hard work and patience would have been for nothing. Their only hope was a close-up kill; it would be the only sure way to terminate Salah El-Din. But it was the most dangerous kind of hit because they seldom had fool proof escape routes. They had lost active Knights in the past because escape routes had become compromised. He couldn't afford to make any mistakes on the sanction.

His selection of Knights had been based on the assumption that the kill would be done close up. The Indian, John Wolf, had proved himself time and time again and was fearless in close-quarter kills. Now the Russian had also proved himself. St Clair had, rightly, banked on the fact that the Russian had been hardened by the guerrilla war he had fought and the hell he was imprisoned in. His ghost man and Dominique were two of the most reliable Knights he could have around in a bad situation. However, it was Jonathan that held the key to the sanction. Jonathan was the only one who had seen Salah El-Din's face. St Clair was about to gamble the lives of four Knights, and his own, in the hope that the ex-priest would be able to recognise the man when the time came – and hold it together. He hadn't told anyone his plan, least of all Jonathan. He would not tell the young American for his own sake. It was a lot to ask of him, but then again, there was a lot at stake.

* * *

Dominique also had trouble sleeping. Her mind was full of images and the ex-priest featured in them all. He was an unwanted presence in her very private life, but the subtle exuberance she felt when she was with him would not go away. Since becoming a Templar, she had always resigned herself to the fact that she would have no time for men, but he was changing all of that. She had liked him the first time they had met and had, probably for the first time ever, struggled to focus on her job in hand. Extracting information from him whilst masquerading as an agent from a bogus insurance company had been hard for her. And then again at breakfast at the hotel, she had watched him; she knew then that she liked him. Feelings are a funny thing, she thought; when they want to air themselves, there is little or nothing we can do to control them. Try as we may, they tend to have a mind all of their own. It was at times like this that she missed her father. He was once a major presence in her life, but not now. She knew she must concentrate on the job in hand. Dominique cleared her head of Jonathan and her nascent feelings.

Chapter 15

Search For The Ark

Place: A hidden location in Cairo, Egypt

Salah El-Din's scholars worked sixteen hours a day trying to unravel the mystery of the Ark of the Covenant's final resting place. They followed every lead, every twist and every turn in its journey. They read everything there was to read. Looked at everything there was to look at. Spoke to everyone there was to speak to and researched everything there was to research. Their labour was intense and focused on one outcome and one outcome only: to reveal to their paymaster where the Ark had gone. Anything less would not have been acceptable and every one of them was in no doubt what failure would cost them.

Salah El-Din was no fool. Shrewd, cunning, cautious and educated, he was also a murderer without conscience or moral and legal boundaries. For years he had believed that the ultra-secret organisation called the Knights Templar still existed. Over the years he had received a number of reports of a particular type of professional assassination. They all carried the same traits. All concerned religion in some way, and always the same assassin's mark was left on the bodies, a small red cross on the foreheads of the deceased. These were not the only frustrating clues he had uncovered over the years, but each clue was so obscure that, unless someone was looking, really looking, they would miss them; and even if they were really looking, had the skill, knowledge, resources, time, money and resolve, they could still miss them. He believed it was the Templars that had carried out those killings, but his efforts to find the secret organization had always failed and there were many around him who thought their paymaster was chasing empty shadows. Tenacious and ruthless, he worked day and night to uncover their whereabouts. For him, there was no other answer to the mystery of where the Ark went. It could only have gone to one place: the Templars. And he wanted the Ark, yearned and ached for it; it engulfed him. He had bled for it and he had bled others for it – many, many others. He believed it should be his. He believed he should be the master of the Ark and when he had it, he would be the most powerful man on the planet.

Salah El-Din had caught a lucky break a few years back. He had found out that some very old scrolls, almost hidden in amongst a bundle of ancient Coptic codexes, had come on to the market in Cairo. Their provenance a mystery, he believed the scrolls could be significant in his search and so he made it his business to get them. He learned that they had been first sold in 1996, in South America, then Ireland and then Berlin, before turning up some years later in Egypt. The person who was selling them in Egypt was a well-known Syrian illegal antiquities dealer, who had his shady offices just off Khan el Khalili souk, Cairo. There was lots of interest in the codexes because of their religious content in relation to Egypt's secular make-up. The only serious bidder for the scrolls was an international criminal by the name of Fayad Ali Sulima. Sulima mysteriously disappeared and was never found.

Over the years, in his search for the Ark, Salah El-Din had gathered together a disparate group of scholars who were experts in their fields. They were rich in knowledge and eager to take his money – for most, there was no alternative. The group, split into three teams and each headed by a senior scholar, focused on tracing the Ark's historical, theological and scientific references in order to determine its final resting place.

Hans Goutman, an East German history professor and author of several books, led the historical team. He had once had a promising career, until, that is, an indiscreet affair with a young female student. She had an exceptional IQ; she was admitted to the university three years early; she was attractive. Such peccadilloes were not uncommon, but, unfortunately for Goutman, the girl happened to be the daughter of a senior politician, and happened to be just fourteen. This was before German Unification in 1990 and back then politicians still wielded absolute power. His exit from the campus was swift; his exit from East Germany swifter, with the secret police hot on his trail.

Tariq abu Taha, an Arab scientist, led the science team. Originally from Jordan, Taha had enjoyed a brief spell at the Jordanian Ministry of Defence, until, along with two others, he was tempted to try to make more serious money by selling state secrets to a rather convincing CIA agent. Now he was on the run. His two accomplices hadn't been so lucky and their disappearance had been terminal. Finding sanctuary with the wealthy Arab, he was grateful to take his money and his protection. It suited Taha that there was absolute secrecy about their work and, more importantly for him, absolute secrecy regarding their whereabouts.

The final senior scholar led the theological team. He was an ex-Catholic priest and an experienced theologian. Henry Brubecker, an American citizen, had been a central suspect in the 1986 FBI investigations into child abuse within the Catholic Church. Facing twelve charges of indecent assault and rape against boys as young as ten, Brubecker had fled Michigan, where he had worked as a senior cleric and professor of theology. Salah El-Din found him in Columbia. Like all of the people that worked for him, Salah El-Din was quick to spot his potential and his weakness; he then made him an offer he couldn't refuse. Brubecker had been with him since the beginning and was the longest-serving member of Salah El-Din's scholars.

Each of the three men led teams of people who spent countless hours investigating, searching, reading and examining an endless sea of information and misinformation. Henry Brubecker and his team searched for references to the Ark, obvious and hidden; they looked for any clue that would show them the Ark's journey. They knew that ancient accounts were, more often than not, written in code so that the location of sacred treasure and details of religious practices would not fall into the hands of enemies. Finding, and then being able to separate fact from fiction, and then unlocking the code, was an overwhelming task that had beaten every authority that had tried to locate the Ark. Brubecker's scholars studied every version of the Bible, the King James Bible, the Greek Septuagint, the Vulgate, a fourth century Latin translation by St. Jerome, the Canonical Bible and many, many more.

It took Hans Goutman and his team nearly two years to study the *Egyptian Book of the Dead*. Some of Goutman's team laboured over works by the tenth-century Arab scholar, An-Nadim. They discovered many references to hidden treasure written on parchment and papyrus. However, these references laid false trails, dealing inconclusively with the mystery of *barabi* (pyramids), but nothing could be overlooked in their needle in an historical haystack.

Goutman and Brubecker combined their efforts when it came to looking at the Dead Sea Scrolls. The eight hundred scrolls, of which only half have ever been published, have changed the view of Christianity. However, once they had laboured over these, they quickly moved onto another collection of manuscripts, found not far from Luxor, in Egypt, the *Nag Hammadi*, written in Coptic, an ancient language extinct after 1600 AD, and buried at one of the most important times in Christian history. But, whilst fascinating, they were not leading them to the Ark.

Even the story of King Arthur was thoroughly researched by Goutman and his team because of its references to the Ark. Tariq abu Taha dispatched three of his team to Viroconium, a Roman City in Shropshire, where Arthur is said to have ruled. Whilst there they discovered the discrepancies between the two popular calendars, the year of Christ's crucifixion and the Anno Domini calendar, If

Geoffrey, the man most associated with the Arthurian legend, confused the two, then Arthur would have been alive around 500 AD. This fact would place him as a historical figure, but they could not find any scientific evidence or any factual link with the Ark. Abu Taha knew not to over-indulge himself in too much hypothesis. Early on in the research, his paymaster, Salah El-Din, had killed one of his team in a wild rage about the lack of progress. The unsuspecting scientist had endeavoured to explain to their benefactor that progress was hampered by the enormity of the task: 'like chiselling away at granite' were the words he had used. In a quiet voice, Salah El-Din had calmly explained that even if a tiny amount of water fell between the cracks in a granite rock, when it became frozen, it would expand and split the hardest of rock. Then he shot the researcher through the mouth.

Now all the scholars were focused, after that incentive, hidden away in Egypt where Salah El-Din had them housed. They wanted for nothing and regular deposits were made into bank accounts set up by their wealthy Arab benefactor. However, whilst they were relatively rich men now, they could not enjoy the rewards of their labours. Forbidden to go out of the palatial mansion situated on the outskirts of Cairo, they remained incarcerated and isolated from the rest of the world. Loyal servants to Salah El-Din, he saw to their every need and no expense was spared to ensure that their minds remained sharp and focused on their task: the Ark.

The whereabouts of the Ark burned a hole in Salah El-Din's soul; it felt to him that he had been searching for it for most of his life. As his criminal empire grew, so did the funds available to search for the Ark. The quest devoured him day and night. Never once did he question its existence. Never once did he believe he wouldn't find it: for him, it was just a matter of time.

All the fractured facts the scholars had, all the information Salah El-Din's money could buy: papers, endless books, ancient manuscripts, the bribery, the threats, the deaths, and their hard work, all led them to the same conclusion. The Nine, the original Nine

Worthies, had spent nearly twenty years excavating and searching the subterranean vaults and catacombs of Solomon's Temple. They had found the Ark, which had been hidden, and then carried it out of the Holy Land when they returned to France.

They unearthed the true story of a man called Wilson. Back in 1864, a contingent of British Royal Army Engineers, led by Wilson, was ordered to carry out detailed mapping of Jerusalem, by Sir Henry James, Director General of the Ordinance Survey. This included a detailed survey of the ruins of Solomon's Temple and a similarly detailed survey of the Islamic Dome of the Rock, which protects the Sakhra. They knew that Wilson's survey would be impossible today because of the complex divisions in Jerusalem, but even back then, religious sensitivities and mistrust had precluded any type of archaeological research. However, Wilson, already a veteran of many expeditions, was a persuasive man, and he somehow won the trust of the Turkish authorities that governed the land. What Wilson discovered was startling: Templar swords, spurs and a small Templar cross were found deep inside excavated tunnels that had been cut centuries before, artefacts that had no historical right to be there. However, despite all his efforts, Wilson left the Holy Land frustrated.

Two years after Wilson's discoveries, another young adventurer, a twenty-seven-year-old fellow Royal Engineer, Lieutenant Charles Warren, again attempted to unravel the mysteries of the birthplace of Christianity. Warren had been banned by the Ottoman authorities from excavating, but despite this he was still able to sink vertical shafts down into the ground around the Temple. Twenty-six metres below ground level he found, at the base of the original Temple platforms, Phoenician inscriptions which still remain a mystery to archaeologists. Like Wilson before him, he also found signs that the Templars had been there before him, but like Wilson, he, too, left the Holy Land no further forward.

Abu Taha, Brubecker and Goutman all agreed that it was the Templars that their paymaster should look to. However, the burning question was, did they still exist? Salah El-Din believed they did, but that they were so secret the world could not penetrate their veil of secrecy; he could not penetrate it, no matter how hard he tried. References to the secret Order were almost as ambiguous and frustratingly sparse as the journey of the Ark itself. However, finally, Salah El-Din's money had bought him two scrolls, which had left him and his team in no doubt that the secret Order still existed.

What they had yet to figure out was that the scrolls, which had once belonged to the Templars, had been stolen by one of their own, a man the Order now only referred to as the Fallen Knight. His real name was banned from within the Order. Through a network of brokers, specialising in the sale of religious artefacts, the Fallen Knight had sold the scrolls to a wealthy American in South Africa, for his private collection. He had stipulated that a sale could only be made if the documents never went public. This was agreed. However, the American unexpectedly died and his estate was savagely fought over by his five children and the scrolls were sold to a man in Berlin, with limited checks being done on the new buyer.

When he finally obtained them, Salah El-Din had not realised that the man who originally sold them must have had a connection with the Templars. It was Brubecker and Goutman who had suggested, some time after he obtained them and after unravelling a small part of the code, that the man must have had a very strong connection or was one of the Order. However, after preliminary searches, Salah El-Din had received the news that the man who had originally sold the scrolls had died, in Ecuador. The deaths in Greece and Birmingham proved he was getting closer to the Templars, but he knew he had made mistakes. Costly mistakes. Dukes might have been able to give him information, but he had him tortured without questioning him. He still hadn't listened to Courtney's tape. One of his men had broken into Jonathan's house before Meeks was able to get there. But Salah El-Din hadn't listened to the tape. He had not made the connection.

* * *

Date: August 2008
Place: The merchant ship *Efach II*

Captain Allan Murry sailed his ship on a true course through the Straits of Gibraltar. The weather was fair and the sea was calm. He would make his final destination as agreed. Already he could feel the sterling bulging in his pockets. He didn't know the fate of his brother yet, Bill, aka Pit Bull. The only person who could have told him about his brother's demise had every reason not to: Salah El-Din needed Allan Murry to make Israeli waters as agreed.

Murry knew what his true cargo was, but he was the only one. The rest of the crew thought that they might be carrying illegal arms. Murry's escape plan, once depositing his cargo, was simple, but they, his crew, didn't have one. He would request emergency docking from the Israeli Port Authority. They would insist that he weighed anchor some way off their shores. This didn't matter. He would be close enough: the wind would do the rest.

He would ask to be set ashore to negotiate a mechanics crew to repair his ship, which, of course, would be perfectly seaworthy. Once ashore, he would make for another ship, which he knew from international shipping agents he had contacted before leaving Liberia would be due to sail about two hours after he set foot ashore. He knew the first officer by reputation; a handsome payoff would secure his berth. Once the authorities had discovered what had happened, he would be in international waters and outside of their reach. Anyway, by then it would already be too late.

Israel would be the first country to suffer; it was Salah El-Din's natural choice. Then Great Britain would be targeted next, but he would offer a trade for the British lives. It would be the Templars' choice if the people died there. The trade would be to spare the lives of tens of thousands of British people in exchange for the Templar's

215

Charge. Having seen the deaths of the Jews, the Templars would have no choice but to make the trade.

However, things were not going as he had planned. He had taken the news about the Birmingham killings badly. He was a hunter who had become the hunted and he didn't like it. The Knights Templar had made their move and left their mark: they had left it for him. He hoped it wasn't going to get worse.

Date: 11th August 2008
Place: Timothy Crowthorp's home, Canterbury

Timothy Crowthorp QC was an outcast within the legal fraternity. Other lawyers disliked him and he disliked them – the feeling had always been mutual. He had shaken the foundation of their puritanical values and brought shame on their profession. His approach to the law was, to say the least, questionable. His practices challenged the fundamental tenet of 'I swear to tell the truth, the whole truth and nothing but the truth'. He made a mockery of the term 'law-abiding'. He provoked lengthy debate amongst the clerks of the court. They based their lives on traditionally accepted values and legal applications; he based his on money and greed. They saw him for what he was, a crooked lawyer; a pariah within the legal system. Since his appointment to the Bar, he had alienated himself from all of his colleagues and others that knew him. His association with his mysterious client was frowned upon. He had, it was whispered, turned native, become a crook like the client he represented. He had destroyed the popular consciousness of legal boundaries and stepped over the line with both feet.

Timothy Crowthorp had a nurtured disdain for the courts. Like all lawyers, he had started out on his career full of moral intention. He studied hard and was initially proud when he had passed the Bar exam, but greed was his weakness, and finding someone's weaknesses was Salah El-Din's speciality. Somewhere in

Crowthorp's make-up, his genes were flawed and at some early point in his career, the fault line fractured. Those who knew him best said that the turning point came when he started representing a wealthy Arab client. It was small pieces of litigation at first, but it was enough to hook him. It wasn't long before he had become trapped in Salah El-Din's world and the recipe for disaster had been mixed, left to stand and, finally set – he had become a crooked lawyer.

Whilst his peers laboured away in case law and the law of statute, he enjoyed the full accruements of crime. Truth, he would often mumble, has a tendency to impinge on one's finances. His newfound truth, he would muse, was not related to the truth promulgated by stuffy old men in silly wigs, spouting their wisdom on corpus knowledge: his truth lay in his accruing wealth. He was a master at creating 'reasonable doubt', even if it meant unreasonable lies. He saved many of Salah El-Din's criminals the inconvenience of doing time. He twisted fact and made supposition real. He would destroy accusers: 'I put it to you, Miss Smith, that this is in fact a case of regretted sex, not rape and that ...' The reasonable doubt was always just enough.

Crowthorp eased himself back into his favourite chair and turned on the TV. Life was good; he was rich and lived well in his Canterbury penthouse.

Dominique and Jonathan watched St Clair leave the car and head off down a side road, a mile or so away from the affluent St Dustan's Mews where the barrister lived. The business card Dagmar Grey had given them had located the man they hoped would give them the information they so badly needed: how Salah El-Din intended to get the Ark, and what his plan was. She put the car into first gear and pulled away onto the Whitstable road. Six minutes later she had found a safe place and parked the car 600 yards away from the barrister's house. She reached for the large blue bag on the back seat and told Jonathan it was time to go.

It was a chilly evening. St Clair pulled the lapels of his overcoat tight around his neck and shuddered. Endless shops and bars stood lit for nocturnal trade, their signs enticing, but not to St Clair. The breeze died. On the opposite side of the pedestrianised main high street, a gang of youths, heavy with alcohol, loitered menacingly, discharging empty beer cans in any direction that took their fancy. St Clair did not linger; he had no time for boisterous juveniles on this night. Moving with speed, St Clair passed the lifeless-looking houses of St Dustan's Mews.

The picture on the television set flickered: outside Crowthorp's phone line had just been cut.

Dominique pressed her cell phone keypad once; St Clair felt the single vibration inside his overcoat pocket.

The knock on the door was deliberate and authoritative. Crowthorp cursed loudly, forgetting that the entrance intercom hadn't buzzed, nor had he let anyone into the building. He rose from his chair. Again the knock at his door. Crowthorp muttered to himself and removed the security chain.

His flat was the top-floor penthouse of an exclusive block. Inside it was decorated to the highest standard and furnished with the most expensive furnishings. The only failing was his desolate window box, a poor relation compared to all the others in the block. He had tried to cultivate a passable window garden, when the mood took him, but he had achieved almost nothing. The planted greenery had long since given up on life and now there was little sign of it ever having existed.

Crowthorp was a small man, five foot five, with a balding head. He was thin and stooped when he walked. An only child, he found social pleasantries difficult and had a disagreeable habit of smacking his lips every time he spoke. He was unmarried, but had a series of girlfriends, all much younger than his fifty-six years. The fact they were only interested in his money never bothered him. He was a realist who liked to have young, pretty women on his arm when he was out. Tonight, though, he was in and alone.

Crowthorp had already convinced himself that it was a Jehovah's Witness. No one else would have the bad manners to disturb someone at this time of night, surely.

He opened the door and opened his mouth, pomposity at the ready. "You can jolly well piss o ..."

St Clair's fist closed it before the expletive got out. Crowthorp recoiled and fell over. St Clair stepped inside, pushed the door to behind him, left the television on and closed the curtains.

Dominique was irritated. She had stood silent and still, hidden in the shadows of the trees, with Jonathan. She had scolded Jonathan twice for nervously rattling the change in his pocket. Two dogs whined loudly. Their copulation over, they had become stuck. They stood facing opposite each other, tail to tail, still connected by their sexual organs. She was concerned that they were about to wake the whole mews with their whines and growling.

"Can't you stop them?" she whispered to Jonathan.

"What to do you mean, stop them? They've just finished."

"I know what they've just done. I was ten feet away. I got growled at twice. There're going to wake the whole place if you don't shut them up."

Jonathan took a tentative step towards them. "Hey," he whispered, "psst, get out of here, shoo!"

Dominique shook her head in dismay. Then she hurled a small stone in their direction. The dog happened to be in the way. With a yelp he took off, dragging his one-night stand behind him. Like a hideous crab, the dogs disappeared into the night. Dominique's gaze went back to Crowthorp's building. She waited for the signal.

St Clair had secured a groggy Crowthorp by tying him to one of the dining table chairs with nylon rope. The apartment was secure. He gave the signal.

Her cell phone vibrated once. Dominique and Jonathan made their way to the block of apartments. The front door was already open, left slightly ajar by St Clair. Inside it was dark. St Clair had already removed the hall and stairwell light bulbs. They crept silently past the other apartments.

At the top of the stairs they entered Crowthorp's apartment. Once inside, there was no conversation between them; they each knew what they had to do. St Clair administered the sodium thiopental straight into Crowthorp's main vein in his left arm. It would take about fifteen minutes to work. Dominique set up the video camera and tapped the microphone – it was all working perfectly. Jonathan looked at Crowthorp's bloody nose and winced.

The barrister was beginning to rouse. St Clair placed a blindfold over his eyes. He knew that when using a truth drug you had to know what the right questions were before you could get the answers you wanted. He didn't know the right questions; he would feel his way and keep his fingers crossed.

Crowthorp felt funny. He was aware that there were at least two people in the room, but his blindfold prevented him from seeing their faces. The first question came and it was easy. He had no reason to lie.

"What is your name?"

"Timothy Crowthorp and I'm going to sue the balls off whoever is paying you, old boy."

"Who do you work for?"

There was no way he would answer this one. "Salah El-Din." Horrified, he heard the words leave his mouth. What was he doing? This would get him killed. The punch, which had hit him hard, must have shaken him more than he had realised. He must gain control. He was a trained lawyer, the survivor of hundreds of bloody court cases, and he was not going to get caught out again.

"Where is Salah El-Din?"

"I spoke to him last night, at his Knightsbridge offices."

He gave the address. The questions went on and on and gradually it dawned on Crowthorp what was happening: they had administered a truth serum. Now everything he knew would come spilling out of his mouth. Salah El-Din would kill him for this. His life was over. For two hours he told St Clair the answer to every question he asked.

The Templars already had more than they needed on videotape to put Crowthorp away for a very long time, but they didn't have what they really wanted: how did Salah El-Din plan to take the Ark? The question couldn't be asked directly. They wove their questions carefully. If he didn't know about the Ark, they didn't want to alert him. Crowthorp knew nothing. Seemingly Salah El-Din had never disclosed his plan to him. But St Clair was persistent. Surely there was something he knew, no matter how small, something that would give them even the slightest hint as to Salah El-Din's plans? Then Jonathan suddenly remembered something. It was a long shot, but worth breaking the agreed silence for.

"Who is Allan Murry?"

Crowthorp raised his head, which had slumped onto his chest. It was another man's voice, a young man he thought, softer and mellower than the first questioner, American.

"A merchant seaman, a captain who has been on Salah El-Din's payroll for the last six months."

"Why?" Jonathan asked.

"I don't know why."

"Who would know, other than Salah El-Din himself?"

Crowthorp thought about it for a second or two.

"Stranks. Bob Stranks knows everything."

As they left Crowthorp's apartment, St Clair made a call to Clay. He told him that they needed to know the whereabouts of Bob Stranks; they needed to question him urgently. Clay didn't know where Stranks was, nor did anyone else except Salah El-Din himself. All Clay knew was that the log which logged people in and out of the building, indicated that Stranks would be gone for the next two days. This was not what St Clair wanted to hear. He had a bad feeling of foreboding that made him very nervous and it was getting worse.

Chapter 16

The Trade

Date: 12th August 2008

Place: 890-923 Knightsbridge Court Crescent, London

Salah El-Din read the details on the website, his computer screen the only light in his darkened room. He'd read the contents of the website many times, and many more like it – he'd read hundreds of websites on Israel. His eyes searched the words; they pierced the description with hatred.

'... *The State of Israel (Madinate Israel), split into six districts, covers an ever expanding 8,029 square miles. Today anyone wanting to follow in the footsteps of the father of the Jews, Abraham, would need four visas, for Turkey, Syria, Jordan and finally Israel...*'

'... *It is a secular state, made up of a religious populous of 85% Judaism, then Sunni Muslim, Druse, then Christians.*'

For Salah El-Din, 85% was 85% too many. He knew that the ratio would never be in favour of the Arabs. However, he had a way to make a start, but it would not be for the Arabs' cause alone, it would be for his own gain.

Salah El-Din despised all religions, but he particularly hated the people of Israel, for it was they, along with the British and Americans, that had evicted his family and many more like them from their home in Har Megiddo during the resettlement of the Jews so that the Hebrews could live on Arab lands and in Arab houses.

The cacophony of languages he heard in the busy souks

whenever he was in the country grated on his ears. Hebrew, Arabic, Yiddish and English intertwined in a corrupt parlance. Not being religious, he couldn't use that crutch upon which to rest his prejudices; he just hated. But he particularly despised the fact that the Jews considered themselves a special people, chosen by God to be the vehicle of His revelation.

He read the final paragraph on the website.

'... *For centuries they would be confined to ghettos, made to wear distinctive clothing and excluded from societies. Their harsh and desperate struggle was sealed in the Shoah (Holocaust).*

'*Prejudice begets discrimination, discrimination infects people and infected people persecute. Persecution is the haunted spectre that blights Israel's history and its people. Singled out by some factions as a power-hungry, demonic race, the Israelis are just people, people like everyone else.*'

The author of the website had added a footnote:

'*Hath not a Jew eyes? Hath not a Jew hands? Organ, dimensions, sense, affection, passions? Fed with the same food, hurt with the same weapons, subject to the same diseases, healed by the same means, warmed and cooled by the same winter and summer, as a Christian is? If you prick us do we not bleed?* – The Merchant of Venice, lll.i.63.

Salah El-Din turned off the website. He'd read enough. He poured himself a brandy and then eased into one of the leather recliners. In the background the music of Mozart played melodically.

Place: 890-923 Knightsbridge Court Crescent, London

Ted Skinner had to make the second call of the evening to his boss. He didn't want to make it. He desperately hoped Morgan Clay would arrive early for his shift, but he knew that was a false hope. The deaths in Birmingham were major blows for his boss; that call had been bad enough. This call, he suspected, had all the makings of being cataclysmic. He punched the four-digit number on the internal phone that would connect him with Salah El-Din's private suite. Skinner told him about the barrister, Crowthorp. He told him that their police informer had said that the police had reviewed the damning evidence against Crowthorp on a videotape that had arrived anonymously. They had put out photographs of Crowthorp at all the port exit points. He was arrested walking through departures at Heathrow in the early hours of the 12th as he was about to catch a plane for Portugal. Their informer said that the intruders into Crowthorp's flat, of whom there were at least two, maybe even three, had entered earlier that evening and had administered pentothal, the truth drug, into his system. They had also painted a small red cross on the door of Crowthorp's apartment. He told his boss that their informer said that Crowthorp couldn't remember much of what he had said to the intruders, but the police had the video recording of his confessions. The informer went on to say that he thought Crowthorp would be going away for a long time. Skinner relayed the message exactly as the informer had told him.

Salah El-Din exploded into a rage. He had no need to ask who the intruders were. It was all too obvious to him now. He knew Birmingham was the Templars. If it had been a regular hit, then the perpetrators would have taken the drugs and the drug money. Besides, they had left their mark, the red cross, and, they had left it for him. In Zakynthos they had also left their mark. Now Crowthorp. They were getting close to him. They knew more than he had thought: they knew too much.

He started shouting, spewing out his rage. He swore to destroy the Templars. He swore to burn every member of the clergy; burn their very bones. He swore to slit the throats of all his incompetent staff. He slammed the phone down and stared wildly at his bodyguards, who had entered his room because of the commotion.

Salah El-Din stretched and rubbed his eyes. He had already spent over four hours on the telephone. He had made twenty-three phone calls, all connected with Unity. He struggled to keep the other criminal bosses together. They were stupid and they were greedy, but he needed them. He needed Unity to stay together until his end game played out: he needed attention on Unity, not on him. The news about Crowthorp was a devastating blow. He had spent a long time meticulously planning every intricate detail of his plan. Now he would have to act sooner than he had wanted. The Templars had changed the rules. He could trust no one. Everywhere he turned he saw incompetence, but too much was at stake to fail. Now he would do the job himself.

Salah El-Din ordered one of his bodyguards to pick up Stranks and bring him back to the offices in Knightsbridge. He told him to tell Stranks to retrieve all of the information from the mainframe computer and send it on to France. He gave the bodyguard the addresses where Stranks would be. The bodyguard checked out of the building via Ted Skinner, as was protocol, telling him he was going to Bristol and then on to pick up Stranks. He then logged the two destinations into the secure 'locations' file.

Salah El-Din's anger still raged at the fact that the Templars would now know where his UK headquarters were. Crowthorp would have told them everything. He needed to move quickly, and he needed Stranks to secure his files – the files that detailed all his complex money laundering, through hundreds of banking transactions, all over the world. Once he had secured the files, Stranks would wipe the hard drive clean, including all of the computers in the last nine offices, the offices of Salah El-Din's illegal empire. The remaining offices in the building, the offices of his legitimate businesses, would continue as normal. Salah El-Din had other secure offices in Paris, Washington and Cairo. Each was connected to the others electronically, but he couldn't risk sending his data that way. There were too many electronic eyes.

Twenty minutes after one of the bodyguards had left to try to find Stranks, Salah El-Din had packed and left the Knightsbridge building with the second of the two bodyguards. His Mercedes left London and headed for a private airfield near Manston airport in Kent. Less than three hours later he was in France.

Despite parts of his operations now being targeted by the Templars, he was sure he could still get what he wanted, if he moved quickly enough. If he moved before they did. His original plan was to place the ad so that the Templars would see it in one of the daily papers, after his captain, Allan Murry, had murdered the Jews. After that he would make the threat against Great Britain. Once the Templars had seen the carnage in Tel Aviv, they would have no option but to make the trade. Thousands of British lives spared, for their Charge. It was that simple. But they were now too close for comfort. Now he would have to make the trade against the lives of the Jews, instead of killing them. For the time being at least, Great Britain was safe. Bringing his plan forward was a risk, but it was a risk he was prepared to take. However, its success now all rested on Murry.

Salah El-Din placed the ad in the newspaper that same day.

Ted Skinner knew there was a problem, a big problem. His monitor was going crazy. Inside the apartment of Salah El-Din there were no video cameras, unlike the rest of the floor, just thermal imaging cameras that showed people as red dots on his security monitor. Salah El-Din always detailed how many people were to be in his apartment at any time. Today there were three in the log. Skinner checked the log again: the three occupants were booked to be there all day. One of the bodyguards had left in a hurry and now he watched as the other two red dots disappeared off his screen, and then the light to Salah El-Din's personal exit went on.

The unexplained activity worried Skinner; it breached all the protocols. He called Morgan Clay for help and advice. Clay answered the telephone almost immediately and Skinner told him what had happened.

"The screen's gone crazy. He's gone and he didn't check himself out first. You know that he never leaves or enters without checking in and out, no one does; he doesn't allow it. Something's wrong, Clay, and I'm not sure what to do. What do you think? Can you come in?"

"Stop worrying," Clay said. "Happy to help." He saw his opening; it was too good an opportunity to pass on. He crossed his fingers. "We really need Stranks. Do you know where he is? You keep everything battened down there and I will get Stranks. We'll get this sorted, don't worry." He held his breath.

Skinner checked the 'locations' file. "We are only supposed to use this in case of emergencies. I could get fired for this. Got it. Stranks is at the same place the bodyguard has just gone, but the bodyguard is going to an address in Bristol first." He gave Stranks's address to Clay.

The Templar ghost man then made the call to St Clair. St Clair agreed that Salah El-Din was now out into the open.

"He's making his move, Morgan. He's playing his end game, but we have to act quickly. I'm still on my way back to Scotland from Crowthorp's, and I'm stuck in heavy traffic on the M8. There is no way I can get to Stranks."

"How about John?" Clay asked. "He might make it if he chartered a plane. If he can get there before the bodyguard, who's going to Bristol first, then we might learn what our friend is doing with a corrupt sea captain."

"I'll call John now. Good work, my old friend. I think your time there will soon be over." St Clair hung up. He then called John Wolf and gave him Stranks's addresses and told him to rent a charter plane, and hurry.

John Wolf was in the air in some forty-five minutes.

Date: 13th August 2008
Place: France

By the next day Stranks and the bodyguard had still not reported in, but the Arab had little concern for them. Stranks had disappeared before, lost in his world of perversion. The bodyguard would find him eventually.

Date: 13th August 2008
Place: MI5 Headquarters, London

Normally the decoding section of MI5 would spot the shrouds, ads placed in the personal columns of newspapers that are coded messages, and Salah El-Din's four by four column was no exception:

> *Box wanted, part made of acacia wood, part gold,*
> *in exchange for Revelation 1.7*
> *Reply to: Ikhwan al-Sufa*
> *The Priory of Sion @*
> *The total of the 'final destruction of the Temple'*
> *The total of Strathmore*
> *The total of 'Verily, in Joseph and his brethren are signs'*

Given enough time, the vast majority of shrouds are decoded, or at least a fix will be determined on their content, or the origin of their text. However, this one was giving them a great deal of trouble. All they had come up with was Ikhwan al-Sufa, meaning Brethren of Purity. Things were not going well. The ad didn't fit any known red-flagged organisation and they were becoming seriously concerned: something about the shroud had spooked them. The code section head at MI5 notified her commander that they might have a problem. The commander called his counterpart in MI6, who then made his way to Bletchley Park.

Date: 13th August 2008
Place: Bletchley Park

The Government's Communications Headquarters, GCHQ, was

called in to help. One of its senior members, Proctor Hutchinson, had, for the last five years, also advised on the Communications Electronic Security Group of GCHQ. CESG advises various government departments and armed forces on the security of their communications and information systems. Proctor Hutchinson had also been a member of the Order of Knights Templar since the age of twenty-nine. And, for the last fifteen years, one of The Nine Worthies, but of course his employers were not aware of this fact.

Hutchinson saw the request for assistance come in on the SIS intranet system. He guessed the possible origin straightaway. The religious connotation and the clue threads had all the hallmarks of their enemy and Templars' sanction target, Salah El-Din. Hutchinson waited for a couple of hours before suggesting the use of the organisation known to SIS as Pi.

From time to time, like secret intelligence services all over the world, the UK's SIS uses private outside agencies that have Omega 1 clearance to carry out certain classified assignments. The thing that made Pi substantially unique was that it truly was of an unknown source and it was known to have advanced intel and a communications network that spread worldwide. Not all of the work was accepted by the secret organisation Pi and, on occasions, it was they who provided intel to the intelligence and security services. They had last been contacted, and had dealt with, a security issue on the Greek island of Zakynthos.

As a precautionary measure with their new problem, the Joint Intelligence Committee approved using Pi's help in determining and deciphering the shroud that had their intelligence services so spooked. The telephone call was placed in the usual way, via the normal covert lines; the call would eventually re-route to an unknown address in Islington. The caller from MI5 spoke slowly, as he knew his call would be recorded. Later, the recording was replayed to St Clair by the Templar communications controller in Islington.

Date: 13th August 2008
Place: Glennfinch Castle

Again all of the Knights, except the Indian, John Wolf, who was trying to find Bob Stranks, had gathered in the control room, deep beneath the castle. The computers were working overtime. The plasma screen flashed with a thousand words and images. Jonathan's juxtaposition idea, used so successfully on the Greece problem, was tried again, but this time it was inconclusive. For nearly two hours the Templars worked to solve the ad. It was pretty clear whom it was from.

> *Box wanted, part made of acacia wood, part gold*
> *in exchange for Revelation 1.7*
> *Reply to: Ikhwan al-Sufa*
> *The Priory of Sion @*
> *The total of the 'final destruction of the Temple'*
> *The total of Strathmore*
> *The total of 'Verily, in Joseph and his brethren are signs'*

'*Box wanted, part made of acacia wood, part gold*' was, of course, the Ark. '*Reply to: Ikhwan al-Sufa*' was, they had decided right at the outset, a false trail. But that was it. After two hours they were no nearer to solving the puzzle than the decoding team at MI5.

It was Dominique who made the suggestion to switch off all the computers. The others were surprised. She told them that the only way they would crack the problem would be to use old-fashioned brainpower. The problem was not a set of random words; it was a puzzle, set by a human mind and therefore a human mind – or four, to be precise – was going to solve it.

The control room seemed eerily quiet and lifeless without the computers. Only the mainframe continued to operate. It churned away with a low hum in the background, still monitoring law enforcement agency communications from all over the world.

St Clair liked the idea of switching off the computers. Besides, his eyes were tired of the binary language that was spewing out of the monitors every second. He suggested they work in two teams. Dominique immediately announced her team, herself and Jonathan. The Russian looked at St Clair and raised an eyebrow. She never worked with anyone unless told to and then she would complain bitterly about it for days.

St Clair was the first to give an insight into the type of person who had composed the riddle by solving the third line. "The 'Priory of Sion' or Prieuré de Sion, is a centuries-old secret society," he said. "However, for those who know, the real secret of Sion was held in the place they would meet, a church in Rennes-le-Chateau, in France." Dominique knew all about the Priory of Sion, but for the Russian and Jonathan it was a history class.

"During a restoration of the small church at Rennes-le-Chateau, the priest at that time, Father Francois Saunière, was said to have discovered something hidden in a hollow column. After the discovery, they say that Saunière took his find to Paris. There he sought out a well-known esoteric leader called Emma Calvé, rumoured to be a High Priestess of an underground movement banned by the authorities.

"When he returned from Paris, Saunière began to make changes to his church. He erected a statue to the demon Asmodeas, who is the custodian of secrets and king of demons."

"From the Deuterocanonical Book of Tobit," Jonathan interjected.

"Indeed. And over the entrance of the church he inscribed the words 'Terribilis Est Locus Iste' – 'This place is terrible', or 'This place is terrifying'."

"When did all this happen?" the Russian asked.

"Saunière died in 1917. But after his death it was discovered that this poor priest from a French backwater had spent in the region of twenty million pounds building roads and sanitation systems and erecting a round tower called Tour Magdala, the Tower of

Magdalene. "Saunière is in good company. Other leaders of the Priory were Victor Hugo, Robert Flood, Sir Isaac Newton and Leonardo da Vinci."

"So you think the 'The Priory of Sion @' is Renneslechateau@?" Dominique asked St Clair.

"I do."

It was Jonathan who made the second breakthrough. "The total of the *'final destruction of the Temple'*. It has to be the Temple of Solomon, which was destroyed in 586 BC." He wrote the numbers down on a writing pad: 5+8+6. "The answer is nineteen," he informed them.

Then Dominique, realising it was numbers they were seeking, suddenly figured out the second. She ran over to her computer and switched it on and within a minute she had the second clue. "The total of Strathmore refers to The Earl of Strathmore, the seventh Grand Master of English Freemasonry in 1733." She wrote out the sum underneath Jonathan's' answer, 1+7+3+3. "The answer is fourteen."

St Clair had been scribbling on a note pad; he told them that the next figure was also nineteen. He wrote out the sum, 12+7. "The total of *'Verily, in Joseph and his brethren are signs'*. It's a quote from the Koran, Surah twelve, Joseph, verse seven.

Now they had a total number, 191419. They thought at first that it was a PO Box number, but decided it would be too obvious. They knew that Salah El-Din had created the conundrum so that the intelligence agencies would not be able to decipher it and a PO Box number was much too simple. Dominique thought that the clue, 'Reply to: *The Priory of Sion @*', was interesting because Salah El-Din had used the symbol @ instead of the word 'at'. This would have been deliberate.

Nickolin thought that the answer had to be some kind of address. "What's the use of the ad without a reply address? It must be an e-mail address, safe and untraceable. He wants us to reply to him via an email address, but what is the Priory de Sion?"

Now St Clair wrote out the e-mail address, changing the Priory of Sion to Renneslechateau@191419. Dominique finished it. She told them it needed a country, so as Rennes le Château was in France, they added '.fr'. Now the e-mail address was complete, Renneslechateau@191419.fr.

Now there was only one part of the puzzle left. What was Salah El-Din offering to exchange for man's greatest treasure, in exchange for 'Revelation 1:7'. Jonathan quoted the scripture from memory. "Look, he is coming with clouds, and every eye will see him, even those who pierced him."

Despite two more hours of intense debate, the Templars could not agree on what 'coming with clouds' meant. It was left to St Clair to decide what to do next and he had no hesitation. They would go along with Salah El-Din. They needed to know what the exchange would be and they needed him out in the open. It was imperative that the Indian found Stranks now.

Their reply e-mail was brief; this time, however, there was no need for codes. St Clair wrote it, then read it out to them. "Son of Ayyub, what would you trade? Surely if the box existed the price would be beyond any man's reach."

"Ayyub?" Jonathan asked.

"He was Saladin's father", St Claire replied.

Dominique typed in the message and hit the send button.

234

Chapter 17

End of Days

Date: 14th August 2008

Place: Luton

Wolf thought that his day couldn't get any worse, but Stranks was about to prove otherwise: the news would be devastating for the Templars.

Wolf had found Stranks at the address Clay had given St Clair, a male brothel-house just outside of Luton, a place where male prostitutes, as young as seventeen, could be bought for sex, any kind of sex. Stranks was a frequent visitor.

The doorman welcomed Wolf. The one hundred pounds entrance fee had been inflated by an extra twenty pounds – the doorman had done well that night. Wolf moved into a large, dimly lit room with erotic murals adorning every wall. There he found an assortment of degenerate customers, drinking heavily and eyeing up the boys; the perversion of his surroundings made him uncomfortable.

After a few minutes Wolf nodded to a young man, no older than eighteen. The young man led Wolf away. They made their way up the wide staircase and onto the first floor. A dimly lit corridor revealed a series of rooms on either side; for most, the red lights outside their doors were on. The young man made for one of the green-lit vacant rooms, but Wolf stopped him and asked him if he knew a man called Stranks. He gave the boy a fifty-pound note. The young man pointed to a door ten yards down the corridor, the red light was on. He didn't have to be told to leave.

Stranks's young prostitute had half-filled the small plastic bottle with water, and then covered the top with silver foil and secured it with an elastic band. He lined it with some ash from a cigarette and then crumbled the soft, cream-coloured, substance onto it. He lit the contents and smoked it through the shell of a ballpoint pen, which was sticking out from the side of the bottle. The boy had lost half of his body weight, but that didn't matter to him anymore; it hadn't done for a long time. A cloud of pale smoke rose up the shell of the ballpoint pen. The boy inhaled the heady, sweet taste from the fumes. He felt the rush even before he had finished breathing it in. Within seconds the overwhelming dizziness had gone, replaced by a sensation of clarity and calm, a direct hit to the nervous system.

Stranks supplied the boy with the drugs. The boy, once high, would agree to anything Stranks wanted and, more importantly, he would beg Stranks to do it. With a drug-induced partner, Stranks was able to indulge himself in violent sexual acts and lose himself in his own abhorrent world.

It was a desperate scene and incongruous to Wolf as he walked into the room. He lived his life believing in the righteousness of man's respectful treatment of his fellow man. Shaken, he made the sign of the cross over his chest upon entering.

"Blessed are the peacemakers, for they shall inherit the earth," he whispered underneath his breath.

Stranks, indignant at the interruption, rose and hurled abuse at the intruder. His pitiful, wiry little body was already sweaty.

The young boy, who had lain underneath Stranks just moments before, made for the door. Wolf stood aside for him. The boy ran out of the room and then Wolf slammed the door shut. He hit Stranks twice on the side of the head with his fist and Stranks went silent.

"Do you want to further amplify your complaint, you low life?" Wolf barked.

Dazed and trapped, Stranks recoiled. The pain shot down his neck and confusion swirled around his head. Then he attempted to make for the door, but Wolf kicked him between the legs, and Stranks sank to the floor in a gasping heap.

Less than three minutes later, Stranks had answered the question that had been troubling St Clair all this time. The question Jonathan had asked Timothy Crowthorp; the question that would reveal Salah El-Din's end game. What did the Arab want with a crooked sea captain called Allan Murry? Now the Templars knew.

"God, what have you people done?" The horror of what Salah El-Din was planning hit Wolf like a tidal wave. "Tell me everything you know about the anthrax," he demanded of Stranks, "or I swear to God, I will put a bullet through your skull right now. And I mean tell me everything."

Stranks began to mumble, barely audible. "It's an acute infectious disease, caused by a spore-forming bacterium called *bacillus anthrax.*" He had trouble breathing; the pain from his groin was severe, but as ever, the computer genius was precise and methodical, almost clinical in his recital. "It's normally found in cows, sheep, goats and camels, and other herbivores. Humans contract it if they have been exposed to infected animals. It can be contracted through the skin, inhalation or gastro-intestinally. If it's not treated it leads to death. Inhalation is the worst, though, because it causes symptoms much like the common cold so victims are unaware of their fate. After several days breathing becomes difficult, then shock sets in. Meningitis frequently develops. Then it's too late. Inhalation of anthrax is normally fatal. It does not smell or taste and its spores are too small to be seen by the human eye. People don't have time to seal up their windows because by the time they have finished, they will already have been infected."

John Wolf was thrown. This was unlike anything they had dealt with before. Bullets and explosions are instant, chemicals normally act within seconds, but biological attacks can fester for days without anyone knowing that they are probably already as good as dead. His heart sank. He then asked which form of anthrax Salah El-Din intended to use. But he knew, deep down, what the answer would be.

"Inhalation, the deadliest. He has a lot of it."

Stranks had just confirmed his worst fears.

Wolf made the call to Scotland. This time he didn't route it via Islington for security; there wasn't time. This time he called direct. The clock was ticking: they now had a potential cataclysmic disaster on their hands and Wolf had no idea what to do next. He just hoped and prayed St Clair would. He told St Clair everything; the call was short and precise. He then made a call to Morgan Clay and brought him up to speed. They agreed a time and place for Clay's pick up. Clay would now put his exit plan into action. Wolf would pick him up the next day. Wolf placed his cell phone back into his pocket and looked in disgust at Stranks. He had got just about everything he was going to get from him. The computer freak was a crumpled, sobbing heap on the floor. Stranks felt no shame or pity for the thousands of Jews who were about to die, only pity for himself.

St Clair had told the Indian to leave after he had everything from Stranks. Wolf now had everything he wanted, including all of the passwords for Salah El-Din's computer network. St Clair hadn't told Wolf to terminate Stranks, but then again, he hadn't told him to let him live either. The image of what Wolf had seen upon entering the room was still imprinted on his mind. Snapping Stranks's neck would be so easy. His life would not be mourned by anybody.

Outside the room a floorboard creaked faintly. Wolf moved to one side; the handle turned and the door opened. Salah El-Din's bodyguard stood in the doorway. His eyes searched the room, assessing the scene. In less than a second he had already concluded that Stranks had talked to the unknown stranger. He had caught Wolf unaware. The bodyguard was a large powerful man, like his twin brother. He had entered the room with his gun in his hand. Wolf's gun rested in the holster, strapped to the left of his ribcage. The bodyguard's gun, a Beretta 92, was the most tested and trustworthy weapon in the world. There was no way his semiautomatic was going to fail when he pulled the trigger.

Wolf had been in many tight situations over the years. Sanctions had gone badly wrong before, but he had always managed to secure a sanction and get out without a scratch. This, he pondered, may well have to be the exception. He intoned a prayer in his native Onondagon language and asked the spirits of his forefathers to protect him. Brave to the last and true to his Shawnee blood, Wolf took out his knife and, holding it in the palm of his right hand, beckoned the bodyguard with a flick of his other hand. The bodyguard smiled, a big, broad grin. Wolf could see he was interested.

The bodyguard dropped the gun and kicked it outside the room. Wolf moved instantly, fast. He caught the bodyguard on the arm and cut him. From the pocket of his long, black, leather coat, the bodyguard drew his knife. It was seven inches long with a carbon fibre base and a thumb-stud for grip. He raised it, and then went for Wolf, catching him on the neck. The cut was deep, but Wolf, his concentration too intense, scarcely noticed.

The two men cut and thrust their blades at each other ferociously. Round and round they circled, stabbing and slicing in an ever-decreasing circle, their eyes never leaving the other's. The bodyguard was good, a naturally gifted knife fighter, quick thinking and fearless at close-quarter combat.

Wolf had already been cut four times, but he was still alert and faster. The bodyguard, thrusting his knife at Wolf's face, over-compensated for Wolf's response and slightly lost his footing. Wolf, anticipating the move, hit the floor with a perfectly executed forward roll and then, on his way back onto his feet, drew his blade across the back of the bodyguard's knee joints. It was a powerful slicing action that inflicted maximum damage. The bodyguard's cruciform ligaments and sinews severed, all stability went from his legs. He toppled. Instinctively, he looked for his gun, but it lay ten feet away outside in the corridor. Blood poured from the back of his legs.

Stranks watched the horror unfold. He knew that if the bodyguard won, he might be able to convince Salah El-Din that he hadn't talked, but if the Indian won, then his life would surely be over. He could make a dash for the gun. It seemed so close, almost within reach. If he was fast enough, he could get it and do the Indian before he realised what had happened. The bodyguard was watching Stranks, willing him to get the gun. Wolf followed the bodyguard's eyes to Stranks and saw where Stranks was looking.

"I'm done messing with you two!" roared Wolf, his anger boiling over.

The fourteen-inch, bone-handled knife hurled through the air at an explosive pace. Sleek and aerodynamic, the knife hit the bodyguard in the neck, cutting his main artery like cotton. Blood spurted from the wound and he lay dead in an instant.

At that moment, Stranks scuttled across the floor to within reach of the Beretta. His hand stretched out and his fingertips touched the handle. One last effort and his hand grabbed the gun, tightening around the grip. "I'll fucking do for you, you fuck ..."

Wolf's foot hit him in the middle of his back. Dazed, he registered the weight of Wolf on top of him. The twist was made in one flowing movement. The neck gave way and snapped instantly. Stranks would never bother young boys again. Wolf made the sign of their Order on the foreheads of the two dead men, a small cross, bloody and red. Then he left.

Date: 14th August 2008
Place: Glennfinch Castle

St Clair had listened in horror at the other end of the phone as Wolf relayed what Stranks had told him. Murry was carrying enough anthrax on board his ship to wipe out the population of two cities, all of it bound for Tel Aviv. The bacterium had been prepared so that it could be released into the atmosphere: inhalation anthrax, the deadliest kind. Now the last part of Salah El-Din's ad made sense to the Templars. The final part of the puzzle they couldn't get: - *the box in exchange for revelations 1.7.* Revelation 1:7 *'Look, he is coming with clouds, and every eye will see him, even those who pierced him'.* They had worried about the words 'with clouds,' which had sounded ominous. Now they became horribly clear: anthrax spores would be released into the atmosphere to kill thousands of Jewish men, women and children.

Wolf had told St Clair that Stranks had made the purchase of anthrax for Salah El-Din. Using a series of false Internet sites, he had been able to hide his communications and the shipment order went undetected by the various law enforcement agencies. A well-organised gang of African smugglers, out of the Congo, had moved the anthrax overland until it had arrived in a Liberian port, the night before Murry sailed.

St Clair had told Wolf to pick up Morgan Clay and then make their way back to Scotland. Now that the end game was known, it was too dangerous to leave their ghost man inside Salah El-Din's organisation.

Calls were then made one after the other. St Clair contacted MI5 and MI6. The Templars, known only as Pi by the two UK intelligence agencies, were known to be reliable and their integrity beyond doubt. The news was taken as fact and thus treated with extreme seriousness. St Clair relayed a set of instructions to the agencies. Within less than thirty minutes of St Clair's phone call, both agencies would be given the authority by the Joint Intelligence Committee to co-operate with the Pi proposal. The hunt for the ship, *Efach II*, was all that mattered now.

The Israeli authorities were alerted. Civilian biodefence strategies were put into place. Bioterrorism planning and response manuals were brought down off the shelves. Health Agencies, Disaster Relief and National Security all went into overdrive. Israel was on code red emergency: full alert. They braced themselves.

* * *

Place: Bahrain

Twelve Navy Seals, on joint US military exercises in the Sultanate of Oman, received their first injection after being flown to Bahrain. Upon their return, each Seal would be tested by isolating any anthrax from their blood, skin lesions from respiratory secretions or by measuring specific antibodies in the blood. However, the Seals knew that the injection administered in Bahrain would do little to protect them if they were exposed: it would be too little, too late. But they each volunteered to join Operation Roulette Wheel anyway.

After the injections they awaited the arrival of an operative who would lead their mission, for which, as yet, they had no details. The Russian, Nickolin Klymachak, was on his way to Bahrain one hour later, in a jet supplied by the RAF. He left Scotland from RAF Golspie, just north of the Moray Firth, and would be in Bahrain in just over four hours.

American spy-planes, on active service in the Middle East since the Iraqi invasion of Kuwait marshalling the no-fly zone, reset their flight plans and started their scan of the Mediterranean. Interpol was immediately contacted and the two junior detectives sent the frequency details of their anode which they had placed on Murry's ship. The two young detectives, who had thought that their days at Interpol were numbered because they had lost Murry, now assisted the American Navy and Air Force. At the same time, there was a lot of comms traffic between various law enforcement agencies regarding Unity. However, St Clair had now worked out that Unity was a red herring and had been used by Salah El-Din to divert attention away from himself and his real end game.

Now the search was focused on the Mediterranean. The American Navy and Air Force scanned and swept vast areas of sea, hoping to pick up the anode's signal – a long shot by any stretch. GCHQ put their electronic mastery to land coverage. Six hours later it paid off. They had intercepted part of a telephone conversation made between two cell phone users. One was from a land base in Europe, the originator, and the other, from some kind of vessel in the Mediterranean, the recipient. It had been faint, but they believed they had enough to confirm it was the target. The Americans mobilised everything they had available to get a visual on their target. A telexed transcript of the brief conversation was relayed back to Pi. It read:

Recipient: *'It will be pushing it.'*

Originator: *'Then push it, Captain. You must move your plan forward. The cargo must be in the target location by the 16th or the deal will be off. It must be ready to deliver to the Jews by the 16th. Then you are to hold offshore and await my instruction.'*

Date: 14th August
Place: The merchant ship *Efach II*

Allan Murry's cargo ship sailed on with him oblivious to the furore that was ensuing. His destructive cargo lay sealed and dormant in the depths of the ship's hold Number 4. Murry, still unaware that his brother was dead, could smell the sterling that would make them both rich men.

The change of plan did not concern Murry. Instead of weighing anchor in the Aegean Sea for a number of days, as previously planned, he would now sail straight for the waters off Israel; he would be there by the 16th. He left the wheelhouse and made his way below decks to cargo hold Number 4. To crates marked 'Agricultural Chemicals', he attached the explosives. The explosion would tear a hole in the side of the hull about fifteen feet wide. The shore winds would do the rest. It would carry the cloud of odourless and tasteless *bacillus anthrax* spores through the air and towards Tel Aviv. He knew his boss was trading something really important not to release the anthrax. He didn't know what. But he also knew that once his boss had it, he had instructions to release the bacterium anyway. He set and armed the timers in cargo hold 4. All was going to plan. He would be long gone off the ship by the time the explosions started, but his crew would not.

Date: 14th August 2008
Place: Glennfinch Castle

St Clair, Dominique and Jonathan stood around the control room waiting for the email to come in from Salah El-Din. There was nothing they could do other than drink more coffee and wait. Thanks to John Wolf, the Templars now knew Salah El-Din's end game. He would offer the lives of thousands of Jews in exchange for their Charge, the Ark of the Covenant.

St Clair knew that if the Arab believed his plan was still secure then he would want to make the trade soon. However, if he found out that they had got to Stranks and knew about the death ship, then he would go to ground and they would never get to him.

"What happens if they don't find the ship before he wants to make the trade, St Clair, what will we do then?" Jonathan asked.

There was no hesitation. St Clair had already made up his mind, despite the unacceptable risks to their Charge. "I will take our Charge from its hidden sanctum and we will meet with the Arab."

Dominique was quick to react. "That's crazy. People will die."

"And if I don't, Dominique, people certainly *will* die. Whenever and wherever the meeting is, if the Russian hasn't taken the ship, then I must take our Charge out of hiding. The Arab will want to see it for himself and, whilst this exposes our Charge, it also exposes him. We need him out into the open so that we can kill him. If he wants to see it, he will need to get close enough to look at it. All we have to do is make sure he doesn't get it.

"If the meeting is soon, it may not give Nickolin time to find the ship. If the meeting is later, then the chances greatly increase that Salah El-Din will find out about Stranks, but those are the cards we have been dealt."

For the next few hours no one moved out of the control room, their eyes fixed on Dominique's monitor. Then, five hours later, the message box flashed 'new message'. Dominique hit the 'open box' icon on the screen and they all gathered round it. Salah El-din's e-mail was short:

Hasidim, (Pious Ones) *a nation of people spared in exchange for the box. You have 30 minutes to reply.*

Murry's cargo ship was not in position yet, but if they didn't find it soon it would be too late. St Clair needed to buy the Russian more time. His fingers worked the keys. He had no choice; he had to go along with it. He hit the send button:

Hic Amittitur Archa Federis (Here is yielded the Ark of the Covenant). *Tell me where and when.*

Date: 15th August
Place: Bahrain

The twelve Navy Seals met their mission leader. Their sergeant wasn't happy about an alien leading his team. The twelve had trained hard together, and an outsider could jeopardise their mission, especially one they had never met before. The sergeant had informed his men that once they were on board the ship, he would assume command. He would not risk the lives of his men for a stranger. He would not risk his own life for some desk-based brass the Pentagon thought might be useful. However, the desk-based brass turned out to be a war vet with more combat experience than all of them put together, and harder and meaner than anyone they had met before.

The drop was made. Thirteen men splashed into the sea, the plane looped once and then disappeared into the horizon. Parachutes were reeled in and the inflate cords on the two Raider inflatables were pulled. The thirteen men would spend all day practising in the inflatables for a craft-to-craft sea boarding.

Date: 15th August 2008

Place: 890-923 Knightsbridge Court Crescent, London

Morgan Clay entered the building in Knightsbridge. The glass phial he had in his coat pocket would not raise the alarm when he entered the basement and passed through the metal detector.

On his last scheduled inspection of the day, Clay entered the room containing the powerful mainframe and carried out all the checks as usual. Then he copied all of the data, using the passwords Stranks had given Wolf. He then placed the phial at the back of the mainframe and attached a small plastic charge to it. Once the charge was triggered, it would take less than five seconds to empty the contents of the phial through the back grid of the mainframe's casing. The highly corrosive acid would begin to eat away at everything and eventually render the whole of the mainframe inoperable and beyond repair. Salah El-Din's lifeblood, his communications network, would shut down terminally. Without Stranks there, any inspection by an untrained eye would simply reveal a mass of electronics that had just burned out. By then it wouldn't matter, because Clay would be long gone and on his way back to Scotland with John Wolf. A swipe card to get to the top floor of the Knightsbridge building, along with the copied data, would be sent to Scotland Yard before they left London.

Later that day, and after finishing his shift, Clay met Wolf at the agreed meeting place. Wolf had parked the Range Rover just off Belgravia. Wolf had already been to Clay's apartment, picked up his things and wiped the apartment clean. Clay wouldn't be returning to the flat he had used for over a year.

Their plan was to wait in London until St Clair called them. Then they would drive to the offices of a courier service. There the copied data, the codes and full instructions would be couriered to Scotland Yard. Wolf eased the Range Rover into the traffic and the two Knights mingled with London commuters.

Date: 15th August

Place: Glennfinch Castle, 10 p.m.

The e-mail from Salah El-Din flashed on the screen.

Let's trade tomorrow. 7 a.m. Bring the box in a white rental van. You are allowed one other car to protect your cargo. Once we have confirmed the authenticity of your cargo, I will give you the location of my cargo. A nation will thank you. Map Ref ...

The e-mail went on to give the location of the meeting point. Now St Clair knew for sure that he would have no other choice than to take their Charge from its secret hiding place to the meeting with Salah El-Din. He needed to move fast; there was much to be done. He made the call to Islington and over the next few hours a task force of armed Knights began to gather at a small private airfield in Yorkshire. The next call he made was to Morgan Clay. He gave the instructions for him and Wolf. Now St Clair's own end game was finally being played out.

Date: 15th August 2008

Place: Somewhere in London

The call came through from St Clair, routed via the controller in Islington. After hanging up, Clay pressed the small detonator in his pocket; the phial would shatter in five seconds. Wolf turned the Range Rover around and they headed for the offices of a local courier services company. After depositing the package, they would drive through the night and head for the meeting point with Salah El-Din, which St Clair had now given them.

Date: 15th August

Place: Bahrain

It was getting dark. The Seals had been practising for most of the day.

They were wet and tired. The sound of a helicopter became audible – thirty minutes early. The mission leader went on the comms. The message came back: Murry's ship had been found, The mission was a go.

The death ship had been put somewhere within a hundred mile radius, thanks to the cell phone interception. Naval intelligence then cross-referenced every ship known to be sailing in the heavily congested waterways against their highly sophisticated nautical gridding maps, but it was still a needle in a nautical haystack. A hundred-mile radius at sea is a long way, and not all the ships spotted could be traced back through their last port authority. Not everyone was registered and not every port authority was friendly. Finally, it was a small anode-tracking device, no bigger than a cigarette lighter and with a restricted range of thirty nautical miles, which had given them Murry.

The American plane was returning to its base after endless, fruitless sweeps of the vast blue ocean to refuel. In a zone referred to as zone f33, on the nautical gridding map, the discovery was made. But they still had a problem. If Murry was spooked for any reason, he could still blow his cargo and release the anthrax spores into the atmosphere anyway. It was unlikely, but everyone was extra nervous. With the wind and thermal currents, the spores could still reach one of two landmasses. The ship had to be secured -before Murry, or any of his crew, had any chance of releasing their killer cargo and making their escape.

The helicopter hovered above the Navy Seals. Their mission leader received the new orders through his comms earpiece. They were now being picked up and told that the next day they would be flown directly to the theatre. Their assault would now be from the Chinook helicopter. The sea around Murry's ship was forecast as rough seas – too rough for a craft-to-craft sea boarding. They would abseil from the hovering helicopter, straight onto the deck of the cargo ship.

Nickolin shook his head, then told the wet, cold men of the new plan.

"Practise for a parachute drop and wet assault and then end up doing it from a dangling rope. It's good to see the army hasn't changed," he said.

One by one they were winched aboard the helicopter and checked their weapons and ammunition. For the assault everyone would carry stun grenades: 'shock and penetrate' was their plan. Simple, but with the element of surprise, it's a deadly, effective offence.

Date: 15th August 2008, 11 p.m.
Place: Glennfinch Castle

The Templar team had about eight hours to get ready and to make it to the meeting place, a small abandoned farm in Cumbria. Now, more than ever, they needed the Russian to secure the ship. Dominique had worked her technological magic again and determined that Salah El-Din was already back in the UK and working the e-mails from a laptop, via a cell phone connection, re-routed through a computer in France.

St Clair's cell phone rang; the call was from the unlisted number in Islington.

"I think we have another problem." The voice was troubled. It now troubled St Clair.

"You think we have?" he said, his mind racing.

"I don't know. I can't be sure."

"I need to know, Controller. This is really important."

"I know. I've been following the comms between you all."

"Tell me what's been happening."

"Well," she began, "it's not a breach, but someone is listening into our comms." She paused. "But it's happened twice today, and both times they have been listening into Luther's cell phone."

"Controller, I need to know. I need you to be sure." He lowered his voice. "Our Charge will be out in the open."

"They have all the right passwords. They're old ones, but still

Date: 15th August 2008, 11 p.m.

operable in the system. The funny thing is, I can't get a fix on the origin. I've cross-checked every comms device we have operational and nothing matches. None of them is the source."

St Clair never swore, but now he did. "Shit, give me your best guess."

"I ... I think it's coming from somewhere in ..."

"Where?"

"Scotland! And there's more. I have just received a call which came from a pay phone ... I think you're going to want to hear it."

She played the tape recording she had made only minutes before. It was a female voice, American, confident and strong.

"I have a message for Payne St Clair. Your scrolls are in Cairo." The anonymous caller gave the address. "I've seen the house. It's accessible, but they're armed. Here are the names of the people who have been working on your scrolls. These are your primary targets. Hans Goutman, a German with an appetite for young female students. An Arab called Tariq Abu Taha. I know the Jordanian authorities would love to get their hands on him. And a real nasty piece of work called Henry Brubecker. The CIA operatives out there would be happy to take him off your hands."

The controller's voice was back on the phone. "I ran the voice analyses, cross-checked twice and came back with a ninety-eight per cent location ranking. The accent is from ..."

"Washington," St Clair interrupted.

"Yes, it is. Do you know who the voice belongs to?"

"I have a pretty good idea who made that call. This is going to get interesting, Controller. It seems that we're not alone in this anymore!"

"What do you want me to do? I could run more voice recognition searches."

"No, there's no point. No time to explain, Controller. We need to concentrate on the scrolls." He then gave her a set of instructions for his friend and member of the Templar Higher Order, André Sabath.

The controller called André Sabath, who had lived in Cairo for more than thirty years and knew the city intimately. Shortly after speaking to the controller, ten Knights in Egypt were called to arms by Sabath, who would control the raid in Egypt from their Cairo safe house. He would move the operations to a mobile unit once the other agencies had arrived.

Pleased to be active again, if only from a control unit, Sabath then made two calls; one to a CIA operative working out of Cairo and the other to an old friend in the Jordanian secret police. Both would soon be joining Sabath and the ten Knights.

Place: Glennfinch Castle, 11:30 p.m.

In the great hall the candles flickered away in a relentless dance, the shadows pirouetting across the walls and ceiling. Dominique had just briefed Jonathan. His heart pounded away at his chest, adrenalin rushing through his body like a torrent: he would finally meet his sister's killer. The plan seemed too simple, but what did he know? He was just an ex-priest.

Time dragged as they waited, sitting together at the table, alone in the vast room. Jonathan watched Dominique methodically cleaning her gun, a Heckler Koch .40. The minutes ticked away slowly.

"Will you stop doing that!" she snapped.

"What?"

"That change business."

"What change business?"

"You rattle the coins in your pocket when you're nervous."

"I do not."

"You rattle the coins in your pocket when you're nervous. You walk flat-footed. Whenever you have to stand for some time, you always have to find something to lean on and you lean slightly forward whenever you're trying to make a point."

"I do not," he said, learning slightly forward. "Anyway, anyone would be nervous around this place. What am I doing here? I'm a schoolteacher and an ex-priest who apparently leans on things and walks flat-footed. Why on earth did St Clair think I would be of any use to him at all?"

"Because, Jonathan, you are the only one who has ever seen Salah El-Din. That's why."

Now it dawned on him. His role in what had happened and what was to come was based on the fact that he was the only person who could recognize the killer. The pressure had just built.

"And," she continued, "St Clair likes you and he thinks he's going to help you with your salvation."

"And what do you think, Dominique?" he asked, settling back in his chair.

"Me …" She stalled. "Well … I like you, too, I guess I mean … I do …"

"No, I meant about my salvation."

She turned away, embarrassed.

11:45 p.m.

A white rental van drove through the open courtyard and round to the back of the castle. St Clair loaded a large alloy box onto the back of the van. Despite its size, the box was almost weightless. Four figures, all dressed in black and with black facemasks, guarded St Clair as he loaded the van. Eight other armed figures remained hidden throughout. After securing the van, St Clair disappeared inside the castle with two of the figures. The others remained guarding the van.

Midnight
Place: Small private airfield, Yorkshire

A small elite group of active Knights had gathered at a small airfield in the Yorkshire Dales. Four Puma helicopters waited on the landing strip, fuelled and ready to go. Their leader, Luther Coates, had been an active Knight for fifteen years. He had been in South Africa when Dominique had been shot in 1996; it was Luther who had saved her life that day.

Luther, a stocky forty-four-year-old ex-SAS serviceman, remained cool and calm as they waited for the signal from St Clair. Despite only having had a few hours notice the previous evening to select and call to arms twenty active Knights, he was ready and so were the Knights.

Luther and another active Knight had once been the most successful close protection team the Order had in operation. The understanding between them, when on a mission, was legendary in the Order. Rarely would they need to use comms to let each other know what the other was doing; instinctively they would know. They had worked together for so long and in so many dangerous situations that their sense of one another was highly tuned. But that was before the other Knight left with the scrolls and disappeared. He was presumed dead, but Luther could never get rid of the feeling that the 'fallen' Knight was still alive.

Midnight (GMT)
Place: Cairo, Egypt

In Cairo three CIA operatives had arrived at the Templar safe house, where Sabath was waiting for them. They were armed, but with orders to take Brubecker alive and arrange for him to be taken back to the USA via the back channels. There he would finally face the charges of gross indecent assault against the young boys whose lives he had ruined over fifteen years ago. A little later, the two-man Jordanian team arrived. Sabath's friend, the one he had made the call to, was leading them. They were also armed, but with orders to terminate Taha and then to dispose of the body. Sabath and the fifteen men waited in the safe house. It was going to be a long night.

Now everything rested on the Russian and the twelve Navy Seals.

Chapter 18

The Four Miracles

Date: 16th August 2008, 6:30 a.m.
Place: An unoccupied farmhouse, Cumbria

It was early when the Templars arrived. The meeting was at 7 a.m.; they were there by 6:30. They stopped halfway down the farm road, as instructed. Their eyes strained to see into the distance, but could discern nothing.

Dominique switched off the engine of the white van. St Clair pulled his Jaguar just up behind them and stopped. Jonathan sat nervously in the passenger seat next to Dominique. She took off her mirrored Ray-Bans and placed her hand on his, smiling. The feeling of foreboding swept over him and the sick feeling, deep in the pit of his stomach, left him weak and nauseous.

"Are you scared?" she asked.

"I've got a list: frightened, panicked, afraid, terrified, petrified, nervous, worried, anxious and, oh yes, scared."

Dominique laughed. "That's quite a list." Her voice softened. "Don't be scared, Jonathan."

"I just don't want to let you all down," he said.

"Jonathan, stop beating yourself up. You won't let us down."

"But I did on Zakynthos. I froze. You could have died and it would have been my fault. I … I couldn't bear it if anything hap …"

"Nobody ever promised us a tomorrow, priest. You take what you can from each day. The rest is down to whatever plan

254

God has for each of us. Don't worry, it's all going to be just fine."
She squeezed his hand again.

6:50 a.m. (GMT)
Place: The merchant ship *Efach II*

The Russian was first down the rope, a thirty-foot slide. It was a textbook exit. The Seals watched him land and then move into position to cover their descent. They had considered him some desk-based brass the Pentagon thought would be useful; now they knew differently. Now they knew a professional was leading them. He gave his directions through prearranged hand signals: the landing was swift and exact.

The first of the thirty-three stun grenades exploded in the wheelhouse. The two men on watch had apparently neither seen nor heard the helicopter. The sea was rough and they were lazy. Murry hadn't had the luxury of being choosy with his crew. The two crewmen saw the door open and then their world imploded. Disoriented and staggering backwards, they offered no resistance. The masked Seals cut the engines; the ship would take just under three miles to come to a halt.

Murry, asleep in his cabin below decks, woke with a start and panicked. Thinking it was an explosion in the ship's engine room, he was desperate to get to the charges in cargo hold Number 4. He didn't relish the thought of anthrax spores spilling out all over his ship, not whilst he was still on board. Dressed only in jeans and barefooted, he left his cabin and made his way down the narrow steel corridor that led to the cargo holds. Four Navy Seals, who were systematically clearing the quarterdeck that contained Murry's cabin, watched him approach. His brain didn't register straight away. The sight of the four Seals, dressed in black and wearing chemical respirator masks, shook him. The sound of twelve more stun grenades systematically exploding in different parts of the ship intensified his panic.

Then gunfire erupted, short rapid bursts from semi-automatic machine guns. He made an attempt to retrace his steps back to his cabin, where he kept a loaded rifle and a handgun. The 7.62 calibre round entered his body at the same time as the Russian terminated the two crewmen on duty in the engine room.

Both men, realising the engines had been switched off seconds after they had heard the explosion on deck, had confronted the Russian. One had an iron bar in his hand and the other a length of chain. The iron bar had not hit its mark. It was a wild swing and the Russian seized it, spun it around in his left hand and buried it deep into the man's torso. Impaled, the crewman fought for his life, the pain crippling his senses. He made an attempt to pull the iron bar from his body, but his strength had gone: his death was slow.

By now the second crewman was already making for one of the four metal doors that offered an escape route. The Russian's sidearm was equipped with a spotter. The thin red beam hit the back of the crewman's head. A second later it was followed at high velocity by a 9mm round. At the same time, the 7.62 calibre round entered Murry's back, leaving a small diameter hole. It left, taking half his ribcage out and his right shoulder blade: Murry had just joined his brother.

A young crewman had foolishly rushed to the wheelhouse with a pistol in his hand. One of the two Navy Seals left on deck spotted the man. The short burst of fire sprayed seven 9mm rounds into him.

The Russian was now in the next cargo hold. Stealthily, he systematically cleared cargo holds 1 and 2; now he was in hold 3. A sound, muffled, caused him to stop. He didn't move. He closed his eyes to increase his other senses. He could hear the other man, feel his breathing. He crouched low and then slowly inched forward. A Navy Seal entered the cargo hold by another door. The Russian saw the crewman as soon as he stood up to fire at the Navy Seal, who fell as two 9 mm rounds hit his shoulder and side. Nickolin's bullet caught the crewman in the calf; the crewman fell, but managed to hold onto his machine gun. He fired widely, but the Russian ran straight at him as if oblivious to the bullets now speeding past him. The Seal reached for his sidearm. He aimed and released two rounds before the pain in his shoulder forced him to drop his gun. One of the rounds caught the crewman on the side of the head, grazing his forehead. He recoiled, and then screamed. It was enough of a distraction. The Russian charged with all his might at a stack of heavy wooden crates. They toppled, smashing the crewman's upper body and head.

The whole operation had taken less than twenty-three minutes. Murry and seven crewmen were dead. The others were now being held under armed guard in the galley. After helping the wounded Seal and making his way up onto the deck, Nickolin sent up the green flare. Less than fifteen minutes later, an American Naval Hunter vessel was mooring alongside the cargo ship. Naval biological handlers and a four-man bomb disposal team boarded the ship via a deck-to-deck crossing, perilous in the choppy seas, but perfectly executed.

The Navy Seals would remain on board to guard the remaining crew and assist with the 'make safe' operation. Until that was done, everyone was at risk. The Hunter remained moored alongside the cargo ship, its three hundred and twenty-three crewmen and women also at risk. It would take a little over an hour to locate and inspect the anthrax, then to secure and disarm the bomb before the ship could be declared safe. The team worked with diligence and great skill in cargo hold Number 4.

On deck, the Russian radioed the agreed call sign from a hand-held radio. The Chinook helicopter arrived and a winch harness was lowered. The Navy Seal sergeant mustered his men on deck. Murry's remaining crewmembers were now under martial law from the Hunter's naval police.

Throughout their time together, the sergeant and the ex-Russian Special Forces man had only exchanged a few words, but now the battle was over the sergeant approached the Russian, shouting to be heard above the melding sounds of ships, sea, wind and the hovering helicopter.

"I don't know who you are and I know better than to ask, but it's been an honour and privilege to serve with you, sir."

The Russian shook his hand. He removed his black assault coveralls and webbing, laid his weapons on the deck of the ship and, turning to the Seals, saluted them.

7 a.m.
Place: The farmhouse, Cumbria

The farm, five hundred metres away and disused, had seen better days. Falling livestock prices and the crippling epidemic of foot-and-mouth disease some years back had have tested the resolve of the previous occupier.

Finding the location had been a simple exercise for the Arab. He had used the same ploy on many occasions, calling up a selection of estate agents specialising in farmland and farm property, telling them he was interested in buying – the hook always worked. With the poor state of the agricultural property market, he had no problem finding what he wanted. A fax detailing his criteria: 'unoccupied farm, isolated and a long wide approach road', then a few more requirements, just to make the enquiry look authentic, such as 'grazing land suitable for a stock count of about 300, mainly beef, with rotating pasture usage, worked every time.

Salah El-Din had received three potential locations, all north of Lancashire. He would have preferred somewhere south, close to major port exit points. He had checked the property on the Internet. The estate agent, eager for a sale, had posted photographs on their websites and whole sections dedicated to statistics for the farm and the area; he studied the photographs and ignored the rest.

The approach road was a firm, well-worn track, undulating and with deep ruts from tractor use. To the right and left of the track there was some three to four hundred metres of open ground before hedgerows on either side broke up the visibility arcs. The dilapidated farmhouse, at the end of the track, was accompanied by an equally dilapidated barn building. The two buildings were surrounded by a railed fence, rotting and fallen in places. To the right of the farmhouse, and past the barn, was a small coppice of mixed trees.

Salah El-Din watched them arrive. He could see everything from the vantage point of the coppice. From there he could be sure that they had followed his instructions. Murry had his orders. If the Templars doubled-crossed him, Murry would carry them out without hesitation. Once the Templars arrived, there would be no place for them to run, no place to hide. He could deal with three or four Templars – he had all his bases covered.

Salah El-Din had to be the one to authenticate the Ark himself. He could have sent others, but this was his victory. He wanted to taste it, savour it. He had spent so long looking for the most ancient religious artefact of all time. He would not trust this to anybody else. He stood silent, watching them through his binoculars. The Templars looked uneasy. His eyes moved to the right of the farmhouse and barn. Behind him, thirty heavily armed mercenaries remained hidden. He scanned along the hedgerow to the left. There was no sign of life, no sign of the sniper, but he knew he was in position, awaiting his orders. The sniper's telescopic sight was trained and ready to slaughter the Templars on his command.

7:15 a.m.

It was a warm summer's morning; the sky was a deep blue with tints of red. The Templars had been waiting for forty-five minutes. They watched the entrance of the main road, the 'For Sale' sign obscuring the first five feet or so.

The car came towards them slowly. The Mercedes looked menacing in the dawn of the day, white with blacked-out windows. St Clair got out of the Jaguar and walked over to the passenger door of the white van. Jonathan opened the door.

"Well, Jonathan, it's that time." St Clair's voice was calm and reassuring.

Jonathan looked back at Dominique. She smiled and then he left the van: Operation Roulette Wheel was nearing its conclusion.

The Mercedes stopped ten feet or so away from where St Clair and Jonathan were now standing. The passenger door opened and a man got out. Jonathan strained to see. He hoped his memory would not let him down. He had spent so long trying to forget that night, blaming himself for his sister's death. Now he needed those images. The images of the man who had been standing next to Senator McGregor when the senator was talking to Courtney at the Christmas Eve party.

St Clair's hand slid inside his trench coat and closed around his gun, the pre- cocked hammer system giving him some comfort. He had two guns, both carried in a specially designed dual holster he wore around his upper body. Each gun, lying top to top to each other, was ready to fire. Dominique had chosen a pump-action 12-gauge shotgun, designed for smaller shooters. It had a seven-shot magazine and a specially modified handgrip stock. Inside her shoulder rig, she also carried a backup gun with a 13-round magazine.

"Well?" St Clair whispered, peering into the fading dawn.

Jonathan stood motionless. The man before him was Middle Eastern-looking, in his mid-fifties. He was tall with silver hair, sharp features and piercing black eyes. Jonathan needn't have worried. The images of the man, the senator and his sister, all standing together in the senator's house, came flooding back to him like a burst of light. Now he would finally justify the trust St Clair had placed in him all along.

"It's him," Jonathan whispered. "That is Salah El-Din."

St Clair smiled and placed a hand upon Jonathan's shoulder. "Remember, Jonathan, we are not alone, but we have to buy the Russian some time. Just follow my lead and it will all be ok."

St Clair could not give the signal to Luther and his men until the

Russian had the ship. If they acted too soon, thousands of Jews would die. It was far from ok; he had to play for time.

Salah El-Din's bodyguard waited in the car for the signal. His orders were that all the Templars were to be killed. It would be quick, and it would be silent. The silencer would buy him valuable seconds as he left the car and started shooting. Salah El-Din's mercenaries, entrenched in the coppice behind the Templar position, would do most of the killing, though. And the sniper would secure the success of the massacre. The Templars were trapped, with nowhere to go other than to their graves.

"My master wants you to deal with me, *Franji*." Salah El-Din used an old colloquial Arabic word from the time of the crusades that designated Westerners.

Hearing his voice, Jonathan felt a surge of rage. He was face-to-face with the man who had killed his sister, or had ordered her death by having her throat cut and her eyelids removed. For the second time he was right there in front of him. Jonathan's palms sweated and his teeth clenched as he stared at El-Din. His heart beat fast and hard.

St Clair was uneasy. He had a bad feeling and he always trusted his feelings, no matter what lay in front of him. He watched the Arab's every move, fully aware that at least one other person was in the Mercedes. The Arab would have other gunmen, but he had placed himself and Jonathan there as bait: the roulette wheel was now spinning for the final play.

"Let's just get this over with, shall we?" he said.

"My master will be pleased you are so eager to trade, my friend."

St Clair laughed. "Your pretence is wasted. We know who you are, what you are and what you have done. Do you think you are that clever? Personally, I have never met a clever criminal. They tend to fall into two categories, greedy or stupid, and you, Salah El-Din, are both."

Salah El-Din couldn't hide his shock. He hadn't realised that he would be identified. He had always been so meticulous about his identity; anonymity had always secured his safety. Momentarily he was thrown, but then he recognized the man standing next to the Templar and he eased slightly.

"Ah, of course, the priest from Washington. I had not recognised you. So you found your saviours, did you, priest – the Knights Templar? Have they helped you, like they helped the incompetent Dukes? Have they helped you get your faith back again? I wonder what poisonous drivel they have filled your small-minded head with? Him, God? How's your sister? I hear she met with a very nasty end."

Dominique's hands tightened around the shotgun as she watched Jonathan freeze, unable to move or to speak now that Salah El-Din had spoken to him directly.

"And you, Templar, you disappoint me. I expected more from you. I expected a more worthy opponent. I have played you like a fool all along, as it should be, and as you would expect from a great leader. As it's been since the time when rapiers and lances stirred the coals of war in my homeland. Ever since your defeat at Hattin and when Saladin conquered Jerusalem from you mongrels, and the Lion Heart betrayed the Muslims. You are as inept as the Templars that have gone before you."

St Clair raised his hand and pointed a finger at the murderer before him. "Saladin died at the age of fifty-five in Damascus. You are not him, you're just a petty thief. You would take his name, a warrior, a great man, a wise man who led his people? Who protected his people, not stole and abused them. He would revile you. Disown you. You're just the son of what I would imagine are disappointed parents. There is no lineage link between you and Saladin. There is no greatness in you, just hatred and greed. You disgust me. You disgust life."

The insult from St Clair about no lineage to the great Arab leader Saladin would have meant nothing to a rational person, but to Salah El-Din it was the worst insult and his anger, stirred, started to vent forth.

"Enough of these empty words, Templar," he spat back. "The

Ark for the lives of thousands of Jews, that's the trade. One call, Templar, one call and it will be stopped, but if I don't make the call for any reason, then their blood will be on your hands." He held his cell phone aloft as if to emphasise the gravity of the situation.

"Give me the Ark."

St Clair still had to play for more time. He had to buy time for Nickolin; it was all down to him now. St Clair still didn't know if the death ship carrying Salah El-Din's anthrax had been secured.

"Why would an atheist, a killer, a low-life like you, believe that the Ark ever existed? Surely the Bible is just a book full of stories to you, written long after Moses and long after Jesus." As St Clair spoke, he studied the terrain, looking for signs of the Arab's killers, who would certainly be hidden out there. He saw nothing, but he could feel their menacing presence and he prayed that Clay, John Wolf and Luther were in position close by.

"You're like all the religious fools, Templar." Salah El-Din's agitation grew even further. "You think everything has to revolve around your faith, your beliefs, and your book. Just because the Ark is powerful it has to be your God that created it. You believe that your God created everything, made the world in six days, but the great Muslim Egyptians believed that matter had always existed and that the world began when order came to it. Today the theory of chaos almost mirrors these beliefs. Mathematical designs repeat within unstructured events. Spot something missing in the theory of chaos, Templar: your God. Remember Zalmovia, the Thracian who was the slave of Pythagoras? He wrote that his master could foretell the future by numbers and ciphers. A natural science based on a natural universe. Again, see anyone missing?

"When Pythagoras founded his scientific order in Croton, in Southern Italy, he believed in the Orphic mysteries. His message was simple: all things are numbers and the principles of things are the principle of numbers. The essence of number is the principle of the universe created by geometrical rules. Understand numbers and understand the beginning. Read the secret books of Phoenician wisdom, Templar, and you will see gospels there that have esoteric teaching. No, not everything has to come from your God, including the Ark. Despite it being in your book, it is also in many other books. Keep your God, Templar, but I will take the Ark."

Salah El-Din believed he was desperately close to the thing he craved more than anything, the thing he lived for, the Ark of the Covenant – that immense, all-encompassing source. He wanted to see it, to touch it. He did not, for a minute, believe that it had never existed; now he wanted it. His eyes moved towards the white rental van.

7:28 a.m. (GMT)

As soon as he was in the recovery helicopter, Nickolin made the call to Islington. Seconds later, Dominique's phone vibrated. She pressed the receive button and lowered the hands-free volume control. The controller's message was short.

"The Russian is on his way home. The ship and its cargo are secure. Proceed." There was a pause, and then the controller added, "Tell St Clair our problem is still here and it's now in your vicinity. Whoever has been tapping into our comms is close to you now. Be careful."

Dominique hit the three-digit number and St Clair's cell phone vibrated twice in his inside coat pocket. He didn't move or show any sign that he had just received the best news he dared hope for, the news he had been praying for. Now, he thought, it is time to end this, time to stop this roulette wheel spinning.

7:29 a.m.
Place: Islington

The controller now followed the instructions St Clair had given her the previous evening. Her first call was to Luther, who, along with his armed Templars, was waiting in the helicopters a few miles away. The second was to Bill Meeks in Washington, who, directly after placing down the receiver, called a trusted friend in the Justice department. Thirty minutes later, twenty-five US Marshals armed with arrest warrants entered the headquarters of the FBI. Eight arrests were made in all, including the two supervisors from Black Ops who had been watching Courtney ever since she had pulled the McGregor file. The Controller then called André Sabath.

7:30 a.m. (GMT)
Place: Templar safe house, Cairo

After placing down the receiver, Sabath moved the operation to a waiting mobile unit. Three of his Knights were already at the target location, on the outskirts of the city. The remaining seven Knights, who had been called to arms by Sabath, moved their equipment into one of the two waiting vans. Three CIA agents and two men from the Jordanian secret police, also moved their equipment into one of the vans. En route, one of the vans stopped. A Templar got out and moved quickly along the street to a disused factory. There he waited and watched.

Ten minutes later, the united forces of fourteen armed men moved onto the house. Two Knights fixed a small amount of plastic explosives to the lock of the front door and then retreated, the electric detonator ready. Sabath was on the comms and checked everyone was in position. Everyone came back affirmative. Sabath then gave the signal to the waiting Templar at the disused factory. He, the Knight, set the timer on the explosives he was carrying in a large black rucksack to fifteen seconds. Throwing the rucksack through a broken window and into the disused factory, he ran from the scene.

A few minutes later, following the explosion, Sabath heard the sirens of the police and fire service. The decoy was working.

The door blew and the fourteen-man team entered the house of Salah El-Din's scholars. Inside mayhem erupted. Tariq Abu Taha was the first to die. Stunned by the noise and explosion, he had made for the back door exit. One of the Jordanian secret police was covering the rear escape route, whilst his colleague had entered by the front. Abu Taha tried to flee, but the Jordanian recognised his mark, pulled the trigger and Abu Taha was dead. Only two more shots were fired.

The German, Hans Goutman, and an Egyptian bodyguard were seen racing for arms that lay on a table in the dining area. Four Knights had seen them. Two bullets were fired and Goutman and the bodyguard lay dead. Henry Brubecker put up no struggle. He was found hiding underneath a bed, crying.

In less than three minutes the house had been secured. The Jordanians left straightaway. The three CIA operatives bundled their mark into the back of one of the vans and drove into the Cairo suburbs. The mark would be shipped back to the US via a covert route, and would stand trial for his crimes against young boys. Sabath and the remaining Knights packed up all the computers, scrolls and texts and placed them into the back of another of the vans, then left.

7:30 a.m.
Place: 890-923 Knightsbridge Court Crescent, London

Scotland Yard officers, along with three people from the Financial Services Authority, following the instructions they had received via courier the previous evening, waited outside the premises of 890-923 Knightsbridge Court Crescent. At 7:30 a.m., the call came through from the unlisted number in Islington: they were given the all-clear to move. Using the swipe card supplied by Morgan Clay, they gained access to the top floor of the building and to the offices of Salah El-Din's legal and illegal offices. All the employees would be interviewed; most would be sent home. However, none of the people who worked in the nine offices that administered the Arab's criminal business dealings would be allowed to leave. A total of nineteen staff would be charged with a series of criminal offences. Down in the basement, the screen monitors were going crazy. Skinner, who was working his shift, thought that there was an electric fault. The detective who arrested him cleared up the mystery for him.

7:30 a.m.
Place: The farmhouse, Cumbria

St Clair's plan was in motion in Cairo, London and Washington. Now it was his time to act. But he needed Salah El-Din just a little closer. Now he would take his biggest gamble yet.

He moved to the van and opened its doors. Jonathan hadn't noticed anything being put into the van before they left, but then again, he had been busy most of the night being briefed by Dominique and being sick in the bathroom. He helped St Clair lift the alloy box out of the van and placed it on the ground, surprised by the lack of weight. St Clair pressed the tips of his fingers against the side of the alloy box so that his fingerprints were held flat on the alloy, then whispered something and the sides slowly folded down into small, one-centimetre concertina sections, taking its lid with it. Jonathan strained to see inside. Salah El-Din moved closer.

Salah El-Din was now directly in the line of fire between them and the Mercedes so that there was no clear shot for the driver of the Mercedes. St Clair would soon be able to give the signal to Dominique. She would start the van's engine and hit the accelerator pedal full on. With five metres to go, she would jump from the van, just seconds before it hit the Mercedes with full impact. This was a manoeuvre they had all practised time and time again.

"There's nothing in it!" Salah El-Din shouted.

Jonathan couldn't help but be disappointed, although he had given up hope of any proof of God.

Salah El-Din's anger erupted once more. "You're a liar and a fool, Templar. the Jews will die and you will die, too. Do you think you can mock me?" He held the cell phone ready to make the call.

"You mean the Jews in Tel Aviv, from the anthrax spores Murry was going to release from his ship?"

Salah El-Din's look was enough; he had been out-manoeuvred.

"Oh, we were fooled by Unity for a while, but it didn't last. Let me help you with this. You look a little confused." Every second St Clair could buy now was a precious second Luther and his men would need.

"For over a year now there has been a Templar Knight in your headquarters in London. He has been there all that time. You have even spoken to him. He was on your security staff, by the way, I particularly like that bit. Your friends in Unity are being rounded up as we speak. We have your cargo ship and your cargo. Murry is dead, just like his brother. Crowthorp is in custody and Stranks, well, let's just say he and your bodyguard will not be seeing any more sunrises.

"Your Knightsbridge headquarters should be swarming with Special Branch officers and FSA roundabout now and your scholars have nothing left to study. The house in Egypt is empty. As for the people you bribed in the FBI and other agencies, warrants are being served and arrests made at this moment. Oh, and by the way, just so that you know, Templars do not lie. Now tell me, is all this too much information for you?"

Salah El-Din turned to the Mercedes, shouting his instruction, but he was in the line of fire. However, the sniper hidden in the trees had a better shot; his rifle was surgically accurate with its telescopic sight. The butt of his rifle eased into his shoulder, his head lowered and his eye looked into the crosshairs of the scope. There wasn't a clear headshot; his victim was turned in the seat and leaning. There was a crack, then the sound of a bullet piercing the van door. Seconds later the van door opened and Dominique fell out, blood pouring from her leg. She dropped her firearm and it crashed to the ground. Her hands reached for the area that now burned. Quickly, she undid her belt and fastened it around her leg as a tourniquet.

Jonathan, watching, saw her fall out of the van. He watched her firearm fall away. He watched as she scrambled to tighten the tourniquet: she was alone and fully exposed. He froze, anchored to the spot. Panic gripped his body, just as it had done on Zakynthos – he stood shocked into immobility. She was bleeding, but the flow was slowly stemming. She looked around for her firearm, and then their eyes met. The edges of his peripheral vision darkened. Now all he could see was Dominique, fallen and bleeding, her eyes on him. For a few seconds it was deathly quiet. In seconds the sniper would fire again and Dominique was a sitting target. Jonathan's legs were like jelly. Nausea ripped at him. He lifted one leg and stepped forward, then the other. He opened his mouth and said *the* name, the name he had forsaken for so long, the name he now needed the most.

"God, please help her!" he screamed.

He started to run, his movement fuelled by his desperate desire to save her. His eyes fixed on her. The sound of shouting erupted around him, but his concentration drowned it out. He reached down and collected her firearm. Then he ran with adrenalin pumping round his body like fuel. There was no time.

He reached her, falling to his knees beside her. He shielded her with his body, positioning himself between her and the direction of the faceless assassin.

He heard the crack of the rifle being fired. His chest erupted with a searing pain. His hands reached for his chest, then his body crumpled to the ground.

Dominique tried to pull him up, hauling with all her might. He made it to his feet with her support. He staggered a few paces forward before his strength was gone and he fell.

St Clair saw him fall. Dominique, covered in blood from the wound to her leg, was learning over Jonathan, screaming at him to get up. The man who had just saved her life lay still, blood pouring from his chest wound. She screamed at his bloody, limp body to move, but it made no difference. Jonathan was dying.

7:35 a.m.

John Wolf had pulled the Range Rover to a halt about one thousand metres away from the meeting point. They had barely made it. Scanning the open terrain in front of him, Wolf had seen the two flashes from the sniper's rifle. Quickly out of the car, he raced across the open field and then disappeared into the shape of the hedgerow.

The sniper slid the bolt back and loaded another round into the chamber, his sights now fixed on St Clair. He breathed in deeply, exhaled half the air in his lungs, then stopped, his finger resting on the cold metal of the trigger.

Wolf crept the last fifty metres. He had heard the first two rounds and saw their flashes, but had no idea who the targets were. The sniper started to pull the trigger again. Wolf's Glock 22 took the man's skull at high velocity and shattered it. The sniper did not get his third round off. He fell from the tree to the ground with a low thud.

Morgan Clay was older than Wolf, but he could still move with speed. Salah El- Din's bodyguard, who'd had no idea that his twin lay dead in some seedy male brothel in Luton until St Clair had just told Salah El-Din, jumped out of the Mercedes. He hit the ground, then rolled, his sub-machine gun cocked and ready. His legs spread for balance. he brought the sub-machine gun under his chin.

Dominique, still on her knees beside Jonathan's bleeding body, tried desperately to stem the blood flow. He was losing too much.

St Clair didn't have time to fire his gun. Salah El-Din dived for him. Both men hit the ground hard and were winded. At that very same moment, from the coppice to the right of the farmhouse and barn, came the thunderous burst of gunfire. A salvo of bullets hailed on the Templars.

Dominique grabbed Jonathan. Her right leg still bleeding and painful, she tried to pull him away. His frame felt like lead, impossible to move from where it had fallen. Her fingers closed around the sleeves of his jacket and she gripped as hard as she could. Ignoring the burning pain in her leg, she learned back and pulled with what strength she had left. Around her the noise of gunfire was deafening. She pulled and tugged for all she was worth. Slowly, inch-by-inch, she hauled Jonathan round to the side of the van for protection.

The mercenaries had made their move. In V formation, they advanced on the Templars. The Templars, desperately outnumbered and pinned down by the incoming rounds, had minutes to live.

The bodyguard aimed and then fired a short rapid burst towards Jonathan and Dominique. The rounds fell wide, smashing into the side of the van, but she felt their rush as they sped past her head. The bodyguard turned the sight switch up two notches. Dominique could feel the gun barrel on her. Crying, she held on tight to Jonathan, covering as much of him as she could.

The hole in his chest was excruciating and the searing pain caused him to fall in and out of consciousness. He sensed her body on his, protecting him. Her face was next to his. He opened his eyes and smiled.

"Seems we're out of time ... I .... I just wanted you to know that I think I lo ..." His voice was a low whisper. The pain shot through his chest again and he groaned with its agony. She held his face in her hands and kissed him, tears streaming down her face. His eyes closed and he went limp.

St Clair and Salah El-Din were in a desperate struggle to the far right of the rental van. St Clair looked across at Dominique and saw Jonathan's body beneath her. She was beating his chest, screaming, "St Clair, help me, please help me, he's..."

Across the open field the figure of Wolf came running towards the Templars. Although he was too far away, he was firing his weapon in a desperate bid to attract the bodyguard's attention away from Dominique. Some of the mercenaries spotted the Indian. Training their sights on him, they opened fire, but Wolf was skilled and he was lucky. He zigzagged across the open field, dodging their bullets.

Clay aimed his gun. The fully automatic belt-fed machine gun spewed out its bullets.

St Clair heaved Salah El-Din to the ground once more and forced his foot into the Arab's ribs. At the same moment he heard a heart-wrenching cry from Dominique. He knew the priest was dead. The bodyguard, alerted by the click of the weapon, turned to see Clay, his gun pointed and about to fire.

Salah El-Din fought like a wild animal. The Templar's foot caught his rib cage for the second time as he bit, scratched, kicked and punched. Cursing and screaming in rage, he attacked every part of St Clair's body he could reach. St Clair was desperate to finish it. Jonathan was dead. Dominique clung onto him, exposed. She could be next.

The bodyguard opened fire first and Clay had to dive to the ground. Rounds sped past his head with frightening closeness. Clay fired his weapon, and a salvo of bullets hit the Mercedes. The bodyguard, tall and menacing, rose to his feet. Finger on the trigger, he ran at Clay, firing a hail of bullets back at him. Clay, the ghost man, was unflappable, with nerves of steel honed after years of dangerous undercover work, but he had never been in a frenzied shoot-out before.

Dominique stroked Jonathan's forehead, tears still falling from her face and onto his. He lay still.

Clay was unable to raise his weapon to release the hail of bullets. Wolf's fist hit the back of the bodyguard's neck like a train and he fell, his weapon rolling away. He tried to get to his feet, but he was disorientated and Wolf was already on him. The Indian delivered four powerful blows to his head and he lay on the ground, dazed. Wolf then rushed over to Jonathan and Dominique. Crouching beside them, he returned fire on the advancing mercenaries, screaming at her to get out of there, but she would not move.

The bodyguard shook his head, his senses returned, and he scrambled to his feet. Retrieving his gun, he turned it towards Wolf. Before he had time to use it, the bullets ripped into him, piercing his heart, lungs and kidneys. He was dead in seconds. Clay lowered his weapon, the barrel still warm. Wolf turned to see the bodyguard fall and he nodded to Clay; the ghost man had just saved his life.

Clay joined Wolf and the two Templars returned a barrage of fire. The barrels of their weapons were hot, but they knew that they had no chance of winning the firefight. There were too many mercenaries advancing on their position. The van, which had protected them, was now in flames and risked being blown up if the fire caught the fuel line. It was getting perilously close.

Unable to reach for his firearm, St Clair took out a small four-inch blade from an ankle sheath. Salah El-Din tried to block the thrust, but the Arab's strength had been sapped by the bloody battle with the Templar. The steel slid into his side and he turned and writhed with the pain.

The noise of the firefight was deafening. Wolf knew that he needed to do something and fast. He broke from his position; two bullets instantly hit his arm and leg, but he kept on going. Scrambling into the Jaguar, he turned on the engine. With a screech of the wheels, he put the car between the mercenaries and St Clair. St Clair dived into the car and again the wheels screeched as Wolf pulled up by the side of the white van. Wolf screamed at them to get Dominique into the van. Refusing to move, she was sobbing, holding Jonathan's dead body close to hers. Now the Jaguar was under fire. One of its wheels blew and then another as the mercenaries closed in. Wolf exchanged a glance with St Clair without speaking. No words were needed. They knew they were about to die.

7:42 a.m.

The gun battle that raged had muffled the rotor blades of the four

273

Puma helicopters. Luther Coates and his team of twenty Knights sprang from the hovering machines. Within ten yards they had reached the back of the derelict farmhouse. Luther split the Knights into two groups. The first fifteen Knights made their way to the front of the farmhouse and immediately began to open fire on the mercenaries. Instantly, four mercenaries fell. The rest hit the ground, turned and returned fire. Luther and the remaining five Knights made their way behind the farmhouse and the barn and onto the edge of the coppice where he moved them into position for a classic crossfire.

Now that the firefight was focused on Luther and his armed Knights, the other Templars left the Jaguar. Clay grabbed the two extinguishers out of the van and sprayed the flames with foam; within seconds the fire was out. St Clair checked Jonathan's pulse. There wasn't one.

"Get him to the Ark, Wolf, quickly!" St Clair barked. The Indian grabbed Jonathan's limp body.

St Clair knelt by the empty space the alloy box had left after it had concertinaed into a small silver cube. He made the sign of the cross and started chanting something. The Grand Master of the Order of Knights Templar spoke in an ancient tongue. The Indian laid Jonathan down over the empty space. Clay, the Indian and Dominique fell to their knees.

"Pray, Knights!" St Clair shouted. "Pray with all your hearts."

Luther's fifteen Knights were now held down in a torrent of bullets. Two more mercenaries lay dead. Luther and his men were working their way around the coppice: thirty more metres and they would be in position. But then two snipers, who had been left in the coppice to cover the mercenaries' retreat route, opened fire. Luther and his Knights hit the ground, forming a semi-circle, but there was no cover and they couldn't see the snipers. They lay as flat as they could, their weapons trained on the trees. They had become sitting targets. Luther looked around for a way out, but it was all open ground. They would be cut to shreds if they tried to run for it.

There was a crack of a fallen branch breaking, then some way off Luther caught sight of the silhouette of two masked figures running towards the snipers' positions. The figures, dressed in black, were making their way along the hedgerow, keeping low, but moving fast. The person in front was much taller, broader than the other.

One of Luther's men shouted that he had a clear shot at them, but there was something about one of the figures. Luther told him to hold his fire. The two masked figures split up, the smaller of the two disappearing into the coppice while the taller hugged the treeline. The tall, lone figure moved with stealth, his rifle bedded into his shoulder, poised in the fire position. Every ten paces he stopped, knelt down on one knee and listened. Then another shot was fired; one of the snipers had barely missed the Templar to Luther's right. The young Knight rolled out of position and tried to return fire, but it was useless because he couldn't see the sniper's position for the trees. Luther, watching the lone figure moving in on the snipers, barked at him to hold fire.

The figure had seen the flash from the rifle and had its position. Now he moved in. He ran ten more paces, then knelt, his right hand gripping the trigger stock, his left nestling in the underside of the breach block case. He took aim. His round hit the sniper in the head. It was a perfect shot; the sniper died instantly. The figure was now hunting the second sniper, moving fast and low along the treeline again.

"I know that run!" Luther exclaimed. "I know that run. It's ..."

Then another crack. The second sniper had spotted the figure and the bullet just missed his shoulder. The figure dived, his reflexes sharp. He rolled forward and lay in the prone position, his sights fixed. Luther, quick to react, stood up, now fully exposed with his rifle tucked into his shoulder. He squinted down the sights and fired on the second sniper's position. He knew he was too far away, but he was drawing the sniper's fire away from the figure. Then his men stood up, one after the other, and started firing. They were all open targets now.

With the fire power of six Knights aiming in his direction, despite being too far away, the sniper panicked and tried to make his escape. He dropped his weapon and jumped from the tree that had been his vantage point. He only managed ten paces. The second masked figure stood in front of him. Without hesitation, the person raised their gun and fired.

From out of the woods the first masked figure raised his firearm above his head and made for Luther and his team. Then he raised his hand to Luther in gesture. Luther smiled at his friend.

"Who is this guy?" one of Luther's men asked.

Luther couldn't help the big broad grin on his face. "That, gentleman, is St Clair's brother, Zakariah St Clair, the fallen Knight."

Still breathing hard and sweating, Zakariah removed his ski mask. He smiled at his old friend. "I'm sorry for all the trouble I've caused, Luther."

Luther shook his hand. "How did you know how to find us?"

"I'm afraid I've been monitoring your comms for a few weeks now. I used old codes to hack into your cell, but I managed it."

Luther laughed. "So you're the one that has had the Controller so worried. She's going to want to have words with you."

Then, the second masked figure came out of the trees. Smaller than Zakariah, the person had executed the kill with extreme professionalism, just the way they had been trained by Zakariah for the past six months.

Just then a bullet sped past them, followed by several more in quick succession and they hit the ground. A small handful of mercenaries was firing on them as they tried to make their escape.

"Well, you two, you had better reload your weapons," Luther called above the din of the renewed gunfire. "This fight is not over yet, and it seems we need every Knight we can get. Good to have you back, old friend."

Dominique knelt, along with Wolf, Clay and St Clair, in front of the empty alloy box. The four members of the sanction team stayed motionless, praying hard. Every one of them waited for something to happen, their thoughts, hearts and souls focused on one thing, the space the alloy box had left.

Then, without warning, a blue smoke appeared. Small at first, it began to grow. A strange rumbling noise, like faraway thunder, seeped out of the empty space before them. Then a shimmer appeared, slowing forming a shape, hazy and gleaming, transparent, yet there. A square shape began to form. It was gold, then silver, then a myriad of colours, all fusing into one another like a rainbow exploding in front of their eyes. The thunder intensified. St Clair raised his voice above the noise, the ancient words spoken at speed. The shape grew more pronounced. And then the Ark appeared, magnificent and glorious in its grace.

The Ark was made of acacia wood and overlaid in pure gold. There were four gold rings attached to it and on the lid two gold cherubim faced each other. The cherubim wings spread upwards, overshadowing the cover.

"Put the priest on the Ark," St Clair called above the thunderous rumble.

The Ark hovered above the ground; a brilliant white light radiating from its core. Then Jonathan was placed on top. The Four Knights bowed in reverence to the Ark.

The remaining mercenaries didn't stand a chance. They faced fifteen well-armed, well-trained Knights Templar to their rear and six more Knights and one small figure, still masked, to their side. When the firefight had finished, one of the Templars saw the light of the Ark and called to Luther.

"It's the Ark! Our Charge is here."

Dominique felt the strange sensation overpowering her, melding her senses together in a euphoria of emotions she had never before experienced. Her heart pounded and the blood rushed through her veins with lightning speed.

Then an eerie silence fell. No sound, no light, no smoke – just a total quiet. The Ark was still. Jonathan moaned. Then, very slowly, he began to open his eyes. With difficulty, he raised himself up and looked around. Unsteady on his feet, he stood before them.

St Clair moved to his side. "Take it easy, Jonathan. I think you're going to be pretty shaken up for a while."

The first miracle, the miracle of life had been given back to him through the Ark of the Covenant. Jonathan's face changed from ashen grey and slowly strength returned to his body. His wound had been sealed; the power of the Ark had fused it.

"Do you believe now, Jonathan Rose? "St Clair asked. "Have we given you your faith back?" St Clair laughed. "Is not our Lord God a merciful God?"

Jonathan looked down at the miracle that had taken place on his body.

The Ark was still there, peaceful, tranquil and still in its Holy splendour.

Jonathan couldn't take his eyes off the religious icon. So many times he had read the word 'Ark'. Now, it was in front of him,. God's work was there in front of him, tangible proof of the Lord God Almighty.

"Can I see them?" Jonathan asked St Clair, his voice trembling. "Can I see the two stone tablets of the Ten Commandments, the words of God?"

St Clair could see the other Knights now arriving from the gun battle. "Of course you can, Jonathan, but the Ark will not stay too long. It never does." He removed the golden lid and moved away, leaving Jonathan to peer inside.

The remaining Knights had now arrived. Some fell to their knees before their Order's Charge. St Clair saw him, the fallen Knight, whose name was banned from utterance within their Order, his brother.

"He saved our lives," Luther told St Clair. "If it wasn't for him, we would have been picked off one by one. He saved the lives of many Knights on this day, St Clair."

St Clair lowered his head in acknowledgement for what Zakariah had done for Luther and the other Knights. Then he placed a hand on his brother's shoulder.

"It was you, wasn't it? You gave us the location of the scrolls in Egypt," St Clair asked.

"It was my wrong to right," Zakariah replied.

"Then consider the wrong righted. Welcome back, my brother."

Zakariah turned to the stranger amongst them.

"I had help," he said.

"I know," St Clair said. "I figured it out yesterday when the controller told me about the telephone message that was left for me. We are in your debt." He embraced the stranger, who had removed her mask. Then he excused himself and made his way back to the Ark.

Jonathan was staring inside the Ark, seeing a most wondrous sight. There, in the Ark, lay the Ten Commandments of Moses. He went to touch them, but looked at St Clair for approval. St Clair nodded. Jonathan could feel history at his fingertips: centuries of time, the ancient ones: the people of the Promised Land. He felt the hand of God.

He lifted one of the tablets, It was weightless – as the Ark when it had been inside the alloy box. Then, to his astonishment, in between the written words of the Ten Commandments, he saw additional lines of faded symbols that seemed to lift from the stone. He looked at St Clair in puzzlement.

"What, Jonathan? What do you see?" St Clair asked, keeping his voice low and hoping beyond hope that there was another in their midst.

"I see thousands of symbols and images, I see ..."

"And tell me, Jonathan." St Clair slowed his words down. He moved closer beside Jonathan, wanting to be clear. "Is there anything else?"

"Yes."

"What do you see?" St Clair asked, not daring to hope.

Then the second miracle happened. "It's like ..." Jonathan staggered slightly, unsteady on his feet, but the grace of the symbols seemed to support him. "It's like I am looking at them through running water. They are there but distant. It's like they are alive, like the symbols are alive."

He saw them moving and rotating; lifting themselves from the stone and slowly forming a three-dimensional orb. The symbols dismantled as they touched each other and then spun off at great speed to form another. Strangely, he didn't recognise the symbols and yet he could make out some of them.

"Look," he said in a hoarse voice. "The resurrection."

St Clair smiled. "You are truly blessed because only a few people have the gift to be able to read them. They are Law and the Lore of numbers, geometry, science, astronomy, the universe, chaos, sincerity and healing. They are the esoteric knowledge. You are looking at the blueprint for the most perfect celestial plan – *Spiritus Mundi* – the Breath of the Universe. They are the sacred science.

"For centuries they have been with us and over those years we have been trying to understand them. Templars in France first discovered their presence. but we still have much to learn about them. We know but a small part of their meaning."

Jonathan had been staring at the orb all the time St Clair had been talking. Despite his weakness, he was transfixed by the animation of the three-dimensional orb that had formed out of the transient symbols and equations hovering above the stone tablet.

"You mean you cannot read them?"

St Clair nodded. "Sadly, I don't have the gift."

"They're so beautiful, St Clair" He scanned the symbols. "It's ..." His words faltered in his excitement as he read: "Here is the Scripture of the thirteenth Apostle." He looked up at St Clair. "Do you know who Mary Magdalene really was? This is going to change everything."

St Clair took his arm. "Not here, Jonathan. Not now. Our Order has only ever had a handful of Knights with the seer's gift. Dominique's mother was the last of them. We will have much time to talk later, but for now, see, the Ark is beginning to fade. It never stays long."

Throughout Dominique had knelt just yards away from Jonathan and the Ark. She did not look around, she did not move, but stayed with her gaze fixed on Jonathan, the man she loved. Now she stood, euphoric with relief. She looked around at the Knights that had joined them. Then, the third miracle of the day happened. She saw him.

"Hello, princess. It's been a while," Zachariah said.

"Dad!" Dominique cried. "How? ... I thought you were ... You're back."

"Seems that way and not a moment too soon. It looks as if you finally found someone you like." He glanced towards Jonathan. "Guess someone had better introduce us."

"This is Zakariah," St Clair said, "my brother and Dominique's father. We all owe him a great debt, Jonathan. He saved Luther and his men. If not for him and his friend, we would probably not be standing here."

Jonathan smiled and shook his hand. He knew he was going to like Zakariah.

"How are you feeling, Jonathan?" Zakariah asked him.

"Alive, I think but a little shaky. So much has happened I can't really make sense of it all, but I'm OK."

"Good," Zakariah said. "Then let's hope this next shock doesn't kill you all over again!" He smiled and turned to his accomplice in the mask who was standing behind him. "Jonathan, I want you to meet the person who helped me. She has sacrificed a lot for you this year. She is a brave lady. You should be very proud of her."

And then the fourth and final miracle of the day happened. The woman removed her mask and, his sister Courtney held out her arms. She called his name and a torrent of emotion welled up inside him. Laughing and crying, he reached out and held onto her.

"How could you be alive? I thought …"

"I'm so sorry we couldn't tell you," Courtney said through tears.

"But … but I went to your funeral. I don't understand how this. You were dead!"

"So were you, Jonathan!" she replied. "But we are both standing here."

"I'm afraid it was my idea," Zakariah said. "We had to make it seem like she was dead, and she had to stay dead. The Arab had a contract out on her life. If we hadn't arranged our ruse when we did, she wouldn't be standing here today."

Dominique moved to Jonathan's side and put her arm around him. He closed his eyes, the happiest man alive. *Thank you, God*, he said silently. *Forgive me.*

It seemed like the perfect ending to Operation Roulette Wheel. However, the wheel was still spinning.

They discovered Salah El-Din had disappeared.

Chapter 19

A Cold Trail

Date: September 2008
Place: Glennfinch Castle

In the days that followed the gun battle in Cumbria the Templar stronghold was abuzz with activity. St Clair carried out a full debriefing of all the Templars who were involved in the operation; André Sabbath did the same in Cairo.

A number of Templars received medical attention for wounds incurred during the battle. Wolf underwent minor surgery for wounds to the arm and leg, and he was soon up and about. Dominique's leg injury would take longer to heal. Meeks had finally spoken to Courtney, overjoyed to learn that she was alive. Luther Coates and Morgan Clay had caught a flight out of Glasgow directly after the debriefing and headed for London. Once there, they fully briefed Proctor Hutchinson and gave him a full account of Operation Roulette Wheel. The senior member of GCH then briefed the Joint Intelligence Committee, GCHQ, the Communications Electronic Security Group of GCHQ, MI5 and MI6.

After the debriefing, most of the Templars made their way back home. Some stayed as they were moving on to other operations and would stay active for some months to come as part of the Unity mop-up. Some stayed for training and refresher training and others stayed on for a few extra days to be closer to their Charge and pray before it in its sanctuary.

* * *

Jonathan had learned much since Cumbria. He had spent long hours with St Clair, understanding the Order, the work they did and the intricate networks and control centres they had all over the world – their eyes and ears. He spent time with Wolf, who he liked very much, before the Indian returned home to his native America, his wounds fully healed.

Dominique taught Jonathan much about their communications, computers and logistics, and with every day, they grew ever closer.

Jonathan helped Nickolin, the Russian, to improve his technical English. Whilst his conversational English was perfect, the Russian would need a greater command of technical language in the months to come. It had been agreed that with no next of kin, he would remain at the castle until he decided where he wanted to base himself. The Russian offered to teach Jonathan some combat skills, and so did John Wolf, but Jonathan declined. He knew that he had a part to play in the Templar organisation, but it was not as an enforcer. He considered himself an ordinary person, but he had been placed in an extraordinary situation. That was not going to change. There were going to many more extraordinary situations; how could there not be? They were the Knights Templar; they protected the Ark of the Covenant.

Jonathan had wondered much about the tablets of stone since that day in Cumbria. About the images and symbols he had seen, their meaning and purpose. The narrow margin that separated them from just shadows and real substance lay heavy on his mind. Not much had been said by anyone about what had happened that day. Like the scrolls, which had arrived from Egypt a week after the battle, the Ark was back in its sanctum, deep within the castle. He had not asked to see it, despite the fact he so desperately wanted to. Whilst Jonathan could not fully comprehend what the Ark was capable of, he did know that the Templars believed that they had only scratched the surface of the possibilities and of its purpose. He wanted to help them. He wanted to know. But St Clair had spoken about it only once since their return. So he waited. He had learnt that St Clair always had a reason for everything. There was always purpose behind his silences and always purpose behind the words he spoke. Often he would speak in metaphors, antonyms and oxymorons: 'always make sure danger is safe,' he would often say. St Clair was a good and methodical teacher and Jonathan admired his sanguine, confident nature and his consideration for others. When St Clair was ready to speak about the Ark again, he would.

A number of days had gone by before Zakariah could call them together: St Clair, Jonathan and Dominique. They'd all been really inquisitive to know how Zakariah had pulled off Courtney's non-death. Now that most of the demobilisation tasks had been done, and life in the castle was getting back to normal, he could finally bring them all together.

Zakariah, Courtney, St Clair, Jonathan and Dominique gathered in the great hall around noon on the fourth day. And, over a pot of coffee, some honey and home-made biscuits, Zakariah finally revealed how he had managed to pull off his audacious bait-and-switch just under a year ago, which started the whole thing off.

"I'd been searching for the scrolls," he told them. "I was frantic to get them back, never thinking that they would get into the wrong hands. I found out that my original buyer's children had sold them after he died, and there were rumours that they had fallen into the hands of a criminal. I was stupid and naïve. I should have known better than to think they would ever be safe.

"I didn't know who had them. I couldn't get a name. I'd followed loads of leads; travelled halfway around the world and back. I was getting nowhere.

"In December last year, I was in Dubai following what turned out to be a false lead when I started to see messages on a few dark Internet sites regarding the scrolls. The author wanted to meet. With no real leads left to follow in the Emirates, I caught a plane and headed for DC.

"I'd been in DC six months earlier and had made connections with an assortment of dubious characters and general low-lifes. I'd put a reward out for ten thousand dollars for information about ancient scrolls being sold or talked about. I'd been to see one of my contacts one day, a thug by the name of Willy Browning. Over a few bourbons, Browning told me he was going to make good money by carrying out a hit, and wanted to know if I was interested in doing the job with him. The contract had been placed on a young woman's life. He told me the name and how the killing had to be done. I made my excuses and left and completely forgot about it.

"Then I met Courtney at the La Bohème eatery," he said, "but it wasn't until she told me her name that I realised that she was the mark for the contract killing that Browning was talking about. Then, when she told me who had the scrolls, it all started to fit together. Salah El-Din had the scrolls; he had also ordered the hit on her life. I was distraught because the scrolls could not be in worse hands. Plus, how was I going to save this woman's life? We were, for good or for bad, now joined in a race to get the scrolls back and to save her.

"I knew that if I didn't do something to help her, she would soon be dead; and the best way to keep her alive was to kill her. Well, at least to make it look that way. So I took a gamble. It was the only play open to me. I arranged for her to go to the McGregor party. I had a contact. He got the invite for me." Zakariah explained. "We got lucky, I guess. Actually, we got lucky a number of times."

"Once inside," Courtney said, taking up the story, "my job was to try to locate Salah El-Din, then to get to him, to rile him, anger him. Zakariah figured that as soon as he learned who I was, the minute I left the party the Arab would have me followed and killed. We both figured that he would have some men outside in the

286

mansion's car park, and at least one inside with him, so there were more than enough people he could send to do the job. So that was it. I was the bait. That was the gamble."

"You must have been so scared," said Jonathan.

"The hardest thing for me was not being able to tell you." Her voice wobbled and Jonathan put his arms around her.

"It damn near broke her heart," Zakariah said, "but the only chance we had of pulling it off was for her to stay dead and that meant dead to everyone. Neither of us, least of all Courtney, expected you to do what you did and try to find her killer. I was told you were, well, a bit of a stay-at-home-ish kind of guy!"

"So, if she was the bait, what was the switch?" St Clair asked.

"That week before the Christmas party, I bribed the night technician at the city morgue," said Zakariah. "There were a number of Jane Does in the morgue for processing and one was about the same height and build as Courtney. The deceased had no next of kin and her body was waiting to be transported to a public cemetery.

"Browning had told me that the killing had to be done a certain way: it required her eyelids to be removed and her throat was to be cut. So, whilst you and your sister were ensconced inside the McGregor mansion, the technician removed the body of the young woman from the refrigeration unit and, as I instructed, removed the eyelids, made the incision to the throat and prepared her for removal, altering the log sheets and medical records so that it looked as if she had already been buried."

"So, Courtney, that's why you disappeared at the party: to find McGregor and Salah El-Din?" Jonathan asked.

"Sorry, Jonathan, yes, that's why I went off and left you alone. It didn't take me too long to find the people I was after. I introduced myself as a fan and a vote the senator could count on. He was more than happy to spend a moment or two with me after that opening. Two or three minutes into polite conversation I dropped the 'goad question', as Zakariah and I had planned it, and it worked. I asked him if he had heard of old scrolls being sold to an Arab criminal. That's when the senator realised who I was. I suspect the Arab standing close by him had already figured it out. Obviously skilled as an orator, debater and all things regarding spin and question avoidance, the senator smiled and told me, no, he had no such knowledge. I then dropped the bomb-shell question, again as we had planned. I asked him if he knew a man called Salah El-Din because I wanted to ask him some questions, serious questions about theft, bribery and fraud. The senator's eyes turned to the man that had been standing close by. It was momentary, but it was enough for me to confirm it was him. The senator, agitated, leaned over to me, his politician's smile still fixed, his composure still impeccable and, in a hushed voice, advised me to leave.

"I had got what I went for, to meet the crooked senator, to identify the man whose name appeared in the files, the files that got wiped, and ultimately, to trigger my own assassination. Now I needed to be the bait that left the party."

"In a pre-selected location, by the side of a railway track, fifty miles from the Vale," Zakariah told them, "I burnt the corpse of the Jane Doe, at an extreme high temperature. I had to burn the body to make sure the autopsy would not expose the real identity of the corpse. By placing the body next to Courtney's car and leaving all of her belongings there, plus emptying a phial of Courtney's blood around the scene, blood I had taken from her arm the day before, I hoped to turn her disappearance into a murder. All these factors played their part in the coroner's assumption that the body had to be that of Courtney Rose. By removing the eyelids and making the incision in the corpse's throat, I hoped it would be enough to fool Salah El-Din into thinking she had been killed. That was our whole play; our only play.

"Courtney had left the party on her own and drove her car to a remote location where we had arranged to meet. The assassin tailed her all the way as I had hoped. At our agreed meeting point, a deserted spot alongside a lake, she got out of the car and hid behind a clump of spruce trees. As the assassin pulled up to her car, I stepped out from my hiding place and fired two shots to his head. The gun's silencer veiled the hit. After checking the man was dead, I moved the shift stick to neutral and then rolled the car into the lake, where it sank out of sight.

"I later found out that the assassin worked for a capo called Donald Cert, or 'Donny The Mouth', as he was known."

"I've heard of him," Jonathan said, remembering what Walker had told him. "Nasty guy."

"Very nasty," Zakariah confirmed. "He had taken his boss to the party and had despatched one of his men, a local knucklehead called Steadman, to follow and kill Courtney. We got lucky on two counts: one was when the killer failed to show after a few days, it didn't seem to raise any suspicion. I guess he'd gone AWOL before. We also figured that Cert probably took the money from his boss for the contract killing and kept it for himself. His greed worked in our favour. The second piece of luck was that Cert must have figured that Steadman had burnt the body because he was worried that his DNA might be all over it."

"It seems the cards were stacked in your favour, brother," St Clair said. "And I assume you arranged the stay at Mary Thomas's?"

"Mary Thomas's?" Jonathan asked.

"I did. I arranged for Courtney to go into hiding at Dominique's old school. It's a private boarding school for girls, Jonathan. It's called Mary Thomas's, in the heart of the Derbyshire countryside. There she worked as a classroom assistant in both computer sciences lessons and maths. And it was from there we both finally tracked down the scrolls in Egypt.

"I stayed in a B&B in a nearby village, so we spent a lot of time together, tracking down the scrolls and preparing for what was to come.

"In the months that passed, we kept ourselves busy by building on Courtney's FBI training in self-defence and combat training. I taught her about the Templars, and taught her how to handle weapons and she became a really good shot."

"A very good shot," St Clair said, remembering what she had done for Luther and his men. You trained her well."

"Yes, and I kept him fit by going on long runs on the Derbyshire Dales," Courtney said. "I even managed to get him to give up smoking."

It was Tuesday night and, as always, the wind outside played its inclement tune as it buffeted the walls and passageways of the castle. Jonathan had spent all day with St Clair in the library discussing the Order's history. The teacher in him made him a good student because he was hungry for knowledge and he caught on quickly.

Courtney and Dominique had been into the city to furnish Courtney with a complete new wardrobe of clothes. Her sparse wardrobe, since having to leave all of her own possessions behind when she faked her death, was in much need of addition. Jonathan liked the fact that his sister and Dominique got on so well. They had become good friends, and for once Dominique didn't feel isolated in a predominately male castle. They were in the computer room, both immensely interested in computers, they were working on a full systems upgrade, which would take days to complete. Zakariah walked with Jonathan to the great hall where they were to eat. They were the only ones who were eating. Dominique and Courtney were completely ensconced in their world of technology and data and nobody wanted to disturb them for fear of getting it all explained to them. The Russian retired early and St Clair had a number of calls to make.

Jonathan liked Zakariah; he saw much of him in Dominique – the more human side. But it bugged Jonathan that he didn't understand why Zakariah had taken the scrolls and potentially risked the Templars' anonymity. It didn't make sense to him. He could see how the intensity of what the Templars did, what they were, could build and weigh someone down. It also bugged him that he had been told that there had been other seers, but no one had explained further. As it had been a few weeks since the battle, he decided it was time to do some digging.

"St Clair called me a seer," he started. "He told me that in his lifetime the destiny of the seers has not been a happy one. Those were his words and he said it in a very matter of fact kind of way, as he does. But I don't know what that means and it's worrying me. He told me that in the last forty years they have only had three with the seer's gift, and the last of them was Dominique's mother, your wife."

"And you need me to tell you what happened to them, the seers?" Zakariah said.

"Yes, I do. Would he mind, St Clair I mean, if you did?"

Zakariah laughed. "No. That's what he wants to happen. If he didn't he would have told you himself and he would have asked me not to say anything."

"There's a reason behind everything he does, isn't there? And doesn't do."

"That's Payne for you. You'd better get used to it if you are going to stick around."

They reached the table in the great hall and sat near to the burning fire for warmth.

Zakariah began. "My wife was a Templar. That's how we met. She was Italian. She was a maths professor at Milano University, but she was also an active Knight. Not in combat, but she was a crucial planner and strategist in many of our most successful sanctions. She was attractive. Had a great sexy smile, and she could light up a room, just like Dominique can, when she allows herself not to be so serious. She had black, long and curly, wild Mediterranean hair. Your sister Courtney has similar hair.

"My wife's name was Sophia. She was a beautiful Italian lady with a passion for life; she loved people. She loved the grace in what we did; loved our calling.

"Back then we lived in Tuscany, not far from where she was

born. Dominique was ten years old when her mother died. She was the apple of her mother's eye; she was the apple of my eye, still is.

"Don't think that Salah El-Din is our only enemy, Jonathan. We have lots of enemies. You might think he is the meanest, baddest sociopath and psychopath that we have faced. Not true. We have faced worse: we will face worse. Our Order goes back a long way, over eight hundred years. That's a lot of time to build up a list of enemies, especially if they think you have secret and divine knowledge, and stashes of money; especially if they know you have!"

Jonathan remembered sitting with St Clair for the first time; he also remembered when he sat with John Dukes in his oppressive apartment on the dangerous street. He'd had a sense of foreboding on both of those occasions which had frightened him. He had the same feeling now.

"We have an enemy, Jonathan, that has been fighting our Order since the beginning, almost 900 years. They were already there in Jerusalem when the first Templars went there. We have been fighting them ever since; they have been fighting us ever since. They are incredibly dangerous. They are called the Abaddons."

Jonathan thought he recognized the name. "Why would I think I know that name, Zakariah?"

"Because you were a priest; because you know your bible; because, like the Ark, that's where they are from, biblical history."

He could not place the name Abaddon, though, not exactly. "And which part of the bible would I know in relation to this?" He was afraid to ask because he suspected he already knew the answer. There could only be one place in the bible. There could only be one place that Zakariah was referring to.

"The Apocalypse of John, or as it is more commonly called, the Book of Revelation. Revelation 9:1-11. … *And he opened the bottomless pit; and there arose a smoke out of the pit, as the smoke of a great furnace; and the sun and the air were darkened by reason of the smoke of the pit.*

"And there came out of the smoke locusts upon the earth: and unto them was given power, as the scorpions of the earth have power ... And they had hair as the hair of women, and their teeth were as the teeth of lions.

"And they had tails like unto scorpions, and there were stings in their tails: and their power was to hurt men ... And they had a king over them, which is the angel of the bottomless pit, whose name in the Hebrew tongue is Abaddon ..."

Oh my God, Jonathan thought, *here we go again.* He shook his head, his hand rattling the change in his pocket. "Great! And your wife?"

Zakariah sighed ruefully. "For Dominique and I, our lives changed irreversibly one New Year's Eve about twenty-two years ago. Abaddon assassins kidnapped Sophia, leaving Dominique for dead. I was away on a sanction in Hong Kong. I had only been gone for two days and was due back, but I had stayed an extra night because there were some loose ends to tie up, but I could have left. I should have left. The Italian police found Sophia's body four weeks later, after a nationwide police hunt. She had been tortured, her elbows smashed, her ankles broken and her ears, eyes and lips had been removed before they finally disembowelled her."

"What! Oh my God!" Jonathan said, shocked. "And Dominique, she knows all this?"

"She had hit her head during her mother's struggle and fell from the bedroom balcony down onto the lawn. They left her for dead: she nearly was. It took years for her nightmares to stop. And yes, she knows what happened to her mother; she knows it all."

"Zakariah, I am so, so sorry. I don't know what to say to you. That is terrible, so horrific. I don't have the words. How do you get past something like that?"

"You don't. I don't think you ever really do. And then when Dominique got shot on a sanction in South Africa, ten years later in 1996, I just couldn't take anymore. She was only twenty, her injury was very bad and she nearly died. If it weren't for the quick actions of Luther, I would have lost her too. She had not been on a sanction since. This was her first in twelve years. So I guess at the time I was scared and wanted some peace. I wanted out. Maybe I lost it a bit, but I missed my beloved Sophia. I miss her so much it hurts every day and I nearly lost Dominique again. I guess that's why I did it. So I took the scrolls so that I would have something to sell and flew to South Africa to see Dominique, who was in hospital. I begged her to leave the Order and come with me, but she wouldn't. So as soon as I knew she would make a full recovery I left and I disappeared."

Zakariah moved uneasily on his chair. He shook his head, shaking away the images, the bad thoughts, the thoughts that had resurfaced time and time again over the years; the thoughts of guilt that he had stayed one extra night and had he not done so … The thoughts that eventually drove him to seek a life away from the Templars, from the constant reminders of the loss of the love of his life and the terrible circumstances in which she died; the thoughts that eventually drove him to take the scrolls and seek peace away from the Order and his pain. He cleared the thoughts from his head, but they would return: they always did, they always would.

"My wife, Sophia, she was the third seer that St Clair and I have known. She had the great gift of understanding the time paradigms the Law and Lore has encrypted deep within its core. Her understanding of maths, physics, gravitational time dilation and relativity offered us glimpses into what might be possible. Her work offered the possibility of a way we might complete our Order's reason for existing.

"She died because she was a seer. Our most feared enemy, the Abaddons, were her murderers. They are our crown of thorns. They naturally decay goodness, they corrupt the human soul and they are savage. The other two seers, our brothers Dumoun and Philippe, crossed over to them in the early sixties. Their treachery cost the lives of many Knights and our Order entered into a bloody, dark time. Without a seer, our work has been slow. It has been frustrating and at times counteractive, as we struggle to understand the complexities of something that can never be truly understood. Then you came."

Jonathan knew he was *there* yet again, in that emotional place: shocked, stunned, scared, disturbed, distressed and yet so utterly excited. There, in the middle of it all, yet again.

St Clair entered the room. Zakariah told him that he had just briefed Jonathan about the other seers and the Abaddons.

"Ah, good," St Clair said. "Now, Jonathan, French onion soup or the salad?"

Chapter 20

The Russian Sanction

Date: Late October 2008
Place: Derbyshire

The trials of both the estate boss the Templars had left for the authorities at Birmingham train station and the crooked QC, Timothy Crowthorp, had taken place, their cases put to the top of the pile. The estate boss was sent away to serve out a fifteen-year sentence for the possession of narcotics, a charge from a previous case that had been pending and an additional three years for the drug money he was carrying at the station.

The trial of Timothy Crowthorp QC lasted just four days. The judge sent him to prison for seven years. Some said that the lawyer defending Crowthorp gave the case less than his best and didn't seemed too sad about the outcome.

At the same time, indictments, charges, trials and sentences were taking place against a number of people in the US. People from the FBI, DEA and some from a number of police precincts were all being tried in what was known in the newspapers as the 'Unity Trials'. Guilty verdicts were handed to every defendant and many were sent away for a long time.

For most of the Templars involved in the gun battle in Cumbria, their wounds were healed or they were well on their way to a full recovery. As days went by and time wore on, Jonathan began to feel an air of calm in the castle that he had not felt before. It was tangible, yet oddly he could not put his finger on it. People seemed more relaxed. He himself felt more relaxed. The tension of the sanction began to ease from all their thoughts, for now. Most of the people there were getting on with what needed to be got on with. Some took time in prayer and contemplation and this constantly reminded Jonathan that these were pious people, religious people. They were good people. Others were busy with maintenance and repairs to equipment. Some were monitoring international law enforcement commutations, whilst other carried out numerous training exercises. A small group of Templars, led by St Clair, had been busy collecting, collating and preparing information and evidence used by authorities in the UK and the US during the prosecutions. But slowly, one by one, the Knights began to leave the castle and return to their lives. Jonathan saw fewer and fewer people about the place and this ebbing began to give the castle a hollow, empty feel.

He was pleased when Dominique suggested over breakfast that they get away for a while, take a long drive and get some fresh scenery. He hadn't felt his old self since his sister's murder but not murder, as he now referred to it. Doing something normal was just what he needed. She'd suggested they take a small road trip; there was someone she wanted him to meet. She said they would be gone for a day, maybe two. He didn't ask whom or where; it didn't matter. He just wanted to get out and be amongst the normal world again.

He'd packed a small bag and was ready twenty minutes later. He sat waiting for her by the front door, the same large arched, double oak door he had stood in front of back in June, when he was deciding if he should ring the bell or run and get away as quickly as possible. He was glad he had stayed.

St Clair, Zakariah and Courtney came out onto the courtyard to see them off. Jonathan smiled to himself, seeing his sister standing there, alive, on a courtyard of a castle in Scotland. How life can change on a dime, he thought.

St Clair tapped his window. "Say hi for me." And that was it. Then he walked off in the direction of the castle's keep.

Jonathan laughed. "He's the strangest guy…"

For the first part of their journey they travelled along wet and soggy Scottish roads. They drove down to and then out of Glasgow, through South Lanarkshire and Dumfries. When Jonathan had driven up through Scotland in search of St Clair, at the end of June, he had seen the splendour of the bracken, fern and heather, efflorescent in shades of vibrant browns, reds and yellows. Then, miles of it lay outstretched before him either side of the road, stretching out of sight like a rustic carpet. Then he had driven in brilliant sunshine towards the craggy ranges of the Moorfoot Hills and the Pentland Hills. But now it had all changed. The British clocks hadn't been put back yet, that wouldn't happen until the last Sunday that month, but it was beginning to get dark early. Winter was drawing in. It was late autumn and the brown and golden leaves were already hanging onto their last leases of life. Patches of mist hung over the lowlands and glens like a ghostly veil and the car's windscreen wipers made easy work of the moist, damp air. The black 3-litre BMW made the journey more palatable. It was comfortable, but the road was long.

When they entered Lancashire, well into England, they stopped for petrol and to take a restroom break. Dominique paid for the petrol and bought bottles of water and some snacks. Jonathan filled the windscreen water bottle and wiped the headlights and rear lights clean. They fastened their seat belts and she hit the accelerator again and the automatic quickly went through the gears with ease. He watched her as she drove. Dressed in black, she wore a little make-up, but not too much. And, as always, her Ray-ban mirrored glasses were firmly fixed to her head. She checked the rear-view mirror, pulled out and overtook a line of traffic.

"So how did you know?"

"How did we know what, Jonathan?

"That the Ark would do what it did, that it would help me. How did you know?"

"We didn't. We were all as surprised as you."

"St Clair hadn't done it before?"

"No. What do you think he is, a magician! Normally he can't even get the lid off! We know very little of what the Ark can do; we certainly didn't know it could do that. It came as a total surprise to us all. Personally, I have no idea what happened. You were dead and St Clair shouted to us to place you on top of the Ark. We prayed: hard. You opened your eyes. All I know is that you have The Nine Worthies all worked up and St Clair has not shut up about it since. They want him to allow you to start to study the Ark, but he has told them that you are not ready. He thinks you need time to come to terms with who we are, who you are now."

"But I am ready, and really eager to see it again, to learn more."

"Priest, it's not going anywhere. It will be there when the time is right. You will know when that is and so will St Claire." She turned the wheel sharply and missed a dawdling hedgehog by about six inches.

"I hear my father told you about what happened to my mother, Sophia?"

"He did and I am so, so sorry. I cannot imagine what you must have gone through. It such a dangerous world you have been brought up in."

"It is a dangerous world anyway, Jonathan. Look what nearly happed to Courtney. There is evil everywhere in this world. The difference for us is we go and find it, before it finds others."

"Do you remember it, that time?" Jonathan asked. "Don't talk about it if it's too painful." He turned the car heating down a little.

"Of course, vividly," she said, turning the heating back up again. "There was no reason for *them* to kill my mother. She was not an active Knight, she was a civilian and they will have known that. She was a seer, though, and that's why they wanted her. We had lived there for so long, in Italy, my parents thought we were safe. They were careful. No one knew us, of us, what we did. For years we lived there. Anyway, it seems not careful enough because they found us and they took her. I guess she would not tell them what they wanted to know and, well, the rest you know."

"How do you get over something like that?"

"You don't, of course. You can't get over it. It becomes part of your life. It becomes part of the fabric that is you from that point on. It is in your thoughts, in your psyche, in your forever. And eventually you learn to get on. Like I have said before, Jonathan, no one ever promised us a tomorrow. We have to make the best of each day and hope we are getting it right."

She indicated and turned right through a small village made up of stone-built cottages and a small flint church. She eased out and overtook the local postman's bicycle propped up against the curb by its pedal. He was emptying a small red wall-post-box. He straightened and tipped the peak of his cap in thanks. She waved, put her foot down, and the postman became a small dot in the rear-view mirror.

Miles of English countryside, B roads, villages and towns rolled by as they journeyed deeper and deeper into middle England and on into the county of Derbyshire.

The private road she had now taken was wide and tree-lined; it went on for about a mile. The sign on the side of the road had been almost hidden by that year's growth of ivy. It read 'Mary Thomas's Boarding School for Girls'. The road became gravel as they neared its end and their arrival would have been clearly heard across the surrounding wood. Then, all of a sudden, the school came into view. It was a magnificent Georgian building with wide marble steps that led to the main entrance. It stood in grandeur in over sixty acres of woodland and arable land. Jonathan looked at Dominique for an answer, but she just smiled a knowing smile back at him.

A young lady, dressed conservatively in a blue school uniform, stood waiting in the car park. She was tall and pretty, with short-cropped black hair. She had greeny-brown eyes and a soft oval face. Dominique stopped the car. She waved to the girl. Jonathan didn't recognise her. Leaving Jonathan by the car, Dominique went to meet her. They hugged and chatted for a few seconds, then they both walked over to Jonathan – and now he did recognise her.

Dagmar Grey looked different, refined and calm. She smiled at Jonathan, and then she hugged him.

"I told you she needed someone to look after her," Dominique said.

"Did you do all of this?" he asked in amazement.

"A week after we met Dagmar, and with help from the psychologist, Dr Glen Fox, we made arrangements for her to be enrolled here, under a scholarship paid for by a certain someone who, some would say, resembles a very famous actor and likes to dish out annoying nicknames!"

"I want to …" Dagmar began. Her voice was less harsh. Gone were the swear words and the cynicism that had embittered their last conversation. Gone were the torn jeans and dirty T-shirt. There was a trace of her rough accent, but it had mellowed. "… I want to thank you for what you did that day. For treating me like an adult and not a child and for keeping your promise about not telling anybody what I said. It was because of you that I eventually went to the police and told them everything. I'm told that there haven't been any drugs on the estate for months now, and for now at least, there is no estate boss."

"And Tony?" Jonathan asked, turning to Dominique.

"Oh, we found him a great rehab clinic in Dorset and he's doing fine now. He's been clean for a few months and he's even started dating a local girl down there. Seems it might be serious. Plus, his sentence was reduced down: no jail time," Dominique replied.

Dagmar took his hand. "Thank you, Jonathan. It was you and your kindness that started all of this. It's like the Pit Bull and what happened that night is from a different life, I owe you a lot."

Jonathan smiled. "You owe me nothing, Dagmar. I am just so pleased to see things have worked out for you and thrilled that Dominique has been able to give you this opportunity. This place looks fantastic. You deserve it. You deserve the break." He turned to Dominique. "But isn't this the place where Courtney was?"

"Yes. Courtney even taught Dagmar, but of course they never knew the link and, it seems, neither did we. Life, eh!"

Jonathan laughed out loud. "It's good to see St Clair and Zakariah can fool each other, right under each other's noses. Life can certainly be stranger than fiction."

A school bell sounded and droves of girls of Dagmar's age and dressed in the same blue uniform started past them.

"I'm sorry, I have to go. The next lesson is chemistry, would you believe it. Living with my family should ensure I'll get good marks when it comes to narcotic powders and their elements!"

Dagmar hugged Jonathan again. Then she walked off and joined several other pupils. Jonathan watched her walk down the gravel pathway towards a block of classrooms to the right of the main school. She seemed to have fitted right in, and it was obvious from how the other girls were with her that she was popular. At the entrance to the classroom block, Dagmar hesitated before going inside. She turned around with a big broad grin and called, "By the way, if you two get married, I want an invitation." Then she went inside.

They left the grounds of Mary Thomas's School and drove back down the gravel road and onto the B roads. The miles passed and the tension in the car increased at a pace all of its own. But finally, after several miles of silent discomfort, Dominique's impatience gave way. She pulled the car over into a lay-by and turned off the engine. She took off her mirrored Ray-Bans and turned to Jonathan.

"Are you ever going to take the initiative? You've sat there for the last half an hour, with your hand in your pocket doing that coin thing again, rattle, rattle, rattle! Do I have to do everything around here?" She learned across and kissed him.

At first Jonathan just sat there, staring out of the muddy windscreen. He was not good with the opposite sex, never had been. He was no longer a priest, but he hadn't had much practice with girls; he was in unfamiliar territory. She had kissed him once before, but that was in the heat of a firefight. He had been semi-conscious, bleeding badly, but still, he remembered how soft and sweet that kiss had been. He contemplated his next action. He put his hand inside his pocket and rattled his change again. Dominique sighed loudly in exasperation, and placed her hand on the ignition key. His hand closed around hers and stopped her turning it. Then, he finally did what he had wanted to do for months. He leaned over and he kissed her.

Her cell phone rang. They all had that same specific ringtone programmed into their cell phones and it meant one thing: it was St Clair, and there was an emergency. Call straightaway. Jonathan's heart skipped a beat or two. He felt the spectre of his new reality close in again.

"Relax," she whispered. Then she got out of the car and took the call. He watched her expression for any indication of just how bad, bad was going to be. She paced, her face serious. The car's engine ticked over idly as he waited. He wanted to know what was going on, yet he didn't want to know what was going on. She seemed to be out there an age.

The call ended and she stood motionless for a minute or two, just peering into the distance. He knew her well enough now to know from her look, her stance, the slight nuances of her mannerisms that she was in sanction mode. It was chilly out. She pulled the collar of her coat up around her neck. Then she made two calls, one longer than the other.

The interior light went on and she got back in the car. "Good news," she said, "we're taking a longer road trip."

"Anywhere good?" He resisted the temptation to say, 'And the bad news?' because he knew it was coming anyway.

"Yep. Just booked the midnight ferry from Harwich to the Hook of Holland, Hoek van Holland, Rotterdam."

"And then?" His hand reached for the change in his pocket.

"Russia."

"Russia?"

"Luther, the Russian and Zakariah have already left."

"Another sanction then?"

"Nope."

"But if Luther, Nickolin and Zakariah are going …"

"News has just come in that a criminal, described as extremely dangerous and red flagged on many of the intelligent services comms, is helping certain Russian drug barons expand their business. Stories are circulating that this person is not of Russian descent, but is extremely well connected for a *иностранец*." Jonathan looked at her. "A foreigner."

"Why is this Templar business?" Jonathan asked.

"For two very good reasons, Jonathan. It would seem that he has a particular penchant for stealing and collecting revered religious objects and, apparently, he thinks he is the old Muslim tribal leader, Saladin! It's the same sanction, Jonathan."

"Oh boy!" was all he could muster.

"Don't worry, Jonathan. I won't leave you alone for a second on this trip."

"You going to find that difficult if we're going on an overnight ferry!"

"Nope, not really. I just booked our passage – and a double cabin."

"Oh boy!"

She released the handbrake and pulled away – to the sound of rattling coins.

THE END

Printed in Great Britain
by Amazon